Shelby was tormented by the way she felt when Michael was around.

She was tormented by the way she felt when he *wasn't* around. On more than one night she had fallen asleep dreaming of Michael, of loving him, of being loved by him. Watching him interact with her nephew Rio pushed her fantasies even farther. Fantasies of families, of couples with children, of a house full of little Chandlers, filled her mind.

She hadn't planned on anything beyond getting into Michael's home and getting her nephew. But now that she knew he wasn't an ogre, the future looked frightening. Frightening because she not only stood the chance of losing Rio, but because any shared future with Michael would be destroyed the moment he discovered her deception. And it was only a matter of time....

Dear Reader,

The weather's hot, and here at Intimate Moments, so is the reading. Our leadoff title this month is a surefire winner: Judith Duncan's *That Same Old Feeling*. It's the second of her Wide Open Spaces trilogy, featuring the McCall family of Western Canada. It's also an American Hero title. After all, Canada is part of North America—and you'll be glad of that, once you fall in love with Chase McCall!

Our Romantic Traditions miniseries continues with *Desert Man*, by Barbara Faith, an Intimate Moments-style take on the ever-popular sheikh story line. And the rest of the month features irresistible reading from Alexandra Sellers, Kim Cates (with a sequel to *Uncertain Angels*, her first book for the line) and two new authors: Anita Meyer and Lauren Shelley.

In months to come, look for more fabulous reading from authors like Marilyn Pappano (starting a new miniseries called Southern Knights), Dallas Schulze and Kathleen Eagle—to name only a few. Whatever you do, don't miss these and all the Intimate Moments titles coming your way throughout the year.

Yours,

Leslie J. Wainger
Senior Editor and Editorial Coordinator

Please address questions and book requests to:
Silhouette Reader Service
U.S.: 3010 Walden Ave., P.O. Box 1325, Buffalo, NY 14269
Canadian: P.O. Box 609, Fort Erie, Ont. L2A 5X3

CHANDLER'S
CHILD

Anita
Meyer

Silhouette® INTIMATE MOMENTS®

Published by Silhouette Books

America's Publisher of Contemporary Romance

SILHOUETTE BOOKS

ISBN 0-373-07581-2

CHANDLER'S CHILD

ANITA MEYER

lives in Denver, Colorado, with her husband and two children. She had no interest in becoming a writer until her ninth-grade teacher made her enter an essay contest. She took second place in the county and has been writing ever since. Her passion for writing and her experience as a former teacher led her to establish a publishing center in a local school, where elementary students come to edit, rewrite, illustrate and publish their own stories. When not writing or working at the school, Anita likes to head for the tennis courts or the ski slopes.

To Carol Rusley,
the real "Guardian Angel"

Prologue

Yucatán Peninsula, Mexico
April 1994

The sweat-soaked T-shirt clung to his back and mosquitoes buzzed in his ears as he climbed to the top of the ridge. He hated the damn heat. He hated the damn bugs. He hated the whole damn country.

Patience, he reminded himself. That was what kept him alive in this business. Taking his time, doing it right. Impatient people got sloppy and made mistakes. Mistakes they paid for with their lives.

He swiped a grimy arm across his forehead and slid his duffel bag to the ground. Leaning against a tall *sapote,* he surveyed the area. Nothing. Nothing but miles of snake-infested jungle creeping along either side of a ribbon of road.

He pulled a cigarette from his shirt pocket and lit it. Inhaling deeply, he let the smoke fill his mouth and throat. It was hard to tell which was more addictive—the taste of tobacco or the taste of success. He thrust one hand deep into the bag and rummaged around the bottom. Gently extracting a dirty bandanna, he pushed the cloth aside and stroked the miniature jadeite statue. It didn't take an expert in Mayan artifacts to know that this one was a beaut. And he knew a half-dozen collectors who would give their eye teeth to own it.

The faint sound of an engine interrupted his musings. His senses tingled and every nerve came alive. It was time. He smiled and slowly rewrapped the statue, laying it carefully on a nearby rock.

Taking one last, long drag on the cigarette, he tossed the butt on the ground and crushed it under his boot. Reaching once more into the duffel bag, he slowly and deliberately withdrew the long-range rifle. It was almost over. Soon he'd be out of this godforsaken place.

He slipped in one shiny brass cartridge and slid the bolt home. The sound of the engine grew louder and he braced the rifle against his shoulder, pointing it toward the bend in the road. An old bus came into view and he tracked it through the scope as it labored up the mountainside. The cross hairs centered on the rear wheel while his forefinger caressed the trigger. Slowly his finger tightened, squeezing it more and more. A single shot rang out, startling the birds who took to the sky en masse.

The bus careened out of control. For a long moment, it clung precariously to the side of the mountain. Then it tipped, slid over the edge and disappeared from view. The wail of a young child echoed in the still, humid air.

He put the rifle back in the duffel bag, and smiled.

Chapter 1

San Francisco, California
May 1994

" The Court finds and determines that Michael A. Chandler, being the maternal uncle of the minor orphaned child, Rio Michael Sky, is a fit and proper person to have temporary guardianship of said child, pending a hearing to determine the heirs of the deceased, Rebecca Chandler, a.k.a. Gloxinia, and appointment of a permanent guardian."

Michael Chandler sat with his back to the attorney and stared out the window of his twenty-three-story office building. In the distance, the sparkling waters of San Francisco Bay captured and reflected the glowing rays of the setting sun. Usually his emotions mirrored this view. A stormy sea made him restless, calm waters brought him peace, crashing waves gave him renewed determination.

Today the shimmering water had no impact. His eyes blurred with fatigue, and his head rested against the back of the high leather swivel chair as he tried to relax the knotted muscles in his neck and shoulders.

"So now he's legally mine, right?" he asked, still facing the window.

"He's temporarily yours." The attorney folded the document and returned it to its envelope. "Without a will, no one can do anything until the court determines the rightful heirs. And it will take four months to get a hearing." He dropped the Order for Temporary Guardianship into a file. "You won't be able to touch the estate until the court decides that you are the only heir. But don't hold your breath on that one. The so-called estate doesn't amount to much. As far as I can tell, your sister didn't have insurance, and once you pay the funeral expenses and any outstanding debts, you'll be lucky to break even."

Michael spun around in the chair and slapped his hands on the desk. "I don't give a damn about the money, Sid. You know that. All I want is the child."

Sid dropped the file into his briefcase. "Michael, have you really thought this through?"

Michael planted his elbows on the polished surface of the desk and massaged his temples with his fingers. He hadn't felt this frustrated in years, not since he was a teenager looking for a fast way out. He felt angry and powerless, like a six-foot-three-inch mainspring ready to snap. But he had no right to take his anger out on his old friend. Harshness gave way to resignation. He slumped back against the chair and closed his eyes. "Yes."

"What is a forty-one-year-old bachelor going to do with a three-year-old kid?"

"What do you think I'm going to do with him?" Despite the audible exhaustion in it, Michael's voice revealed the force of his conviction. "I'm going to see that he gets the best of everything. He'll have his own nanny, a whole fleet of them if that's what he needs. I'll send him to the right schools. He'll have a safe home, a warm bed, food, clothes, toys, opportunity. That boy is my nephew and I swear he'll never want for anything."

Sid waited a long moment before answering. "You can't bring back your sister by buying off her child," he said softly. He raised his hand when Michael tried to interrupt. "Hear me out, Michael. First of all, you are Rio's *temporary* guardian. Second, in determining permanent guardianship, the court is going to look at a lot more than just your bank account. Precedents are being set every day in this area. Many courts are ruling in favor of the real family, with parents, emotional security, trust, love."

"So you're saying I don't measure up?"

"As your attorney, I'm pointing out all the possibilities. This child had a father and that family has as strong a claim to the boy as you do."

Michael shook his head. "We don't even know who the father is. Isn't that how I got custody?"

"We didn't know at the time we filed the petition, but I have a pretty good idea now. I received a preliminary report from the authorities." Sid pulled a file from his briefcase. "Whenever an American is killed in a foreign country, there generally follows a very thorough investigation. This one is turning out to have some fairly interesting and unusual wrinkles."

Michael was instantly on the alert. "What kind of wrinkles?"

Sid flipped back the cover of the file. "There were five people involved—one man, two women and two children. All five were members of the commune. The communally owned vehicle—a beaten-up old bus, badly in need of repairs—was returning from the town with a load of supplies. A tire blew out and the bus flipped. The man and your sister were killed. One child was critically injured. The other woman and your nephew escaped with minimal lacerations and contusions."

No matter how many times he heard the words, no matter how coldly or officially the facts were presented, the images of Rebecca and that bus were more than he could bear. Michael pushed himself out of the chair and strode across the room to a built-in bar. "You haven't told me anything new," he said stiffly.

Sid turned around in the swivel chair. "It wasn't an accident, Michael. The tire didn't just blow." He paused, groping for the right words, but there was no way to lessen the impact. "It was shot out," he said bluntly.

The coffeepot Michael was holding froze in midair. He put it down on the glass-top table and turned slowly to face his attorney. "What did you say?"

"The police recovered a bullet, a..." Sid shuffled through a few sheets of paper. "A 7.62 NATO in the rear tire, which they suspect came from a Remington M700." He met Michael's piercing stare without wavering. "It's a heavy-barreled sniper rifle."

Michael shook off the prescient fear that had doused him like a wave of cold water. He poured himself a cup of coffee and sat back down behind the desk. "That doesn't make sense. Why would a sniper be shooting at a busload of crazy hippies?"

"The authorities wondered the same thing, so they've extended their investigation substantially. The commune itself checks out clean. Basically it's a back-to-nature, New Age religious group led by some guru-yoga teacher who believes the road to spiritual awareness can be discovered by studying the cornflowers."

"Cornflowers?" Michael made a face. "Corn *flakes* is more like it."

Sid smiled. "Be that as it may, the commune welcomes anyone without asking a lot of questions. Besides Gloxinia—I mean, Rebecca—the other two adults on the bus were a woman called Tiara something and a man named Elias Sky. The Tiara woman moved into the commune with her husband and two children about six months ago."

"Let me guess," Michael interrupted. "Disillusioned yuppies wanting to throw away the old value system. Right?"

"Close enough," Sid said. "But the interesting one in all of this is Elias Sky, the man who was killed. According to the commune people, he was a Caucasian male, late twenties or early thirties. He wandered into the commune approximately four years ago. Never volunteered any information about his life on the outside, and no one was interested enough to ask. He was fairly well liked, and he did a little bit of everything—carpentry, poetry, painting, farming."

"Terrific. The original jack-of-all-trades," Michael said sarcastically.

"That's one way of putting it," Sid quipped.

"Meaning?"

"Meaning he dabbled in a lot of things—basic scams, insurance fraud, robbery, occasional extortion." Sid tossed the file on Michael's desk. "An impressive list, wouldn't you say?"

Reluctantly, Michael picked up the file. "Why didn't we know about this sooner?"

"Because the authorities had a tough time identifying the body. After the accident, the Mexican police took fingerprints from both of the deceased in order to identify them. Fortunately, the people in the commune knew something about Gloxinia. They knew she was an American who had a brother named Michael living in San Francisco. So the American authorities ran her prints through the Department of Motor Vehicles and matched them to a print on an old driver's license. She was identified as Rebecca Chandler and that led them to you."

"Didn't they have any leads on Sky?"

"Too many. One person thought he was from Australia. Another said he had gone to college in England. No one knew exactly who he was. And it's not surprising," Sid said, reaching across the desk and retrieving the file. "He probably didn't know himself. He's been called Linc Kellogg, Lester Kellogg, Ken Lester, Ken Lewis, Lewis Kent . . . the list goes on and on. He disappeared about five years ago, but he's wanted for questioning in a half dozen different cases, and there's an existing warrant for his arrest in Florida for armed robbery." Sid pulled a sheet from the file and slid it across Michael's desk. "It's all here. Read it yourself."

Michael fingered the edge of the police report, trying to digest everything Sid had told him. "So you're saying Rebecca died because of this...this...person?" He turned his chair away from the desk and stared moodily out the window. The white triangle of a sailboat bobbed on the choppy blue-green water.

"It looks that way. And that's only part of it. According to the members of the commune, Elias Sky latched on to Rebecca." Sid took a deep breath. "They said he was Rio's father."

Michael whirled and surged to his feet. The sudden movement sent the chair crashing against the credenza. "Can they prove it? Is there a birth certificate?"

"Michael, I think you should—"

"Is there?" Michael thundered.

"No."

"A marriage license? Anything like that?"

"We haven't found one. But it's still possible that someone from Sky's family could come forward and claim the child."

"Never!" Michael's outrage exploded in the quiet office. "*If* Sky was his father—and that's a hell of a big 'if'—that man was a fugitive, a felon wanted for armed robbery. I'll rot in hell before I ever turn my nephew over to someone in that family!"

Sid waited a long moment before answering, letting the fire in Michael's words return to a smolder. "To begin with, we don't know if there *is* anyone in Sky's family." Sid lowered his voice but never took his eyes off Michael. "And your own past is hardly without blemish."

"That was a long time ago. I was just a kid."

"Agreed, but that doesn't make it go away. It could still be used against you in court, especially in a custody case."

Michael leaned against the window, one arm braced high against the frame, his hand clenched. A brooding silence enveloped him.

"Michael, the police have turned their attention to the sniper. They're trying to determine who shot out that tire and why. But I think we should continue investigating Mr. Sky. We need to find out if he has any parents, grandparents, siblings—anyone who might oppose your petition."

"No." Michael's voice was deathly calm. "I want it dropped."

"That doesn't make any sense . . ."

"It makes perfect sense. First, I don't want Rio to ever know his father was a criminal. And second, as soon as you start digging into that creep's life, looking for relatives, they'll come flocking out of the woodwork. I don't need people lined up from here to San Diego with sob stories about their long-lost kin. Investigate the accident all you want, but don't go looking for relatives. I want all references to Rio's father kept quiet. As far as the press is concerned, my sister died and I was appointed guardian of her son. Is that clear?"

"I think you're making a mistake."

"Maybe. But that's my decision." Determinedly, he sat down at his desk and began sorting through a stack of files.

Sid shrugged, then sighed loudly and stood up. "Okay, you're the boss." He picked up his briefcase and walked to the office door. "But if you change your mind, give me a call." Sid let himself out, quietly closing the door behind him.

Michael jerked the knot of his tie loose, then leaned back in the leather chair and closed his eyes. Memories engulfed him and he was powerless to keep them at bay. Memories of a twelve-year-old boy looking at a baby so small and fragile. *Baby Becca.* That was what his mother had called her. And he was the big brother. It was his job to protect her.

But he couldn't protect her from the father who ran out on them shortly after she was born. And he couldn't protect her from a stepfather who hated them both. For a while, Michael's stories sustained her. He fed her dreams of living like a princess in a big house with servants and fancy cars. He vowed someday he would make all those dreams come true. But at fifteen, he'd given up and run away, leaving her with nothing more than a promise.

Michael held his head in his hands. He'd tried to keep that promise. After the successes, after he had the big house and the fancy cars, he went back for her. But by then it was too late. Becca had taken off, the same way he had. He spent years looking for her. Tracking down every lead, no matter how far-fetched. Always believing that someday he'd find her. Never imagining it would be her death that brought them together again.

His fingers curled around the police report Sid had left lying on the desk. Not wanting to curb his anger, Michael crushed the paper into a tight wad and flung it across the room.

Damn that sniper. Damn the commune and the bastard called Sky. He damned them all for taking away the only part of his life that was really good. The last time he'd seen Becca she was three years old—the same age as Rio was now. The significance of that wasn't lost on him. Fate had seen fit to give him a second chance. He would get permanent custody of his nephew, and he would let nothing—*no one*—stand in his way.

"Mr. Chandler will be right with you," the secretary said politely, seating herself behind the gleaming chrome-and-wood desk.

Shelby McMasters glanced up from the magazine she was pretending to read and smiled. "Thank you," she said, then mindlessly gazed down again.

Shelby stared at the pages in front of her. Then she stared at the thick cream-colored carpeting around her. Finally, she laid the unread magazine back on the glass coffee table and smoothed an invisible wrinkle from the slim skirt of her blue linen suit. It had been quite a while since she had worn an interview suit, and her physical discomfort only heightened her nervousness.

For the third time, she folded her coat neatly over her arm and tried to tuck a stubborn lock of blond hair into place. She had passed the first round of interviews with Michael Chandler's associates and was now ready to meet the man himself. Everything depended on getting this job.

Reaching into her purse, she withdrew a small clipping from the Mérida *Excelsior* and unfolded it, carefully smoothing the creases with her fingers.

DOS MUERTOS, TRES HERIDOS EN UN ACCIDENTE

Quickly she scanned the article, reading for the umpteenth time how a bus had overturned, claiming two lives, including that of a young woman known as Gloxinia. Sole remaining relatives were a son, Rio, and a brother, noted shipping importer and entrepreneur, Michael Chandler.

Shelby jumped reflexively as a harsh buzzer sounded on the secretary's desk. The woman stood and opened the door to the office. "You may go in now, Ms. McMasters."

Drawing a deep breath, Shelby slipped the article into her purse. With confidence and determination, she stepped through the doorway and crossed the spacious and elegant office. Her gaze took in the room in one thorough sweep—a small Turner seascape framed beneath a portrait light, a large pair of lapis lazuli bodhisattvas on either end of a walnut credenza, an Imari vase filled with dried flowers and, on his desk, an exquisite chacmool carved in stone. Two things were clear. Michael Chandler had a taste for antiquities, and the wherewithal to procure them.

Shelby stopped in front of the oversize walnut desk and waited for the man to look up from the file he was reading. Covertly, she studied him.

His picture had appeared in enough magazines for Shelby to recognize him anywhere. The photos were virtually the same, each a study in perfection—the right suit, the right tie, the right hairstyle, the right pose. That was his image. She had assumed the real Michael Chandler would be more . . . real. She had assumed wrong.

The Saville Row suit was tailor-made to fit his broad shoulders, and the blue-and-red silk tie added just the right touch of color. Overhead lights glistened on his thick, dark hair, neatly layered and brushed away from his face, looking as soft and luxurious as sable. The shadow of his lashes fell across the rugged lines of his cheeks. Even his hands, strong and beautifully groomed, added to the image. Everything about him was picture-perfect. *A little too perfect,* Shelby thought grimly.

Without looking up, he motioned in the general direction of a swivel chair upholstered in a sea-green fabric. "Sit down."

His voice was like a cello, deep and melodic, yet tinged with forcefulness. A voice reeking of power and authority, demanding respect, accustomed to giving orders. Shelby shivered as she thought of that voice raised in anger.

"Are you cold?"

Shelby stared into a pair of cool gray eyes. The well-tanned face and firmly sculptured features showed lines around the eyes, nose and mouth—not deep, but enough to indicate he was no longer a youth. He was probably in his late thirties or early forties. He had dark eyebrows above eyes the color of liquid smoke, a square jaw and a firm, generous mouth.

Annoyed with herself for even noticing, Shelby folded her hands in her lap and forced her voice to be calm and smooth, in direct opposition to her emotions.

"No, sir. Not at all." Subservience didn't come easily to her, but drastic times called for drastic measures and "sir" seemed the appropriate touch.

He looked her over critically, seeming to photograph every detail of her face and clothing in a split second. "Your credentials are excellent, Ms...." He paused, flipping to the front page of the résumé.

"McMasters. Shelby McMasters." Her poise retrieved, she lifted her chin to meet his steady gaze. There was a lot more than just a job at stake.

"Hmm. I see you've only recently left your position with the Ashbaughs."

"The youngest child is now old enough to join his brothers at boarding school. There was no longer a need for my services."

"Their recommendations are glowing. I'm impressed." He smiled slightly and for a moment Shelby's mind blurred like a camera out of focus.

This wasn't like her. Stress, that's what it was. All the stress of getting this far had seeped into her brain cells and altered her normal pattern of thinking. Now a simple smile was fogging up her sanity.

"Since you were with the Ashbaughs quite a while," he continued, "I assume you've had experience with small children."

"Yes," she replied, and then winced inwardly. She didn't sound like herself. Her voice was high and tight. *Please*, she begged. *Please don't let me blow this interview.*

He leaned back in the plush leather chair, his gold cuff links catching and reflecting the sunlight that streamed in through the windows. "Yours is the first résumé I've seen that indicates that both your English and Spanish are flawless. Are you familiar with the particulars of this position?"

Shelby struggled to concentrate. "The registry said the position required live-in, full-time help for one child, a boy, age three."

"That's basically correct. The child is my nephew, who has recently been orphaned. He's still in Mexico, where his mother was living. Since it is unknown whether the boy speaks English or Spanish, I require someone fluent in both languages."

He paused suddenly, and Shelby's heart slammed into her rib cage as his penetrating gaze locked onto hers and refused to let go.

"However," he continued obdurately, "I am not looking for 'help.' I am looking for a primary caretaker. My business interests allow me no time for familial involvement. The person I hire will have complete responsibility for every aspect of the child's life and will be paid accordingly."

Shelby's eyes narrowed. A chill engulfed her. Michael Chandler was handsome, rich, powerful . . . and one of those men who believed you could make any complication disappear if you threw enough money at it . . . even if that complication was an innocent little boy.

"I see," she clipped, her heart thundering in righteous anger.

His look deepened to a stare. "Is that a problem?"

"No, sir," she said, surprised at how calm her voice sounded. "I have no problem with that. I am quite accustomed to taking matters into my own hands." She smiled at the accuracy of her words.

"Good." He gave a final glance at the résumé then closed the file, looking her over appraisingly. "How do you really feel about children, Ms. McMasters?"

The question caught her off guard and she hesitated before answering. "Excuse me?"

"Your references describe your abilities—efficient, conscientious, meticulous, organized. I'm asking about your personality. Are you caring? Loving? Creative? Spontaneous?"

Shelby blinked. The conversation had taken a strange and unexpected turn. The same man who coldheartedly said he didn't have time to waste on familial involvement was now questioning her ability to be a loving, caring nanny. Perhaps she'd misjudged him. Perhaps a human being hid beneath the surface of the ruthless entrepreneur, after all.

"I'd like to think I'm all of those things," she said slowly. "And as for how I really feel about children . . ." Shelby drew a ragged breath. "I believe children are a precious and irreplaceable gift. They are our link to the past and our hope for the future. They are open and honest, giving freely of themselves and asking little in return. Once touched by a child, a life can never be the same."

She looked at Michael Chandler and held her breath. The desperate need to get this job gave her words a passion she hadn't anticipated. But if her little speech moved him, he didn't show it. Apprehension quickly flooded her. Maybe she'd gone too far, overstated her case. . . .

"Are you married?"

"No."

"Are you currently involved with anyone?"

"I beg your pardon?"

"I asked if you are currently involved with anyone."

"I fail to see the relevance of . . ."

"I'm not interested in your seeing the relevance. I'm interested in the answer."

Shelby felt her cheeks redden with suppressed wrath. So much for thinking he might possibly be human. He was nothing more than a master gamesman—deceptive, overbearing, rude, not to mention intrusive. He couldn't legally ask those questions, and under any other circumstances, she would have hit him in the face with an Equal Employment Opportunity complaint. But this time she held her tongue. She would do whatever it took to get this job.

"No," she said with quiet firmness. "I am not currently involved in a relationship."

"Good. Keep it that way." His lips formed a confident smile that could easily be mistaken for arrogance. "These interviews have already taken far too much of my time. I have no intention of repeating them." He stood, and Shelby quickly followed his lead.

"Does this mean I have the job?"

"It does. Pending a reference check with your previous employer, you will be on a three-month probation starting tomorrow." He crossed the room in quick strides and opened the door. "Speak with my secretary on the way out, and she will arrange to have someone pick up you and your luggage in the morning."

Shelby paused at the door. "Goodbye, Mr. Chandler. Thank you." She held out her hand and he shook it, his grip firm but not familiar. The touch of his warm, broad hand left her slightly off balance, and she felt strangely disappointed when he broke contact.

She let out a long sigh as she exited the Chandler Office Complex. Turning the corner, Shelby McMasters headed for the public library. She had less than twenty-four hours to learn how to be a nanny.

Chapter 2

One of Michael Chandler's lackeys arrived early the next morning in a full-blown limousine to drive Shelby to the Chandler estate. Despite her determination to remain unimpressed by anything Michael Chandler did, said or owned, her resolve slipped a few notches as the limo whisked her off to her new home in northern Marin County.

Through the tinted window, Shelby surveyed the area. The Chandler estate was built on a ridge overlooking the Pacific Ocean. A brick wall, at least fifteen feet high, enclosed the grounds, reminding her of a castle wall. A computerized security system monitored the main gate, and the limo paused just long enough for the driver to be recognized before proceeding slowly up the long driveway.

In her thirty-three years, Shelby had had many opportunities to rub elbows with the wealthy. She was a frequent speaker at their parties and fund-raisers, always ready to plead her cause for the preservation of historical artifacts. Over time, she had developed the opinion that people were a lot like their homes. The gaudy, pompous, ridiculous-looking houses generally had occupants to match. The ones that screamed fashion design usually had owners who were all veneer and no substance. It was a blatant stereotype, and she knew it, but nevertheless, she truly believed you could tell a lot about an individual by examining his surroundings.

It was more than idle curiosity then, that made Shelby lean forward and crane her neck to get a glimpse of Michael Chandler's home. When the limo pulled away from the gates and rounded the turn, it was what she *didn't* see that surprised her the most.

There were no cherub-topped fountains carelessly spewing water in ways that would make a conservationist cringe. No ridiculous marble statues loomed in the middle of formal gardens. No ostentatious display of wealth. No bundles of money thrown around in an attempt to cover up what could only be described as bad taste. Nothing about Michael Chandler's property shrieked nouveau riche and Shelby had to dump her prejudice on the spot.

The Chandler estate was lovely. The grounds were landscaped with an elegant simplicity designed to imitate and complement the natural beauty of the land. Dominated by fifty-year-old cypress trees, the indigenous flora had been retained, moved into beds along the front of the house where their riotous colors fought one another for attention. Hydrangeas with white corymbose clusters lined the steep driveway leading to the two stone lions that flanked the entrance to the house.

Shelby's breath caught in her throat as she stepped out of the limousine and stared at the building before her. Beautiful. Except for the lions, the two-story, white stone structure was unadorned, with two wings spreading out from the main building at the sides. Set against the backdrop of a cloudless blue sky, its austere elegance dazzled her.

A maid opened the massive front door, admitting Shelby to an airy entryway of white travertine marble and black granite. Directly in front of her was a free-standing curving staircase leading to a second-floor open walkway. It was gorgeous . . . and anything but childproof.

"Wait here, please," the maid said softly, taking Shelby's two suitcases from the chauffeur. Shelby watched her carry the bags up the luxurious moss-green carpeted stairs, cross the railing-flanked walkway and disappear into the rooms beyond.

The marble flooring extended from the foyer in both directions. To the right, Shelby could see part of a formal living room. To the left, the marble curved past a large, bright sun room, then disappeared under the stairs.

Shelby shifted uncomfortably. Now that she was actually here, the magnitude of her deception weighed heavily. She had always been proud of her honesty and straightforwardness. Yet, she had paid someone her life savings to falsify records and to provide her with a portfolio of bogus credentials. She had convincingly passed herself off as a professional nanny, feigning respect and subservience to an arrogant man whose ego matched his wallet and whose values she could never accept. And she had turned her back on a career that had taken a lifetime to build.

All for the sake of a child.

She hated what she had done, the way she had acted. But she believed her reasons were just, and under the same circumstances she'd do it all over again.

A young man, looking for all the world like one of the Beach Boys in a preppy suit, appeared in the foyer. "Ms. McMasters? I'm John Callahan, Mr. Chandler's personal assistant. This way, please."

Shelby took a deep breath and followed him along the marble path, past the sun room, under the stairs and through a handsome wooden archway to the library. The impressive room spanned the width of the wing, with an enormous fireplace at one end and an oversize desk and bay window at the other.

Michael Chandler and another man sat talking. Shelby was determined not to divert her attention from the business at hand, but the artifacts displayed in this room revealed much about her new employer. Most people collected art indiscriminately—a painting, a piece of furniture, a vase, a rug—whatever was in vogue at the moment. And admittedly, the floor-to-ceiling bookshelves were interspersed with a few antique curios. But it was the glass case above the bar that caught her attention, heart and soul. In it stood one of the finest collections of Mesoamerican clay figures she had ever seen. Collections this specific were rarely the work of an art dealer, and it irked her to think that, ego and money aside, Michael Chandler also had a discerning eye and exquisite taste.

The conversation ceased, and the stranger stood as Shelby crossed the room. Michael Chandler remained seated behind the desk.

"I'm Sid Bryce," said the short, balding man, extending his hand, "Mr. Chandler's attorney. You must be Ms. Mc-Masters. Please, have a seat."

Shelby shook his hand, nodded politely to both men and took the offered chair. Too bad her new boss didn't have Mr. Bryce's manners. Michael Chandler leaned way back in his chair, his well-built physique relaxed and powerful. His biceps strained the fine fabric of his shirt as he tented together his fingertips and watched her.

Some men talked about their power. Michael Chandler wore his. The attorney may have been conducting the business, but there was no doubt who was really in charge.

"I have here an employment contract for you to read and sign," Mr. Bryce said, handing Shelby a legal-size document. "Since you've no doubt seen these before, let me tell you this one is standard except for paragraphs 5d, 16a and 30."

He flipped to the second page of his copy and indicated she should do likewise. "Paragraph 5d," he continued, "specifies the financial compensation. Mr. Chandler has agreed to provide medical and dental insurance in addition to a monthly salary which is considerably above the going rate. I think you'll agree he has been quite munificent in that department."

Munificent was an understatement. Shelby stared at the number until the line of zeros blurred together. Since the average nanny didn't pull down this kind of salary, something else had to be going on. But what? She shot a glance at the man in question, but he remained silently aloof.

Shelby arched an eyebrow. "Mr. Chandler is indeed generous."

It was strange talking about him in the third person, as though he weren't even in the room, when all the time he sat in his leather chair like a king on his throne, the master of all he surveyed. Shelby's skin prickled.

She leveled her most genial smile at him, then turned to the lawyer. "What other services does Mr. Chandler expect me to provide in order to earn this salary?"

Mr. Cool-and-Distant Chandler didn't even blink. He sat there stoically, his face as unflinching as the granite that lined his hall. Whatever he was thinking or feeling was carefully hidden from view. Shelby kept her smile in place with a struggle. Something about this man set her teeth on edge, and if she wasn't careful, she'd be fired before she even got started.

"The additional services are specified in paragraph 16a on page four," the lawyer answered smoothly. "Mr. Chandler realizes his house is not presently equipped to meet the needs of a child. Your responsibilities, as set forth in this contract, will include the complete outfitting of the nursery and play areas. Bedroom furniture, decorative accents, linen, clothing, toys. Everything will be left to your discretion. There is an expense account over which you are to have complete control, and an automobile will be made available for your personal use. Basically, you are authorized to do everything necessary to ensure the health and well-being of the child."

"Shall I prepare a list of proposed changes?"

Michael Chandler's voice broke into the conversation. "No," he interjected. "I don't have time to approve every little detail. Just have it finished by Saturday."

Shelby blinked. "All of this is to be done in less than a week?"

The attorney nodded. "You will be flying to Mexico on Saturday afternoon and returning with the boy on Sunday morning. Mr. Chandler recognizes this does not allow you much time. Naturally," he added, "no expense should be spared to get the job done."

"Naturally," Shelby echoed, struggling to hide the resentment steadily building inside her. Michael Chandler made it clear he didn't have time to be bothered with the needs of his nephew. So he would pay her a ridiculously high salary, and she was to "spare no expense" to take care of this irksome little problem.

All the more reason for her to be here.

The leather desk chair wheezed softly as he shifted weight. Shelby turned in that direction to find herself under intense scrutiny. He was studying her, sizing her up.

"You *can* handle the job, can't you?" he questioned.

Shelby uncrossed her legs and straightened her spine. "Naturally," she said, a slight smile taking the edge off the word. She was pleased she could look him straight in the eye.

Michael suppressed the grin that tugged at the corners of his mouth. First the crack about her services and salary, and now this. No doubt about it—Shelby McMasters had backbone.

Most of the people he dealt with were cowards. Out of deference to his money, power and prestige, they bowed and scraped and carried on until he was sick of it.

But this lady was different. She showed real spunk, moxie. And that was refreshing. Too bad he wouldn't be spending much time with her, because under any other circumstances . . . He smiled in spite of himself.

"Yes. Well, now," Sid said, clearing his throat. "The final difference in the contract is in paragraph 30." He paused, allowing Shelby time to find the appropriate place. "This section contains a nondisclosure and confidentiality agreement. Although the Chandler name is well known throughout the business community, Mr. Chandler values his privacy. If you sign this agreement, you will be committed to strict confidentiality as to everything you witness on these premises."

Shelby swallowed hard. This wasn't part of the plan. She hadn't anticipated being bound by a bunch of legal restrictions.

A deep voice invaded her thoughts. "Is that a problem?"

He was studying her again, those steel-gray eyes mocking. Was she imagining things or was he really taunting her, daring her to match him? Shelby had never in her life backed down from a challenge, and she wasn't about to start now. She'd known going into this that it would be an uphill battle. One more charge wouldn't make much difference.

Without a word, she stood up. Slowly and deliberately she approached the desk. She lifted a gold-plated pen from the handsome desk set, and turned around to face the lawyer.

"Where do I sign?" she asked smiling, the set of her jaw the only clue to her seething determination.

"Michael, my boy, you've restored my faith. You are indeed a man of the future." Sid dropped the contract into his briefcase and snapped the lid shut. "No gray-haired grannies with warm milk and cookies for you," he said, grinning broadly. "No, sir. We're talking champagne and canapés." He helped himself to a glass of ice water from the crystal decanter on the side bar, then took a seat. "I had about given up on you these last few years, after that mess with Gina and all. But now I see I was mistaken. I take back every unkind word I've said about you." He held up his glass in salute. "That is the loveliest nanny I have ever seen."

"I hadn't noticed," Michael lied calmly, already turning his attention to a stack of mail on his desk.

"Hadn't noticed!" Sid exclaimed, nearly spilling his drink in his lap. "Come on, Michael, it's me you're talking to. I could hear your hormones standing up and shaking off the dust halfway across the room. A blind old man with one foot in the grave would have noticed that lady. And contrary to popular opinion, you're neither."

"Popular opinion?" Michael asked, his eyebrows raised in amusement.

"Well, Catherine's opinion," Sid replied, drawing himself up in defense of his wife. "She said you wouldn't notice a pretty woman if she jumped up and bit you on the nose. And you're about as socially active as a cranky old man."

A smile stole across Michael's face. "She's right on both counts," he said, chuckling. "I'm too old and too busy for this romantic nonsense. So, before your lovely and well-intentioned wife gets any ideas, you tell her Ms. McMasters comes from a top-notch agency and has excellent credentials."

"No argument there," Sid said. "Hair the color of golden honey, eyes as bright as sapphires, legs so long they..."

Michael laughed out loud. "Give it up, Sid. You're an attorney, remember? You're supposed to have a heart of stone, not the soul of a romantic."

"And what's wrong with a little romance? Just because you spend all of your time dreaming of overfunded pension plans and hostile takeovers doesn't mean the rest of us do. Just imagine what it's going to be like living with her...day after day." He drew out the words in a way that could not be misinterpreted.

"We will not be living together," Michael replied firmly. "She's a paid employee, just like Hodges, Callahan or any of the others." He pushed the chair away from the desk in a single thrust and strode quickly across the room to a series of handsome rosewood drawers that covered the bottom portion of one wall.

"Oh, I don't know," Sid drawled. "It seems to me you're just a tad more tense now than you were this morning when you were barking orders at Callahan and telling Hodges to clean out the guest rooms."

"I am *not* tense," Michael growled, rummaging through the cabinet files. "I'm overworked."

Sid's tone softened considerably as he put aside the teasing. "You've lost Becca, found her son and now have a child and a beautiful woman moving into your home, all in a few weeks. It's not your work that's upsetting you, Michael. It's the change. You don't like it and you never have."

Michael felt the knot in his stomach tighten. Sid knew him too well. Sid and Catherine had been a part of Michael's life from the time they pulled him off the streets—a reckless, impatient kid, no longer a child and not yet a man.

Sid was the one who had recognized Michael's tremendous drive and ability. Sid had guided and encouraged him like the father he'd never known. And, although they rarely spoke of it, Sid knew the dark aching in Michael's soul that nothing seemed to fill. Over the years, Michael had learned to cope with the emptiness, convincing himself that an ordered, disciplined life was all he needed.

He expelled a long breath. "I like my life the way it is…and I don't intend to change it."

"I'm sorry, friend," Sid acknowledged quietly. "But you can't control this one. Your life is never going to be the same. Mark my words."

"I'd like to mark your words on the Peterson contract," Michael grumbled, glad to have an excuse to change the subject. "It should have been done two days ago."

Sid grinned and sifted through the files in Michael's box. "It was," he said, tossing a file with a bright green label into Michael's lap. He picked up his briefcase and headed for the door. "Oh, by the way, Catherine said to tell you she still expects you for dinner next week, and your nephew, too, if he's up to it. And of course," he called over his shoulder, "you could always bring the new nanny…."

The door closed before Michael could reply.

Michael remained rooted to the spot for a long time, examining the papers in his hand. Finally, he tossed the file aside. He had read the same paragraph three times and still hadn't the slightest idea what it said.

He picked up a small, hand-carved jade bowl, one of his earliest acquisitions, and held it up to the light. The deep green color was the essence of life—pure, rich, vibrant. Perfection. But not at all like life, which was messy, unpredictable and constantly changing.

Sid was right. As committed as he was to giving Becca's child the best of everything, he still wasn't ready to accept the changes his life was undergoing.

Michael stared broodingly out the window. The house sat on a small knoll and the grounds in the back sloped gently away from the house. From the vantage point of the library window, Michael could see everything. To the left—the swimming pool, gardener's cottage and greenhouse. To the right—the garage, with half a dozen fine cars within and a small apartment above. And beyond it all, out past the cliffs and the rocky coast, lay the Pacific Ocean. He was drawn to this view, drawn by the water that crescendoed into mammoth waves and pommeled the shore. Pulled to this spot by an emotional undertow born of fear and allure, both attracted and repelled by the element he could never control. The ocean was his constant reminder of how far he had come.

His father had been a shiftless dockworker, a man who had abandoned his family when Michael was barely twelve years old. As a child, Michael had had nothing. Now he had it all, and he'd learned his lessons from the sea.

Some people called him powerful, but his power was nothing like the harnessed power of water that had driven men and machines for a century.

Others thought him ruthless, but even he couldn't compare to the devastation wreaked by a stormy sea that unmercifully destroyed everything that stood in its path.

Many envied his wealth, but his riches could never compete with the bounty of the ocean.

He looked out to the thin line on the horizon where the water met the sky and the two merged as one. This view, this visual combination of everything and nothing, kept Michael Chandler's life in perspective.

And then he spotted them—Callahan and McMasters—coming from the greenhouse. After she'd signed the contract, Michael had instructed his assistant to show her the rooms that she and the boy would occupy, and then take her around the estate and introduce her to the rest of the staff. Michael's eyebrows knit together as he watched the couple cross the lawn and head toward the garage. Young Callahan was showing a lot more enthusiasm for this assignment than for his usual duties.

And who could blame him? Shelby McMasters was an attractive lady. Tall and slender, she wore a plain knit T-shirt dress, belted at the waist. It wasn't much of a dress, really. It was the kind of thing that depended entirely on the person wearing it. And on her it looked terrific. It clung in all the right places, molding her hips and caressing the swell of her breasts.

There was dignity in her chiseled profile. Even at this distance, he could see the high, elegant cheekbones, the straight, delicate nose, the cleanly angled jaw.

Yesterday she had worn her hair pulled back in an intricate braid, but today the blond mane tumbled in waves around her shoulders. The wind blew silky tendrils across her face, and she swept them away with her hand as she walked.

About that, Sid was right. She had great legs and a damned sexy walk. She didn't wiggle or swing her hips the way a lot of women did, but there was grace and energy in her step. She walked with confidence and determination, a woman who clearly knew where she was going. And to Michael Chandler, *that* was sexy.

Instinctively, he stroked the silky jade bowl, running his fingers over its smooth curves, playing with its intricate carvings.

Michael tore himself from the window and retrieved the abandoned file. He tried to force his mind back to business, but when another twenty minutes lapsed unproductively, he gave up. He couldn't work here today. Maybe he'd have better luck working in the city.

He picked up the phone to call Pasig and have the limousine brought around, but then thought better of it. He needed to clear his head, and a good hard drive in the new Jag might be just the thing. Michael grabbed his jacket and headed for the garage.

"This is some car," Amelia Benedict said from the passenger seat. "I can't believe he gave you a brand-new Jaguar to run around in."

"Why not? I have a lot to do and very little time to get it done." Shelby downshifted as they approached the entrance to the parking garage. "But for the record, he didn't give it to me. I took it."

"Terrific," Amelia said with an exaggerated sigh. "You're in town less than a week, and so far you've impersonated a nanny and stolen a car." She shook her head, her shoulder-length earrings dancing in the air. "When I get back to my office, remind me to take out an ad for a new friend. Nothing fancy... just someone normal and legal."

"It's not like it sounds," Shelby said. She maneuvered the dark green car into a tight parking space and switched off the engine. "Chandler said he would make a car available for my personal use, but when I got to the garage, there wasn't much to choose from."

She reached around into the back seat and retrieved her purse and a notepad. "I didn't want the limousine," she explained, "because I didn't want some driver knowing every move I make. And the little two-seater sports job wouldn't hold half the stuff we need to buy."

Shelby locked the doors, double-checked them, then headed for Geary Street. "A couple of the cars were classics," she said. "You know, the kind you only haul out on special occasions when you're absolutely certain the sun's not too hot, the air's not too cold, the wind's not too strong and there's a less-than-zero-percent chance of rain. I wasn't about to take any of those. So that left the Jaguar. It's the closest thing to a station wagon the man had."

"I don't know about this," Amelia said, shaking her tangled mass of red curls.

"You *do* know about this. If it hadn't been for you, my dear *Mrs. Ashbaugh*, I wouldn't have gotten this far." Her tone turned serious. "I owe you one, Amelia, and I won't forget it."

"Hey, you don't owe me squat. And even if we were keeping score, which we're not, this wouldn't come close to making up for all the times you bailed me out. I'd be angry if you *didn't* ask for my help." Amelia gave Shelby a quick hug. "You're doing the right thing. And you're going to breeze through this with your eyes closed." She took Shelby's arm and hurried her off the sidewalk and into a store. "Now, come on, lady. We've got work to do."

Michael Chandler drew in a furious breath and expelled it in a hiss. "She took what!"

"She took the new Jaguar, sir. Not more than twenty minutes ago." Ralph Pasig, full-time chauffeur and part-time mechanic, nervously shifted his weight from one foot to the other. "She said you promised her a vehicle."

"A vehicle—yes. A brand-new, customized Jaguar XJS— No!"

"I'm sorry, sir. I didn't know."

Michael stood in a wide stance, his clenched fists planted on his hips. "You should have checked with me," he barked.

"I would have, sir, but Mr. Callahan said it was all right." Pasig stared at the ground, unable to look his boss in the eye.

"Callahan?"

"Yes, sir," Pasig said, trying to shift the blame. "He and the young lady came to the garage together. He practically *ordered* me to give her that car."

Michael doubted that. It was more likely she had come waltzing in, all warmth and smiles, and Pasig had told her she could have any car she wanted. He would probably have given her the Crown Jewels, no questions asked.

"Find Callahan and tell him I want to see him in my office *now!* And remember I give the orders around here—not John Callahan. You check with me before you hand over the keys of my cars to anyone. Got that?"

"Yes, sir!" Pasig said, obviously relieved that the boss had found a new vent for his anger.

Michael Chandler stormed back to the house. Shelby McMasters had been in his life only a few hours. First, she took over his thoughts. Now, she had taken his car. And he didn't like either one bit.

"Shelby Kelland, I'm an interior designer, not a miracle worker." Amelia slid into the café, dropping an armload of carpet samples, cloth swatches and wallpaper pieces on the bench seat.

"McMasters," Shelby corrected. "Remember? New name, new identity, new credentials, the works."

"Sorry," Amelia said apologetically. "It just slipped out. But it would still be a whole lot easier if I could *see* the place I'm supposed to be decorating."

"I've described the rooms, I've drawn sketches of them and you're going to have to work from that. I don't want you at the house," Shelby said, more harshly than she intended. For a long moment an awkward silence stretched between the two friends. "Now, *I'm* sorry," Shelby said quietly. "I didn't mean to snap at you. You're my best friend, and I know you'd never deliberately ruin this for me, but . . . to be honest . . . I . . . I . . ." The blunt words tumbled out in a rush. "I can't risk your snooping around."

"I never snoop," Amelia said indignantly. "I wanted to see the place in order to give you the best possible service." A sly smile played across her face. "And while I'm there, I might notice a few other changes I could suggest to Mr. Chandler."

"Absolutely not."

"Come on, Shelby. I just want to meet the man. Think of what it would mean to claim the famous Michael Chandler as one of my clients. It would be a real boon to my business."

Shelby shook her head. "Take my word for it, Michael Chandler is not the kind of man you'd want to work for. He's a cold, self-centered, power-hungry chauvinist...and those are his good points."

Amelia chuckled. "Sounds better than the guys I've been dating."

"I'm serious, Amelia. You could lose your business by being on his bad side."

Amelia sighed audibly. "Okay, okay. Let me see the list again." She took the notepad and began checking off the items. "You've selected the new carpet and the guy will come tomorrow morning to measure the rooms. Royal blue will work very well," she said, lapsing into a comfortable role. "Primary colors are known to stimulate children's minds, plus it won't show the dirt."

Shelby grinned. "I'm sure Michael Chandler will appreciate the practicality of my choice." She signaled the waitress and placed an order for two iced teas.

Amelia continued, undaunted. "You'll need to wallpaper at least one wall in the playroom, but leave the walls in the bedroom as they are, except for the border of dinosaurs and the matching dinosaur curtains." She slumped against the back of the seat and studied Shelby. "Are you sure you want dinosaurs? I mean, they're so...obvious."

"I really want dinosaurs."

Shaking her head, Amelia picked up a swatch of material and stared into the face of a sneering pterosaurian. Shelby suppressed a laugh as her friend made a face and frowned right back at the brightly colored flying reptile. "If you went with Laura Ashley, you could..."

"I want dinosaurs."

"You and about thirty million other people," Amelia muttered. "Why not try something more original?"

"I want dinosaurs."

"But—"

"Amelia," Shelby said, loudly enough to cause three customers and a waitress to turn their heads and stare. "I want the dinosaurs."

"Fine," Amelia said, throwing up her hands in a gesture of submission. "It was just a suggestion." She took a long drink of her iced tea before continuing. "Nancy will come tomorrow morning at ten to measure the windows. If she drops everything else, she can probably have the curtains, the window-seat cushion and the bedspread done by Friday. And I'll send the paperhanging crew to the house tomorrow right after lunch."

Shelby tore a sheet of paper off the pad and began scribbling. "I need to contact a construction company about building a safety fence around the outdoor pool. That pool is an accident just waiting to happen. Also, I'd better talk to Jules about ripping out all those California buckeye bushes. Poisonous fruit," she added knowingly.

"Who's Jules?"

"Jules Hodges, the gardener. His wife, Anna, is the housekeeper and cook. They live in the cottage at the back of the estate. The Hodgeses, John Callahan and Ralph Pasig are the only live-in help. The rest are day-timers." Two stuffed dinosaurs and a brontosaurus nursery lamp/night-light threatened to spill into her lap and Shelby leaned against the stack of purchases to hold them up.

"The jungle gym and the sandbox will be delivered and installed the day after tomorrow," Amelia added. "And the day after that, you get a truckload of sand and the bedroom furniture, assuming the carpeting and wallpapering are done on time. I think that takes care of all the big stuff."

"I hope so." Shelby propped her elbow on the table and stared into her glass, mindlessly stirring her tea with the long spoon.

"Are you okay?"

Shelby looked up and offered a faint smile. "I'm nervous, excited and scared to death of facing the 'Wrath of Michael Chandler' once he finds out who I really am. Other than that, I'm fine."

"Maybe you should give up this idea and go back to the dig," Amelia said, chewing on her bottom lip. "I mean, have you really thought this thing through? What if you can't pull it off? What if you get caught?''

Shelby frowned. "This morning you said I would 'breeze through with my eyes closed.' Now you don't think I can pull it off. Thanks for the vote of confidence."

"It's not that. It's just…well…you don't exactly look like a nanny."

"Looks are deceiving," Shelby quoted. She drank the rest of her tea and slid the glass to one side. "I wouldn't back out now even if I wanted to—which I don't." She stood and began gathering the packages. "Michael Chandler has ordered me to make his home a safe and proper environment for his nephew and that's precisely what I'm going to do." Abruptly, Shelby sat down and stared blankly at her friend.

"Now what's wrong?" Amelia asked.

"Car seat. We forgot to buy a car seat." Shelby looked at all her purchases and groaned. "It will never fit in the car with all this stuff. Do you think I could get it delivered?"

Amelia laughed. "Honey, tell them it's for Michael Chandler and they'll deliver it to the moon."

A picture of the handsome man sprung unbidden to Shelby's mind. The memory of his slate-gray stare sent the blood rushing to her toes. "I wonder how Mr. Chandler will feel about having a car seat installed in his limousine," she said, her eyes sparkling.

"I don't know," Amelia said laughing, "but I have a feeling you're going to find out."

Chapter 3

Michael Chandler doubled forward, then stretched out his legs, pushing hard against the wall, the force propelling him far out into the pool. There was something hypnotic about the steady rhythm of his arms whistling through the air, entering the water with barely a ripple, then grabbing the water and pulling it back behind him to start the cycle yet again. He approached swimming as he did everything in his life with intensity and aggression.

Like Janus, the Roman god with opposite faces, Michael had divided himself into two separate and distinct individuals. His professional persona looked forward, into the future, a continuous stream of challenges and ventures. He thrived on the chaos that tested his business acumen and forced him to change tactics, change directions, change plans almost daily.

But his private life faced the other way. It was quiet, orderly, regimented and constant. There was no room for upheaval, no need for change. And swimming was a critical part of his personal routine. It cleared his mind and pushed his stamina to the limit. It removed the pent-up frustrations of the previous day, and prepared him mentally and physically for the one to come.

Michael hit the wall and swam underwater much farther than usual. He surged to the surface, gulped air into his lungs, then plunged under again. It was taking a long time—a very long time—to get rid of yesterday's frustrations.

His thoughts turned automatically to his newest employee, and reflexively he hauled himself a little faster through the pristine water. He had been furious when he discovered she had taken his Jaguar, and had intended to have it out with her when she got back. But his meeting with the officers of the Peterson Company about the proposed asset acquisition had gone on all night. By the time he'd gotten home, he'd been too tired to confront anyone.

The delay had given him time to cool off, and in retrospect Michael realized he had little cause to be angry. Since everything had to be done by Saturday, she had to get started right away. He appreciated her efficiency; he just wasn't used to *not* having things his own way—right where he wanted them, when he wanted them.

Michael allowed himself a small sigh as an uneasy feeling washed over him. He didn't believe in premonitions, but he had the sinking feeling that the missing Jaguar was only a small taste of what was to come.

He had lost count of the laps some time ago, but having finally laid to rest yesterday's hassles, he was just starting the second stage of his routine when he heard a low rumble, like the sound of distant thunder. He glanced up, but the blue sky was cloudless and rich with the light of the early-morning sun.

Michael did another flip turn and headed for the far side of the pool, slicing through the water with quick, clean strokes. Then he heard the noise again. It was louder this time, and unlike thunder, it was continuous, and growing in intensity.

Then he saw the source. A cement truck lumbered around the back of the house, it's loaded cylinder turning slowly. Dumbstruck, Michael watched as the truck plowed through a low hedge, crushed a full bed of azaleas and eased to a stop some twenty-five feet from the edge of the pool. A large section of manicured lawn was steadily sinking under the heavy weight.

Anger replaced shock as Michael hauled himself out of the pool and strode quickly to the vehicle, rivulets of water running down his body. "What the hell do you think you're doing?" he demanded, ripping open the door to the cab and yanking out the wide-eyed driver.

The man stepped away from Michael's menacing stance and retrieved a work order from the cab. "Chandler, right?" He pointed to the clipboard. "Says here we're supposed to put in a fence."

"I didn't order any fence." Michael grabbed the clipboard out of the hands of the astonished driver. He flipped quickly to the signature page. Shelby McMasters. "I'll be right back," he growled. "Meanwhile, get that truck off my lawn and park it by the garage."

"Look, mister, I ain't got all day, you know."

Michael silenced him with a scowl, and continued glaring at the man until he reluctantly did as he was told.

A breeze from the ocean whipped around him, but Michael was too heated to feel a chill. Without bothering to retrieve his robe or towel, he stormed into the house. "Callahan!"

Michael left a trail of puddles and wet footprints that started on the lanai, slopped through the halls and dead-ended in the library. He grabbed the phone and buzzed the security guard at the gate. "Who the hell gave you permission to let a cement truck onto my property?"

Before the guard could answer, John Callahan dashed into the room. But he was stopped short by the sight of his boss, clad only in swimming trunks, bellowing into the phone, while all around him, water dripped on the plush carpeting and was absorbed like a sponge. "You . . . called for me, sir?"

"Find McMasters. I want to talk to her—now."

"Yes, sir." Callahan headed for the door, then turned back to his boss. "May I get you a towel?"

"I don't want a towel, damn it. I want an explanation!"

Callahan fled the room, and Michael returned to the telephone conversation with his guard.

"Until someone else starts signing your paychecks, you'd be well advised to remember who you work for," Michael said, his voice filled with silky menace. "No one gets onto this property without my permission. And if you can't handle that, I'll find someone who can."

Shelby stood in the doorway, listening to the one-sided conversation, but her eyes were focused on the taut, well-tanned body before her. Michael Chandler looked more virile and dangerous than any man had the right to look. She gazed at the wide shoulders, the narrow hips and the muscular legs that were the trademark of an athlete. His dark hair glistened like black silk and droplets of water clung to his lashes. Suddenly, he looked up.

"Come in and sit down, Ms. McMasters. We have a few things to discuss." His voice was overly courteous, frighteningly so. He tossed the work order in her lap. "What can you tell me about this?"

"It's a work order for the new fence."

"I know *what* it is. What I don't know is why you ordered it. I didn't realize your talents extended to landscaping."

"You ordered me to prepare your home to meet the needs of your nephew. It is a statistical fact that in the warm weather states of Arizona, Florida, Texas and *California,* drowning is the leading cause of accidental death of children under the age of five. The U.S. Consumer Product Safety Commission estimates that two hundred and sixty children under that age drown each year in residential pools and spas."

"Which is precisely why I hired you," Michael countered. "It's your job to look after the boy."

"Mr. Chandler," Shelby said slowly, "a child can drown in less than three minutes. *Three minutes,*" she emphasized. "The majority of those drownings could be prevented with adequate protection around pools. Are you suggesting I should risk your nephew's life for the sake of a few plants?"

Michael opened his mouth, then closed it again. There was no refuting her logic. "Of course not," he replied. "But you should have mentioned this to me beforehand."

"You specifically said you didn't have time to be bothered with details."

"Ms. McMasters—" Michael planted his hands firmly on the desk and leaned toward her "—a loaded cement truck parked in the middle of my flower bed is hardly a 'detail.'" Droplets of water fell from his chest and arms, landing on the files that littered his desk. Michael straightened abruptly and tried to shake out the papers, his wet hands sticking to everything they touched. "I will contact a landscape architect and have the area redesigned to include a fence," he said calmly.

Shelby stiffened and pushed her case a little harder. "Mr. Chandler, I apologize for the errant behavior of the driver and I intend to see it does not happen again. However, your nephew will be here in three days and I seriously doubt that even you could have the area redesigned, materials ordered, delivered, and installed, and have the landscaping redone in seventy-two hours." She pulled a drawing from her clipboard and placed it on the desk in front of him. "Following the recommendations of the C.P.S.C., I have arranged for the pool to be completely fenced in. The fence will be five feet high, and the gates will be self-closing and self-latching." Shelby paused for breath. "The men from the fence company should be here shortly," she continued. "Given the time constraints, I suggest you let them install the fence. If you don't like it, you can have it redone or, for that matter, completely removed, when your nephew is a little older."

Michael took a deep breath and expelled it slowly. Arguing with her was like fencing with a foilmaster—for every lunge she had a parry. "Fine," he said. "Finish it. But in the future, you will check with me before removing, replacing or refurbishing anything." His voice was dangerously low. "Is that clear?"

Shelby met his icy gray eyes without flinching. "Of course, sir. Is there anything else?"

"As a matter of fact, there is. My Jaguar..."

The loud mutterings of Anna Hodges cut short what he intended to say. Wielding towels and a terry robe, the Scotswoman marched into the library and propped her fists on her sturdy hips. "I've been mopping that floor from here to the pool, Mr. Michael. You told me yourself not to put any chemicals on the marble, and what do you think that pool is filled with?" The woman's eyes widened as she surveyed the area around Michael's desk. "And just look what you're doing to the carpet!"

"Mrs. Hodges, this is not the time—"

"I know you're a busy man, Mr. Michael, but if I don't get the water up now, it'll ruin the carpet for sure." The older woman thrust the robe into his hands and dropped to her knees, blotting the carpet with her towels. "It won't take but a few minutes."

"Perhaps I could help you," Shelby offered, stooping beside the portly woman.

"Heavens, no, miss. That's not your job. You've got to get ready for Mr. Michael's nephew. I can handle this all right. As my Jules always says—"

"Excuse me, Mr. Chandler," John Callahan said, venturing into the room. "There's a gentleman here who wants to see you about a load of cement."

"Out of here, all of you," Michael roared. "Callahan, tell that idiotic driver to go to hell. Mrs. Hodges, I will call you when I am finished in here. And as for you," he said, turning his fury on Shelby, "we will continue this discussion about my car later. Now, everyone, get out!"

The room emptied in a flash.

"That man is impossible," Shelby muttered as she headed for the pool and the delinquent driver. "Not to mention the fact that he has the personality of a goat."

"Don't you pay him no never-mind," Mrs. Hodges replied, the load of towels supported by her ample bosom. "Mr. Michael's not that bad. He just takes a bit of getting used to."

That was the understatement of the decade. Shelby tipped her head and looked sideways at the housekeeper. She seemed normal enough. But Shelby couldn't imagine any sane person putting up with Michael Chandler. "How long have you worked here?" she asked.

Mrs. Hodges rubbed her wispy gray hair. "Nearly fifteen years," she said. "Yes, indeed. Mr. Michael had just made his fortune and built this house for himself. He hired Jules and me straightaway and we've been here ever since. Although I don't mind telling you, we were sure afraid for our jobs when he married the missus."

Shelby halted. She hadn't known he'd been married. But more surprising than the knowledge was the disturbing effect it had on her. "I didn't realize there *was* a Mrs. Chandler," she said slowly, hoping to encourage the older woman into talking.

"Nasty woman, that one, and good riddance, I say. Mr. Michael's better off without her."

Shelby wanted to know more, but Mrs. Hodges bustled off to the kitchen, leaving Shelby to deal with the truck driver. The cement wasn't supposed to arrive until after the fence posts were in place and that couldn't be done until the holes were dug. It was only seven-thirty in the morning and already she had faced down one angry man and was about to face another. Shelby sighed. If this was any indication, it was going to be a very long day.

Michael knotted the sash around his thick, terry robe and cinched it tight. Through the library window he watched Shelby as she marched past the pool and headed for the cement truck parked in front of the garage. The driver sat on the bumper smoking a cigarette. He tossed it into the grass when Shelby approached.

Michael watched as Shelby pointed to the offending butt and forced the careless driver to pick it up. The lady had moxie—pure and simple. She stood up to Michael without batting an eye and now she was giving the cement truck driver the tongue-lashing of his life, jabbing at his chest with her finger. And damned if he wasn't taking it. She had the finesse of a diplomat and the determination of a bulldozer. Her talents were wasted as a nanny, thought Michael. She could have been a boardroom executive, a CEO at the very least.

The buzzer on his desk sounded and Michael punched a button on the speaker.

"Mr. Chandler? This is George at the front gate. There are three guys here with a truck from J & A Fencing. They say they're supposed to install a new fence. Should I let them in?"

Michael hesitated, but there was no avoiding the fact that his pool needed to be fenced. "Yes," he said finally. "Let them in." He was about to ring off, when another thought struck him. "And tell them to keep their truck in the driveway where it belongs," he warned.

"Yes, sir."

The speaker clicked off. Michael watched until the truck rounded the back of the house and came into full view. Shelby moved in front of the vehicle, waving her arms like a senior officer of the Signal Corps. He couldn't hear her words, but her actions were crystal clear. With the men standing around her, she pointed to the pool, or more accurately, to specific spots around the pool. She gave them a sheet a paper and stood there while the men studied it. She marched them over to the trodden azalea bed and all three men turned to look at the poor cement truck driver, who shrugged helplessly. Finally, she pushed up her sleeve and pointed to her watch. Michael chuckled. CEO was too mild—she could have been Chairman of the Joint Chiefs of Staff.

Michael sat down at his desk. Watching the circus was a pleasant diversion—as long as he wasn't part of it—but he had work to do. A lot of it. He pulled out the Peterson file and his mini-recorder and began dictating.

"Memo to Sid Bryce. Re: Peterson Asset Acquisition Agreement..."

The intercom buzzed again.

"Yes?"

"This is George at the front gate. Sorry to bother you, Mr. Chandler, but there's a lady here from Decorating Designs. She says she has to measure some windows. Do I let her in?"

"Yes," Michael barked.

He picked up the hand-held microphone and started again. "I'm concerned about Peterson's proposed representations and warranties about their qualified plan..."

Buzzz.

"Mr. Chandler? This is George at the front gate. There's a guy here who wants to measure some rooms for a new carpet. Should I—"

"Yes," Michael said with exasperation, punching the intercom button and silencing the guard. He replayed the tape and tried to pick up his train of thought. "Because of the spin-off of their Pacific operations, I'm concerned their pension plan may be underfunded. Let me see the backup...."

Shelby knocked softly on the half-open door and, without waiting for an invitation, let herself in. "Excuse me, Mr. Chandler. I'd like your permission to have Mr. Hodges remove and destroy all the California buckeye shrubs."

Michael slumped back in his chair and looked at her blankly. "The what?"

"California buckeye. They look like a small horse chestnut tree and have a glossy brown seed similar to a nut. The nut, if eaten, is fatal."

"Fatal?"

"Yes, sir."

Buzzz. Michael propped his elbows on the desk and held his head in his hands.

"Mr. Chandler, this is..."

"...George at the front gate," Michael said in unison with the voice on the speaker.

A week ago, Michael was in control of his life. It was ordered and disciplined. His staff was ordered and disciplined. A week ago, Michael would have handed George his head. But that was a week ago, a lifetime ago. Today everything was different. "Don't bother me anymore," he said simply.

"But, sir, you said—"

"I know what I said and I'm changing my mind. I'm the boss. I can do that." Michael glanced at Shelby, who was standing erect in front of his desk. A smile spread across his face as an interesting idea entered his aching head. "From now on, George, whenever someone arrives at the gate, you are to buzz Ms. McMasters and ask *her* permission." His smile broadened and he tipped his head politely to Shelby.

"But, sir," George said, "she already gave me her permission."

"What?"

"First thing this morning, Ms. McMasters gave me a list of all the people she was expecting, their approximate times of arrival and where they should be directed."

Michael looked up at Shelby, who tipped *her* head politely and smiled back. He shook his head. "Uncle," he said, half under his breath.

Shelby suppressed the laugh that bubbled in her throat. The look on Michael's face was priceless. For the first time since she'd met him, Michael Chandler looked human.

The voice of the confused George came over the speaker yet again. "Beg pardon, sir?"

"I said, I'm an uncle." Michael flipped off the intercom.

"About the California buckeye..."

Michael sat up straight in his chair. "If the seeds of those plants are hazardous and lethal if eaten, then I suggest you see to their removal." He turned to his business, dismissing her with his inattention.

Shelby stood there, staring at him. The man wore a suit of armor. For one brief moment, he had raised the visor long enough for her to glimpse the man under the helmet. Then, just as quickly, he had slammed it down, preferring to joust with some corporate dragon, instead. Shelby chuckled at the image. Armor—maybe. Saintly knight—never.

"Is there something else?" he asked with cool, unruffled resolve.

"No, sir," she said smartly. When Michael turned his back on her, she snapped to attention and offered him a mock salute. She pivoted on her heel and left.

Outside the library, Shelby found the carpet man waiting for her. She showed him Rio's bedroom and playroom and waited while he took the measurements. The carpet was in stock, and for Michael Chandler, the company had agreed to install it the very next day. At least that much was going as planned.

Shelby glanced at her watch. The assistant from Amelia's store should have been here by now. She signed the final purchase order for the carpet, then escorted the man to the front door.

"Oh, there you are," Amelia said, popping out of the sun room and hurrying over to Shelby.

"What . . . ?"

Amelia flashed Shelby a broad conspiratorial wink, and spoke up loudly. "It's so nice to see you again. I'm so delighted you selected our little company and we're thrilled to have the opportunity to work with you. Now, this morning I'll measure the windows for the curtains. Dinosaurs, right? Wonderful choice. That dinosaur pattern is one of our most popular prints. I'm sure your little one will just love it. And my, what a lovely home you have. Perhaps there are a few other items . . ."

Shelby regained her composure and ushered Amelia through the foyer and toward the staircase. "I realize you don't have much time, Ms. Benedict, so I'm sure you'll need to get started right away."

"No, no, not at all. I'm completely at your disposal," Amelia said, balking as Shelby tried to push her up the stairs. Craning her neck, Amelia continued to scan the room, her eyes adding up items like a cash register.

"I insist," Shelby said through clenched teeth. "Right this way." She took Amelia's arm and didn't let go until they reached the second floor and were safely in the bedroom, well out of earshot. "What are you doing here? You promised me you'd stay away."

"I never actually promised, and besides, Nancy was . . . unavailable."

"Look, Amelia. I'm in no mood to play games. I will stand here until you measure these windows, then I will personally escort you out. I have already had two run-ins this morning with Michael Chandler and I have no intention of repeating the performance."

Amelia shrugged, removed a tape measure from her purse, and began measuring the windows. "He didn't seem so bad to me," she said, recording the numbers in a little book.

Shelby gasped. "You met him?" She grabbed Amelia by the shoulders and spun her around. "You didn't say anything to him, did you?"

"Of course not. Well, I said good morning." She studied the look on Shelby's face. "Come on, what did you think I would do... stick my tongue out at him? I'm your friend, remember? I'm not going to give you away."

"Shh. Keep your voice down." Shelby sighed and plopped down on the window seat. She scooped up one of the stuffed dinosaurs and hugged it close. "That man drives me crazy. One minute I'm scared half to death, and the next I want to punch him in the nose. And as soon as I think he might actually be part-human, he turns into an overbearing ... baboon."

"I think he's cute."

"Cute?" Shelby made a face. "He's rude, arrogant..."

"... Rich, gorgeous ..."

"... condescending, self-centered ..."

"... tall, blond..."

"... insensitive, overbearing ... *blond?*" Shelby's eyebrows shot toward the top of her head. "Who are you talking about?"

John Callahan chose that moment to enter the room and Amelia's smile could have put Pacific Gas & Electric out of work for a week. "Him!"

Chapter 4

"*Him?*" Shelby asked.

"Hem," Amelia said quickly. "How much of a *hem* would you like in these curtains?"

John Callahan cleared his throat. "I'm sorry to interrupt you, Shelby," he said, "but the fence installers need to talk with you."

Shelby eyed Amelia. "Thank you, but Ms. Benedict isn't quite finished. It will be a few more minutes before I can show her out."

"Nonsense," Amelia countered. "I'm sure someone else could point the way. Perhaps this gentleman could help me, Mr...?"

"Callahan," he said, extending his hand. "John Callahan."

"Amelia Benedict," she chirped, taking the offered hand, "owner of Decorating Designs. I can redesign any room in your home, complete with custom-made curtains, draperies..." Reluctantly, she released his hand. "...bedspreads," she added with undue emphasis. "In fact, I have some samples with me that I would be happy to show you."

Shelby shoved Amelia toward the windows. "Yes, well, I'm sure Mr. Callahan has other things to do."

"Not at all," he said, grinning broadly. "I'd be delighted to stay with the lady until she's finished here."

"There, you see," Amelia exulted. "You run along, Ms. McMasters. I'll be done and out of here *tout de suite.*"

Shelby flashed Amelia a neon look that screamed "don't-you-dare-do-anything-stupid," and hurried to the pool to see what new problem awaited her.

The rest of that day and the next two passed in a flurry of constant work. Shelby talked to Jules Hodges, who obligingly tore out the California buckeye. She monitored the installation of the jungle gym and the sandbox. She deftly deflected Amelia, who showed up again that afternoon under the pretense of supervising the paperhanging crew. The carpet was installed Thursday morning, the furniture arrived that afternoon, and on Friday Amelia delivered the bedspread, draperies and a covered cushion for the window seat. It was amazing the number of doors that swung open for the name "Michael Chandler."

The man himself had stayed clear of the estate, and Shelby hadn't seen or talked to him since their confrontation Wednesday morning. For all she knew, Michael had moved out completely—not that it bothered her, of course. In fact, she was relieved he was gone. She didn't need those icy gray eyes peering over her shoulder, that smooth voice criticizing every decision she made, that imposing form sparring with her at every turn.

Still, when she happened to say something to John Callahan about Michael's absence, he said the boss was frequently away. And when she casually mentioned it to Mrs. Hodges, the lady had said, "No sense looking for trouble. If Mr. Michael wants something, he'll let you know. In the meantime, you just do your job."

Now it was Friday night, and tomorrow she would fly to Mexico to get Rio. Her heart lurched at the thought of the orphaned little boy. He was the real reason she had worked so hard. She gazed around the room she'd prepared—all of this was for him. But it was going to take a lot more than a new bed and dinosaur curtains to make up for his loss. Let Michael Chandler give him all the material stuff. She was going to give

Rio what he needed most—someone to love, and someone to love him.

Shelby settled the dinosaur lamp/night-light on one end of the dresser, plugged it in and turned it on. She smiled as the endearing character warmed the room with its soft glow. She put the few items of clothing she had purchased into the drawers and arranged the toys and books on the shelves of the built-in bookcase. A kelly-green stuffed brontosaurus fell to the floor. Shelby picked it up and sat down on the edge of the bed. She ran her fingers down its roller-coaster neck, up and over its back and down to its tail. Finally, she placed it gently in the center of the bed, its head lying on Rio's pillow.

The course of both their lives had changed forever, all because of one horrible, stupid bus accident.

"May I come in?" Michael asked, eyeing her curiously.

Shelby jumped at the sound of his voice and blinked away the tears that had gathered in her eyes. "Of course," she said, her voice husky with suppressed emotion.

"I'm sorry if I startled you."

"No, you didn't. Well, maybe a little," she confessed. She smoothed out the wrinkles in the bedspread and turned to face him.

Michael looked up at the border of colored dinosaurs that marched around the room and the matching curtains hanging at the windows. "Dinosaurs, huh?" he said. "They look . . . nice."

"Thank you. Rio will love them . . . I mean, I hope he will," Shelby added quickly.

"I'm sure he will." He continued looking around the room, staring at the bookcase, the oak dresser and the bed.

"I kept records of everything—what I purchased and how much I spent," Shelby said, defending herself against his silence. She picked up a notebook from the window seat and offered it to him. "I think you'll find everything in order."

"I'm sure everything's fine," he said, ignoring the book in Shelby's outstretched hand. "You've proven yourself quite competent in these matters."

No one would ever characterize a baby dinosaur lamp as being romantic, but Shelby could feel its soft, mellow warmth spreading throughout the room. Or maybe it was her own inner warmth she felt, glowing from his compliment. As improbable as the idea sounded, he *had* paid her a compliment.

The small lamp darkened his eyes and dappled his hair with flecks of burnished copper. It put parts of the room in shadow, but Michael's shadow loomed largest of all, soaring up the wall and across the ceiling. Real dinosaurs never looked so big.

He strolled through the connecting door that led to Shelby's room and flipped on the light. "You didn't change anything in here," he said. "You could have redecorated your room, as well."

"There was no need," Shelby replied, putting down her notebook and straightening a picture that hung on Rio's wall. *No need to waste money changing a room I won't be staying in for very long,* she thought. She moved to the doorway and smiled. "The room is quite nice the way it is."

In fact, her room was lovely. The airy corner room had a dormer and window seat like Rio's. Striped yellow wallpaper covered two walls and white curtains matched the quilted comforter on the double bed. She had forgotten how luxurious it felt to sleep on a real mattress with sheets that weren't gritty with sand. And it was wonderful slipping your feet into your shoes without first having to shake out the spiders. Here you didn't have to wait your turn to take a shower, and there was always plenty of hot water. Living in civilization went beyond "nice." It was heavenly.

"It's nice enough," Michael commented, his eyes narrowing. But it was also odd. She had made his nephew's room warm, cozy, welcoming, but her own room remained untouched. At first glance, there was nothing to indicate anyone even used this room. The dresser was void of combs and makeup and jewelry. There were no plants or photos or books. Nothing at all to make it her own, to make it look lived-in—except for a slinky red something-or-other that lay across the foot of the bed. "I guess I'm surprised you haven't made this room more...personal," he said, eyeing the garment, "with your own mementos and such."

Shelby brushed by him and scooped up the flimsy camisole. Every piece of clothing she owned was practical, serviceable and guaranteed to last forever. After all, when you spent your time tromping through a tropical jungle, you didn't need sexy lingerie. But all that had changed when she'd come back to the States. One of the first things Shelby had done was to give in to her one weakness. It was a proven fact that sexy underwear built confidence and self-assurance, and Shelby had needed a bundle of both in interviewing with Michael Chandler. But then, she wasn't about to tell him she'd been wearing this self-same item the day she'd marched into his office and landed the job.

Shelby tucked the silky garment into a dresser drawer. "I haven't had much time," she said tersely. She also wasn't about to tell him she didn't have much in the way of "personal mementos." Everything she owned could fit into two suitcases and a couple of footlockers—and they were still back at the dig. "Was there something you wanted?" she asked.

The curtness of her tone cut short Michael's attempt at small talk. "Yes," he said. "I wanted to talk with you about tomorrow's trip. You'll be flying in my private jet nonstop from San Francisco to Chetumal. Pasig will drive you to the airport and escort you to the plane."

Shelby blinked. "Your private jet? Isn't that a bit extravagant?"

"If you prefer, you could leave San Francisco at one in the morning, fly to Houston and sit there for three hours waiting for a connecting flight. Would you like me to change the arrangements?"

"No, of course not," Shelby said, reddening.

"Then it's settled." Michael pulled a fat envelope from the inside pocket of his suit jacket and sat down on the edge of Shelby's bed. He withdrew a sheaf of papers from the envelope and carefully unfolded them. "My pilot will fly you directly to Chetumal, which is the capital of Quintana Roo, one of three Mexican states in the Yucatán peninsula," he explained, handing Shelby her itinerary.

Reluctantly, she sat down beside him to study it. Having Michael Chandler nose around her bedroom was one thing—sitting next to him on the bed was quite another. She was uncomfortably aware of the powerful shoulders that seemed to dwarf her, and the length of hard, muscled thigh only inches away from her own.

"There will be a driver waiting to take you due west across Quintana Roo into Campeche," Michael continued. "Just over the Campeche-Quintana Roo border is a small town called Xpujil. It's about sixty or seventy miles from Chetumal. In Xpujil, I've arranged for a guide with a four-wheel-drive Jeep to take you the rest of the way. The commune leaders know you're coming, but they may be reluctant to give up the boy.

They're a strange group—uncooperative, tight-knit, never give a straight answer. These papers authorize the boy's release into your custody. If you run into trouble," he said, handing her a smaller piece of paper, "call this number and ask for Eduardo Villegas. He's a lawyer in Chetumal and is familiar with this case."

He moved a fraction closer and she caught the tantalizing scent of soap and spice. A muscle tightened in her jaw. "I'm sure I'll be fine."

Michael nodded. "No doubt," he said, "but regardless, it's best to be prepared. If all goes as planned, you and Rio will spend tomorrow night in Xpujil and return home on Sunday. Do you have your passport?"

His tie hung loose around his neck and the top button of his shirt was undone. "Yes," she said, dragging her gaze from the faint white line of a scar that stood out against his tanned throat.

"Good. And here is the consular certificate you need to bring Rio out of the country." His arm grazed hers as he handed her the paper.

Shelby stiffened. Leaning over his desk, he was intimidating. Leaning over her, he was downright overwhelming. The first one she could handle, the second left her all but paralyzed. Her fingers slowly closed around the document and she put it with the others.

"The flight will be a long one, over seven hours. I told the pilot you'd be ready to leave San Francisco at ten tomorrow morning, which means you will have to leave here by eight. Will that be a problem?"

A tingling sensation rippled along her spine and Shelby briefly considered leaving for the airport right now. "Not at all," she said.

"Good." Michael tugged on one end of the tie and it slid slowly around his neck, the silken colors cascading into his strong hands. "Any questions?"

It was hard to come up with a question when your brain had turned to dust. "None that I can think of," she answered truthfully.

"Well then, I guess that's it." The bed shifted suddenly as he stood, and Shelby scrambled to her feet. "I'll see you when you get back. Good night."

With that, he left, and relief nearly knocked Shelby to the floor.

Shelby sucked in her breath as she stepped aboard the sleek private plane. So this was how the other half lived. Correction—the other half of one percent. Not everyone could take a basic 737 and turn it into a flying penthouse that rivaled a suite at the Fairmont. Rose-colored carpet, two inches thick, cushioned her feet as she entered the lounge area. The deep, burgundy-velvet wing chairs were designed for comfort, and silk curtains were drawn over the oval windows. There was a game table of burled wood and a formal bar hosting tiers of crystal decanters.

"Pretty impressive, isn't it?" A smartly dressed flight attendant slipped Shelby's overnight bag into a closet.

Shelby grinned. "Was I that obvious? What gave me away— the bulging eyes or the gaping mouth?"

The attendant smiled and glanced over her shoulder before answering. "Actually, it's a pleasant change seeing someone who isn't bored by all of this."

Shelby nestled back in the velvet-cushioned chair and surveyed the compartment. Comfort was a high priority with people who traveled frequently, but Michael's plane made first class look like a slave galley. Not that she'd had much experience with first class—her idea of comfort was a scratchy blanket and a neighboring empty seat. But it wouldn't take much to adapt to this kind of luxury. Shelby shook her head. "How could anyone ever become bored living like a king?"

"You'd be surprised." The attendant pulled a small stack of magazines from the magazine rack and replaced them with some new ones. "We'll be departing shortly," she said. "Our estimated flying time is seven hours and thirty-five minutes. Skies are clear this morning and no turbulence has been reported. Mr. Chandler has given you full use of the plane, so please feel free to explore, once we are airborne. As you can see," she said, with a sweep of her arm, "this is the drawing room. The kitchen and the crew's compartment are forward, the rest of the compartments are aft. There are playing cards," she said, pointing to the game table, "music via the CD player, movies and a library. If there is anything else you need, just ask. Lunch will be served at one o'clock. Is that acceptable?"

Shelby nodded.

"Fine. In the meantime, would you care for a late breakfast or a cocktail, perhaps a Mimosa, Bloody Mary, champagne?"

"Could you conjure up a glass of ice water?"

The attendant smiled. "I think I can manage that." She poured the water into an elegant glass, placed it on the small table next to Shelby, then turned to leave.

"Wait, please," Shelby urged, seizing the opportunity to learn more about her new boss. "Could you answer a few questions?"

"I'll try." The attendant perched on the arm of one of the wing chairs. "What do you want to know?"

Shelby took a deep breath. She was great at digging into other people's lives—as long as those people were already dead. But snooping into the actions of a live person was an entirely new experience. "About Mr. Chandler," Shelby began hesitantly. "Does he travel a lot?"

"Well, he doesn't travel as much as some, but he does make regular trips to New York, London and Tokyo. He has businesses in those cities."

"I see." Shelby took a long, slow drink of her ice water. So, even living in San Francisco, the best Rio could hope for was a long-distance relationship with his uncle. "Do you always accompany him?" she asked, trying to visualize Michael soaring across continents with a squadron of gorgeous attendants. The image came far too easily.

The attendant smiled. "Unfortunately, no. I belong to a select group of attendants who service only private planes. It's handled through an agency and whoever's next on the roster works on whichever plane is leaving. It's completely arbitrary, unless a patron requests specific attendants."

Shelby didn't miss a beat. "And does Mr. Chandler ever request specific attendants?"

"Not in the three years I've been here."

"Oh." Shelby swirled her glass and carefully studied the clinking ice.

"It's Steuben."

She looked up blankly. "What?"

"Your glass. It's Steuben crystal." The attendant shrugged apologetically. "I thought you were wondering."

Shelby frowned. Who cared if the stupid glass was Steuben, Waterford or plastic? She didn't need a flight attendant to tell her he was rich. She already knew all his statistics, how he had parlayed a small import company into an international conglomerate, how he had risen from a street-smart punk to star status. It was the success story of the decade. The fact was, she had read every last word on Michael Chandler and still knew nothing at all about him. There had to be something—some skeleton in the closet, some dark side—that she could uncover. But if she didn't soon figure out the right questions to ask, she would lose her opportunity to pump the attendant for information. "Yes, of course," Shelby said hastily. "I was just admiring it. It's quite lovely. Tell me," she added, "do people ever party on these planes and fly to exciting places, like Rio de Janeiro or Monte Carlo or Saint Moritz?"

"Oh, sure, all the time . . ."

Shelby mentally patted herself on the back.

". . . but not Mr. Chandler. He's all business."

Shelby sighed. Didn't the man have any vices? "You sound as though you like him."

"I do. He has very high standards and demands the very best, but he treats us as professionals. He has a temper and is short on patience, but if you do your job and do it well, he'll see that you're well paid." The attendant eyed Shelby skeptically. "But then, you already know that, don't you?"

Shelby gave her a look that she hoped appeared innocent. "Not exactly," she said. "I've only been working for Mr. Chandler since Tuesday. There's still a lot I don't know." *And a lot more I intend to find out.*

"Ah, so you're nervous," the attendant said, nodding her head reassuringly. "I was scared witless the first time I flew with him. He can be pretty intimidating."

"That must be it," Shelby agreed. She tried to steer the conversation in another direction. "Do you know why we're going to Mexico?"

The attendant shook her head. "All we know is that we're supposed to fly one of his employees down, and two back."

"Employees?" Shelby echoed in disbelief. "I'm going down there to get a child."

The wide-eyed look on the attendant's face defied description. "His child?" she gasped.

"Not his son," Shelby corrected. "His nephew. I gather you didn't know about Mr. Chandler's sister. She died in an accident, leaving an orphan son."

"No, I didn't know. How awful."

A gentle bell tolled, and the attendant stood and straightened the chair she'd been sitting on. "I have to get back to work, but if you need anything else, use the call button." She exited through the doorway and closed the cabin door behind her.

Shelby buckled her seat belt as the plane began taxiing toward the runway. *"How awful,"* the attendant had said. She didn't know the half of it. Both of Rio's parents were dead, he would be yanked out of the only home he had ever known and shipped off to live with a man he had never met, in a country whose language he could barely speak. "Awful" didn't begin to describe what had happened to that poor little boy.

Shelby pulled back the curtains. Lemon-yellow sunlight streamed through the cabin windows, warming her skin. Far below sparkled San Francisco Bay and the beautiful boats that dotted its surface. She watched intently as the plane left the city behind and continued its journey inland over the patchwork colors of the San Joaquin valley. All too soon, they reached their cruising altitude and clouds obscured her view.

Shelby curled up in the wide seat and tucked her feet under her. By evening she would be in Mexico and by nightfall she would be with Rio. She didn't relish the thought of uprooting the child. She also didn't think much of taking him to live with a total stranger who, sight unseen, considered him a nuisance. But the bottom line was she had no choice. Shelby sighed. Seven and a half hours was far too long a time to sit and think.

She stood up and stretched. The attendant had encouraged her to explore the plane and now seemed as good a time as any. With a little luck, she might find something she could use against Michael Chandler. Maybe he was into gambling, or X-rated films, something—*anything*—that would strengthen her case.

She opened the first cabinet and peeked inside. Situated to the left of a built-in VCR unit, it contained dozens of videocassette tapes. Shelby ran her fingers along the titles—*Coconuts, The Big Store, Go West, At the Circus, A Night at the Opera, Duck Soup... Duck Soup?* She looked again. No mistake. Michael Chandler had an entire collection of Marx Brothers movies. Shelby's eyebrows furrowed. She had assumed he had a couple of fine qualities hidden somewhere, but never in a million years would she have guessed a sense of humor was one of them.

She opened the next cabinet—a few brand-new decks of cards and a couple of racks of poker chips. So he gambled. It was something, but not much. She closed that door and tried the next. This one was filled with CDs—Bach, Corelli, Daquin, Handel, Locatelli, Manfredini, Telemann, Vivaldi—a baroque-lover's dream come true. Shelby frowned. You couldn't hang a man for liking classical music.

She slumped against the cabinet. This was going nowhere. She gave up on the drawing room, and moved to the next compartment. It was a richly paneled office and library. A large desk took up most of the room, but what attracted her were the handcrafted bookcases filled with books of every size and color. Shelby scanned the shelves. The library was extensive, with a distinct emphasis on history and philosophy, mostly by people she hadn't read since college. The list was as impressive as it was surprising.

Then another book caught her eye. Tucked away at the end of a shelf, half-hidden from view, was a dark green book with gold lettering. She carefully pulled it from the bookcase. *Mesoamerican Artifacts* by Gregorio Davila. Davila was a renowned expert in his field and the leading authority on Mesoamerican antiquities. Her own precious copy of this book was packed safely away. Few people outside archaeological circles had ever heard of Gregorio Davila. It was unusual, even for someone as widely read as Michael Chandler, to be familiar with Davila's work. Shelby thumbed through the well-worn pages of the book. Then she remembered the glass case of fine Mesoamerican clay figures prominently displayed in Michael's study. Not so unusual for a man with his own private collection, she thought.

Leaving the library, she discovered the bathroom—complete with a small shower—and at the far end, a bedroom cabin, with the door slightly ajar.

Shelby pushed open the door and peeked inside. A wide and welcoming bed dominated the room. A navy blue satin quilt covered the bed, and pale blue sheets were turned back over the quilt. She felt like a trespasser, a sneak, but she couldn't stop herself. She walked slowly around the room, trailing her fingers along the streamlined walnut credenza, running her hand over the back of another wing chair, coming to a stop in front of a small closet.

Part of her said there was no reason to be snooping through his clothes. Part of her said there was no reason not to. Curiosity won out and she gingerly opened the door. The closet wasn't large enough to hold much. There were a half-dozen white dress shirts and an equal number of silk ties. Shelby fingered one of them, then without thinking pulled it from the tie rack and draped it around her neck. Was it just last night Michael had sat next to her on the bed, his tie loose and dangling down the front of his crisp white shirt? She held the tie to her nose and inhaled deeply. It was there—the faint but unmistakable scent she had come to associate with Michael Chandler.

Michael.

The man made her blood boil in more ways than one. His arrogance was infuriating. His intimidating demeanor left her ready to kick him in the shins. And she didn't want to get started on his attitude toward children.

But Lord, he was handsome. The erect posture proclaimed an unshakable confidence; the lean, muscled body proved he was more than a weekend warrior; and his voice . . . His voice was deep and arresting, one that could speak with authority or drop to an intimate whisper. The kind of voice that kindled a fire in the pit of her stomach.

Maybe that was the problem. Maybe she had spent too many years at the bottom of a sandy pit. So many years searching through artifacts of the dead that she had forgotten what it felt like to be alive. She wasn't used to falling apart just because a man looked at her. Or sat next to her. Or leaned close. Usually, she put them in their place. And their place was definitely and firmly outside her emotional borders.

Until now. Being around Michael Chandler was changing that, and Shelby wasn't at all sure it was a change for the better.

She pushed aside the business shirts and suits until she came to a thick terry robe, much like the one Michael had worn that first morning after his swim. Hastily undressing, she slipped into the robe and pulled it tight around her. She turned up the collar and buried her face in its softness.

Sometimes even the staunchest mind was vulnerable to lonely thoughts, and now was one of those times. The king-size bed loomed empty before her. Impulsively, her mind conjured up the vision of Michael sleeping there, his dark hair thick against the big down pillow, his bare shoulder revealing smooth, deeply tanned skin, one strong arm thrown over the coverlet.

Shelby's breath slowed.

The air of the cabin was cool against her heated skin. She could imagine the gentle rise and fall of the covers with each shallow breath. She traced the outline of the quilt along his firm, lean body and down his long legs. They were all alone, the two of them, thirty-five thousand feet above the earth.

The moment, like the robe, seemed to wrap around her, drawing her closer, urging her forward. She slipped out of the robe and slid between the pale blue sheets. Being in Michael's bed seemed utterly right. She felt protected and safe. She needed his strength, the solid feel of sinew and muscle and power. She wanted his strong arms holding her, wanted his lips on hers.

She snuggled farther into the comfort of the bed and closed her eyes. A vision of Michael came easily, and she knew exactly how it would be...

There was an invitation in his eyes, in the way his gaze lingered on her mouth and trailed down her throat. She felt it in the touch of his hand as he reached for her, in the way he leaned close enough for her to sense the desire building inside him. His fingers, long and strong, drifted across her stomach and thighs. He drew her into his arms and covered her mouth with a passionate kiss. The powerful image of herself moving beneath him made her body feel as if it were touched by fire. The thought of being held and caressed and made love to forced her heart to pound wildly in a way that was almost painful. Desire swept over her, and made her tremble with need.

The plane hit a pocket and dipped, abruptly ejecting her from her fantasy. Her face flushed with embarrassment as she struggled to her feet. Thank God, no one was here to see her, to see what a fool she had made of herself. She threw on her clothes and rushed from the room, slamming the door behind her.

She collapsed in the nearest chair. Being in Michael's bedroom did strange things to her mind, and, for the sake of her sanity, she vowed to spend the rest of the flight watching the Marx Brothers.

* * *

Mexico.

Shelby peered out the window as the plane flew in a wide arc over Chetumal. In a few minutes they'd be landing, and in a few hours she would be with Rio. She couldn't wait to see him, to hold him, to talk to him about his uncle and to tell him all about their new life in the States. She intended to do everything in her power to ensure Rio's happiness in his new country.

The moment the wheels touched the tarmac, the attendant rapped softly on the closed drawing-room door and announced that Shelby's car was ready.

Shelby gathered her things and followed the attendant to the waiting driver. A sultry breeze wafted around her as she climbed into the car. She had been away less than a month, and had already forgotten how hot and humid the weather was, especially during the rainy season.

Before long, they had left the city behind, moving steadily along the curving road of Highway 186 across the state of Quintana Roo. Driving into the thick, lush rain forest, Shelby craned her neck, her eyes delighting in the tall *sapote* and *campeche* covered with wild jungle vines. This part of the Yucatán reminded her of an untamed paradise with tranquil blue lakes and abundant rivers sparkling in the waning light of the sun.

Blooming *flamboyanes* marked the way, their wide-spreading branches covered in clusters of brilliant orange-red flowers, while fallen scarlet petals carpeted the road before them. Shelby breathed in the heady fragrances of the plumeria, and marveled at the morning glory creeping and climbing over bushes and trees.

She could feel her anticipation and nervousness growing as they logged in the miles. She willed the car to go faster, wanting to get to Xpujil before nightfall. Driving through the Yucatán at night would be foolish for anyone unfamiliar with the area. The highway had no streetlights, and road shoulders were nonexistent.

Shelby eyed the driver skeptically. She wasn't worried about being found out—not yet away—for in a city the size of Chetumal, she was anonymous. But she did question the driver's abilities. Regardless of the fact that Michael had arranged her transportation, she knew from experience there was no guarantee the driver was competent this far away from the city.

In fact, she would have preferred to rent a car and drive herself, but Michael never would have allowed that without her supplying a darn good explanation. And explanations were something she was a little short on right now.

She tried to stretch in the cramped quarters of the old Ford. Weariness from the many hours of traveling plagued her muscles, but she was too close to her destination to demand they stop.

Dusk was settling around them when they reached the small village of Xpujil. The driver slowed, but had not fully stopped when Shelby bolted from the car.

"*Señorita,* wait. We must find your guide."

Shelby paused and cast furtive glances around the sleepy town. She had to find the guide and get out of Xpujil, get out before anyone recognized her and started asking questions she wasn't prepared to answer. Michael Chandler's connections stretched out like tentacles, reaching far and wide, perhaps even this far into the Yucatán. And if he ever found out...

An Indian man rounded the corner of a small building and hurried toward them. He stopped dead in his tracks when he spotted Shelby.

"Felipe?" Shelby's voice was barely a whisper. Sensing the approach of the driver behind her, she rushed forward to meet the familiar Indian. "*Perdoneme, señor,*" she said loudly and in flawless Spanish. "Are you the guide?" She pleaded with her eyes, praying he would understand her hidden message.

"*Sí, señorita,*" he said formally. "I have been waiting for you. My Jeep is parked right over there."

Relief washed over her like early-morning rain. "I'll be fine now," she said to the driver. "This man will take me to the commune. We'll meet you here tomorrow for the return trip to Chetumal."

The driver nodded, got back into his car and disappeared into the rapidly approaching night.

"Felipe, I can't believe it's you," Shelby said, embracing the Indian warmly. "Thanks for pretending you didn't know me."

Her friend returned the hug. "You have much to explain," he admonished, "but I would never question the intentions of a friend." He picked up her bag and started toward the Jeep.

"Wait a minute," she said. "I have to find the real guide and explain that I won't be needing his services."

Felipe's dark eyes shone with amusement. "I *am* the real guide," he said. "Señor Chandler pays very well, no?"

"How do you know about Michael Chandler?" Shelby gasped.

Felipe laughed. "It would seem we both have much to explain. Come. It is growing darker and we can talk on the way. We will have to hurry if you want to reach the commune tonight."

Shelby nodded and climbed into the Jeep. There was no need to tell him that from this point, she could find the commune in her sleep.

A collared peccary trotted across the dirt track, briefly illuminated by gossamer moonbeams that sliced through the jungle darkness. The jouncing stopped as Felipe slowed the vehicle to avoid hitting the pig.

"So, it was just coincidence," Shelby said, "that Michael hired you to be my guide."

"Not at all," Felipe answered, drawing himself up. "Señor Chandler ordered the very best—and that was me."

"Of course," Shelby said, giving his arm an affectionate squeeze. "I see nothing has changed since I've been gone."

Felipe's tone turned serious. "When you left, you said you needed to return to America for personal reasons. Since you are back in Mexico, does this mean you will be returning to the dig?"

Shelby shook her head. "Not yet." She studied the young man, trying to decide how much to tell him. "Felipe, what do you know about all of this?"

"Very little. The representatives of a rich American named Michael Chandler came to Xpujil looking for an experienced guide to drive someone from the town to the commune and back. I was recommended, they offered me a great deal of money and I graciously accepted." He looked at Shelby out of the corner of his eye. "Now, it is your turn to explain."

Shelby nodded and took a deep breath. "One of the children at the commune is Michael Chandler's nephew. Mr. Chandler is paying me a great deal of money to take the boy to California and see that he is well cared for."

Felipe's eyebrows furrowed. "You were not happy with the money you made at the dig?"

"It had nothing to do with money." She turned in her seat to face her friend. "Felipe," she began hesitantly, "do you remember how I spent all of my free time away from the camp, sometimes for the afternoon, sometimes overnight?"

Felipe nodded. "Of course," he said, grinning broadly. "We assumed you had . . . how shall I say . . . a friend . . . in the village."

"Not in the village, Felipe. I have a friend in the commune. He has blond hair and gray eyes and is nearly three and a half years old. My 'friend' is Mr. Chandler's nephew. When I learned his uncle wanted him to live in America, I took it upon myself to make sure he would be all right." A parrot flew directly overhead and settled in the thickly covered branches of a flowering tree. "Do you understand?"

"I suppose so, but—"

"Enough talk about that," Shelby interrupted. "Tell me all about the excavation. I don't miss this heat or the bugs, but I do miss the work." That was an understatement. Archaeology was her passion and she had spent most of her life pursuing her dream. She hadn't thought there was anything that could take her away from it. Glancing down at her smooth, clean hands, she realized that she even missed the feel of dirt under her fingernails.

She turned quickly to Felipe. "Tell me everything that's happened since I left. How is the work going? Have you finished clearing the second tier? Have you uncovered any new artifacts?"

Felipe laughed. "Too slowly, almost and none of any significance. The jadeite figure you discovered is still the best find. I will take you there in the morning and you can see the progress for yourself."

Shelby shook her head. "I can't, Felipe. First of all, I'd prefer that no one from the dig know I've been here. If they think I'm still in the States, I won't have to answer a lot of questions. And second, I'm expected in California tomorrow night. In fact, I'm already behind schedule. I was supposed to get back to Xpujil to spend the night, then leave for Chetumal first thing in the morning. As it is, we'll have to spend the night out here. Will that be a problem for you? I know most of the people who live in the commune, and I guarantee they'll make you comfortable."

"I will accept their hospitality with great pleasure, Señorita Shelby. But you have come so far. It would be a shame to go back without seeing everyone at the dig. You are very much missed, you know."

They passed a small, cultivated grove of orange trees and approached a clearing where a row of little cabins stood out against the moonlight.

Shelby turned to her Indian friend as the vehicle slowed to a stop. "Remember, Felipe, I don't want anyone else to know I was here. Promise me you won't say anything. Okay?"

He never had a chance to answer, for at that moment, a little boy tore across the compound, shouting, "Tía Shelby! Tía Shelby!"

She sprang from the Jeep and scooped the child into her arms. Tears rolled down her cheeks as the little boy threw his arms around her neck.

"I'm back now, Rio," she rasped, her voice choking on the tears. "And I'm never going to leave you again."

Chapter 5

Shelby gave Rio one last hug and kiss. "Now you have to go to bed or you'll be too tired to fly on the plane tomorrow."

Rio scrambled down from Shelby's lap. "Night-night," he called, racing toward the half-dozen pallets at the far side of the open room.

"Aren't you forgetting something?" Zenith pulled a bedraggled red teddy bear from behind her back and offered it to the little boy. He snatched it out of her hand and clutched it to his chest before settling down on one of the makeshift beds.

Zenith tossed her long braid over her shoulder and picked up the hand-carved toys scattered across the plank floor. "He must be excited if he could forget his *osito de peluche*. A couple of days ago, he lost it and I was afraid we'd never find it. After the death of his parents, I couldn't bear to see him lose another thing, not even that ratty old stuffed animal. Fortunately, one of the men found it at the edge of the orange grove."

"How in the world did it get out there?"

"I don't know. The best I can come up with is that Rio left his bear in one of the farm trucks and, during the unloading of the crates, the bear fell out."

"Well, the main thing is that he got it back." Shelby held open a burlap sack and Zenith dropped in the toys. Zenith pulled the drawstring tight, then set the bag inside the wooden cupboard. "It's so quiet around here," Shelby said. "Where is everyone?"

"We thought you might want to be alone with Rio tonight, so Eamon took our children to the empty cabin. I'll join them as soon as you're settled. Rio hasn't spent much time in his parents' cabin since the accident, but if you'd rather stay there..."

"No," Shelby said quickly. "I'd rather be here." She looked around the spacious room, filled with the love and warmth of Zenith's family. All the cabins were pretty much the same—plank floors swept clean every day; wooden table, chairs and cupboards that were strong and functional; quilts for the pallet-beds made from scraps of old clothing. This cabin contained evidence of the day-to-day living of decent, caring, hardworking people. The other one contained only memories, and Shelby wasn't ready to deal with them yet. "Thank you for all you've done for Rio," she said quietly. "It helped a lot to know you were here taking care of him."

"Gloxinia was part of our family, Elias too, and Rio is like our own son. We were happy to keep him." Zenith took two oranges from a woven basket and handed one to Shelby.

"I know." Shelby dug her nails into the plump fruit and began peeling away the rind. "Does Rio understand what happened?"

"Somewhat. He knows his parents aren't coming back, but he doesn't understand why." Zenith glanced over at the little boy, already asleep, and lowered her voice. "He also knows you're going to take him to see his new uncle, but I don't think he realizes he isn't coming back here—ever."

"You don't know that," Shelby protested. "The situation will change."

The long braid jumped from side to side as Zenith shook her head. "Be realistic, Shelby. Just because I choose to create and live in an ideal world doesn't mean I'm naive. His uncle will never let him live here." She put the orange peels in a bucket to be taken to the compost.

"I'm going to bring him back here to visit as often as I can, and his uncle won't have a lot to say about it... not after I'm appointed Rio's guardian," Shelby stated flatly.

"*If* you are appointed guardian," Zenith corrected. She looked at Shelby with a mixture of compassion and concern.

"Why didn't you tell the authorities Elias was your brother? Why haven't you claimed Rio as your nephew?"

A slice of orange caught in her throat, and Shelby swallowed hard. "I've never heard you be so blunt," she answered evasively. When Zenith failed to respond, Shelby shrugged. "It's a long story."

"Time is no stranger to us," Zenith said. "And I am a very good listener."

Shelby took a deep breath and let it out slowly. "How much do you know about Linc, about our past?"

"Nothing. But Elias came with a troubled soul, of that I am sure."

Shelby smiled sadly. "My brother and trouble have been synonymous for a long time. For as far back as I can remember."

Zenith said nothing, letting Shelby tell the story at her own pace.

"My parents were basically good people," Shelby began, "but they were greatly misguided when it came to raising their children. They wanted what most parents want—to give their children a better life, to provide them with opportunities and things they themselves never had. To that end, they worked, both of them, day and night. Linc and I had everything we could ever want, but we grew up alone. Our parents never once made it to a soccer game or a band concert, a scout meeting or a school play. They didn't seem to understand that we needed *them,* not their money. We longed for parents, but what we got were automated tellers."

Shelby stopped, trying to control the painful memories that threatened to escape the darkest corner of her mind. "With no one to guide or encourage or discipline him, Linc ran wild. He was picked up for truancy, disorderly conduct, malicious mischief. My parents bailed him out and pretended nothing was wrong. After a while, he dropped out of school and began running scams and con games. He got in deeper and deeper until he couldn't see any way out. In the end, he was a fugitive, wanted for armed robbery, grand theft, and probably a lot of other charges I don't know about."

Drawing up her knees, Shelby circled them with her arms and stared at the little boy sleeping in the corner. "A few years ago, he tracked me down at the dig. He told me about the commune and Gloxinia and how he was about to become a father." Her voice emerged in a ragged whisper. "He said he was happy. Happier than he ever thought possible."

"Did you believe him?"

"I wanted to."

"But..."

Shelby gripped her knees even tighter. "But he was a professional con man. He'd lied to me so many times, made me believe what he wanted, how could I ever know when he was telling the truth?" Shelby felt the lump in her throat mushrooming. "And now...now there's only Rio. He's the only thing in this world that matters. I know what he needs. And it's not his uncle's money or power or prestige. He needs love and trust and acceptance. He needs a family. All humans do. And if they don't have a traditional one, they'll seek out a substitute. Gangs, clubs, motorcycle groups...they're all families of one sort or another."

"Like communes," Zenith added.

"Yes," Shelby admitted, "like communes. Maybe this is where Linc found his family." She swallowed past the lump in her throat. "I'd like to think the time he spent here meant something, that Gloxinia and Rio meant something, that I..." She let the words trail off. "That's why I didn't claim his body. I knew it would be returned here, to the only place where he found peace."

Zenith put her arm around Shelby and gave her a hug. "Rio's not the only one who's suffered a great loss," she said quietly. "You must give yourself time and room to heal."

Shelby tried to dismiss the jolt of pain that slashed through her at Zenith's words. "There is no time. Not with Michael Chandler breathing down my neck." She crossed the room and pulled Rio's blanket up over his shoulders.

Zenith picked up a basket of sewing. "Tell me about him. What is he like?"

"He's hardworking but cold, aloof and short-tempered. Sounds just like my parents, doesn't he? Michael will probably give Rio all of his money...and none of his love." Shelby shook her head. "But that doesn't make him a monster. And so far, I've found nothing I can use against him in court."

Zenith pulled a length of thread from the spool and broke it off. "Courts of law are inconsistent and unpredictable. There is no guaranteed outcome."

Shelby grimaced. "Perhaps not. But consider this. . . ." She raised her hands and began ticking off the items on her fingers. "One—Linc was a fugitive and a felon. Two—I would probably be considered an accomplice or an accessory since I knew where he was hiding and didn't turn him in. Three—I don't have the stable home and financial security that Michael has. And four—" Shelby turned her head, unable to look Zenith in the eye "—I used my brother's old connections to buy a new identity." She turned back to the older woman. "Be honest, Zenith. If you were the judge, would you give me permanent custody of a child?"

"If you are uncomfortable with your decision, then why did you do it? Why did you choose this path?"

"Because I wanted to be close to Rio. Because he needed some continuity in his life. I couldn't stand by and watch him be taken by one complete stranger and delivered to another. He'll have questions about his parents and I can help with that. I wanted to make the transition as easy as possible for him. I had to see him safely settled in and cared for, just in case . . ." The rest of the sentence hung suspended between them.

Zenith glanced at Shelby out of the corner of her eye. "You will always be welcome here."

Shelby shook her head. "No, thanks. I respect the life you've built for yourself, Zenith, but it's not for me." For a long moment she watched Rio as he slept. "Rio and I have to carve out our own future," she said quietly.

Zenith stood and put away her mending. "Your future will be awake and ready to go at first light. We'd better get him packed."

He stood in the shadows and leaned against the side of the airplane hangar. Even the shade provided no relief from the hot, sticky air. He scratched the two-day stubble on his face, and pulled a cigarette from a dirty pack. Last one. The pack crumpled in his sweaty hand and he tossed it to the ground.

As soon as that plane was in the air, he'd blow this stinking hellhole. Everything had been so easy, it was as if it was meant to be. First, getting his hands on the statue. And then, taking out Linc Kelland. That was a stroke of genius. Not only had he eliminated any possible competition, but it turned out that Kelland's kid had a rich uncle in San Francisco who was sending his own private plane to get the brat. No one would suspect them of smuggling artifacts out of Mexico. It was all so easy. All he had to do was get the statue on that plane.

He'd been here since dawn—waiting...watching. He probably should have stayed away. He had already done everything possible. But he had to know they were on the plane. He needed to be sure. So, here he stood, drowning in his own stinking sweat. The plane had been fueled and ready for hours and he had already verified it was going to San Francisco. So, where the hell were they?

Panic surged through his veins. Maybe they'd had a flat tire. Maybe the car never showed up. Maybe the damn driver drove them off the road and they were lying in a ditch.

No. He inhaled deeply on the cigarette, finding a bit of calm as the smoke enveloped him. Panicking wouldn't help. He needed to be patient and wait—even if that meant camping out here for the next three days.

He straightened abruptly as two men pushed a set of stairs across the field. It meant they were here. Nothing had happened to them, after all. He had worked himself into a near frenzy just because they were a little late.

He held his breath as the men adjusted the stairs and threw open the door to the jet. Two pilots and a couple of attendants crossed the field and hurried into the plane. Then a porter appeared carrying several small bags, which were handed to an attendant at the top of the stairs.

Any minute now. He could feel the tension building inside him. Sweat ran down his back and soaked his shirt. He felt like a shoplifter, seeing the exit door a few feet ahead and wanting to bolt through it; knowing he was this close, but forcing himself to go slowly; not daring to breathe until he got through those doors.

Then he saw them coming out of the building—the woman holding the kid. She put him down and took his hand, leading him toward the plane. They were almost there when the kid dropped his teddy bear and pulled back on her hand to stop. She turned around and stooped to pick it up, and that was when he got a good look at her.

Kelland? It couldn't be. He blinked away the sweat that clouded his vision and looked again. No mistake. It was Shelby Kelland. What the hell was she doing with the kid?

A wicked smile crossed his face. This was getting interesting. So, Shelby Kelland had left the dig to become a nanny for the Chandler brat. He watched them climb the stairs and disappear into the body of the plane.

Fate had just handed him a big, fat bonus.

After a few minutes the plane rolled to the runway and he watched in silence until it was safely in the sky. Everything had gone according to plan. And then some.

A jaunty mood came over him as he sauntered back to the car. He stuck his hands in his pockets and began humming. "San Francisco, here I come..."

"Why?"

"Because Uncle Michael is your uncle."

"Why?"

"Because he and your mother were brother and sister."

"Why?"

"Because you ask too many questions, that's why." Shelby grabbed the child around his waist and threatened to tickle him, while squeals of laughter filled the drawing room of the private plane. The wrestling ended with both of them collapsing into a chair.

"You know," Shelby said, switching easily back and forth between English and Spanish, "I have to tell you something about your Uncle Michael. He doesn't know that you and I have known each other for a long time. He thinks we just met yesterday. I don't want to confuse Uncle Michael, so I think we should play along with him and pretend we're new friends. Do you think you can do that?"

Rio nodded solemnly.

"Good," Shelby said with a sigh of relief. The language barrier would protect them for a while, but she knew Rio would pick up English pretty quickly and she wasn't about to risk the whole thing falling apart. "I think you'll like being at your Uncle Michael's," Shelby said. "He lives in a nice house where there are lots of toys, and he has the biggest car you've ever seen, with a special little seat in it just for you."

"Is he like my daddy?"

The question came out of left field. She had known there would be questions eventually, but not this soon...not now, when her own wounds were still so painfully raw. She closed her eyes for a fraction of a second, then opened them to meet Rio's steady gaze. "No, honey. He's nothing like your daddy. He's quite tall and has very dark hair," Shelby said, latching on to the physical differences.

Rio was silent for a long moment. "I miss him," he said softly.

"So do I, sweetheart. So do I." Shelby held the little boy close, cradling him in her arms. She could feel her pain welling up inside, but there were no tears. Maybe she'd grieve later. But then again, maybe the tears would never come.

"Do you know what I think?" she asked. She was changing the subject and she knew it, but at that moment she would have done anything to alter the course of the conversation.

"What?"

"I think you should take a little nap."

Rio shook his head vigorously and pointed out the window. "It's not nighttime."

"I know. But we've been traveling since early morning and it will be very late when we reach your Uncle Michael's. If you rest now, you'll be wide-awake for the ride in his big car."

Rio looked doubtful.

"Let's read a story first," Shelby suggested. "What will it be, *The Haunted House* or *The Frog Princess?*"

"Frog," Rio shouted, jumping up and down.

"It's in my bag. Can you get it?"

Rio dug through the totebag and triumphantly pulled out the dog-eared book. He settled comfortably in Shelby's lap as she began reading.

"Once upon a time, there was a frog
named Lily. She told everyone she
was going to be like her great-
great-great-great-great-great-
great-grandfather, the . . ."

"Frog Prince," Rio sang out as Shelby slowly turned the page.

"That's right, the Frog Prince." Shelby read through the story twice, and the enchanting words soon produced the desired effect. Rio's head leaned heavily against her shoulder and his hand loosened its grip on the stuffed bear. She put aside the book and lifted him easily into her arms. At the back of the plane, she jabbed the bedroom door with her foot, and it swung open before them. Holding Rio with one arm, she pulled back the covers, then settled him into the middle of the bed and tucked the blankets around him.

"Tía Shelby?" Rio's voice, soft and heavy with sleep, drifted up to Shelby.

"I'm right here, honey," she said, sitting down on the edge of the bed.

"... love you ..."

Her heart did a strange double flip inside her chest and she swallowed the lump in her throat. "I love you, too, sweetheart. Now, close your eyes and go to sleep." She brushed the thick golden locks away from his face and stroked his forehead with a light, soothing touch.

It wasn't fair.

It wasn't fair that any child should lose his parents at such a young age. It wasn't fair that Michael had been appointed temporary guardian and would probably be awarded permanent guardianship, as well. It wasn't fair that she was forced to use lies and deceit just to be close to the nephew she loved.

Her heart overflowed with love and tenderness and compassion. She knew firsthand what a young boy needed in his life. All she asked was a chance to give it to him. She wanted to be there for Rio, to share in his triumphs and to comfort him when things went wrong. She intended to help him discover the world's many mysteries, and to teach him how to find joy in the face of life's adversities. Her feelings didn't stem from duty, or obligation, like Michael Chandler's. She had a pretty sound idea of what was in store—raising a child was tough work under the best of circumstances. Being willing to do it alone took courage and determination ... and Shelby knew she had a lot of both.

Quietly she slipped off the bed and dropped into the chair by the small, oval windows. As far as she could tell, Michael Chandler didn't give two hoots about his nephew. She didn't hate the man, or begrudge him his success, but what made her see red was how he could be so totally blind to Rio's emotional needs. To hell with all his money and prestige and the "opportunities" he could give a child. Michael didn't love Rio, and that was the bottom line.

Outside the windows, the earth below seemed tiny and inconsequential, and she wished they could keep flying forever. The sky was slowly changing from cerulean to the orange, crimson and violet of sunset, the perfect backdrop for the way she felt.

The setting sun brought closure to her old way of life. There was no doubt she'd miss the dig and the chance of uncovering a tiny piece of history. But now she was responsible for a tiny piece of the future—Rio. Getting custody of him would mean making major changes in her life. She would give up the on-site work and instead concentrate on teaching or perhaps writing about current discoveries. Studying the past had been her life's ambition, but until now, she'd never known the thrill of having an impact on the future.

Shelby closed her eyes. Every minute she hurled through the sky, brought her closer to Michael Chandler.

Her frustration with him was fueled by the deep primal instinct of a mother protecting her young. There had to be a way to get custody of Rio. And it was up to her to find it.

Michael pushed back the cuff of his shirt and checked his watch. He had been waiting nearly an hour, and this was the first time in years he had been forced to wait for anything. What on earth had possessed him to come to the airport?

Sid. Well-meaning, troublemaking Sid had dropped by this afternoon on the pretext of delivering some papers, and had hung around to talk Michael into coming to the airport and meeting the plane. As Rio's uncle, Michael had a moral responsibility, Sid said, an obligation to be there when his nephew arrived.

Sid was right. Any kid who had been yanked out of his home and tossed onto a plane for eight hours with a total stranger was bound to be confused and scared, even if the stranger was as entertaining as Shelby McMasters. Michael shook his head. He thought he'd had a rough time growing up, but it was nothing compared to what this child was going through.

He stretched out his legs, leaned his head against the back of the uncomfortable airport chair and closed his eyes. *This child.* As long as he called him "the child" or "the boy" or even "my nephew," it somehow seemed less real. The boy had a name and Michael was going to have to start using it.

"Rio Chandler," he said out loud. Well, that was one way of continuing the Chandler name into the next century, because it sure didn't look as though he was going to have any children of his own.

He stood up and paced across the floor of the private lounge, then stopped and looked at his watch again. Time dragged too slowly when he wasn't working. He wasn't cut out to be a one-man welcoming committee. He should be home catching up on some of his work—like the Peterson deal. Given the way he'd been behaving lately, old man Peterson was having second thoughts about letting Michael acquire the company. His work was erratic, he couldn't focus and he was way behind schedule. Michael wouldn't blame the old man if he pulled out of the deal completely.

Michael glanced at the briefcase lying unopened on the coffee table. Who was he trying to kid? Chances are he wouldn't be able to concentrate any better tonight than he had in the last week.

Had it only been seven days since Shelby McMasters had turned his life upside down?

In the beginning, he'd thought he couldn't work because of all the noise. His quiet, stately home had been taken over by carpet layers, wallpaper hangers, curtain makers—not to mention the fence installers. He had done what any sensible man would and retreated to his office. But he couldn't work there, either. He had spent all of his time wondering what was going on back at the estate.

Finally, two days ago, everyone had cleared out, including Shelby. Once again he'd had the place to himself. He could come and go as he pleased. He could swim laps or exercise without interruption. His house was peaceful, quiet.

It was too peaceful, and too damn quiet.

He'd found himself stomping around the house slamming doors and banging closets, trying to break up the interminable silence. He would have given a month's salary for one good argument.

And it wasn't for lack of trying. He lit into Pasig for leaving a smudge on the side of the limousine. He tormented Callahan until the young man packed up his files and fled to the nearest public library. He'd even tried to bully Anna Hodges, but the old biddy just stuck her hands on her hips and walked away. Not one of them would stand up to him. Not the way Shelby had. The God's honest truth was he couldn't wait until she stepped off that plane and they could go toe-to-toe once again.

A warm smile creased his face. He had half a mind to tear into her because the plane was late, knowing damn well she wouldn't put up with any of his guff. Her blue eyes would flame with anger and defiance. Her full round breasts would raise as she drew a deep breath to prepare for her verbal assault. He knew it was a cliché, but she was beautiful when she was angry. And he would have deliberately provoked her, if it weren't for the fact that his nephew would be witness to the scene.

He stood in front of the large windows and watched the sun disappear behind the horizon. It was a glorious sunset—streaks of red and gold split the sky, then faded into the dusk that was now enveloping the airport. *You would have missed this beautiful sunset if you hadn't been here,* nagged an inner voice. Michael nodded his agreement. *And how much more of life have you missed because of your self-imposed isolation?*

He shook off the question with a snap of the locks on his briefcase. If he was going to wait here, he was also going to have something to show for it. Determinedly, he pulled out a stack of papers, but before he had read the first one, his mind had wandered.

It didn't make sense.

A few weeks ago his home was just the way he liked it. He lived and worked alone, and actually enjoyed the solitude. Now, the same place felt . . . empty . . . almost lonely, and those were words that had never bothered him before.

Even when Gina walked out, he hadn't felt lonely. If anything, he had felt relief. After four years of marriage, they had ended up polar opposites. She had reinforced what he had learned as a kid—people only want you for what you can give them. And as soon as she'd found someone who could give her more money, more prestige, more of everything, she had packed her bags and left.

His father . . . Gina . . . the myriad business piranhas he'd encountered over the years—they were all the same. Users. And the more powerful he became, the more often people tried to use him. It was easier to keep the world at a distance than to risk being used and discarded again.

But fate had ripped open his cloistered life, and he couldn't keep the world out any longer. Shelby had blown into his home like a fresh summer breeze on the ocean shore, warming his frozen soul. In truth, there were two reasons why he now stood impatiently waiting for the plane. One was to meet his new nephew . . . the other was because he didn't want to wait until morning to see Shelby again.

He was still staring into space forty-five minutes later when the private plane rolled to a stop outside the lounge window. An attendant opened the doors to the accordion tunnel connecting the plane to the terminal and Michael stood as Shelby and Rio entered the room.

She was surprised to see him; there was no doubt about that, but was there also a hint of pleasure in her blue eyes? She looked very tired, and Michael cursed himself for insisting that she make such a demanding trip in two days.

He stood, transfixed, as she approached him. "Rio, *este señor es tu tío*. This is your Uncle Michael," she repeated in English. Rio ducked behind Shelby, then peered up at Michael from around her leg.

Unable to move, Michael remained rooted to the spot, seeing the little boy for the first time. The thick, honey-blond hair must have been his father's contribution, but the rest of him was pure Chandler. He had a small square jaw, firm mouth and cool gray eyes that watched Michael warily. In his right arm, he clutched a ragged teddy bear, while with his left hand he clung to Shelby. It was like looking into a mirror—a thirty-eight-year-old mirror.

Finally overcoming his paralysis, Michael squatted in front of Shelby. "I'm very pleased to meet you, Rio." Even to his own ears, his voice sounded surprisingly soft and quiet, coaxing the child from his position of relative safety.

The little boy smiled shyly. "*¿Podemos ir, mi osito y yo, en su carro grande?*"

Michael looked up at Shelby and gestured helplessly with his hands.

Shelby smiled. "He wants to know if he and his bear can go for a ride in your big car."

"My what?" It took a full moment before Michael could comprehend what she was talking about. "Oh, yes, of course, my big car. You bet," Michael said, nodding his head vigorously. "We're going to ride in the big car."

Shelby looked down at the large man squatting in front of her, his gaze on Rio. Nothing could have shocked her as much as seeing him waiting when she'd stepped off the plane. She hadn't figured he would care enough or even be curious enough to come to the airport to meet them. In fact, she had counted on the long ride back to the estate to steel herself against seeing him again. But she was wrong. Whether he cared, whether he was curious or whether he just felt it was his duty, Michael Chandler was here. And even more amazing was that he seemed to instinctively know how important it was to meet a child on his own level. She stared at the lush thickness of dark brown hair just a hairbreadth away and clenched her fists, resisting the urge to run her fingers through its silky softness. Fate was indeed being nasty. Not only did she not have time to prepare for meeting with him, now they would all have to take the long ride in the "big car" together. At least she wouldn't have to ride with him kneeling at her feet.

As if reading her thoughts, he smiled at Rio, then stood abruptly, his towering body scant inches from her own. The captivating scent of soap and spice filled her head, then, just as quickly, disappeared as he moved away from her. He collected the papers scattered across the coffee table and stuffed them haphazardly into a briefcase. When he finished, he turned to Rio and, for a moment, it seemed as though he was about to offer Rio his hand. Instead, he pushed open the door to the private lounge and held it for Shelby and Rio to pass through.

"Let's go find that big car."

Michael led them down a long corridor to a set of double doors. As they pushed through the doors, a large group of photographers and reporters surged forward. Shelby's eyes glazed as flashbulbs began popping. She heard Rio's startled cry and scooped him up into her arms. Someone grabbed her arm and tried to thrust a microphone into her face, but she wrenched free. Above Rio's cries, a dozen people were shouting Michael's name.

"Mr. Chandler, any comments for the press? Is this the first time you've seen your nephew?"

"What was the commune like? Was he ill treated?"

"Does he speak any English? Will you get him to say something for us?"

"How about a picture of you holding the boy?"

"Who's the woman? Is she the nanny? Will she be living with you?"

A shudder raced down Shelby's back. The last thing she needed was her picture plastered across the front page of some sleazy newspaper for someone to recognize. She had worked too hard to have everything fall apart now. With renewed vigor, she supported Rio with one arm and tried to shield them both with the other. But the reporters persisted. They grabbed and pawed, and all the while flashbulbs popped, continually blinding her.

Someone grabbed her arm again. She struggled to get away, but he held fast. "Stop struggling. Let me help you." An achingly familiar, deep voice shouted near her ear. Michael. She burrowed her head into the soft cushion of his shoulder as his protective arm encircled her and Rio and held them close.

She could feel the rumblings deep inside his chest as he shouted at the reporters. "Out of my way," he roared as he continued to push through the crowd, dragging Shelby and Rio with him.

Rio began squirming in her arms. "No, Rio. I can't put you down," Shelby said in Rio's ear. "You'd be crushed." Rio said something she couldn't understand over the din of the reporters. His struggling became more frantic and he kicked at her with his feet. Through the glass doors about a hundred feet ahead, she caught sight of Michael's silver limousine. Pasig scrambled around to the passenger side and opened the door of the parked car. "Please, Rio," she begged. "We're almost there."

He was screaming and crying hysterically. *"Osito de peluche!"*

This time she heard him. With a feeling of dread, she glimpsed Rio's empty hands. The bear was gone. Somewhere in the middle of that swarming mass of unflinching reporters he had dropped his beloved toy. That bear meant so much to him, and she'd be damned if she'd let her own selfish need for privacy stand between Rio and the precious little he had left in the world. "We've got to go back," she said to Michael. "Rio dropped his bear."

"I can't hear you. Tell me when we get in the car."

"No," Shelby said, pulling away from him. "Rio dropped his bear. We have to go back and get it."

With a flick of his arm, Michael knocked a microphone out of a reporter's hand and cast a scathing look at the group who doggedly pursued him. "I'm not going back there and neither are you." He grabbed the thrashing child out of Shelby's arms and pinned him against his chest. Thrusting his briefcase into

Shelby's empty arms, he grabbed her elbow and forced her through the glass doors.

"But you don't understand," she begged, struggling to pry his strong fingers from her arm. "Rio's bear is special."

"No toy is that special," Michael countered, shoving her into the car. "I'll buy him a whole storeful of bears in the morning." He jumped in behind her and Pasig slammed the door closed on the reporters.

"Osito de peluche," Rio sobbed, kicking free of Michael and throwing himself into Shelby's lap as Pasig started the car. The photographers had given up, but the reporters continued to rap on the windows, jogging alongside the limousine as the immense car pulled away from the curb.

"How dare you toss me in here like a piece of luggage!" Shelby hissed at Michael. "I demand you stop this car so I can go back and find Rio's bear."

"No."

The single word cut through Shelby like a hot knife through butter. Maybe he hadn't understood the importance of Rio's bear. "That bear is about all Rio has left in this world," she said. "I insist you let me go back and look for it."

"You can insist all you want," he said coldly. "But as your employer, I am telling you that you are *not* going back there."

"Of all the arrogant, coldhearted, insensitive, contemptuous…" Shelby bit her tongue as his icy stare sliced through her. "When you were a child," she said, her soft voice almost beseeching, "didn't you ever own something that meant more to you than anything else in the world?"

A stony silence answered her plea.

"Osito de peluche," Rio sobbed.

"I know, honey. I know." Shelby glared at Michael as she lifted Rio into the car seat still kicking and crying, and buckled the straps around him. She wanted desperately to make it better for the dejected little boy, to promise him everything would be all right. But she couldn't lie. The frigid look on Michael's face made it clear that things were far from "all right." For whatever stubborn, pigheaded, idiotic reason, he wasn't going back. For two cents, the moment she got to the estate, she'd grab his Jaguar and personally drive right back to the airport. But reason got the better of her. In his present mood, that kind of behavior was likely to get her fired—and that wouldn't help her or Rio.

"Honey, I can't promise that we'll find him," Shelby said, kissing the child's forehead, "but maybe tomorrow we can go back, after the reporters are gone."

Oh, how she wanted to give Michael a piece of her mind, but she kept her own counsel. Telling Michael what she thought of him in front of Rio wouldn't help anyone, particularly Rio and, right now, that was her main concern. "Guess what's waiting for you at your Uncle Michael's house?" she asked, trying to raise the little boy's sunken spirits. "Dinosaurs." She pronounced the word with far more enthusiasm than she felt. "Three big dinosaurs—a brontosaurus, a stegosaurus and a tyrannosaurus rex. Won't that be great?"

Rio shook his head and wrapped his chubby arms around himself in the timeless gesture of desolation. Silent tears tracked down his cheeks as he rocked back and forth. *"Osito de peluche,"* he begged.

Shelby glowered at Michael as she wiped Rio's face with a tissue. She took back every nice thing she'd ever said about Michael. He *was* a monster and she would never forgive him for hurting Rio.

Michael stared sullenly out the window. He had never expected it to be like this. One minute the three of them were casually walking through the airport, and the next they were caught in the middle of a stampede. He should have anticipated the damn reporters. He hated them with a passion, hated the way they invaded his life. Hated them with the same intensity that Rio probably hated him right now.

He glanced across the car at the little boy who sniffled as he leaned against the side of the car seat. This was a hell of a way to start a relationship with anyone, much less a kid. He'd known from the beginning he wasn't father material and this was proof positive.

Michael straightened his tie and turned again toward the window, staring out into the darkness. Okay. So no one would nominate him for Father of the Year, but that didn't make him a hellhound, either. He knew from experience what an accursed breed reporters were, and he'd done his best to protect Rio from them. He wasn't about to apologize for trying to help. Of course, Rio wouldn't see it that way. He glanced at Shelby, who was still shooting him down with those crystal blue eyes. Neither would she.

And since when did he care what anybody thought of him? Michael sighed. Ever since his mirror image had walked off the plane and asked if they could go for a ride in the big car. Some ride. Rio had silently cried himself to sleep and still the tension was so thick you could choke on it.

By the time they reached the estate, all Michael wanted to do was run...escape. He didn't even wait for Pasig to open the limousine door. He stormed out of the car and into the house, not stopping until the library door slammed closed behind him. Whipping out a bottle, he poured himself a large brandy. He raised the glass, but his hand froze halfway to his lips as one of Gina's constant reproaches rang in his ears. *Well-bred people do not gulp brandy. They sip it.* Michael threw back his head and tossed the fiery liquid down his throat.

He heard them in the hall and on the stairs—Anna fussing over the "wee one," Callahan offering to carry their bags. Damn it! It wasn't supposed to end like this. He was supposed to be out there doing something, helping carry Rio up the stairs, starting to act like a parent. Michael scoffed. He'd already tried that once tonight and look where it had got him.

His throat burned from the drink, but he didn't care. It was late and he was tired, and the image of Rio's hurt look and Shelby's accusing stare haunted him mercilessly. First decent thing he did in years and it blew up in his face. All because of a damned teddy bear. The thing was on its last legs, anyway. He'd buy Rio a new one—a dozen new ones—bigger than the kid himself. In a week's time Rio would forget all about the old one.

Or would he?

Michael poured himself another drink and watched the golden liquid slosh against the sides of the glass. When things got bad, there was always a bottle. He could always get stinking, cross-eyed drunk and turn his back on the rest of the world.

That's what his old man always did.

Michael flung the glass against the wall. The elegant crystal shattered into a hundred pieces and rivulets of brandy trickled down the wallpaper and collected on the carpet. Visions of a child sprang up like a phoenix out of the sparkling shards—a little boy with dark hair and clear gray eyes clutching an old truck. It had been more than thirty-five years and still he could recall every detail of that truck...every dent...every chip...every...

He punched the intercom button on his desk and dialed the garage. "Pasig. Bring me the Jaguar, now!"

With a flick of his wrist, Michael jerked the steering wheel, the rear wheels kicking up a fine spray of gravel as he ground to a stop. He let out the clutch, flipped off the lights and cut the engine. It was nearly midnight and this part of the airport, catering only to private planes, was completely deserted. The hard drive and the cool night air had helped to calm him, but now, surrounded by darkness, he gripped the steering wheel and stared down the length of dark pavement.

A short burst of humorless laughter broke from his lips. This was the second time today he'd been here. The first time had ended in disaster.

Trying not to think about it, he unfolded his tall frame from the low-slung car and left it parked in a zone marked Limousines Only. He pushed through the glass doors and stopped in the area where the reporters had assaulted them. Quickly, he scanned the length and breadth of the room, but there was no sign of Rio's bear.

Michael retraced their steps up the long corridor to the private lounge. He replayed the scene a dozen times in his mind— Rio and Shelby coming through the doors of the accordion tunnel, him stooping to talk with Rio, holding open the door to the lounge so they could pass through. Michael shook his head. He was sure Rio had the bear when they left the lounge, and that meant Rio had to have dropped it when they were bombarded by the press.

He hurried back to the area and looked around again. Nothing. It was ridiculous to have thought that he could find it, anyway. No doubt the cleaning people had thrown it out with the rest of the garbage. It wasn't the sort of thing they usually found in this part of the airport and they might not have thought it was worth sending to the Lost and Found.

Osito de peluche. The words echoed in the empty room as he tried to forget the look on Rio's face. If he could find the toy and give it back to Rio, there was a chance of undoing the damage he'd done, a chance for them to start over. As it was,

Rio would never trust him, and Michael didn't blame him one bit.

Michael swore and lashed out at a freestanding ashtray. It toppled over, emptying cigarette butts and cigar stubs onto the floor. He stared blankly at the mess. The ashtrays were full. They hadn't been cleaned. With renewed hope, he bent down to right the stand and his hand brushed a piece of fuzz on the floor. The carpet hadn't been vacuumed, either.

Wait a minute. That wasn't a piece of fuzz. Michael picked up a clump of cotton and rubbed it between his fingers. It was stuffing... batting. The bear had to be around here somewhere.

A week ago, if anyone had told Michael he would be crawling around a deserted airport on his hands and knees in the middle of the night, holding a wad of stuffing and looking for a decrepit teddy bear, he would have had them certified and locked away.

Ridiculous as it sounded, that was what he did.

He crawled to a nearby circle of cushioned chairs and peered under one. He couldn't see anything without a flashlight. Gingerly he shoved his arm under the chair and felt around—two gum wrappers and a felt-tipped pen. He tried the next one—nothing. Like paper clips to a magnet, the spilled ashes clung to his trousers as he moved around the grouping of seats. Under the last chair his fingers found a soft, nubby fabric.

On more than one occasion, an astute business move had given Michael a real high. But nothing compared to the surge of pure triumph that shot through him as he pulled Rio's teddy bear out of its hiding place. He could have hugged it—well, almost. He frowned at the animal hanging limply from his hand.

As he remembered, it wasn't much of a bear to begin with, and now it was even worse. It was missing an eye and one of the ears was half off, and there was a two-inch tear along the front seam. Clearly it had been trampled in the rush and kicked aside. Maybe Shelby or Mrs. Hodges could do something with it, fix it up a little. For one thing, it would need a lot more stuffing. He took the wad of cotton he had been holding and tried to shove it into the bear's stomach.

Michael's eyebrows furrowed as his fingers came in contact with a small, hard... something. He sat down in one of the chairs and laid the bear across his knees. Tugging at the seam, he easily ripped it open wide enough to insert his hand into the cavity. Slowly, so as not to further destroy Rio's bear, Michael extracted the object, which was wrapped in a dirty cloth.

The fabric fell away, and in his hand lay the most beautiful Mesoamerican figure he had ever seen.

Chapter 6

Michael sucked in his breath as he ran his fingers over the jadeite carving. It was perfect—definitely Mayan, probably late classic period. He expelled his breath in a soft whistle. The last time he had seen a piece even approaching this quality was in the San Francisco State Museum where his friend, Quentin Ingersoll, curator of the Mesoamerican division, had allowed him a close-up look at a small private showing on loan from a Mexican collector. And even those pieces didn't compare to the fine detail and condition of the one he was now holding.

What was a figure like this doing in Rio's bear?

Surprise gave way to shock as the truth registered. He stared at Rio's disheveled bear, still lying in his lap. Artifact smuggling. Someone had used his nephew to smuggle a priceless antiquity out of Mexico. But who? And from where? Michael's head spun as he tried to put the pieces together. Mayan ruins had been uncovered throughout the state of Campeche, and, with the advent of technology, pictures from outer space had revealed many untouched structures within the thick, uninhabited jungle of the Yucatán. The archaeological sites of Haltunchen, Edzna, Hochob and Dzibilocac were scattered across north-central Campeche, and several others in south-eastern Campeche had also been partially excavated and restored.

Michael struggled to remember them and where they were located ... Chicana ... Becan ... *Xpujil*. The word stuck in his throat. His sister's commune was within driving distance of the town of Xpujil, and he'd bet money the archaeological site wasn't more than ten miles from the town. If the statue didn't come from the older Xpujil site, it could easily have come from one of the newer ones.

That helped to explain where it had come from, but it left the larger question untouched. Who could have done this? That anyone would stoop to using a child for smuggling was appalling, and Michael recoiled at the thought of someone turning Rio into an Oliver Twist. But right now Rio was the strongest connection Michael had. The smuggler had to be someone who had known Rio was leaving and where he was going—and that meant everyone in the commune was open to suspicion.

Michael shook his head. That conclusion didn't fit. The police reports indicated the commune dwellers were naturalists, people who were into organic farming and carpentry, not the least bit interested in material items. There wasn't much room in their lives for a Mayan statue or the wealth it could bring.

So, if it wasn't someone from the commune, then who? The possibilities seemed endless. Half the world had read about the accident and knew Rio was headed for the U.S. However, Michael reminded himself, only his immediate household was privy to any of the details.

Running through the short list of names, he immediately eliminated Pasig and the Hodgeses. They wouldn't know a Mexican antiquity from a dime-store trinket. And it certainly wasn't Sid. He and Michael went too far back, and if Sid had needed fast money, he could have found a dozen more inventive ways to get it. Callahan was young and ambitious, but he hadn't been away from the estate in months, and Mc-Masters ...

Michael paused. What *about* McMasters? He really didn't know anything about her, other than the information that appeared on her résumé, and the fact that she'd been pretty eager to get the job as Rio's nanny. But Michael dismissed the thought as quickly as it entered his head. *All* the people he had interviewed had been eager to become Rio's nanny. That didn't mean a thing.

Yet his inner voice wouldn't stop its nagging. He remembered how she had put up a good fight to get back into the airport terminal and find the toy. "You don't understand," she had said. "Rio's bear is special." Michael studied the precious four-inch figure lying in his hand. Special didn't even come close.

He rubbed a hand across his eyes and Shelby's face appeared behind his lids. She couldn't be a smuggler. He'd grant that she was determined and more than a little pushy, but she was also attractive and open and honest. She simply wasn't the smuggling type.

Then again, what exactly was the smuggling type? Michael frowned. When was the last time he had passed someone on the street and said, "Ah, yes. That's the one. Definitely an artifact smuggler." Wasn't that the whole point of smuggling—to be as inconspicuous as possible? Looking pretty and wholesome was a perfect disguise. And if you could ooze maternal love and affection, so much the better. Ma Barker had probably loved her kids, too, he thought grimly.

He shook his head. Logic was quickly deserting him. First he had exonerated Shelby because of her looks, and now he had condemned her for the very same reason. Hurriedly, he rewrapped the statue, slipped it into his pocket and stuffed the batting back into the bear. The answers weren't going to be found in a deserted airport terminal.

Michael sprinted through the glass doors into the moonlit night. He needed to talk with Shelby. And he needed to do it now.

Shelby sank onto the bed, stretched out under the covers and tried to relax. Two days of solid traveling had left her exhausted, and she was glad the evening was finally over.

Even though it was very late when they arrived, the staff had been wonderful. Mr. and Mrs. Hodges had cooed and fussed over Rio as though he were the crown prince, and John Callahan had offered to show him the new jungle gym and sandbox first thing in the morning. Whether due to a lack of understanding, fear, or both, Shelby didn't know, but Rio hadn't said a word since the ride home. He had just clung to her like a lifeline.

It had taken forever to get him to sleep. The change in time zones and traveling had thrown his body schedule way off, not to mention the nervousness of being in a strange home and the trauma of losing his *osito de peluche*.

Shelby sighed. Her anger at Michael had subsided and resignation had set in. He simply didn't realize how important that bear was to Rio. Rio had so little left of his former life that his toy had become an anchor, the one stabilizing facet of a tumultuous life. Unknowingly, Michael had cut him loose, leaving him to drift helplessly along.

Only a parent would understand. If this was the type of behavior that could be expected from Michael in the future, he would never be a real father to Rio. Maybe it wouldn't hold much weight in court, but Shelby intended to relate the incident to her attorney, in the hopes that it would somehow strengthen her case against Michael.

If only she could be sure of getting custody of Rio.

If only Michael weren't so influential and well known.

If only he was a little less attractive and a little more understanding.

If only...

Sleep, restless and shallow, had finally settled upon her when crying from the next room jarred her awake. All traces of sleep disappeared as she bolted through the doorway that connected her room with Rio's. He was still asleep, but deep sobs racked his small body.

"Wake up, Rio," Shelby said, sitting next to him on the edge of the bed and shaking him gently by the shoulders. "You're having a bad dream, honey. Wake up."

Rio sat up and rubbed his eyes, hiccuping softly. He looked around the dimly lit room in confusion, then hugged Shelby and sniffled into her shoulder.

"Do you remember your dream?" she asked, sweeping a lock of curly hair off his face.

Rio shook his head.

"That's okay." She bent down and retrieved the stuffed dinosaur, which had fallen to the floor.

"Don't go."

Shelby's heart wrenched at the sound of anguish in the little boy's voice. She gave him a big hug and kissed the top of his head. "I'm not leaving," she said. "But how about we get you a drink of water for those hiccups and then we'll sit in the rocker for a while?''

Taking her hand, Rio obligingly padded along with her to the bathroom, where Shelby gave him a drink of water. Then she wrapped a blanket around him and sat in the rocking chair, cradling him in her arms.

''Sing a song, Tía Shelby. Please.''

''Will you close your eyes and try to sleep?''

The dove gray eyes completely disappeared behind a scrunched-up face.

Shelby's gentle laughter melted into the night. ''You don't have to close them *that* tightly,'' she said, dropping a kiss on his forehead. Slowly, she rocked back and forth, and began singing a Spanish lullaby she had learned at the commune.

Michael stood in the doorway, mesmerized by the haunting strains of Spanish that filled Rio's room. The feminine voice was light and airy and, although he didn't understand the words, the music touched him.

He had been on his way to Shelby's room to talk with her about the statue and the stuffed bear, when the sound of soft voices and quiet laughter coming from the nursery stopped him. Now he stood in the shadows and watched as she held Rio in her arms and sang him to sleep.

For as long as he could remember, Michael had envisioned this very scene. As a child, he'd dreamed of sitting with his mother, waiting for his father to come home. But his father had quashed those early dreams. He didn't need Michael or a family...he had just needed someone small to bully and to give him a sense of power.

Years later, after he and Gina were married, Michael had imagined himself coming home to a wife and child. But that dream had died, too. Gina didn't have time for a family. She was too busy finding new ways to spend his money. Eventually, he'd convinced himself that he didn't need a family and he didn't want the emotional baggage that accompanied one.

Now, as he stood in the doorway watching Rio and Shelby, an inexplicable longing and yearning stirred inside him. The old dream had returned with a renewed vigor to haunt him once again.

How ironic, after all this time, to finally see the scene played out—not with his parents, not with his own wife and child, but with his nephew and an employee.

That's really all Shelby was, he reminded himself. But he was having a hard time remembering it. From the moment she'd gone toe-to-toe with him over the issue of the swimming pool fence, she had seemed less like hired help and more like an equal.

She shifted her position in the rocking chair and now Michael could see part of her profile. Her unconscious movements charmed him, and the soft light from the nightlamp glowed on her skin, giving her a look that was almost surreal. Her hair shimmered and glistened with gold, and as she rested her cheek against the top of Rio's head, their hair mingled together. The colors were so close he couldn't tell where Rio's ended and Shelby's began.

Seeing her like this with Rio, it was hard to believe she could be involved in anything as serious as artifact smuggling. The hostility and anxiety he had seen in the car on the way home were gone. Now she seemed peaceful, content to sit in a rocker and sing. If Shelby McMasters was really a smuggler, she wouldn't be calmly rocking while a valuable artifact was kicked around the airport.

Or would she?

A thousand questions cluttered his mind, clamoring for attention. And for the first time in a long time, Michael didn't have any answers. At least not where Shelby McMasters was concerned. One minute he was totally, absolutely, one hundred percent sure of her innocence. And the next . . .

Michael glanced down at the mangled bear dangling from his hand. He couldn't give Rio the bear while it looked like this. The child was obviously having a tough time getting through his first night in his new home, and the shock of seeing the bear in this condition would do far more harm than waiting another day. Tomorrow he'd give the thing to Anna and tell her to fix it up.

Rio.

Dear God.

He stole another long look at the beautiful woman holding his nephew and his stomach twisted in knots. If she was responsible for this mess, then he had put Rio in the arms of a vile and coldhearted thief. But if she was innocent and he threw her out, Rio would never forgive him . . . nor would he forgive himself. A choice between Scylla and Charybdis. And that meant no choice at all. Shelby McMasters was a primary suspect, and, without hurting Rio, Michael's only option was to keep a very close watch on everything she did. Silently, he backed away from the door as Shelby's singing faded to a hum.

Michael returned downstairs, and locked himself in the library. Taking the statue out of his pocket, he unwrapped it and placed it and the bear side by side on the desk before him. This was an intricate puzzle, and one that Michael was determined to solve. Anyone who could get close enough to Rio to hide a statue in his bear was a real and dangerous threat.

Michael turned the figure over and over in his hands. The events of the night were taking a toll on his temper and once again he felt ready to explode. He couldn't sit around and wait for something to happen, and pacing a hole in the carpeting hadn't helped.

He had to act. If he couldn't trace the statue from this end, maybe he could start with its origin. Somewhere there was a record of its find—the date, site and person or persons responsible. He needed the complete history of this figure . . . and he knew just the man who could get it.

Michael flipped through the cards in his Rolodex and punched in the number. Impatiently, he drummed his fingers on the desk as the telephone continued to ring . . . three . . . four . . . five. *Come on, Ingersoll, answer the phone.*

" . . . 'lo?" The voice on the other end of the line was slurred and groggy.

"Quentin? We need to talk."

For a long moment, silence answered Michael's demand. "Chandler? Is that you?" The man's voice became decidedly more irritated. "Do you know what time it is?"

Michael hooked the phone between his shoulder and neck and pushed back the sleeve of his shirt. "It's one-fifteen. Are you awake?"

"No. This is all part of my nightmare. What the hell do you want?"

"I want to talk about a Mayan statue, about four inches tall, late classic period, carved of jadeite and close to mint condition."

"Right." The word stretched out, then snapped back like a slingshot. "Get in line, Michael. I know at least ten other collectors who want one, too. You're in great company. Now, if there's nothing else, I have a date with my pillow."

"I'm not *looking* for a statue," Michael said, pausing for dramatic effect, "... I'm holding one."

"Whaat?" As Michael expected, he now had Quentin's full attention. "Where did you get it?"

"That's not important. The reason I'm calling is that I want you to do a little research for me. I need a complete history on this figure." He winced at the quick intake of breath on the other end of the line.

"Michael, don't play me for a fool. We both know every legitimate piece *comes* with a complete history. I repeat the question, where did you get it?"

Michael sighed. "I can't tell you, Quentin. Let's just say I received it under some rather... unusual circumstances, and I need to know more about its origin."

Quentin Ingersoll was nothing if not persistent. "What kind of 'unusual circumstances'?"

"I don't want to go into it right now, but I would appreciate it if you would check it out. And, of course, since this is such a... delicate... matter, I'd like the investigation kept confidential."

"Michael, I want a straight answer. Are we talking about something illegal?"

"Look, Quentin, I would never ask you to do anything illegal or unethical. I'm simply asking for information on a specific piece—date of find, site of find, history since the find and so on. Will you do it?"

Michael held his breath during the ensuing silence. He needed expert help, and he needed someone he could trust to be discreet. Quentin Ingersoll was the only one he knew who filled both requirements.

"I'll have to see the statue. Bring it to the museum in the morning."

Michael grimaced and hastily decided in favor of pushing his luck. "Under the circumstances, Quentin, I'd like the figure to remain here, where I can keep an eye on it. I'll make a point of being home all day tomorrow so you can come at your convenience to inspect it. If anyone at the museum asks, tell them one of your crazy, eccentric collectors—who just happens to be a noted benefactor and patron—wanted to see you personally. That should keep questions to a minimum."

Quentin's voice was tinged with anger. "You should know by now, Michael, I can't be bullied or bought."

"Of course not, Quentin," Michael said smoothly. "I never intended to imply otherwise. I was merely giving you a legitimate excuse for coming all the way out here. Actually," he said, drawing out the word, "now that I think about it, there are several pieces I've been wanting reappraised. Insurance requirements," he added quickly. "I couldn't possibly bring all of them to the museum. I realize you're very busy, but perhaps you could find time to come to the house tomorrow and take a look. No doubt you're as concerned about my collection as I am."

Quentin's resignation came clearly over the wires. "I'm not worried about your collection, Michael. I'm worried about you. I don't know what you've gotten into, but it doesn't sound good."

Michael laughed and shrugged off the somber thoughts. "You worry too much, Quentin. I'll see you in the morning . . . and thanks." He dropped the receiver into the cradle, then sat back to admire the jadeite carving. It certainly was a beauty, and one he'd love to get his hands on. Michael chuckled at his own joke. He already *had* his hands on it—literally at least. But it wasn't his lawfully, and that made a world of difference.

He appreciated and respected fine pieces of art and he was proud of his own private collection. But he would never stoop to stealing works of art that weren't for sale. Some works were destined to be shared with the whole world, not hidden away in a rich fanatic's private vault. It was unlikely this piece had been stolen from a museum, or the whole art world would be buzzing with the news, but if that was where it came from, then that's where it belonged, and he would do everything in his power to see it returned.

But what to do with it until then?

Michael looked around the room. The library-office was his bastion and he spent more time here than in any other room in the house. It was the one place where he worked, where he read, where he came for the solace offered by the magnificent ocean view. Keeping the artifact here meant keeping it close . . . and safe.

Safety was a major problem considering the smuggler would undoubtedly try to recover it. But there was no place on the estate more safe than his own Mesoamerican collection housed in this very room. Michael stared at the glass cabinet on the far side of the wall. Maybe there was a way to kill the proverbial two birds with one stone . . . or in this case, with one statue.

Cradling the statue in his hand, he turned off the alarm and unlocked the glass cabinet that contained his collection of Mayan figures. He placed the jadeite statue inside, locked the cabinet and reset the alarm. Then he crossed the room and pulled open a cabinet door.

Inside, along the wall, was a metal box, about the size of a small fuse box. Using a key he had taken from his desk drawer, Michael opened the box, revealing a series of switches and wires inside. He activated four of the switches and watched four small corresponding red lights come to life.

He glanced up at the tiny electronic eyes barely discernible in the corners of the room between the ceiling and the walls. He smiled and closed the metal door, pocketing the key.

The surveillance equipment had been Quentin's idea and was heartily endorsed by the insurance company. Yes, it was unlikely anyone could sneak onto the estate. Yes, the glass cabinet was bulletproof. Yes, the alarm system was state-of-the-art. And for those reasons alone Michael rarely bothered to use the damn video camera. Besides, it was more hassle than it was worth.

But now there was someone who didn't have to sneak onto the estate. Someone who already had access to his home, who was already insinuating herself into Rio's life, who was already clouding Michael's judgment. And frankly he didn't trust her. His heart swore he wouldn't videotape anything more revealing than Mrs. Hodges and her yellow feather duster.

But his mind wasn't so sure.

Michael gave the jadeite statue a final look, then turned out the lights. When Quentin saw this piece, he would start his investigation immediately. Maybe then Michael would get some answers.

Shelby crawled into bed, her body screaming for sleep, her mind rebelling against it. Every night as she slipped under the covers, she prayed tonight would be different. Yet every night as sleep overtook her, the nightmares began, and she was powerless to stop them.

Maybe now that she was reunited with Rio, the dreams would let up and she could experience the deep sleep of those who were free from worry and fear. For the next few months they would be together, and she'd have all that time to plan her next move.

Shelby closed her eyes and tried to welcome sleep, but as soon as she did, the nightmare started again. . . .

"Do you solemnly swear to tell the truth, the whole truth and nothing but the truth, so help you God?"

"I do."

"State your name for the record."

"Shelby Kelland."

"Please be seated."

Shelby took the indicated chair within the small wooden box and folded her hands in her lap. She was prepared for his badgering questions; she would be careful with her answers.

A faceless man rose from the table and approached the witness box. "Ms. Kelland, what is your occupation?"

"I'm an archaeologist specializing in Mayan culture."

"And where do you live?"

"For the last several months, I have been living and working at the same place—in the home of Michael Chandler."

"Prior to that, where did you live?"

"For three and a half years I lived at the site of an archaeological dig in the Yucatán peninsula of Mexico."

"I understand you have filed a petition for guardianship of the three-and-a-half-year-old child named Rio Chandler, claiming the child is your nephew. Is that correct?"

"Yes."

"Will you please explain to the court exactly how you are related to the child?"

"My brother, Elias, was Rio's father."

"Can you prove that?"

"Of course. There are any number of tests, such as fingerprinting, dental records and so on, which would prove that the man who lived in the commune under the name Elias was actually my younger brother, Lincoln Kelland."

"Ms. Kelland, I am not questioning whether you had a brother, where he lived or what name he used. I am questioning your claim that this man is the boy's father. Do you have a marriage certificate, a license or any document that would prove your brother and Rebecca Chandler were married?"

"No."

"Do you have a birth certificate or any other document that names your brother as the father of Miss Chandler's son?"

"No."

"And you expect the court to believe you are the boy's aunt simply because you say so?"

Don't let him rile you, Shelby told herself. *Stay calm.*

She took a deep breath before continuing. "You don't understand," she explained. "Gloxinia and Elias, I mean Rebecca and Lincoln, were married under the tenets of the commune. Just because there isn't a record, doesn't mean it didn't happen."

"Ah, yes, the commune. Most of us don't have a very good picture of what commune life is like. Perhaps you could enlighten us. This commune is open to anyone, correct?"

"Yes."

"And people wander in and out, stay or leave, as they wish?"

"Yes."

"There are no requirements of monogamy, are there?"

Shelby's palms were sweating and she rubbed them against her skirt. Please, not again. He was leading her on, forcing her to draw conclusions that seemed logical, but that were completely erroneous. She had to make them understand how wrong they were about the people in the commune. If only she could explain—

"The court is waiting for your answer, Ms. Kelland."

"Well, there are no written laws governing—"

"That was a yes or no question. Does the commune have any requirements of monogamy—yes or no?"

"No."

"Therefore, it is quite possible that any of the men from the commune or, for that matter, a transient just visiting the commune, could be Rio Chandler's father."

"No! That's ridiculous!"

"Please, Ms. Kelland, calm down. Ridiculous or not, the fact remains that you simply have no proof of any sort as to Rio Chandler's paternity. Isn't that so?"

Shelby was trapped. She felt small and helpless, like an animal caught in the jaws of a bear trap. "Yes," she said softly. "I have no proof." Grateful for the temporary reprieve, she watched in silence as her nameless, faceless adversary walked back to his table and sorted through a stack of papers.

"Since you are seeking permanent custody of the boy, we can assume that you care deeply for him, that you have only his welfare at heart, that you want what's best for him. Is that correct?"

"Absolutely."

"Ms. Kelland, please describe your home to the court."

Shelby twisted her hands in her lap. "My home?"

"Yes, your home, where your live, your place of residence. What does it look like? What sort of amenities does it have?"

"I live in a tent," she mumbled.

"Speak up, please, the court can't hear your answer."

Shelby lifted her head high. "I said, I live in a tent."

"Indeed. Isn't it a fact, Ms. Kelland, that your tent is located in the middle of a tropical rain forest, a jungle?"

"Yes."

"And your meals, such as they are, are prepared by a laborer in a mess tent where you eat with a dozen other coworkers?"

"Yes."

"And the nearest doctor is miles away and the nearest school even farther. Isn't that correct, Ms. Kelland?"

"Yes."

"And are you telling the court that you believe this is the best environment in which to raise a little child?"

"Of course not. If I am awarded custody of Rio, I intend to quit my job at the dig and provide a warm and loving environment for Rio, one that is stable and secure."

"You want to provide an environment that is 'stable and secure'? Exactly what does that mean?"

"Well…a nice home, with a large backyard to play in, toys, friends his own age, a good learning environment with access to books and other educational materials, things like that."

"And you can provide these things?"

"Yes, I believe so."

"How much money do you have in the bank right this minute?"

Shelby shook her head. "That's not the point—"

"Oh, but it is. A financial affidavit would clearly show that your savings would barely support a loan for a car, let alone a down payment on a house. Isn't that right?"

"I admit it will take a little time for me to get reestablished, but I know I can do it."

"Really? What exactly will you do to support yourself and the child if you are appointed guardian?"

Shelby squirmed in the chair. "Well...I don't have anything definite yet, but with my experience, I'm hoping to qualify to teach archaeology—perhaps at a local college."

"That's interesting. I know people who spend years trying to become college professors, yet you think you can secure this position at a moment's notice because of your vast experience. And when you get this wonderful teaching job, what will you do with your nephew?"

"I beg your pardon?"

"What will you do with young Rio while you are spending your time teaching, or working, or whatever it is you intend to do?"

"Until he reaches school age, I would have to rely on a good day-care service," Shelby admitted reluctantly.

"Tell me, Ms. Kelland, since we've established that you cannot afford to buy a home, where do you intend to live?"

"I'm not sure..."

"Not sure? Come now, you must have some idea. If you were to walk out of this courtroom with Rio right now, where would you take him? To a hotel...a motel...a shelter for the homeless?"

"No!" Shelby cried, pounding her fist on the rail. If only they'd give her a chance to explain. "I've been so busy taking care of Rio at the Chandler estate, I just haven't had time—"

"Yes, indeed, and now that you've broached the subject, let's talk about your work with Michael Chandler. Will you please tell the court who Shelby McMasters is?"

"I am."

"You are," he echoed. "Isn't it a fact, Ms. Kelland, that, using the fictitious name of Shelby McMasters and armed with a fake résumé and other falsified credentials, you insinuated yourself into the home of Michael Chandler?"

"I obtained the position of nanny in the Chandler household in order to be close to my nephew."

"You deliberately deceived and lied to Mr. Chandler in order to get what you wanted?"

"Not really. As his aunt, I believed I was the best one to care for Rio."

"But the information on your résumé and your letters of recommendation were lies, were they not?"

"Yes."

"And you never revealed to Mr. Chandler that you were related to his nephew?"

"No, but I have given Rio the very best care and—"

"Ms. McMasters, excuse me, Ms. Kelland, do you agree that Michael Chandler is the child's maternal uncle?"

"Yes."

"And since, for the past three months, you have been living in the Chandler home and working as the child's nanny, would you say that Mr. Chandler's home provides an environment that is, in your own words, 'secure and stable'?"

"Yes, but—"

"In fact, isn't it true that, after Michael Chandler was granted temporary custody of his nephew, he hired you and ordered you to prepare a nursery and playroom for the child . . .'' He picked up a document from the table, flipped to a marked page and began reading. "'. . . completely outfitted with bedroom furniture, decorative accents, linen, clothing and toys'?"

"Well, sort of. He—"

"Just answer the question, Ms. Kelland. Yes or no?"

"There was an employment contract that—"

"Yes or no?"

"Everything he did was at my recommenda—"

"Your Honor, I ask that you please instruct the witness to answer the questions without giving unsolicited testimony."

Shelby glanced up at the black-robed figure who glared back at her and nodded threateningly.

"Now then, Ms. Kelland, I repeat the question. Did Michael Chandler order you to prepare a nursery and playroom for his nephew? Yes or no?"

"Yes."

"And didn't he further authorize you to do whatever was necessary to 'ensure the health and well-being of the child'?"

"Yes."

"Didn't he even go so far as to have a safety fence installed around his swimming pool?"

"Yes."

"Didn't he agree to the removal of all the plants and shrubbery on his property that might be hazardous if ingested?"

"Yes, Yes, YES!" Shelby held her hands over her ears and tried to block out the accusing questions of her persecutor.

They made Michael look like a saint. They thought all the changes she'd made at the estate were his idea. Shelby wanted to scream. Michael did nothing, nothing! All he did was throw his money around. And he was very good at doing that.

"If you were no longer employed as Rio's nanny, do you believe Michael Chandler would do his utmost to secure a suitable replacement for you?"

"Oh, there's no doubt he would hire the best money could buy," Shelby retorted, not even bothering to temper the sarcasm.

"Precisely. So, you agree that, as long as Michael Chandler is guardian of his nephew, the boy will never want for anything."

"But Michael doesn't love Rio," she shouted. "Maybe he can meet all of Rio's *material* needs, but that doesn't make him fit to be a guardian."

"Really? You still question Mr. Chandler's fitness to be the permanent guardian?"

"Yes, I do."

"Tell me, Ms. Kelland, have you ever seen Michael Chandler hurt, spank, slap or in any way abuse his nephew? Have you ever heard him yell at, scold or even reprimand his nephew? Can you tell the court of one single instance when Michael Chandler acted in a manner that was inappropriate to or inconsistent with the needs of his nephew?"

"As a matter of fact, I can. The night Rio and I arrived in San Francisco, Rio lost his teddy bear in the airport. Michael Chandler refused to go back in the airport and look for it, even after I told him how very important it was to Rio."

"Indeed. But isn't it true that the real reason Mr. Chandler refused to return to the airport was that an unruly mob of reporters, who were undoubtedly responsible for the boy losing the toy in the first place, were still there and threatened the health and safety of his nephew?"

"Well, yes, but—"

"And isn't it also true that Mr. Chandler promised his nephew he would replace the stuffed animal with a new one, first thing the very next morning?"

"Yes, but Rio didn't want a new toy, he wanted—"

"Your Honor, we believe we have clearly proved that—one, Ms. Kelland cannot substantiate her claim of relationship to the minor child, Rio Chandler. Two—although Ms. Kelland may

be sincere in her claim of love and devotion to the child—she
has no permanent residence and no visible means of support.
And three—Michael Chandler has proven he is the natural
brother of the deceased, Rebecca Chandler, and has available
ample means and resources to support his sister's child. He is
well known and well respected as an upstanding citizen of this
community. We respectfully request that he be appointed permanent guardian."

"No!" Shelby screamed. "Wait!" But even as she jumped
to her feet, she already knew it was too late. She watched helplessly as the judge raised his gavel.

"After due consideration of all parties involved, I hereby
order the child, Rio Chandler, to be given over to his uncle and
permanent guardian, Michael Chandler. Case dismissed."

Chapter 7

The judge's gavel crashed down against the desk, and Shelby awoke with a start. Perspiration soaked her body and her nightshirt clung to her breasts. Her eyes ached with the weight of unshed tears and her throat and mouth were dry. She was tense and exhausted, but a quick glance toward the window told her there was no time to go back to sleep, even if she wanted to.

Shelby struggled out of bed and stifled a yawn as she moved to the window. She pushed aside the curtains and her feelings at the same time, with one simple flick of her arm. She'd had a lot of practice these last few weeks keeping her emotions at bay, promising herself she would deal with them later. *I'll think about it tomorrow,* she inwardly quipped. Shelby sighed. As unlikely as it sounded, she and ol' Scarlet had a lot in common. Neither of them was prepared for the trials that lay ahead, and each was too stubborn to give up and turn back.

Shelby looked out across the dew-laden lawn. Linc would have loved this view. He would have stood here reveling in the silence of the early dawn, watching the mist and fog leave the land and head back toward the sea.

Lord, she missed him.

She'd lost touch with him when she was in college. He had always been on the run, and the only news she'd ever gotten was when the police questioned her about some new scam he was involved in. She hadn't known he had fled to Mexico or was hiding in a commune until the day he'd showed up outside her tent. He'd said that he had been living in the commune for over a year and it had changed his life.

He had changed all right—so much so that she'd had a hard time believing it was Linc. He had looked the same—a little older, a little grayer. But his bearing, his attitude, his mannerisms had belonged to a stranger. He'd said he'd come to understand who and what he was. He had given up his old ways and had found acceptance and serenity.

And she had wanted desperately to believe him.

Except for occasional trips to town for supplies, he rarely left the commune, so whenever she could get a free weekend she had traveled there to be with him and his family. He always made the most of their time together. He taught her how to relax, how to balance the stress of her work with the beauty of the land she was living in. He constantly reminded her of the tenuousness of life and the importance of making each day count.

Maybe he'd known what was coming.

Or maybe it had all been an elaborate ruse.

But she remembered clearly the afternoon she'd dashed across the compound and stopped cold when she felt the heavy emptiness that covered the commune like a mantle of stone. She had been attending a week-long seminar in Mexico City and hadn't known about the accident. Her brother was gone. There had been no time to cry and grieve over her loss, because he had left behind a legacy of life and laughter. He left Rio.

A sparrow skimmed the surface of the vast lawn, looking for a place to land without wetting its feet. It was going to be a beautiful day—Rio's first day—and she would not let the recurring dream or the weight of her memories dampen it.

"Tía Shelby?" Rio stood shyly in the doorway of her room, the brontosaurus under one arm and a book under the other.

"Good morning, sunshine," she said brightly. "What have you got there?" Shelby picked him up and dropped him on the bed, then bounced down beside him.

"*Un dinosauro,*" he said, holding it up in the air by its tail.

"So I see. Do you like it?"

Rio shrugged. "It's not *osito.*"

"I know, honey, and I'm so sorry about that." Some of the anger at Michael crept back in, but Shelby vowed not to let it affect Rio. As soon as she could, she would call the airport and see if anyone had turned in the toy to the Lost and Found. It was a slim chance, but it was better than nothing. "What else do you have?" she asked, changing the subject before Rio could be swept away by his own feelings.

"A book. Read it."

"You bet I will." They curled up against the pillows and Shelby read the story of the hungry little worm who ate cantaloupe, doughnuts, hot dogs, pumpkin pie, peanuts, bologna, cheese, sauerkraut, chocolate cake and just about everything else.

"Now, *I'm* hungry," Shelby said.

"Me, too," Rio echoed.

"I think we should get dressed, make our beds and then eat breakfast. What do you think?"

"I want to eat these," he said, pointing to the colorful pictures in the book.

Shelby made a face. "I don't think they would be very good for breakfast. Remember what happened to the worm when he ate all those things?"

Rio nodded solemnly. "He got sick."

"That's right. But I'll bet Mrs. Hodges will be able to fix us a great breakfast. Shall we go see?"

In spite of the fact that it was nearly two a.m. when he finally crawled into bed, Michael was up early that morning. Not early enough to swim laps or put in a few hours of work as he usually did, but early enough to get to the library and check on the statue. It was still there, on the middle shelf of the glass case, right where he'd placed it, and a quick look inside the paneled box revealed no one had gone near the collection during the night. He hadn't really expected anything to happen—after all, no one but Quentin knew he had it. As far as the smuggler was concerned, the statue was still inside Rio's bear.

Rio's bear.

Michael opened a desk drawer and pulled out the all but decapitated animal. If he gave it to Hodges, she could fix it before Rio saw it in its mangled state. He was halfway down the hall when he heard Shelby's voice coming from the sun room. Normally it was as light and clear as bird song, but this morning she sounded more than a little strained.

"Are you sure? Have you checked everywhere?"

Michael froze, his back pressed against the wall.

"No, I've already talked to Lost and Found and the custodial services department. Please, I don't know who else to call."

He wasn't used to this—eavesdropping in his own home—but neither was he about to throw away a chance to find out what the hell she was up to. Michael held his breath, listening to the one-sided conversation.

"I'm absolutely certain he had it when we got off the plane. It has to be there somewhere. It's a small teddy bear, reddish-brown with a cream-colored face. It doesn't look like much, but it's very important. I'm willing to offer a reward..."

Her voice trailed off like a music box winding down, and with it Michael's heart sank.

"No, I understand." Resignation and frustration were evident in her tone. "But if anything comes up, please call me at this number. I'd appreciate your help."

Michael ducked back into the library as Shelby hung up the phone. He listened to her footsteps on the marble floor until they faded away.

Damn. She really wanted that bear, but whether it was for the statue or for Rio he still hadn't a clue. Confronting her with his suspicions would do no more good now than it would have last night. He needed proof... some kind of evidence that she was directly involved in the smuggling. He looked down at the disfigured bear still in his hand. Maybe there was a way. As soon as she was apart from Rio, he would give her the bear and ask her to fix it. The look on her face should tell him everything he needed to know.

Michael tucked the bear back into his desk drawer and headed for the kitchen. At best, Rio would get his bear back. At worst... he didn't even want to think about it.

The laughing, carefree voices stopped him in the hallway outside the kitchen. He couldn't see the people, but he could hear the conviviality and jocularity of his staff eating breakfast.

Rio garbled something that was half English and half Spanish.

"He's an awfully sweet boy, that one is," Mrs. Hodges said. "But I do wish I knew what he was saying."

Shelby laughed, and the anxious voice he'd heard in the sun room became a distant memory.

"He said you're a good 'cooker.'"

"A good cooker, is it? Well, I'll be. Imagine that. Just wait until I tell Jules. He thinks I'm a good cooker, too. And it's going to take a good cooker to fatten that child up. He's too skinny, he is. But isn't it something how much he looks like Mr. Michael? You would swear it was his own son. Even though I didn't know her, I'm mighty sorry about what happened to Mr. Michael's sister, God rest her soul."

Michael stiffened. The last thing he needed this morning was to listen to his busybody housekeeper talk about Rebecca.

"But if you ask me," the older woman continued, "this could be a blessing in disguise. Yes, indeed, as I always say, when the good Lord closes a door, He opens a window. Mr. Michael needs someone in his life. He's been alone far too long, and I've been telling him so, even though he don't pay me no never-mind. You and that boy are going to make a world of difference in Mr. Michael's life, you just see if I'm not right."

Michael scowled. Why didn't the old woman keep her opinions to herself? He didn't appreciate her discussing his private life with Shelby any more than he appreciated the unsolicited advice. And as for Shelby making a "world of difference," that might well be the understatement of the decade.

The sliding glass doors that looked out over the back lawn slid open. "'Morning, everyone." Michael listened as John Callahan strode into the room, sniffing the air. "Pancakes? I knew it, Mrs. H. I could smell them all the way to the garage."

"You sit right down, Mister John. I've got a stack just waiting for you. You dig into these while they're hot."

Michael stepped away from the door. He didn't have to see the people to picture them in his mind. Rio—his neck about level with the table, shoveling pancakes off his plate and into his mouth; Hodges—with an apron tied around her ample waist, bustling around her kitchen and fussing over everyone; Callahan—confident and eager, fitting in easily in any circumstances; and Shelby. It took less time than a heartbeat to conjure up a picture of Shelby McMasters—her blond curls glittering in the morning sunlight, her smooth skin lightly tanned like the color of a pale apricot, her long, lithe legs bared by her shorts, her blue eyes and bright, quick smile. His chest tightened as it hadn't done in years.

"So, champ," John said around a mouthful of breakfast. "Are we going to take that tour of the jungle gym this morning?"

Michael listened as Shelby offered a quick translation.

"I'm sorry," John apologized. "I didn't realize he didn't understand English."

"It's okay," Shelby said. "Rio is a very bright little boy and he understands an incredible amount of both English and Spanish. But there are bound to be a lot of words that he simply hasn't had exposure to. 'Jungle gym' is the first of them."

John nodded. "And what about his speech?"

"Fine," Rio said in perfect English.

The room erupted in peals of laughter.

Michael leaned against the wall and closed his eyes. He wanted to join them. More than anything else, he wanted to waltz right in, straddle a chair and order up a huge plate of hotcakes and black coffee. He wanted to chat and joke with them, but the truth was he didn't know how. He had tried it once or twice before, always with the same results. The conversation shifted and tension tinted the air, people just weren't relaxed or comfortable around him.

He was The Boss. An outsider in his own home.

A chair scraped across the floor and the patter of little feet stopped at the sliding glass doors that led out to the back lawn. "*¿Puedo salir afuera?*" Rio begged. "Pleeze?"

"I can understand that in any language," John said. He pushed himself away from the table. "It will be a while before the slave driver needs me for anything. Will you let me take Rio out and show him the jungle gym? Pleeze?"

"All right, all right. Go," Shelby said, laughing. The patio door slid open. "Be careful," she called after them.

"He'll be fine as long as he's with Mr. John," Mrs. Hodges said. "He's very good with the little ones. And now it's your turn, miss. You haven't had your own breakfast yet. Sit down and I'll whip up another batch of pancakes."

"Please don't go to the trouble. I'll just have a cup of coffee and maybe another glass of juice."

"It's no trouble at all. I enjoy my work and besides, Rio himself said I was a good cooker, now, didn't he?"

"Well, yes, but—"

"No buts. You're almost as thin as he is, poor thing. You both need fattening up and I intend to do just that." The sound of a whisk scraping the bowl drifted into the hall. "And if it'll make you feel better, I'm not doing this just for you, you know. Mr. Michael hasn't eaten yet."

Shelby's juice glass stalled halfway to her mouth. She had forgotten about Michael. After the horrible things she had said to him in the car, she wasn't ready to face him. Not yet. He had behaved very badly, but so had she. She needed time to get her thoughts together, to think of a way to apologize for what she'd said while not apologizing for why she'd said it. The more time the better. Maybe she could get out of here and join Rio outside before Michael arrived.

"What time does Mr. Chandler have breakfast?" Shelby asked, glancing up at the large kitchen clock mounted on the wall.

"Anytime now." Mrs. Hodges pulled a large tray from a closet. "As soon as I get it ready, I'll take it in to him."

Shelby blinked. "He has breakfast in bed? Every day?"

"Lordy, no," said Mrs. Hodges, her laughter rumbling through the kitchen. "Mr. Michael's usually up and swimming before the rest of the world's out of bed. By the time I get breakfast made, he's already put in two hours of work. I serve him breakfast in the library."

Shelby breathed a sigh of relief, but her reprieve was short-lived. A deep voice boomed from behind her.

"Not this morning, Mrs. Hodges. Today, I'll have breakfast right here."

It would have been easy to hastily retreat to the library and wait for Mrs. Hodges to bring him breakfast there. And, for a moment, Michael had seriously considered doing just that. But a yearning, stronger than he had ever felt before, overtook him. He was suddenly aware that, except for business, his life was spent standing in the shadows, being on the outside, watching from a distance. With the unexpected emergence of Rio and Shelby in his life, he had been given the opportunity to change all of that . . . if he was willing to try.

With a forced smile glued to his face, Michael walked into the large kitchen. "There's no need for you to carry a tray to the library, Mrs. Hodges. I'm expecting a visit from Quentin Ingersoll this morning and I probably won't start working until after he leaves." He glanced around the room and located the percolator. "May I?" he asked, gesturing to a cluster of stoneware mugs on the counter next to a freshly brewed pot of coffee.

The portly woman stared at him in openmouthed astonishment. "Of course, Mr. Michael," she said, quickly recovering herself as the smell of burning pancakes tinged the air. "Help yourself."

Michael poured himself a steaming cup of coffee, then took a seat at the table next to Shelby. He had guessed right about the shorts and the long legs, which disappeared under the table, but what he hadn't pictured was the kelly-green V-necked terry top that matched her shorts. As she leaned across the table and reached for the sugar bowl and creamer, her top rode up, revealing the inward curve of her waist. She had the kind of body men dreamed about. Exciting. Ripe. Touchable.

He took a large gulp of hot coffee and clenched his teeth as it seared its way down his throat.

"Cream or sugar?"

He shook his head, the scalding liquid temporarily robbing him of his ability to speak. It was happening again. He felt large and clumsy, and although he didn't consider himself a chauvinist, he felt decidedly out of place in a room that had traditionally been the bastion of women.

"Here you go, Mr. Michael." Mrs. Hodges placed a large plate of pancakes in front of him. "And there's a lot more where those came from." The always-talkative and generally bossy woman fell silent, clearly uncomfortable having the boss watch her as she worked.

Shelby sipped her coffee, studying him over the rim of her cup. He was wearing tailored beige slacks and an open-necked, short-sleeve shirt, and seemed surprisingly calm in spite of the events of the night before. She watched as he spread a napkin across his lap and slid his hands down the tops of his thighs. She could almost feel the strength of the muscles beneath. Never before had she been so aware of a man's looks...so aware of a man, period.

She shook off the disturbing thoughts that coursed through her mind like heat lightning. It was perfectly normal to be unsettled by a man as breathtakingly gorgeous as Michael Chandler. But, she reminded herself, she would never do more than just look, for three very good reasons. First, she hadn't forgotten her gut-wrenching dream last night and the fact that she was always only one step away from losing Rio. Second, sexy was great, but it wasn't enough, not when the man in question turned into W.C. Fields in the presence of kids and small animals. And third, she hadn't forgiven him for the way he had brutally dismissed Rio's bear as unimportant and inconsequential.

It would be a long time before she got over that one.

Shelby stirred a bit more cream into her coffee. For Rio's sake, she needed to establish a decent working relationship with Michael, and that meant clearing the air of last night's argument. In spite of her hidden agenda, she had to be honest with him about her feelings, and now was as good a time as any. She decided to apologize for her angry outburst and tell Michael how much she appreciated his protecting them from the mob of reporters. But she also intended to tell him that she was disappointed in the way he'd ignored Rio's feelings and that, in her opinion, he had failed to explore other options of retrieving Rio's bear. Her decision thus made and her statement rehearsed, she turned to face him.

"Mr. Chandler," she began.

"Ms. McMasters," he said at the same time. His grin was like liquid mercury, slipping away almost before it registered. "Please . . . after you," he insisted.

"I want to talk about last night," Shelby started to say. Suddenly, she felt nervous and shy. It was hard not to stare at him as he worked his way through breakfast, hard not to notice the way his lips surrounded each morsel of food, the way he slid the empty fork from his mouth, the way he flicked his tongue to catch a drop of syrup. Watching him eat pancakes was like an invitation to a bacchanalia.

"Go on," he said, tearing her from her reverie.

She dragged her gaze away from his mouth and looked him straight in the eye. "I would like to apologize for the things I said and the way I behaved last night. My actions were inappropriate and totally unprofessional and for that I am sorry."

"Apology accepted—"

"However," she continued firmly, "although there is no excuse for my behavior, it wasn't without provocation. I believe the way you handled the situation was abominable." He looked at her with raised eyebrows, but she rushed on, undaunted. "I admit it would have been foolish for either of us to fight our way back through the crowd to look for Rio's bear. But there were other alternatives which you refused to consider. Mr.

Chandler, you completely dismissed the feelings of your nephew, and I would be remiss in my duties if I failed to point that out."

From somewhere near the stove she heard Mrs. Hodges gasp, but Shelby could no more temper her words than she could slow down the internal rush of emotion that was steadily gaining momentum.

For a long, frozen moment Michael did not move. Then slowly he reached for the syrup. "Is that so?" he asked with a detached calmness.

His steel-gray eyes impaled her. She faltered, swallowing to wet her stubbornly dry throat. "Yes, it is. During the last few weeks, Rio has gone through unimaginable trauma. He needs support and stability, not rejection and self-doubt. The way you respond to him will have a great impact upon his ability to adapt to his new life." She took a deep breath and let it out slowly, trying to control her racing heart. There was no way she could remain composed where Rio was concerned.

Shelby watched as Michael leisurely finished his coffee. There was something in the air between them. Something so electric that her scalp tingled from it. His eyes locked with hers as he dropped the cup on the table with a dull thud that made her jump. "Thank you for so eloquently pointing out my many faults and defects, Ms. McMasters." His voice was a low silky purr that was far more intimidating than shouting would have been. "Is there anything else you would like to add while we are on the subject?"

In truth, she had barely skimmed the surface, but discretion being the better part of valor, she held her tongue. "No. I think I've said quite enough." *More than enough,* she thought ruefully.

"Fine." Tossing his napkin onto the table, he pushed back his chair and strode out of the room.

"You've done it now, miss," Mrs. Hodges said as she cleared away Michael's dishes and wiped the table clean. "You don't understand Mr. Michael. He doesn't mean to be gruff, he just doesn't know how to be otherwise."

"Well, it's about time he learned," Shelby exclaimed. "Look at this," she said, pointing to the empty table. "He couldn't even take the time to say thank you for breakfast. I've seen rocks with more sensitivity than he has."

Planting her hands on the counter, Shelby looked out the window to where Rio and John were playing. John was trying hard to teach Rio the intricacies of operating a Big Wheel. He sat on the ground holding his legs up in the air, pedaling them back and forth in bicycle motion. When that didn't help, he stood up and bent over the front wheel, put his hands on Rio's feet and pedaled the bike while walking backward. It was funny and silly and so very touching. John Callahan, a perfect stranger, was doing all the things with Rio that Michael should be doing.

Michael. She wanted to grab him by his incredible biceps and shake him. What was wrong with him? Why was it so difficult for him to love a child? Why couldn't he understand what Rio was going through? Her hands clenched into fists and she slammed them on the countertop. For all the world, she could not understand why he was so cold.

She never heard him enter the room once again, but she felt his presence. The hairs stood up on the back of her neck and her skin prickled under his penetrating stare. His hand burned her shoulder as he touched her and she spun around to face him. His face was a mask. Controlled. Neutral. Unemotional. Her heart tripled its rate and she drew an unsteady breath.

He took a step back, an unreadable expression on his wickedly handsome face. "Here," he said, holding out a small brown bag. "Take it."

Shelby looked at him blankly. "What . . . ?"

Michael folded his arms across his chest. "Open it. Consider it *my* apology."

Her fingers trembled as she fumbled with the bag. Finally, with a stunned Mrs. Hodges looking on, she slipped her hand inside the bag and pulled out Rio's bear.

She could have hugged him.

"Oh!" Tears sprang to her eyes and she hugged the bear instead. "I can't believe it. You went back and got it." Shelby held the bear out in front of her, just to make sure it was really Rio's, then crushed it to her chest again. She looked up at Michael through a cloud of thick, wet lashes. "I don't understand," she said softly. "Why didn't you say something? Why did you let me go on and on, making a fool of myself and falsely accusing you?" She nuzzled the bear with her chin. "It seems I owe you another apology."

"Not at all. Everything you said about me last night and this morning is correct, and when I realized it…" He shrugged. "I went back to the airport and found the bear." He looked skeptically at the stuffed animal which Shelby was still hugging. "…or rather, what's left of it."

Shelby unfolded her arms and looked at the mangled little toy. "You're right. It's in pretty bad shape, but I think I can fix it." She turned to Mrs. Hodges, who had witnessed the whole scene with a mixture of amusement and wonder. "You wouldn't happen to have a sewing kit and a spare button, would you? I could go and buy the things, but I'd like to get this back to Rio as soon as possible." Shelby sat down at the table and laid the bear in front of her. "Oh, and I'll need some batting, too, if you have it."

"I've got some pillow stuffing and buttons, everything you need, in the guest house. I'll go get them and be back in two shakes." The older woman trotted off, her apron strings flying out behind her.

Michael watched intently as Shelby stuck her fingers through the hole in the bear's midsection, and began poking and prodding inside.

She looked up and smiled, acutely aware of his staring. "Is something wrong?"

"Wrong? No. I just wondered what you're doing."

Shelby smiled and moved the bear closer for him to see. "The bear's arms and legs weren't ripped, but they were pretty well squashed. I'm taking the batting that was left in the body cavity and moving it out to the limbs. Once they're plumped up, I'll use Mrs. Hodges's batting to restuff the body. Then I'll resew the center seam and with a little luck it will be better than new."

She held it away from her and studied it, but to Michael's eye there was nothing to admire. "You must have had a lot of experience repairing things."

Shelby nodded. She hadn't fixed many toys, but she was constantly mending the knee of her well-worn jeans, repairing a rip in her shirt or jacket, desperately hoping her clothes would hold together until the next time she could afford the trip to Chetumal to replace them. "I've done a bit from time to time," she answered evasively.

Mrs. Hodges burst into the kitchen waving a sewing basket in one hand and large bag of batting in the other. "I was saving this to make a pillow for my Jules," she puffed, "but he surely won't miss what was never there."

The two women wasted no time. Sitting down at the table, Shelby threaded a needle and set to work reattaching the bear's ear, while Mrs. Hodges dumped out a whole jar of buttons and began the search for just the right one.

Michael shifted from foot to foot. He had missed nothing. When he gave her the bear, he'd seen her eyes widen, heard the slight gasp slip from between her abruptly parted lips. The image of her blue eyes shiny with tears had been permanently etched in his mind. When she found the hole in the bear's stomach, he watched as she moved aside the old stuffing and made room for the new.

If she was the smuggler, she didn't show it. No, she was more like a prowler, moving stealthily through his life, unknowingly ferreting out the secret dreams he had spent years learning to hide. Beneath the aggravation they seemed to bring out in each other, there was a powerful attraction. He hadn't felt this drawn to a woman in years.

He liked her. He liked the way she looked and the way she smelled. He liked her honesty and determination. He liked the fact that she stood up for herself and was never intimidated. He liked the way her generous mouth pursed in thought, and he wondered how that soft mouth would taste.

He didn't want to leave . . . but he had no reason to stay.

"I'll leave you ladies to your work. The sooner the bear is fixed, the sooner you can return it to Rio."

Shelby reached up and grabbed his arm. "No," she said.

His arm felt branded by her touch as her smooth, soft fingers brushed the fine hair on his arm. A sharp tingle traveled from those fingers up his arm. "No?"

Her look was one of determination. "You were the one who found the bear, you need to be the one to give it back."

"I'm sure that's not necessary."

"I'm sure it is," she said stubbornly. The pressure on his arm increased slightly. "Please."

"¡Tía Shelby, *mira! ¡Mira!*"

In two strides Shelby was at the window. She smiled in relief when she saw Rio sitting at the top of the slide, grasping the arched handles on either side. "I see you," she shouted back, waving to him. As she watched, Rio let go of the bars and slid into John's waiting arms.

Chandler's Child

Only then did she realize Michael was standing right behind her—so close, she could almost feel the crisp twill of his pants against the backs of her bare legs. So close, his broad shoulders seemed like a wall she could lean back against. So close, his breath tickled her ear.

She turned quickly and sidestepped around him, trying not to breathe in the heady scent of his cologne, trying not to notice the expanse of tanned throat exposed by the open-necked shirt. She dropped into her chair and plunged the last handful of stuffing into the center of Rio's bear.

"He called you *tía*."

"What?"

"Rio called you *tía*. Doesn't that mean aunt?"

Shelby nodded casually. This question she had anticipated and was prepared for. "Ms. McMasters is quite a lot for a little boy to say, particularly for a little boy with limited articulation skills." The needle disappeared under a flap of material and reappeared on the other side.

Michael chuckled. "It's a difficult name for an adult to pronounce," he said smiling, "even someone with highly developed articulation skills."

Shelby returned his smile as her needle dipped again. "Since Rio was calling you uncle, it was a natural extension for him to call me aunt." She winced as the needle pierced her skin. *Okay, so it wasn't exactly the truth... but it wasn't exactly a lie, either.*

He leaned over and wiped away the drop of blood perched on the end of her finger. It immediately stopped bleeding, but only because his overpowering presence had sent all the rest of her blood rushing to her toes.

"Don't you think it's a little strange that Rio is calling us by our first names when I'm 'Mr. Chandler' and you're 'Ms. McMasters'?" he asked.

Shelby felt her face flush. She had hoped it wouldn't come to this, that he'd be more understanding. "Since it bothers you, Mr. Chandler," she said bluntly, stabbing the bear vigorously with the needle, "I will ask Rio to stop doing it." She finished the last stitches and snipped off the thread.

"It's Michael," he said extending his hand. "And, in my opinion, Ms. McMasters, Rio should do whatever is easiest for him."

A smile twitched at the corners of her mouth as she extended her own hand—with Rio's bear still in it. Hastily, she tucked the bear under her arm. "It's Shelby," she said as her hand slipped into his. "And thank you." A delicious shiver raced up her spine, and a timeless hunger stirred to life, coiling deep inside.

"Did you see me? Did you see me?"

Shelby thrust the bear into Michael's hand and he quickly hid it behind his back as Rio bounded into the room.

"Yes, I did," Shelby said, her words a little breathless. "You were wonderful."

"You certainly were."

Rio froze at the sound of his uncle's voice and a look of terror came into his eyes. Shelby saw it, and she knew Michael saw it, too. Rio hadn't forgotten what his uncle had done, nor did Shelby expect him to. But Michael had a chance to change all that, if only he would speak up.

"Rio, your Uncle Michael has something for you." She turned the little boy around to face his uncle, but he shrank back against her.

For a long moment Shelby was afraid Michael was going to turn and walk away. But slowly he brought his hand from around his back and extended the stuffed animal to Rio.

"*Osito,*" Rio squealed. "My bear!" Rio grabbed his toy and hurled himself at Michael. He hugged Michael's knees and buried his face in the sharp creases of Michael's pants. "Oh, thank you!"

Michael reached down and stroked Rio's hair awkwardly. "You're welcome."

Upping the wattage on his smile, Rio ran out through the sliding doors clutching his bear by one newly sewn arm. Shelby watched Michael watching Rio as he ran to show John Callahan his old toy. A sad smile reached Michael's eyes as he turned and exited the kitchen.

As soon as he was gone, Shelby twirled around the room. "You were right, Mrs. Hodges," she said, giving the bewildered woman a hug. "Rio did it. He's turning Michael Chandler into a real human being."

Her own words stopped her cold as a dreadful realization crept over her. The more "real" Michael became, the more likely she would lose the child she loved.

Chapter 8

"So, what do you think?" Michael asked.

"I think you have a lot of explaining to do." Quentin Ingersoll held his Polaroid camera a few inches away from the statue on Michael's desk and snapped a picture. "You don't need me to tell you how good the piece is. You knew that before you called me." A whirring sound accompanied the photo as it slid out of the bottom of the camera. Quentin placed it on the desk next to the others.

"Okay, so we're agreed the figure is superb. What can you tell me about it?"

"Nothing."

"Nothing? Come on, Quentin, you must know something. Don't hold out on me."

Quentin snorted. "Who's holding out on whom, Michael?" He laid the statue on its side and snapped another picture.

"You can badger all you want, but I'm not going to tell you how I got it. If you won't help me on this, say so, and I'll find someone else."

Quentin sighed. "Okay, Michael, we'll play it your way...for now. I don't know where this little guy came from, but I know he *didn't* come from a museum. There have been no reported thefts of a figure even remotely resembling this one, and the statue shows no indication of ever having been restored or even retouched. Given the amount of dirt and grit embedded in the crevices, I would assume it's a very recent recovery."

Michael nodded.

"And, I haven't told you a single thing that you didn't already know, or at least suspect. Right?"

Michael smiled. "Something like that. Can you find out anything more specific?"

"I'll try, but it'll take some time. The figure is definitely Mayan, but there are quite a few people in Mexico working on Mayan ruins. I'll have to contact each group, find out what artifacts have been uncovered and cataloged, and then ask if any of them happens to be missing."

Michael grinned. "I'm sure you'll be the soul of discretion."

Quentin frowned. "This is serious business, Michael. Recent discoveries can only happen in one of two ways—an authorized dig, or an unauthorized one. If it came from an unauthorized dig, obviously there will be no documentation of the find. But quite frankly, the Mexican authorities take a dim view of individuals running around digging up their land and those sites are found out and shut down before the people have a chance to do much of anything. The likelihood of this statue coming from an unauthorized dig is very remote. That means it was probably stolen from an authorized site. And if *that's* the case, I assure you both the thief *and* the Mexican Bureau of Antiquities are out looking for it. Either way spells trouble." He picked up the statue and turned it over and over in his hands. "Let me give you some unsolicited advice. Get rid of it. Take it to the police. Turn it over to the authorities. Tell them what you won't tell me."

Michael shook his head. "Not yet. I want to see what you come up with first." He took the statue from Quentin's hands and crossed the room to the glass cabinet.

"At least let me take the thing back to the museum. I'll box it up and store it in the vault. It'll be completely safe and no one but the two of us will even know it's there."

"Sorry, Quentin. It's a lot easier for someone to get into your museum than it is to get onto my estate. My security system is better than yours, and I have my own reasons for keeping it right here." Michael carefully returned the figure to the glass cabinet, set the alarm and activated the electronic surveillance.

"You're a stubborn man, Michael. Don't say I didn't warn you." Quentin collected the Polaroid photos from Michael's desk and arranged them in a neat stack. "I'll let you know if anything turns up. But don't hold your breath. There's a lot of ground to cover."

"You might want to start with the Yucatán."

"The Yucatán?" Quentin's eyes narrowed. "Why there?"

Michael shrugged. "Just a suggestion."

Quentin eyed Michael suspiciously. "That's where your nephew came from, wasn't it? The one who arrived last night."

Now it was Michael's turn to be surprised. "How did you know about my nephew?"

"What's not to know?" Quentin pulled the morning paper from his briefcase, opened it up and tossed it on Michael's desk.

CHANDLER HEIR ARRIVES FROM MEXICO

The front-page caption screamed at him as he looked down on a picture of himself trying to shelter Shelby and Rio from the mob of reporters. Michael couldn't see Shelby's face, which was half-buried against his chest and blocked by Rio, but there was no mistaking the fear in Rio's eyes and the anger in his own.

Quickly he scanned the article. Nothing had been left out. The story described in great detail how Rio had been orphaned and how Michael had been appointed temporary guardian. They dubbed Rio the heir apparent to the Chandler fortune and joked about the "rags to riches" saga of the Chandler men. Michael grew tense. If this kind of publicity continued, they would have more than an artifact smuggler to contend with. There would be a constant stream of reporters and photographers dogging their heels, harassing them everywhere they went.

A strange, unfamiliar emotion bubbled deep inside him. Like a throwback to some prehistoric time, he felt a desperate need to protect both Rio and Shelby. He hated the way the press hounded him, insinuating themselves into his life, but he knew how to handle it. Rio and Shelby didn't. Rio was an innocent child, small and vulnerable, and Shelby was . . .

Michael stopped, at a loss for words. Shelby was an enigma. She had poise and sophistication, but she was also down-to-earth and homey. She was warm and tender with Rio, yet she had the courage to confront Michael. Her smile could light up the room and her tongue could cut like a scalpel. He appreciated her beauty, and admired her honesty and determination. Whether from physical attraction or verbal sparring, the sparks always flew when they were together.

That curious feeling stirred inside him again, long-dormant feelings of possession and protection, which Michael abruptly pushed aside. He felt responsible for Shelby and Rio—nothing more.

". . . keep it a secret."

Michael's head snapped up. "What?"

"I said, I don't know how you expected to keep your nephew a secret." Quentin tucked the stack of photos into his briefcase and clicked the lid shut. "Half the world knows by now."

Shelby knocked softly on the half-open door, then let herself in. "Michael, I'd like to talk to you about— Oh, excuse me. I didn't realize you had company." She turned quickly and was about to leave when Michael called her back.

"Come in. We're finished." Michael stood and offered introductions. "Quentin, this is Shelby McMasters, Rio's nanny. Shelby, this is Quentin Ingersoll, the cur . . . an old friend of mine."

Shelby took the old man's hand and shook it warmly. "It's a pleasure to meet you, Mr. Ingersoll. I apologize for the interruption."

"Not at all," he said, easily catching the warning look Michael shot him. "As Michael said, we're all through." He picked up his briefcase and looked her over appraisingly. "I must say, though, the photograph doesn't do you justice."

Puzzled, Shelby looked from Quentin to Michael and back again. "I beg your pardon?"

"Nothing," Michael interjected. "Quentin, let me see you to the door." He picked up the coat Quentin had draped over the back of a chair and extended it to him. "I'll be right back, Shelby," he called over his shoulder.

A smile twitched at the corners of her mouth as the sound of muffled voices faded. She liked the ease with which Michael said her name—a nickname given to her by her beloved grandfather. As an adult she had legally changed her first name to Shelby and had insisted on keeping it when the phony ID papers were drawn up. Not only did it honor the one person in her life who had truly loved her, but it also ensured Rio would not accidentally give her away. Not since her grandfather used it had the name sounded so special. Michael's deep baritone voice seemed to caress the consonants, making her name sound almost . . . musical.

She walked comfortably around Michael's library, pleased with the tentative truce they had established earlier. The morning paper lay on his desk and Shelby picked it up. Shock froze her entire body as she stared at the picture on the front page. To steady herself, she sat down on the chair in front of the desk. Rio's frightened face and Michael's handsome one stared back. She read every word of the accompanying article, becoming increasingly angry as she did so. The paper was a respectable daily, so there was nothing demeaning or licentious in its tone. But the feeling of invasion, almost violation, remained. There was virtually nothing in the article about her. She was referred to only as "the boy's nanny." But the entire history of the Chandler family, especially the untimely death of Rio's mother, was laid bare for all the world to see. And even though there was nothing about Linc, Shelby could easily imagine how difficult it must be for Michael to have his private pain so openly displayed.

And Rio.

The fear in Rio's eyes was all but tangible. Shelby had never seen him so terrified. She'd been so furious over the way Michael had treated Rio's bear, that she hadn't realized how serious the situation with the reporters had become. Had it not been for Michael, Rio could have been seriously injured . . . or worse. Her clammy fingers smudged the black ink as she traced Michael's arrogant dark eyebrows and angry eyes. The man's public persona might be hard and cruel, but beneath the veneer was something inherently decent.

"I'm sorry you had to see that."

Shelby jerked her head up as Michael reached her side. She turned the paper facedown in her lap, as though hiding the article would make it go away. "It's all right," she said.

"No, it's not all right," he contradicted, gentling his voice. He perched on the corner of the desk and studied her. She was frowning, worrying her soft bottom lip, pulling it between her teeth. "You're upset."

She didn't try to deny it. "Of course I'm upset. And I should think you would be, too." She picked up the newspaper and waved it in front of his face. "Or do you like seeing your picture and your life story spread across the morning paper?"

Michael chuckled. "Believe me, the last face I want to see over a cup of coffee is my own. But there's not much I can do about it. Over the years I've learned to avoid the press most of the time and ignore them the rest of the time." He folded his arms across his chest and gazed down at her.

Shelby glanced down at the newspaper she was still holding. Her eyes fixed on the article and not on his penetrating stare. "Is it always like this? Everywhere you go?"

"Not all the time, but frequently. The paparazzi used to sit outside the front gate and follow me to work every day, but fortunately they've grown tired of the boring life I lead. Contrary to what they'd like to think, I'm not a rich playboy. I'm an incurable workaholic, and except for a few charity fundraisers, I have very little time for frivolity."

Shelby was acutely aware of the change in him as she listened to his frank admission. The old Michael Chandler would have dismissed her with a brisk wave of his hand. The new Michael Chandler took the time to talk with her and share his experience.

"They keep looking for a scandalous story," he continued. "And I keep hoping they'll find it somewhere else."

"That doesn't sound very likely," Shelby sympathized.

One shoulder lifted in a negligent shrug. "I can handle it," he said. "The person I'm worried about is you."

A curious warmth flooded her body. She drew a deep settling breath. "Me?"

Michael nodded. "If last night was any indication, it's obvious you haven't had much experience dealing with pushy reporters. Some of them are more than annoying. Some are downright dangerous. And now that you and Rio have entered the picture, they'll be after you, too."

Shelby shook her head, refusing to accept that possibility. "I understand why they'd come after you. You're an important personality and your actions affect a lot of people. But why Rio and me? Rio's only a child. What could they possibly want with him?"

"He's today's news," Michael explained. "And to the paparazzi, that's all that counts." He leaned toward her and Shelby's breath caught in her throat. Like an animal trapped by a cobra's stare, she watched transfixed as he took the newspaper out of her hands and tossed it into the wastebasket. His long fingers never touched her, yet she had the sensation of being burned by an intense heat.

He sat down in the leather swivel chair behind the desk and leaned back. "What would you say to a bodyguard?"

"I'd say forget it," Shelby answered with more force than she intended.

His aristocratic face broke into an amazingly streetwise grin. "Now, why is it that I'm not surprised?"

Shelby returned his smile. "What I meant to say is that we don't need a bodyguard."

"I don't want anything like the incident at the airport to happen again," Michael persisted. "Rio is to have the best of everything—including the best in security and safety."

Shelby shook her head. "He needs to learn to take care of himself, to develop his own sense of safety, to experience success and failure." Her voice rose in direct proportion to her rising emotions. "That won't happen if you hire a platoon of people to shelter him from the world."

Michael's fist banged the desk in frustration. "It also won't happen if he's mobbed the first time he steps foot in a public park."

"Rio needs love tempered with discipline, not a simulated—albeit bejeweled—jail cell," Shelby snapped, her temper flaring.

"*Jail cell?*" Michael's voice raised incredulously and he spread his arms wide. "You're calling all of this a jail cell?"

"Isn't it?" Shelby said. "You have high brick walls surrounding the entire estate. You have a guard at the entrance, monitoring everyone who comes in and goes out. And now you want to hire bodyguards to accompany the prisoners you let out on parole. Rio doesn't need that kind of a life."

The abrupt silence was frightening and Shelby was suddenly sure her zealous tongue-lashing had cost her the job. She waited, eyeing him warily. The look he gave her was acutely assessing, but when he didn't speak she switched tactics and prayed for the best.

"Mr. Chandler—Michael—I apologize if I've overstepped my bounds. But I also believe Rio should have the best—the best exposure to life's experiences. There is so much out there for him to explore," Shelby urged, gesturing broadly, "Zoos, museums, planetariums, botanical parks. In a few years he'll be ready for school and he'll need to develop social skills. The best way for him to develop those social skills is to spend time with other children."

"I'm not saying you shouldn't do those things," Michael said, his tone cold and clipped. "I'm merely suggesting we take precautions to protect you and Rio."

"Protect us from what—an aging Bactrian camel or the skeleton of a tyrannosaurus rex?" Shelby made a face. "Following us to the zoo or the museum will be about as exciting as following you to your office. Having a professional bodyguard tagging along would simply draw more attention to us."

"And what about reporters constantly dogging your heels?"

"What about them? If, as you say, they're going to be a constant part of Rio's new life, then the sooner he learns how to deal with them, the better off he'll be."

"And you? How will you feel when they start snooping into your life and speculating on your activities?"

Shelby stopped cold. She hadn't thought about herself. She wasn't thrilled about letting the world in on her secret, but she would risk even that for Rio's sake. The most important element was what was best for him.

"I'll wear sunglasses and a big, floppy hat," she announced. "I'll make myself look so ridiculous that no one in his right mind would suspect me of doing anything remotely interesting."

Michael chuckled at the image that sprang to mind. No floppy hat in the world could contain that soft, shining mass of golden hair. And even hidden behind sunglasses, he felt certain he would see those sparkling blue eyes.

"I can take care of myself," she insisted. "And Rio, too. That's why you hired me, isn't it? The least you can do is give me a chance to do my job."

"Fair enough," Michael said, marveling at the way she rode roughshod over all his objections and somehow came out the winner. "For now, we'll try it your way—no entourage, no bodyguards, nothing. But if *anything* happens, any incident, no matter how insignificant, the deal is off. Agreed?"

"Agreed," Shelby said, and for the second time today her hand disappeared in his large, tanned one. Being with Michael felt different now than it had a week ago. A week ago, that little speech would have cost her her job, but his curt gruffness had slipped a notch or two, allowing her a glimpse of a more tolerant, accepting man. He might not agree with all her ideas on child-rearing, but at least he respected her opinion.

And how much would he respect her when he learned the truth? How would he feel about her when he discovered she intended to oppose his petition for permanent guardianship?

He still had her hand, his thumb caressing slow circles over the rapid pulse in her wrist. Sanity returned, and Shelby pulled her hand away. The tingling warmth disappeared, and in its place came a blast of reality, which enshrouded her hand and then settled around her heart.

As if sensing the change, Michael became suddenly formal. "You said you wanted to talk with me. I gather it wasn't about this newspaper article."

"No," Shelby answered. "I wanted to talk to you about a pediatrician. I . . . would . . . imagine that Rio has not been under a doctor's care. As his temporary guardian, you need to make the decision about his immunizations." She couldn't help smiling at the puzzled look on Michael's face. He reminded her of a small boy trying his hardest to understand adult conversation . . . and failing miserably.

"Immunizations?" he asked.

She nodded. "In the state of California, immunizations for polio, mumps, measles, rubella, diphtheria, pertussis and tetanus are required before a child can enter school. Granted, Rio is a few years away from that, but these immunizations usually begin in infancy and continue through the first five years of a child's life."

Michael nodded solemnly. "Go ahead and do it."

Shelby smiled. "Not only did I need your permission, I also need a recommendation for a good pediatrician. I don't know any physicians in this area. Perhaps you could talk with some of your friends who have children and ask them which doctor they use. Then I'll call and make an appointment to take Rio in."

"Of course. I'll check it out and get back to you this afternoon." Retrieving a pad of paper from his desk drawer, Michael scribbled a note to himself. He tore it off the pad, tucked the note in his calendar and put the pad back in the desk. "I appreciate all the..." he started to say. But when he looked up, she was gone.

Michael stared at the empty seat. Damned if he could figure her out, but Shelby McMasters was the most interesting woman he'd met in a long time.

For one thing, she was the exact opposite of everything he was used to. For a brief time after Gina walked out, he had expended a lot of energy on women, trying to prove to himself and the rest of the world there was nothing wrong with him. His dates had been carbon copies of one another—glossy women who lived in slinky, black gowns and nursed giant trust funds for a living.

Shelby McMasters wore terry-cloth shorts and V-necked tops, and made her living as a domestic.

He was used to women who did what was socially correct, and kept their tongues and their emotions under control.

Shelby McMasters never hesitated to tell him *exactly* what she thought—like calling his home a bejeweled jail cell.

Michael smiled sadly. Little did she realize how accurate that description was. In many ways, his home *had* become a prison. Over the years, he had managed to erect both physical and emotional barriers—barriers designed to lock the world out... and lock his feelings in.

Oh, yes. Shelby McMasters was everything he didn't want... and she'd gotten to him faster than any woman had in a very long time.

He spun around in his chair and grabbed a file off the credenza. Hell, what difference did it make? It wasn't as though he was looking for feminine companionship. He and Shelby would find some reasonable middle ground to spar on, and there was nothing wrong with that.

As long as it didn't go any further.

And it wouldn't.

In fact, the last thing he wanted was someone like Shelby McMasters, with her incandescent eyes, musical voice and tempting body, to complicate his life.

He flipped through his Rolodex. *Friends with children.* That shouldn't be too hard. One by one, he ran his fingers through the cards. He had the names of dozens of single socialites, and the name of every CEO of any significance. He personally knew every member of every board of directors that had any clout in the city, and he had the private phone number of every politician in the state, from the up-and-coming to the over-the-hill.

But he didn't have any real friends with small children.

Eventually, he would locate the best pediatrician in the state. All he had to do was call someone on the board of directors at one of the hospitals and get a recommendation.

But that wasn't the point.

Michael sighed. How had his life become so void of all the things that had once mattered most? Not having friends with children wasn't much in the scheme of things, but at the moment, it seemed pretty damned important.

"I'll look in here," Shelby called. She hurried through the open door of the library without bothering to knock. She didn't have to. During the past two weeks, she and Michael had reached an understanding. They had established ground rules that made it easier for them to live and work together, without getting in each other's way. The rules pertaining to Michael's study were fairly simple. If the door was wide open, she and Rio were welcome to enter and browse through his vast selection of books. If the door was ajar, they were to knock first, and if the door was tightly closed, it meant he was not to be disturbed under any circumstances. They were to stay away and stay quiet.

On this particular morning, Shelby knew Michael was long gone. He had been up early, as usual, and had swum laps for an hour. From her bedroom window, Shelby had watched him churning through the blue waters of the pool while all around, the trees ruffled softly in the breeze, catching and reflecting the early sunlight. She often watched him—sometimes early in the morning, sometimes late at night, when the surface of the unlit pool reflected darkly, except for that one narrow strip where the water churned into a froth.

For weeks she had watched him—watched him swim, watched him eat, watched the procession of businessmen who paraded through his home office at all times of the day and night. She had listened to his side of phone conversations and convinced Mrs. Hodges to let her bring Michael his mail.

And so far she had discovered nothing.

No behavior that the court would call unseemly. No activities that the court would consider questionable. Nothing that would classify him as unfit to be Rio's guardian.

Her attorney had advised her to give up and she was beginning to think he was right. Clearly, Michael was not the ogre she had once imagined. He ate breakfast with them nearly every morning, sometimes starting work late because Rio had slept in. He monitored Rio's progress on the Big Wheel and the jungle gym with a mixture of wry amusement and veiled pride. He was even attempting to learn Spanish, a fact Shelby wouldn't have known if she hadn't accidentally overheard him trying to talk with Rio.

Every day he was becoming more like a father.

Every day her chances of getting Rio dwindled.

She tried unsuccessfully to pinpoint the exact moment his Arctic heart had begun to thaw. Maybe it had happened when he was watching Rio play. Possibly it had started that first morning at breakfast. Perhaps it had begun the night he'd found Rio's bear.

Rio's bear.

That was why she'd come in here. They were on their way to the pediatrician's office for Rio's first checkup and he wouldn't go without his bear. Shelby began a rapid search of the room—under the desk, behind the draperies, in the bookcase—no luck. She stood in the middle of the room, her hands on her hips, her eyes closed, trying to think. The last time she remembered seeing it, Rio and the bear were curled up on the sofa "reading." Shelby pulled the pillows off the couch…and there it was, right where he'd left it. She scooped up the toy and headed for the door. "I found…"

A chill raced down her spine, just as she neared the door. She stopped dead in her tracks and turned slowly to face the glass cabinet mounted on the wall near the sofa. It couldn't be.

But it was.

Staring back at her from its place on the shelf was a small Mayan figure carved of jadeite—the one she had uncovered at the new site near Xpujil. Shelby took a deep, steadying breath and tried to calm the pounding of her heart. Her hand reached out, stopping just short of the glass case, her fingers itching to touch the precious little statue.

It was the same figure, she was sure of it. There hadn't been enough time for someone to make a copy and the bits of dirt embedded in its crevices testified that it was the original. But what was it doing here? When she'd left the dig a few weeks ago, the statue had been completely cataloged, then wrapped and packed for eventual shipping to the world-renowned Museum of Anthropology in Mexico City. There was no way Michael could have gotten this statue. But he had. The proof was staring her in the face.

How?

The word echoed inside her head. It bounced off the walls and ricocheted around the room. How...how...how? Her fingers closed around the arm of Rio's bear, squeezing the toy's limb as anguish squeezed at her heart.

Rio's bear. Helplessly, Shelby looked down at the stuffed animal clenched in her white-knuckled fist. In a split second she compared the size of the statue to the size of the opening Michael had asked her to repair. *A perfect fit,* the nagging voice declared. And it was Michael who had prevented them from going back into the airport...Michael who had kept Rio separated from his bear until the next morning...Michael who now displayed the statue in his private collection.

No, Shelby screamed within, shaking her head against the niggling doubts. *It couldn't have been Michael.* He had never been to the dig. He had never seen the commune. He had never met Rio. He couldn't possibly know that Rio had a bear.

He didn't need to know, the voice insisted. All he needed was an accomplice—someone willing to steal the statue and hide it in Rio's things, someone who would tell Michael where to find it, someone who Michael could easily pay off.

She could find no other explanation, no other reason that he would be in possession of this statue.

Tears stung her eyes and ran unchecked down her cheeks. All this time she had been looking for something to hold against Michael Chandler, something solid that would stand up in court.

Now she had found it...and the pain was almost more than she could stand.

Chapter 9

The pain of betrayal sliced through her. How could he have done this? She'd thought that she knew him, had thought the man was different from the cold, ruthless image he projected. Over the past few weeks, she'd come to respect and even like Michael. She was beginning to trust him. Trust? She laughed out loud at her own gullibility. The slate was wiped clean now, and she was left feeling small and stupid and naive.

Then the pain turned to white-hot anger, cutting and tearing like a knife. All the time she had spent chasing her beloved dream rose up to scream and protest. For years she had studied in pursuit of a degree. For months on end she had endured the dirt and heat of the jungle, subsisting more on passion than on food. And for what? For some moneyed collector like Michael Chandler to snap up a piece of Mexico's heritage for the sake of a good investment.

No. Michael had no right to the statue. No private collector did. It belonged to the people of Mexico, for them to share and cherish, admire and rejoice in. The figure would never have been sold. However Michael had obtained it, he had done so illegally. And worse, he'd used his own nephew to smuggle it in.

With a conscious effort, Shelby shoved aside the anger that blinded her. There wasn't much time and she needed every

minute to compose herself and think. Hastily, she tried to sort
out the myriad thoughts that tumbled through her mind. Reminding herself that she was a highly organized, efficient individual, she set out to formulate a plan. The first thing she had
to do was to contact her friends in Mexico and have them trace
the statue.

Dumb idea.

She didn't need to have the statue traced. She knew exactly
where it was. She was staring at it, for heaven's sake. And besides, it would be tough to contact anyone at the dig. They
didn't have AT&T wired to the pyramids, and the closest she
could get would be a phone call to Xpujil. A letter to Felipe
would take weeks, and she'd have a heck of a time explaining
to Michael why she was receiving telephone calls or letters from
the Yucatán. What she needed was someone to do the work for
her. Someone like Amelia.

Dumb idea number two.

Amelia was a good friend, but she wasn't Nancy Drew. The
image of Amelia, wearing the latest in jungle attire and tromping through the tropical rain forest was comical, but it wasn't
smart. Michael would be facing a whole host of criminal
charges—conspiracy to commit grand theft, transporting stolen property into the country, possession of stolen goods and
who knew what else. If convicted, he would certainly be handed
a jail sentence, not to mention the possibility of extradition. It
wouldn't be fair to bring Amelia into this mess. The situation
was too serious, and Amelia was too flighty for Shelby to even
consider.

Okay, if she eliminated herself and Amelia, then who was
left? The obvious answer was her attorney. Shelby turned the
idea over and over in her mind to examine it from all sides. He
already knew about her relationship to Rio and the fact that she
had infiltrated Michael's home. He didn't condone her actions, but he was powerless to stop her . . . and attorney-client
privilege prevented him from ever disclosing her secret.

He was the perfect choice. She would have to call him, anyway, to tell him what she had discovered, and surely, he would
have access to a private investigator who could check out her
story.

Shelby offered a faint smile to the figure who stood watching her from his position of safety. That little guy was going to

the Museum of Anthropology in Mexico City if she had to smash the glass case and take him there herself.

"Tía Shelby!" Rio shouted as he burst into the room. "Come on." He grabbed his bear and hugged it with one arm while pulling on Shelby's hand. "The big car is here."

With a final backward glance at the statue, Shelby took Rio's hand and hurried out of the library. Her plan was now firmly established in her mind. She would call her attorney from the pediatrician's office and have him begin immediate inquiries at the site near Xpujil. With any luck, he'd have some preliminary information within the week.

Shelby sagged under the realization of what she was about to do to Michael. But the future of *two* little fellows now rested firmly on her shoulders.

"You take this," Rio insisted, handing Shelby his bear as they approached the revolving exit doors of the medical building.

The visit to the pediatrician had been an unqualified success as far as Rio was concerned. He now juggled a large red balloon, a plastic ring and a full sheet of dinosaur stickers, which he was alternately peeling and applying to various parts of his anatomy.

For Shelby, the visit had been far less comforting. Rio's checkup had gone well and she had been greatly relieved when the doctor had pronounced him hale and hearty, but when she'd called her attorney from the bank of phones in the building lobby, their conversation had left her feeling decidedly uneasy.

The lawyer was so delighted with her news, he could hardly contain himself. "Oh, how the mighty have fallen," he said, chortling, and inwardly Shelby cringed. She felt like Brutus stabbing Caesar in the back. "The press will have a field day with this one," he added, insisting she had all but won her case. He readily agreed to send someone to Mexico to verify the statue had been stolen and he assured her he would take no action without her prior consent.

That should have been enough . . . but it wasn't. The whole incident had left her precariously close to tears. All this time she had been searching for something to use against Michael, and now that she'd stumbled upon the statue, she almost wished she'd never spotted it—almost. The knowledge of what he had done weighed heavily on her and she drew a tortured breath. She truly felt Michael had no right to the figure—it belonged to the people of Mexico—and her heart recoiled at the thought of him being so base as to use his own nephew to steal and smuggle what his money could not rightly buy.

During the long ride into the city, Shelby had been blessedly numb, but ever since her conversation with the lawyer, the pain had started seeping through her, growing in intensity as it spread. She had actually thought Michael was changing, becoming more human. She believed she had seen a side of Michael that wasn't visible to others. She was certain they had discovered a new level to their relationship, one carved out of respect and friendship. Her eyes filled with scalding tears and she was powerless to stop them.

If only there was another explanation.

The revolving door closed behind Rio, and, tucking the bear and her purse under her arm, Shelby leaned into the door propelling them forward and out onto the sidewalk. The bright light of the midday sun blinded her, and she squinted as she searched for the silver limousine. Pasig would be waiting for them somewhere nearby.

A teenager with long streaky hair and a black leather jacket sauntered down the sidewalk toward them.

"Come here, Rio," Shelby warned in Spanish and Rio obligingly trotted over to where she stood.

But the teenager wasn't interested in Rio. As he neared Shelby, he reached out and grabbed at her purse, still tucked under her arm.

"No!" she screamed, the word escaping from her lips before she realized she had said it. With slow-motion clarity, she watched the teen drop her purse and yank on Rio's bear. They struggled and she kicked his knee—hard—but he held on to the bear until she feared it would rip in two. She didn't see the limousine arrive, or see Pasig bolt from the car, but she heard his voice and it gave her the strength to hold on a little longer.

With the heavyset driver bearing down on him, the kid gave up. He gave Shelby a final shove that knocked her to the ground, then took off running and disappeared down the street.

"Are you all right, miss?" Pasig asked, helping her to her feet.

"I'm fine." Shelby stood shakily on the sidewalk peering at the spot where she had last seen the young man.

The driver swore. "I'm sorry I didn't get him, but at least he didn't get what he was after." He picked up the discarded purse from the sidewalk and offered it to her.

Shelby looked down at the teddy bear, which she still instinctively clutched. Consciously telling her hand it was all right to let go, she reached out and took the purse from Pasig. She blinked twice and looked at him again. "What did you say?"

"I said, at least he didn't get your purse."

Comprehension dawned. That kid didn't want her purse. He was after Rio's bear. Maybe no one else knew that, but she did. She tried to bring into focus a picture of the teenager's face. She was sure she had never seen him before. How was he connected to Rio?

She looked down at the little boy, whose wide and helpless eyes were filled with tears. "Don't cry, honey," she said. "It's okay." She leaned over to give him the stuffed toy, but the world spun crazily and she would have sprawled out onto the sidewalk if Pasig hadn't grabbed her.

"I think we'd better get you home right now," he said, propping her up with one arm while he opened the limousine door with the other. "You may need a doctor, and even if you don't, Mr. Chandler is not going to like this one bit."

With his back and the sole of one foot propped against a Dumpster in the alley, Thomas Nansen struck a match, cupping his hands around the flame to protect it from the breeze. It wouldn't be long now, he thought, lighting the cigarette and extinguishing the match with a single flick. Paying that punk to grab the bear was pure genius.

He straightened quickly as a teenage boy stumbled headlong into the alley, gasping for breath.

"Well? Hand it over," he barked.

The kid slumped down at the man's feet. "I ain't got it," he rasped.

"What!" Nansen grabbed the kid by the lapels of his jacket and hauled him to his feet. "Look, buster, you better think twice before you try to con me out of another fifty bucks."

"I'm not, man," the kid said, shrinking back from the person who still held him captive. "I swear I never got it."

"I warn you, boy, if you're holding out on me, I'm going to bust your head wide open."

The kid ran a hand through his stringy, uncombed hair. "Look, mister, you can have your money back, but you gotta believe me when I tell you I ain't got it."

"Start talking," Nansen growled.

"Well, I was waitin' outside the building, just like you told me, and I see them come out, only the kid don't have the bear. At first I thought maybe they forgot it, but then I see the broad's got it under her arm." He paused to catch his breath, but Nansen's glaring look forced him on. "Well, I walk up kind of casual and when I get next to her I grab the bear, but she starts yellin' and kickin' at me. She won't let go of the bear and then this guy jumps outta a stretch limo and charges after me. Man, I said, forget this. I knocked her down and just hauled outta there. And that's the truth."

Nansen took the bills from the kid's pocket and stuffed them in his own shirt. "You keep your mouth shut," he said. "Now get out of here." He shoved the teenager onto the pavement and watched as he scrambled to his feet and ran off.

For a long moment he just stood there, letting the anger build up inside him. When he could stand it no longer, he grabbed a wooden crate and smashed it against the Dumpster, gaining release as he watched the slats crack and splinter.

Damn them.

He had been so patient, waiting for the right moment. He had followed them to a zoo and an art museum and a million other places during the last few weeks. But either the kid didn't have the bear with him, or there were too many people around to risk making a move.

Today had been perfect. He had seen Chandler leave early that morning in his hotshot sports car, so when the limousine pulled out a few hours later, he knew it had to be for them. He'd followed the car to the medical building, then watched in glee as Kelland and the kid got out. There was the bear, just like in Mexico. It was going to be so easy.

And then Kelland and that damn driver screwed it up... screwed up his lovely little plan. Well, next time they wouldn't be so lucky. Next time he wouldn't give the job to some two-bit kid. He'd do it himself. And he'd do it right.

He slid the cold metal casing from his pants pocket and deftly flicked the tiny button. With a single click, the knife sprang to life, its long blade slashing the air as it glinted in the sunlight.

Oh, yes, he thought, running a finger along the smooth edge. He'd do it right next time . . . or Shelby Kelland would be one dead lady.

Drawing a deep breath, Shelby limped into Michael's library and silently closed the door behind her. He was standing behind his desk with his back to her, talking to someone on the telephone.

She exhaled a long, silent sigh. Her body ached from the tumble she had taken on the sidewalk that morning, and she had a bruise on her hip and outer thigh that looked like a Technicolor tattoo of the Yucatán peninsula, but it was probably nothing compared to what she would look like when Michael got through with her.

It was late when he'd arrived home, but he had immediately summoned both her and Pasig to the library. Because she was putting Rio to bed, she had been able to delay the confrontation—until now.

"I know all that," Michael said into the telephone. "I've got the report right here." He wedged the receiver between his shoulder and his ear, and leaned over the credenza, reaching for a file folder. Shelby watched with frank admiration as the blue oxford cloth shirt he wore stretched across his wide, muscled shoulders and tapered back.

She tore her gaze away. This was not the time to indulge in romantic fantasies. She needed a clear head. All afternoon, she had tried to fit together the pieces of the puzzle, but so far nothing made any sense. She was convinced that she had never before seen the kid who had bungled this morning's attempted theft. She was also fairly confident that the kid had never in his life been to an archaeological dig. In fact, unless she missed her guess, the chances were fairly good that he didn't even know which hemisphere the Yucatán was in. On the other hand, there was no doubt that he was after Rio's bear and not her purse . . . so he must have thought Rio's bear contained the statue . . . which Michael now had . . . which meant Michael hadn't paid him off . . .

Which didn't make sense.

"It's been more than three weeks," he was saying. "And considering the amount of money I'm willing to spend, I expected your report to tell me a hell of a lot more than this."

Shelby ventured a glance at the glass case by the sofa. The little figure was still there—right where she had seen it this morning.

If Michael had hired the kid to steal the statue in Mexico, then why was the kid now trying to steal Rio's bear? And if Michael hadn't been involved in the theft and smuggling, then how had he gotten the statue? A flicker of hope ignited like a raging inferno. Maybe he hadn't stolen it. Maybe there was a reasonable explanation for his having it. But what could it be? Shelby's battered mind ached as much as her bruised body.

"I'm not going to wait much longer," Michael said calmly into the receiver. "I want that information now." He hung up the phone and tossed the file folder onto his desk.

"You wanted to see me, Michael?"

He turned abruptly, but his gray eyes were unfathomable as he quickly opened the middle drawer of his desk and casually swept the file into it. "How are you doing?" he asked, motioning for her to take a seat. He shoved his hands into his pants pockets and studied her.

Shelby crossed the room slowly and gritted her teeth against a wince as she gingerly lowered herself into the chair. "I'm fine," she lied. She twisted awkwardly in the seat to avoid putting any weight on her bruised hip.

Michael's raised eyebrows made it clear he wasn't buying that for a minute. "Pasig said you took quite a bad fall."

"All I got were a couple of bruises," she confessed. "A small one on my leg . . . and a large one on my dignity." She swallowed the nervous laugh that bubbled in her throat. "Actually, I was more embarrassed than hurt."

In less than a moment he was around the desk, crouching in front of her. "Maybe you should have it looked at. If you don't have a physician of your own, let me call mine. I guarantee I can get him to make a house call."

Instinctively, her hand flew to hide the bruise that was already concealed by her shorts. "That's really not necessary," she said. The thought of exposing her black-and-blue thigh to any of Michael's acquaintances, even his doctor, was more than a little disconcerting. "It's a bit stiff right now, but in a few days it'll be fine."

"Are you sure you didn't twist anything?" He took her ankle in his strong hands and rotated it slowly. The touch of his fingers sent jolts of electricity shooting up her leg, and she stiffened convulsively. "Relax," he said. "You're as tight as a spring."

And that spring was coiling tighter and tighter deep inside her.

His hands moved up to her calf, gently kneading the constricted muscles. He glanced up at her with a look that made her pulse race. "Nothing seems swollen," he commented. "You're lucky to have gotten away with only a bruise."

I'll be lucky to get away at all.

His seeking hands returned to her foot and slipped off her sandal. He massaged first her ankle and Achilles tendon, then rubbed his thumbs against the top of her foot while his fingers trailed the underside of her arch. "Are you in pain?" he asked.

The dull ache of her bruised hip was still there, but it seemed distant, almost detached from the rest of her body, and she could feel skittering tingles under her skin. "A little," she croaked.

He nodded. "This ought to help. Do you know about mechanoreceptors?"

He had lifted her foot up and turned his hands around, so his thumbs now pressed into the soft, fleshy sole of her foot. Her mouth formed the answer to his question, but the sound stuck in her throat. Her ability to speak had vanished as mysteriously as the ancient Mayans. She shook her head.

"Mechanoreceptors are nerves just below the skin surface that relay sensations like pressure, vibration and movement. Our bodies register pleasure when our mechanoreceptors are touched."

Shelby relaxed into the chair as Michael continued the slow, deliberate kneading of her foot. Based on the drowning waves of unbelievable pleasure washing over her, her foot must be loaded with mechano-thingies, and he was touching every one of them.

"The great thing about mechanoreceptors," he continued, "is that not only do they send out pleasure signals, but those signals then block messages from other nerve pathways...especially messages of pain."

His deft fingers stroked and caressed the soft fleshy pads and it didn't take a quantum leap of imagination to picture those hands on other, equally sensitive parts of her body. As if reading her thoughts, he looked up and smiled—a warm, lazy smile that quickened her heartbeat.

"The hairless parts of our bodies are loaded with mechanoreceptors." As he spoke, his eyes left hers and traveled slowly down her body. "Places like the soles of the feet, the tips of the fingers and toes, the palms, the . . ." His voice trailed off and his gaze locked onto her breasts. "Which means they are much more responsive to touch."

Never before had a simple foot massage become so erotic. The soreness in her hip had long since disappeared, replaced by a deeper, stronger ache that was half pain, half pleasure. Her heart was pounding, echoing like thunder in her ears, and her heated blood rushed to every part of her body. She wanted more, wanted him to touch her like that everywhere.

But this was Michael. Michael Chandler. The one person who stood between her and the nephew she had sworn to protect. Fantasizing about Michael in his own private plane was one thing. You couldn't get hurt from a good dose of fantasy. But this was the real thing. And the real thing still had his hands on her while her traitorous body cried out for more.

Her eyes darted around the room, finally landing on the small jadeite statue in the glass case. Its severe look seemed to admonish her, reminding her how foolish—perhaps even dangerous—it would be to get emotionally entangled with the likes of Michael Chandler. She had to disengage. Now.

"Well, thank you for the foot massage and the neurology lesson." She scooped up her sandal, struggled to her feet and hobbled toward the door. "I'll remember how those mechano-things block out pain the next time I stub my toe."

He was between her and the door before she had taken three steps. "Wait a minute," he said. The corners of his mouth quirked up in a strange anticipatory smile. "We're not finished here."

Shelby blanched. "We're not?"

He took her elbow and led her back to the chair, easing her into it with a firm yet gentle push. He leaned his hip on the desk behind him and sat there studying her with distinct amusement. "Now, then," he finally said. "Let's get this thing over with."

Shelby squirmed uncomfortably in the seat, her heart racing. His steel-gray eyes locked onto hers and seemed to look right through her protective armor. She was sure he could peer into her mind and soul and see the lies buried there.

"I'm sure I don't know what you're talking about," she said.

"Don't you?" He laughed—a deep, rich sound that warmed her blood. "You're going to play this out to the end, aren't you?" When Shelby didn't answer, he leaned forward and planted his hands on the arms of her chair, neatly trapping her. "Okay," he said slowly. "Let's talk about your bodyguard."

"My wh-what?" Shelby stammered.

"Oh, come now," he said mockingly. "Surely you haven't forgotten our little deal."

His face was so close, she could see the slight shadow that darkened his jaw and the area around his mouth, and smell the faint essence of his expensive after-shave. "Well, no, but..."

"As I recall, you insisted I give you a chance to prove yourself...to prove you could take care of yourself and Rio. I agreed, with the proviso that if anything happened, our deal would automatically terminate."

A wave of relief broke over her. He hadn't discovered her deception at all. He was back to talking about the morning's incident.

The apprehension she'd felt when she first entered the library quickly resurfaced. Michael was not a man easily put off. Had Pasig told him anything? Did Michael know the thief was after Rio's bear?

"Well?" he prompted.

She smiled shyly at the handsome face positioned scant inches from her own. "Anyone anywhere can be hit by a purse snatcher," she pointed out. "This was a singularly unfortunate experience, and one that will probably never happen again."

He was having none of it. "Regardless of whether you think this experience was 'singularly unfortunate,' the fact remains that either you or Rio could have been seriously hurt. I cannot and will not run that risk again."

Was that real concern she saw on his face? His words were all business. He spoke like a banker having no qualms about repossessing a home, but the tone of his voice was laced with something more—worry maybe?

"I believe our agreement stipulated that any incident, 'however insignificant,'" he quoted, "would terminate the deal."

"It did," Shelby acknowledged. "But surely there are small allowances for extenuating circumstances. You don't always hold to the strict letter of the law, do you?"

Michael's grin was anything but sophisticated. "Always." He straightened and moved away from her, taking a seat behind his desk.

"But—"

"Shelby, there are no but's. Starting tomorrow morning, you and Rio will have a bodyguard accompany you every time you leave these grounds."

"I have no choice in this?" she asked weakly.

"None whatsoever. In fact, I have spent the better part of the afternoon deciding who that person should be and arranging his schedule."

Shelby sighed. There was no way she was going to change Michael's mind on this one. "Fine," she said, steeling herself for a meeting with a large, brawny man who had the mind and body of a brick wall. "What's his name?"

"His name?" Michael laughed again, and the silky richness of his voice sent her head spinning. "His name is Michael Chandler."

Chapter 10

"You?"

He looked at her with a directness that went straight through her. "Yes, me."

"That's ridiculous!"

"Why?"

"You're not trained to be a bodyguard... Are you?"

"No. But what difference does that make? You don't want one, anyway, so I'd be perfect for the job. I can keep an eye on the two of you and at the same time get better acquainted with Rio. It makes perfect sense."

Not to her it didn't. The thought of spending that much time with Michael was unnerving. "What about your business? You just can't take off whenever you feel like it."

"On the contrary. Since it's my business, I can do whatever I want. But for the record, I was planning to take a vacation, anyway. I canceled it when my sister died and I discovered I had a nephew. Now I'll be able take that vacation as well as spend time with you and Rio."

Did he have any idea how dizzy his words made her feel? *Forget it,* her brain said. *Think about it,* her heart said.

This could be the opportunity she'd been waiting for. Spending a lot of time with Michael meant they'd be closer. *Too close*, said her heart. *Close enough to find out about that statue*, said her brain. Shelby tried to tune out the voices and concentrate on what Michael was saying.

"Not that much will change," he said. "At any given time, I have half my work at the office complex and half here. Actually, it'll be nice having everything under one roof. With computer-telephone modems and fax machines, I can work here as easily as in the city, and it will save me a lot of traveling time. There may be a few meetings that require my attendance, but if you keep me informed of your plans, I can schedule the meetings when I know you won't be leaving the estate."

She looked at him through eyes that no longer saw clearly. Gone was the chiseled face etched with hard and bitter experience. Gone were the gray eyes that flashed like steel and were filled with cynicism. Tonight she saw warmth in their soft, smoky color, and his handsome face showed a vulnerability that made him even more appealing.

There was no denying she was drawn to him. Blatant desire swept through her whenever he was near. But she was his employee and Rio's nanny. She had to maintain a professional distance and she had to put Rio's future above all else.

From his position behind the desk, he looked at her, studying her reaction to his proposal. She was definitely not happy. She looked nervous, once again worrying her bottom lip, fidgeting with the clasp on the gold band of her watch. His plans clearly disturbed her, which made it all the more intriguing. "Is there some reason I shouldn't be with you and Rio?" he asked smoothly.

Reluctantly, Shelby looked at him, forcing herself to meet his steady gaze. One winged dark eyebrow was arched. She saw the speculation in his eyes before they went carefully blank. The hard mouth curved in a sweet, disarming smile. Maybe there was a reason they shouldn't be together. Maybe she couldn't trust herself to be with him. A wave of emotion crashed over her, drowning her in her own senses. She closed her eyes and squeezed the arms of the chair.

"Shelby, are you all right?" He was crouching in front of her, cradling her cheek in one of his strong hands.

"I don't know. I guess I'm a little tired. I'm sorry."

"You're as white as a sheet." His arms were around her, helping her up, supporting her as they walked toward the door.

"I'm the one who should apologize. You had a bad scare today and you need to rest. It's my fault for keeping you up so late."

His tone was gentle and his breath stirred the hair on top of her head. Drawn to the smoky voice and the comforting broad shoulders, she wanted to lean into him, to sink back into the protective fold of his arms as he helped her up the stairs. She was tired of being tough and independent, and she wished desperately for someone to share her burden.

But it couldn't be Michael. Far from easing her troubles, being involved with Michael would make her life more complicated and more difficult. He was the one who blocked her path to getting custody of Rio, and he was the one who was in possession of the glorious jadeite statue.

They reached the door to her bedroom, and she struggled out of his arms. "I'm fine now," she whispered, keeping her voice low so as not to wake Rio. "I think I'll soak in a hot bath and then crawl into bed." She leaned against the wall, taking some of the weight off her bruised leg.

He brushed a strand of hair from her face, tucking the errant curl behind her ear, then ran the tip of his finger lightly across her cheek. "If you're sure you'll be all right," he whispered, his breath cooling her flushed face. His thumb traced the line of her jaw, coming to rest in the soft hollow beneath her chin. It took only the slightest pressure to lift her face to his.

The kiss wasn't at all what she expected. The mouth that covered hers was incredibly soft, amazingly gentle and sinfully experienced. His jaw was a bit scratchy against her cheek while his lips subtly coaxed her to respond. She could have deflected a demanding assault, but she was totally defenseless against this smooth persuasion.

Her arms stole around his neck, and his shoulders seemed to swell beneath her fingertips. She plunged her hands into the hair at the nape of his neck, so much thicker and softer than she had imagined. Her moist lips parted on a deep sigh that lifted her breasts against his chest. Her head arched backward and her eyes closed as he kissed her throat. His hands, large and warm on her back, moved from her shoulders to her waist and pressed her against his body. She leaned into him, unable and unwilling to move away.

His tongue delicately and beguilingly stroked her lips. With a moan, her mouth softened and clung to his, savoring the taste of him. The appetite he awakened left her ravenous for a nourishment only he could provide. Her fingers laced through his sablelike hair to hold his head. But as she tried to taste him again, to satisfy the sudden craving, he pulled back, leaving her confused and panicked by the seductive hungers coursing through her.

Eyes the color of a stormy sea searched her face. "Good night," he said. "Sleep well." He opened the door to her bedroom, waited as she hobbled inside, then closed it after her.

Michael leaned against the wall and exhaled the breath he didn't realize he had been holding. A fierce arousal thrummed through his body. Damn, but he wanted her—wanted to slide his hands under those terry-cloth shorts and feel the soft flesh of her hips; wanted to slide his fingers to the top of her thighs and beyond; wanted her naked and writhing beneath him.

And she wanted him, too.

Her response to his kiss told him that and then some. Never before had he seen such pure desire in a woman's eyes—desire that mirrored his own. Never before had his reaction been so complete. And he knew that if he had pursued her, if he had let his hands and mouth continue their slow exploration of her luscious body... well, he sure as hell wouldn't be standing out here alone in a drafty hallway.

None of this made any sense. He'd known beautiful women before. He'd known women who were clever and captivating and more than willing. But he'd never known anyone who could get to him the way she had. Shelby McMasters was an enigma, a fascinating riddle with more questions than answers, answers that he was determined to find.

Maybe it was a natural reaction to the events of the day. Fear was a powerful aphrodisiac, and just knowing someone had tried to harm her had filled him with cold-blooded rage. He wanted to protect her, comfort her. But she was his employee and the primary suspect in the artifact smuggling. He had no right entertaining such thoughts of her...no rights to her at all.

For a long time, he remained in the darkened hallway, listening. He heard the water being drawn and watched the dark shadows limp past the light that shone under the door. The soft light drew him like a moth and held him suspended there—unable to get any closer, unable to back away.

He waited, worried that she might fall or need help, wondering how he would handle it if she did. It didn't take much imagination to know how she would look relaxing in a tub full of bubbles...her hair pinned up...a few curls dangling crazily at her nape...the water swirling around the long length of her sensually curved body.

He turned and strode quickly down the hall to his own room. Forget the damn bath.

What he needed was a cold shower.

"...and tell Peterson he's absolutely right," Michael said into the phone. "We agree with his assessment completely." He gave a few more directions, then hung up with a satisfied smile. Things were going well...very well. He had gotten more work done in the last week than he had in the last month. Most of his meetings were handled with conference calls and he was single-handedly keeping a messenger service company in the black, but all in all it was a small price to pay for the knowledge that Shelby and Rio were safe.

He had escorted them to the zoo to see the new baby rhino, and he had attended the opening of a new dinosaur exhibit at the California Academy of Sciences. He had even visited a bilingual classroom, where Shelby talked to the teachers about the special needs of bilingual children...and he'd thoroughly enjoyed it all.

That fact alone should have been enough to send him running for cover.

But it wasn't. Above everything else, he had a job to do, an obligation to his sister's child. As Rio's self-appointed protector, Michael felt he was paying off a debt that had haunted him for years. And the fact that Rio and Shelby were a package deal made the job that much sweeter. He knew she wasn't pleased having him tag along every time they stepped foot off the estate, but she had accepted it with grace and aplomb, and Rio was absolutely thrilled whenever the three of them were together.

They hadn't talked about the kiss. It was easier to pretend it had never happened. Their relationship since that night had been purely professional, strictly business—more or less. He still felt her presence whenever she entered a room. The air between them still crackled like static electricity. And when they weren't together, he still thought about her.

Constantly.

She was everything he had ever wanted and more. She was bright and witty and passionate. He had watched the way she responded to Rio, always giving him her full attention. She was good at that. She was the type of woman who would make a good mother, a loving mother, and she deserved better than spending her life taking care of other people's kids. She deserved a man whose world revolved around her, a man to sleep beside and raise a family with, a man who would abandon everything else in life to make her happy.

And sometimes, alone, late at night, he wondered if maybe he could be that man. If maybe, with her, he could find the happiness that had eluded him all this time.

But he'd never know as long as the smuggling issue was unresolved.

Michael glanced across the room at the little statue that had caused such an uproar. He now knew the statue had been uncovered at a new archaeological site near Xpujil and, after being properly recorded, it had been packed in preparation for shipping to Mexico City. But he still hadn't a clue as to how it got inside Rio's bear. His operatives were trying to track it down, but so far they weren't having much luck. The archaeologists who worked at the site refused to talk to anyone other than the Mexican authorities.

Contrary to what Pasig had reported, the attack on Shelby was probably not the work of an ordinary purse snatcher. *Somebody* knew that statue was inside Rio's bear, and it stood to reason that the person who put it there would eventually try to get it back. However, from the description Shelby and Pasig had given of a teenage assailant, he sounded too young and inexperienced to have masterminded such a plan.

Michael thumped a pencil up and down on his desk. He felt uncomfortable not warning Shelby of the potential danger, but on the other hand, he still hadn't ruled out the possibility that she was somehow involved. The best decision had been to establish himself as their official bodyguard, and he intended to keep on operating in that capacity until this mess was over. Then things could go back to normal ... and he wouldn't have any excuse to be with them.

He tossed the pencil into a desk drawer and spun around in his chair to face the window. It was a glorious day, and he refused to let melancholic thoughts spoil it. In fact, he felt like celebrating. The Peterson acquisition was finally completed, he hadn't had a run-in with anyone in days, and the white-capped ocean waves swelled and crashed against the rocks, their pounding roar beckoning him like the call of the Sirens. It was the perfect day to take Shelby and Rio out on his boat.

He found them playing outside on the jungle gym. Shelby was pushing Rio on the swing, and the delighted child was yelling "higher, higher" with every push. Michael hadn't even passed the pool when Rio spotted him. At Rio's insistence, Shelby stopped the swing so he could hop off.

"¡Tío Michael! ¡Tío Michael!" Rio dashed across the back lawn as fast as his little legs would carry him. A step or two away, he lunged at Michael, who deftly caught him and tossed him into the air. After another few tosses, Michael settled Rio on his shoulders. "I'm a good swinger, aren't I?" asked the little boy.

"You certainly are," Michael replied, watching Shelby approach.

Shelby felt his gaze slide over her and she became suddenly self-conscious. She was acutely aware of the slight jiggle of her breasts beneath her T-shirt and the way her hips swayed when she walked. She cursed the fact that summer lent itself to shorts and short tops, and made a mental note that from now on she was to dress like a beekeeper.

"Good morning," she said brightly, refusing to acknowledge how much his admiring stare had disturbed her. She glanced up at Rio, who was perched high on Michael's shoulders. He was holding on to Michael's head, and Shelby fought a ridiculous surge of envy as his small hands buried themselves in Michael's thick, dark hair. "What brings you away from your work so early in the morning?"

"You do."

The simple reply sounded incredibly erotic, and her pulse quickened.

"Well...you and Rio," Michael amended. He let go of Rio's legs and tried to reach across to tie Rio's left sneaker. But every time he started knotting the shoelaces, Rio kicked out with his legs, thus not only messing up the bow, but running the risk of falling backward off Michael's shoulders, as well.

Shelby watched in amusement as Michael tried several times to pin Rio's legs with his arm and tie Rio's shoe at the same time. Finally, he looked to her in exasperation. "Do you mind?" he asked.

"Not at all." Shelby stepped close and while Michael's strong hands clamped Rio's small ankles, Shelby adroitly tied both sneakers in double knots.

"Much obliged," he said. "It's pretty obvious I haven't had much experience with three-and-a-half-year-olds. Maybe I should practice on something simple..." He lifted Rio over his head, placed him firmly on the ground and grinned at her. "Like the agitator on a washing machine."

Shelby returned his grin. It was impossible not to. He was trying so hard to establish a good relationship with Rio. She wanted to tell him he was doing a great job—far better than she had ever expected—but the words stuck in her throat.

Ever since she had discovered the jadeite statue in Michael's glass case, her emotions had seesawed uncontrollably. The attack last week left serious doubt that Michael was responsible for stealing the statue, but she had yet to uncover how he came to possess it. And, statue aside, there was still the greater problem of who would get custody of Rio. *Remember*, her mind warned, *the stronger the bond between Michael and Rio, the harder it will be for you to win your case.*

"Did you want to see me about something?" she asked briskly.

"Absolutely," he said, ruffling Rio's golden curls. "I have a proposition for you."

Her heart thumped wildly as some of her more elaborate fantasies sprang to mind.

"I propose we spend the entire day out on my boat."

"Your what?" Her voice and her fantasy cracked at the same time.

"It's a bathtub-shaped thing with a motor. People generally sit in it and float all around San Francisco Bay."

Again that infuriating grin. "I didn't realize you had a boat," Shelby said, properly chastised.

Michael shrugged good-naturedly. "It's not big, but it's perfect for a day-long getaway. And I haven't been out in a long time. What do you say, sport? Do you want to go boating?"

"*Osito*, too?"

"You bet. We're going to spend the whole day having fun and you wouldn't want your teddy to miss that." He turned to Shelby. "Will you come?"

No. Tell him no. You can't risk getting involved.

"Please?" The humorous twinkle was gone from his eyes and in its place was something infinitely deeper and stronger.

"Rio will need a life jacket," she said at last.

Michael grinned again. "We'll have him fitted for one at the yacht club. In fact, I'll bet we can even find an infant-size life jacket for his bear."

"I'll have to *find* the bear first."

"He's on the table in the foyer waiting for us."

"I'll need to pack towels and lots of sun block."

"I keep a cabinet full of beach towels and a drawer full of sun block, sunscreen and suntan lotion on board the boat."

"I'll have to prepare a picnic lunch."

"I've already talked to Mrs. Hodges and at this very minute she is loading a wicker basket with all manner of delectables."

Shelby planted her fists on her hips. "I'll have to get my swimsuit," she taunted. "Or have you already done that, too?"

"I...I..." His grin turned sheepish. "I'll meet you out front in fifteen minutes."

Chapter 11

"I hope you're not expecting the *QE II*," Michael remarked as Pasig dropped them off at the yacht club, agreeing to pick them up again at the end of the day.

"Not at all. I don't know much about boats, anyway."

"Well, people have certain expectations about me—about my house, my cars, my private plane, my businesses—all the things that contribute to one's status." He made "status" sound like a four-letter word. He tightened the straps on Rio's life jacket, then hoisted him down from the counter.

"My boat is different," he continued. "It's not for show and it's not meant to impress anyone. There are no servants, no Jacuzzi and no special amenities. It's what I do for myself. When the world gets too crazy, I have an automatic hideaway. I simply pull up anchor and head for the open sea."

"Sounds great to me." More than once Shelby had felt the urge to run, to find a place to hide where the real world wouldn't intrude. And, in a way, she'd found it. Found it in a career that continuously looked to the past instead of dealing with the present; found it in a job that kept her virtually isolated; found it in a driving obsession that left no time for personal relationships. Only now was she beginning to see the drawbacks of that kind of life.

He led them down a series of docks lined with all types of elegant and festive boats, most of them looking more like cruise ships than private vessels. Near the end of the last dock he stopped before a glistening white boat with forest-green trim. "This is it."

It may not have been Trump's yacht, but it wasn't a rowboat, either. The *Maiden Voyage* was thirty-four glorious feet of fiberglass, burled wood and polished brass.

Michael held his hands wide. "Well, what do you think?"

His ruggedly chiseled features held a very boyish expression. He looked like a small child showing off his first trophy. *You're incredible,* Shelby thought. "It's incredible," she said.

What was truly incredible was the change that came over Michael the minute he started the motor. Before her eyes, he became younger, lighthearted and carefree. The worry lines that frequently creased his forehead faded; the day's frustrations were left in the slip as they putt-putted out of the marina.

The sky was brilliant blue and dotted with puffy white clouds, and sea gulls screeched overhead as they made their way out into the sparkling water. Seated comfortably in the back, Shelby lazily watched Michael and Rio together at the wheel. Before they left, Michael had gone below and brought up a wooden chair for Rio to stand on and had plopped an old, worn sailing hat on the boy's small head. There wasn't much of Rio to see, between the bright orange life jacket, which covered all of his upper body, and the old navy blue hat, which fell partway over his eyes, but he was having the time of his life as he grasped the steering wheel with his two tiny fists.

Once again her inner voice began its nagging. The situation had changed. Michael had changed. The two of them made a perfect pair, the voice said, not uncle and nephew, but father and son.

Shelby dismissed the disheartening thoughts. Michael was trying hard to make this a special day—a day to be enjoyed—and she refused to let the persistent doubts eat away at her happiness.

And she *was* happy. She found great pleasure in watching Michael interact with Rio. She smiled at herself. Who was she kidding? She found great pleasure watching Michael. Period. He had stripped off his shirt and his lithe body was clad only in swimming trunks and deck shoes. Her eyes took in the broad shoulders, the strong muscular arms and the narrow waist. The sun glinted off his dark hair, highlighting the streaks of chest-nut and giving his skin the look of oiled bronze. Shelby was still staring at him when he glanced around, his eyes narrowing against the glare of the sun. He caught her smile and easily re-turned it.

Oh, yes, she was happy. Happier than she had ever dreamed possible. She turned her face to the sky and basked in the sun's golden warmth.

A breeze blew up off the water and played with Shelby's long blond curls. Michael could easily imagine sinking his hands into that thick mass of curls, could see it fanned out on his pillow. She leaned back against the railing and closed her eyes. Her lips curved in a tender smile . . . sensual lips as soft as angel wings that would mold themselves to his own.

She was wearing a red-and-white-striped crop-top that barely met the waistband of her shorts, and the soft cotton fabric outlined the swell of her full breasts. She kicked off her san-dals and shifted position, her white shorts riding up her thighs. A long, beautiful length of tanned leg was exposed to his view.

"If you're working on a tan, you'll have better luck wearing a swimsuit," he hinted broadly.

She opened her eyes and looked at him through sleepy, half-closed lids. "And bare my bruised hip to the light of day? No, thank you."

He cut the motor, showed Rio how to drop the anchor, then settled down on the bench beside her while Rio skipped across the deck with his teddy. "You know," Michael said, fingering the hem of the cotton top, "I rather thought you might have a bikini on under this."

Shelby made a face. "A month ago, maybe. But eating Mrs. Hodges's cooking three times a day has made a mockery of my weight. I've probably gained ten pounds since I've been here."

"You look pretty good to me."

Shelby started to argue, but the look in his eyes silenced her. It wasn't a come-on. He was an honestly blunt man who meant what he said, and he'd said it because he believed it.

Michael watched the change that came over Shelby. Her lids lowered and her cheeks flushed. She'd recognized his remark for what it was—a compliment—and she was clearly pleased by it.

"I'm hungry."

Michael laughed as Rio's voice broke into the conversation. "So am I, sport," he replied suggestively. "So am I."

Shelby felt her cheeks redden and she turned toward the sea to hide her face from his view. But even with her head turned, she could feel his eyes watching her... caressing her... daring her to meet his gaze... a lazy grin spreading across his handsome features. This little excursion was turning out to be a lot more than she'd bargained for.

"Why don't we go below and get those baskets Mrs. Hodges packed?" Michael asked Rio.

They disappeared into the hold, but reappeared a few minutes later laden with two large wicker baskets. A bottle of wine protruded from the open lid of one of them.

Very carefully, Rio put the plastic plates and paper napkins he was carrying on the bolted-down circular table, then ran back down to the galley for the matching plastic cups and utensils.

"It's not Wedgwood and Waterford," Michael apologized, "but under the circumstances, it's a lot more practical."

No sooner had Michael spoken, than Rio appeared at the entrance to the hold. It was difficult for him to see over the fat life preserver he was wearing, and as he approached the top step he tripped, littering the deck with plastic ware.

"You must be prophetic," Shelby said as she picked up the scattered pieces of plastic and hugged the little boy who was trying desperately not to cry.

"Not at all." Michael winked at Shelby as he helped Rio up into a chair by the table. "I've done the same thing myself."

Rio's tears dried on his cheeks as he looked at his uncle in disbelief. "You fell, too?"

Michael nodded solemnly. "At least a half-dozen times."

Shelby smiled as she took a seat next to Rio and began unloading the bulging baskets. It was impossible to imagine the athletic, well-coordinated Michael Chandler tripping over his own feet.

... baked ham... fried chicken... vegetables and dips...

But the way he had helped Rio feel better about himself was wonderful.

... macaroni salad... potato salad... pasta salad...

His compassion and understanding were wonderful.

... fine cheeses... ice-cold shrimp and cocktail sauce...

He was wonderful.

... a large assortment of fresh fruit ... crackers ...

Life was wonderful.

...potato chips... and one peanut-butter-and-jelly sand-wich.

Shelby looked at the table in disbelief. "Who's going to eat all this? There's enough food here to keep us at sea for a week."

"Maybe Mrs. Hodges is trying to tell us something." He grinned wickedly. "Do you suppose she suspects us of running off?"

The indomitable Mrs. Hodges apparently knew what she was doing, for as it turned out, Shelby had seriously underesti-mated Michael's appetite. In no time at all he had polished off nearly half their bounty.

"Just wait," Michael assured her. "It won't be long before Rio eats more than I do. Right, champ?"

Both adults turned in tandem to the little boy seated be-tween them. Propped against the table with his chin resting on the puffy vest, Rio was sound asleep.

"Is there a bed below?"

Michael nodded and Shelby stood, preparing to carry the sleeping boy below deck.

But Michael's hand on her arm stopped her. "May I?" he asked. "I promise not to stumble on the stairs."

Shelby smiled her response and watched as Michael easily lifted the sleeping child into his arms. He was strength and gentleness, power and compassion, all at the same time. She watched until he disappeared below deck, then began clearing the remains of their lunch.

Minutes later, with everything packed neatly away, she stretched out on the deck and sipped the wine from her plastic glass.

"Sorry I took so long." Michael picked up the half-full wine bottle and his glass, and settled down on the deck next to Shelby. "I was worried the rocking of the boat might pitch him off the bed, so I moved a couple of chairs to form a guardrail. Then I was afraid he would clunk into the hard chairs, so I piled up some pillows and blankets to cushion it. He slept through the whole thing. Nothing short of a typhoon will wake him." He drained the rest of his wine, then refilled both their plastic glasses. "I didn't mean to leave you with the cleanup."

"No problem." A cooling breeze drifted across the deck, tousling Michael's hair and making it look eminently touchable.

Shelby turned away and looked out at the vast expanse of sea. Ever since the night of the attack, she had been very careful not to be alone with Michael. It wasn't that she didn't trust him. It was more that she didn't trust herself. She was tormented by the way she felt when he was around. She was tormented by the way she felt when he *wasn't* around. She was tormented by her rampant emotions and felt powerless to stop them.

Biting her lip, she tried to ignore the bronze body soaking up the sun just a few feet away. On more than one night she had fallen asleep dreaming of Michael, of loving him, of being loved by him. Watching him interact with Rio pushed her fantasies even further. Fantasies of families, of couples with children, of a house filled with little Chandlers. Fantasies couldn't hurt you, but reality could be devastating.

Suddenly, she was thinking "future" and that was as frightening as it was new. She hadn't planned on sharing a future with Michael Chandler when she first schemed her way into his home. But somewhere, somehow, that had changed. Feelings she hadn't experienced in years had flared to life with an overwhelming intensity.

But there would be no shared future once Michael found out she had lied and deceived him about her relationship to Rio. The greatest thing they had in common was the very thing that would drive them apart.

The long silence continued, punctuated only by the cry of a sea gull flying overhead and the soothing, gentle sloshing of water against the side of the boat.

Michael withdrew something from his pocket and placed it in the palm of Shelby's hand. "Here."

Propping herself up on one elbow, she looked at the small copper coin. "What's this?"

"A penny for your thoughts," he said, smiling.

She closed her fingers around the coin, still warm from his body. She wanted to do it. More than anything, she wanted to throw caution to the puissant ocean winds and tell him the truth. Only the strength of her conviction and her love for Rio helped her keep her own counsel.

"Actually," she said, "I was thinking about us."

Michael cocked his eyebrow in surprise.

"Do you realize we haven't argued in weeks? It's incredible, considering how we started. It's been good for Rio not to have us fighting all the time." She shrugged and turned her head away from him to stare at a passing speedboat.

He reached out and took her hand, fingering the coin, gently forcing her to look at him again. "I'm sorry it took so long for it to be this way." Waves, formed in the wake of the long-gone speedboat, slapped against the side of the yacht, rocking it gently back and forth.

She glanced down at her hand, still held firmly in his—delightful indeed, but growing increasingly awkward. "It's your turn," she said, neatly extricating her hand and curling his fingers around the coin. "A penny for *your* thoughts."

That infectious grin reappeared. "I was thinking how very little I know about you."

There it was. The one topic she most wanted to avoid.

"I don't know much about you, either . . . other than what I read in the papers," she said evasively.

The sparkle in his eyes was unmistakable. "I'll tell you about my past if you'll tell me about yours."

"Okay," Shelby said, eyeing him suspiciously. "Who goes first?"

Michael fingered the penny in his hand. "Call it—heads or tails." He tossed the coin high into the air.

"Tails," Shelby called out as Michael deftly caught the penny and flipped it over on the back of his hand.

"Tails it is. What's your pleasure?"

Dangerous question. She swallowed the laughter bubbling in her throat. "You first. I want name, rank, serial number and any pertinent information that isn't visible to the naked eye."

He grinned wickedly. "I'm forty-one years old, six feet three inches tall, and weigh one hundred eighty-five pounds. I've had all the appropriate childhood diseases and none of the inappropriate adult ones. I started with a small import/export company and parlayed it into an international corporation. I love boating and art collecting, and I hate politics. I'm on the board of directors of more hospitals and museums than I care to count, and you can undoubtedly find me in *Fortune 500,* *Who's Who* and any magazine that runs stupid lists of 'Most Eligible Bachelors.'" He glanced over at Shelby. "That's it," he said, starting to down the last of his drink.

"Sorry. Not good enough."

Michael choked on the wine. "Not good enough?" he sputtered. "Why, I know a dozen women who would give their eyeteeth for a man with credentials like those."

"Only a dozen?" she teased. "Come on. You promised to tell me about your past, not your image. I already know about that."

His gray eyes hardened as he studied her. "My past doesn't make for a very pleasant story," he said dryly. "Are you sure you wouldn't rather stick with the image?"

Shelby nodded. His comments had piqued her interest and she felt inordinately pleased that he was willing to confide in her. She tucked her feet under her and raised her eyes to meet his steady gaze. "I'm sure."

Satisfied that she was serious, Michael took a deep breath. "I was born here in San Francisco," he said slowly. "My father was a dockworker who drank most of his wages and my mother had to survive on what was left. I had one sister, Rebecca, who was twelve years younger. My father ran out on us shortly after she was born. A year or so later, my mother remarried. My stepfather didn't have much use for me, and my mother had her hands full with my sister, so at fifteen, I dropped out of school and left home."

Even more surprising than what Michael had said, was the way he said it. He was completely indifferent, detached and unemotional. He was not revealing his own painful childhood—he was relating a series of facts. Shelby kept her voice calm, but inside she felt sick. "I had no idea you'd had such a rough childhood."

Michael shrugged impassively. "It wasn't that bad," he lied. "It was just... different. I lived on the streets for nearly two years until I got caught trying to break into someone's home. That someone turned out to be Sid Bryce."

Shelby looked incredulous. "Your attorney?"

"The one and only. Since Sid and his wife, Catherine, interrupted me before I actually stole anything, they refused to press charges. Instead, they insisted that I 'work off' the damage I caused. I was still working for them long after I'd paid off the debt. They were the closest thing to a family I'd ever known. Sid helped me get a job with an import company. I was a dockworker just like my old man. But unlike him, I didn't drink away everything I owned, and I learned fast. I moved from the docks to checking inventory, then to ordering merchandise, all the time turning my salary over to Sid to invest for me. I had an uncanny knack for knowing which products to import, and by the time I was twenty-five, I had enough experience and enough capital to start my own company. Chandler Enterprises took off, and I never looked back."

"What about your parents?"

Michael looked up into the bright blue sky and studied the few cottonlike clouds that hung suspended above them. "After I started working on the docks, I did run into my father once. He didn't even know me. A few months later I heard he'd been killed in a barroom brawl."

He leaned up on one elbow and watched her. He'd seen pity and revulsion in others, but there was none of that in Shelby's lovely features. Her face showed an unflinching compassion. He offered her a half smile. "I was able to provide for my mother during her older years, but she's gone now, too. And Rebecca . . . well, she skipped out before I made it big and you already know what happened to her. I never had the chance to give her the life she deserved. In short, I'm all that's left of the Chandlers."

"Except for Rio," she said softly.

"Except for Rio," he echoed. "That boy means more to me than everything else I own, and I'll fight tooth and nail to keep him. Nothing in this world will stop me from taking care of my nephew."

Shelby's heart caught in her throat. There was no doubt now how he would react to her petition for guardianship. He would never willingly give up Rio, and her lies and deceit had only made her case that much weaker.

But there was no disgrace in what she had done. He, himself, said he would go to any lengths to keep Rio. Why should he expect her to do any different? Shelby stared hard at nothing. At least he was honest about it. No matter how she glossed over it, the fact was, she wanted Rio and she had tricked everyone to get close to him.

Maybe Michael would forgive her.

Not likely, she thought helplessly. In his eyes she would only be after Rio.

So where did that leave her?

Clearly, she had no choice. She had to continue the deception. Her only hope of getting custody of Rio was to prove Michael was somehow involved in the artifact smuggling.

She ventured a look at the man in question. His lonely smile went straight to her heart as he rolled the plastic glass between his hands. "That's enough about me," he said quickly. "Now it's your turn."

Shelby nodded. "What would you like to know?"

"Anything—where do you come from, where did you go to school, what are your hobbies?" The pause was barely noticeable. "Do you have any family?"

Shelby took a deep breath and stretched out on the deck, letting the memories—good and bad—come to the surface. "I'm afraid I've led a very ordinary life," she said. "I grew up in a very small town in upstate New York. My dad was a CPA working as a solo practitioner and my mom was his secretary. They believed it was their duty to provide the very best for their family. As a result, they worked day and night, and I barely knew either one of them. My real family was my grandfather, who was a car salesman and a mechanic."

"That's an odd combination."

Shelby nodded. "It is now, but it wasn't back then. You had to understand my grandfather. He was a fanatic when it came to cars. He couldn't get enough of them. My mom used to say he had motor oil in his veins." Michael chuckled, his warm smile encouraging her to continue. "Anyway, Grandpa opened a small dealership and promptly found himself in the new car/used car/repair car business—the only one in town."

"He sounds very special."

"He was." Tears stung her eyes, and the urge to turn away so Michael wouldn't see her cry was very great. She looked at him through thick, wet lashes. "Like your family, they're all gone now," she said simply.

He reached out and brushed a stray hair from her face. "Do you have any brothers or sisters?"

"Just one, a younger brother, named Lincoln."

Michael tilted a curious eyebrow. "Lincoln as in 'Abraham'?"

Shelby laughed. "No, Lincoln as in Continental Mark IV. I told you, my grandfather was a fanatic when it came to cars. I don't suppose you've ever heard of the 1968 Shelby Mustang GT500? Grandpa used to say it was the best of the pony cars."

Michael's shoulders shook with silent laughter. "You're kidding, right?"

"Afraid not. I was about seven years old when the first Shelby came out. For months that's all he talked about. And then, when Carroll Shelby produced the GT500..." She lowered her voice a full octave. "That Shelby is the car of the future. Zero to sixty in 5.2 seconds flat...V-8 engine with 335hp...front disc brakes...independent, coil spring front suspension...and solid axle, leaf spring rear suspension. Yes, sir, the perfect combination of performance and luxury." She sipped a little more of her wine and resumed her normal speaking voice. "Somewhere along the way, he started calling me 'his little Shelby.' Before I knew it, the name had stuck, and I've been Shelby ever since."

Michael's gray eyes sparkled mischievously. "So what's your real name?"

Shelby shook her head. "Shelby *is* my real name. As soon as I was old enough, I had it legally changed. It was my way of honoring and remembering the one person who meant more to me than anyone else."

"But what was your name before you changed it?" he persisted.

Shelby frowned. "What difference does it make?"

Michael shrugged. "Call it idle curiosity. Come on," he coaxed. "It couldn't have been that bad."

"Sorry. That's one question I'm not going to answer."

"Why not?"

"I have to maintain some mystery," she said jokingly.

Warily, Shelby watched as Michael leaned back against the side of the boat and folded his arms across his broad chest. "Well, if you won't tell me, then I'll have to start guessing." He stroked his chin in thoughtful consideration. "Let me see...is it Agnes? Bertha? Cornelia?"

"No."

"Dorcas? Ethel? Frieda?"

"Not even close."

"Gertrude? Hildegarde? Rumpelstiltskin?"

By now, Shelby was laughing so hard, she couldn't speak.

"You're not going to tell me, are you?" he prodded.

Shelby shook her head, as convulsive laughter racked her body.

"Oh, all right," he said, with mock resignation. "We'll forget it for now. Go on with your story."

"There's not much more to tell," Shelby said, finally catching her breath. "When my brother came along, Grandpa was so tickled with having his own Shelby that he insisted on having a 'Lincoln,' too."

Michael's grin split his deeply tanned face. "And I suppose if you'd had a sister, she would have been named Mercedes?"

"Heavens, no," Shelby said indignantly. She drew herself up tall. "My grandfather only bought American."

He laughed loudly and a star-burst of fine lines appeared around his incredible gray eyes. The hearty sound echoed off the cabin and surrounded her with its deep resonance.

"Shh," Shelby cautioned, clamping her hand over Michael's mouth. "You'll wake Rio."

The gesture was innocent but intimate. Her fingers brushed his beard-roughened cheek as his lips moved in laughter against her palm. The sparkle of mirth left his eyes, and was replaced with smoldering passion.

Shelby tried to remove her hand, but he covered it with his own, holding it against his mouth while his lips caressed the soft flesh.

Their eyes met and held. Tension drew her stomach tight as his gaze dropped to her mouth. Her breath caught and she was swept away on a tide of emotion as vast as the water they floated on.

Slowly, he moved toward her. He couldn't have stopped if he'd wanted to. Every muscle in his body was propelling him toward the inevitable.

He leaned forward, his dark eyes staring into hers. Closer and closer, until his face blurred in front of her eyes. She felt his breath warming the air between them, anticipating the moment when his lips would move against hers.

He pulled her into his arms and gently covered her mouth with his. Her lips were soft and her breath sweet with the taste of wine. She smelled of sea air and perfume. His hand combed through the hair at the back of her head—hair as soft as satin, as rich as spun gold.

Shelby ran her palms up the swelling muscles of his chest, firm and warmed from the sun. She lifted her fingertips to his shoulders and touched the cords of muscle and sinew beneath.

She buried her fingers in the thick dark hair at his nape, far silkier than she remembered.

His hand dropped to her throat, circling it lightly. Every place he touched was racked by a tiny explosion of heat that became a wake of languid warmth as his hand moved on. The gentle rocking of the boat and his sensual touch made her body feel like liquid. Yet inside she was restless and tense, yearning for something just outside her reach.

His tongue swept past her lips, invading her mouth. Her heart accelerated and her legs turned to water as he deepened the kiss with an urgency that snatched her breath away. With a smothered moan she clung to him, surrendering to the force of his lips and the demands of his seeking tongue. Instinctively, he tightened his arms around her, crushing her to his chest, pressing her against the long, hard length of his body. A wild pulse thundered in her ears and swirling heat coiled through her.

He tasted of wine, and she eagerly closed her lips around his tongue. The boldness of her action amazed her, as she drew deeply upon it again and again.

God help her, she wanted him. Wanted to be drenched in the sensations that were Michael—touching his powerful muscles, tasting the salt on his skin, soaking in his scent and his sound. She wanted him more than food or drink or anything else in this world except . . .

"Rio," she murmured as his lips rained kisses over her eyelids and along her jaw.

"Rio is sleeping." His honeyed voice filled her with a lassitude that was delicious and seductive.

"But . . ."

He brushed a kiss across her lips, silencing her objection. His hand slid from her waist up under the crop-top until his palm was molded to her breast. The thin, soft bra was no obstacle as his fingers stroked and caressed and gently tormented her until her breathing turned ragged.

In one carefully controlled move, he eased her on to her back until she could feel the cool smooth wood beneath the deck cushions. She needed that, needed to find something sturdy and unyielding to offset the feeling of being tossed around on a stormy sea. He loomed over her, leaning on one forearm, his hips pressed intimately against the cradle of hers. The sea air was cool against her heated skin, but the contrast only heightened the waves of urgency rocketing through her body.

She was losing her mind. And she didn't care.

How long had she waited for a man like this to come along? A man who could make her stagger like a drunken sailor with just a look or a touch. She was tired of being strong and independent. Tired of feeling so achingly empty while the lonely nights stretched out before her like the endless jungle.

This man stirred in her a passion she hadn't thought possible. She felt it in her breasts, in the tensed muscles of her thighs, in the throbbing of her very core.

He played with the waistband of the white shorts, his palm pressed flat and warm against her bare stomach. A quiver of desire rippled through her and she was powerless to suppress it. His fingers slipped under the cotton material, splayed across her belly, then inched even lower. Her body opened for him, yearned for him, urged him toward the part of her that felt on fire.

And then she heard the cry.

Her eyes fluttered open; it was like being wakened from a deep and dreamy sleep. For a moment she thought it came from within her, her own body crying out, drowning in some strange undertow.

But then she heard it again. Deep sobs, racking a small body. Rio.

In the space of a heartbeat she flew across the deck and down the small flight of stairs two at a time. Rio was lying in the middle of the bed, eyes closed, while his small hands tugged fiercely on the strings of the orange life vest.

Shelby scooped him up into her arms and held him close. "It's okay, honey," she crooned. "I'm right here."

The adrenaline that pommeled her body left a trail of guilt in its wake. How could she have been so careless, so thoughtless, so swept away by her own emotions that she forgot the real purpose for her being here? She could never forgive herself for indulging in her own selfish flights of fancy while Rio struggled alone with the demons that still occasionally haunted his sleep.

"Is he all right?" Michael's voice, deep and filled with concern, came from behind her.

"He will be," she said sharply. She held the child tight in her arms, rocking him with a fierceness that was meant to ease her own pain as much as his.

A lock of hair fell across her face and Michael reached out to brush it back, but she turned away. She didn't want him touching her, or kissing her, or doing anything ever again that would distract her from her purpose . . . from Rio.

Undaunted, Michael tossed aside the pillows that had formed the padded guardrail and sat down beside them on the small bed. "Did you have a bad dream?" he asked.

Rio nodded, his eyes wide with fear.

"Do you want to talk about it?"

Rio wrapped his arms tightly around Shelby's neck and buried his face in her shoulder.

"Nightmares about the b-u-s?" Michael asked, spelling out the last word, his voice pitched low for her ears only.

Shelby nodded. "I think it's best if we go back now," she said coolly.

"Okay." Michael folded the chairs, and tucked them into a storage locker. "But I'm going to need some help. What do you say, Rio. Do you want to drive the boat?"

"I really don't think that's a good idea," Shelby said, but Rio was already scrambling off her lap and reaching for Michael's outstretched hand. She watched in disbelief as the two of them climbed the stairs then listened as Michael reeled in the anchor and started the motors.

Damn him. Her whole life was falling apart and he was to blame. He was the one who had awakened in her a passion she hadn't known existed. He was the one who was slowly and insidiously taking her place in Rio's life. For a few brief moments today, she had actually thought she could have it all— Michael and Rio.

Now she knew it was only a matter of time before she lost them both.

The sun was going down in a blaze of crimson as they approached the yacht club. The air was cooling quickly, and Michael slipped his arms into the sleeves of a cotton shirt, buttoning all but the top two buttons.

He used the motion as cover to glance at Shelby sitting alone at the far end of the boat. She hadn't spoken two words since they started the trip home. It didn't take a genius to figure out what she was thinking, to know that she was berating herself for the way she had acted, for compromising her professionalism. They needed to talk about it, tonight, after Rio was in bed. It might take some time, but somehow he would make her understand that they had done nothing wrong.

The radiance had left her eyes and an overwhelming sadness ravaged her beautiful face. The strained silence tore at his heart and he couldn't look at her without wanting to wrap her in his arms and keep her there forever.

Forever.

There was a word he'd never expected to find in his emotional vocabulary. But then he had never expected to find someone like Shelby McMasters. In a few weeks she had turned away years of loneliness and isolation. Suddenly, words like *forever* were taking on a whole new meaning.

He watched in appreciation as she drew her long legs up against her chest and wrapped her arms around them. Oh, yes, he thought. Tonight they would discuss Rio . . . and a whole lot more.

Shelby watched as Michael cut the motor and the boat floated gently into the slip. Jumping onto the wooden planks, he deftly moored the boat while Rio stood patiently by the railing, clutching his teddy. When the boat was secured, Rio raised his hands and Michael lifted him to the pier.

By the time Michael turned back to help her, Shelby had already hopped the rail and was about to jump the two-foot distance to the dock. Putting one hand on either side of her waist, Michael swept her into the air. Her top was not long enough to completely cover her waist and his hands spanned her bare flesh. She grasped his broad shoulders and felt the ripple of muscle under the cotton shirt. For one last, sweet moment, he held her, suspended, with his breath warm against her throat.

"Come on," Rio interrupted, tugging on Michael's leg. "Let's go."

With a broad smile, Michael set Shelby firmly on the dock, but the feel of his hands on her skin lingered.

"Next stop, the pizza parlor," Michael announced, leading them down the pier, past the rows of moored boats. They were halfway down the wharf when he stopped. "We forgot the picnic baskets. Mrs. Hodges will have a fit if we don't bring them back." He pitched a low, conspiratorial voice to Rio. "Women get very upset about fuzzy stuff growing in their Tupperware." Rio nodded his head in serious agreement, although it was clear he hadn't the slightest idea what his uncle was talking about. "You two go on ahead," Michael said, his deep, baritone laugh rumbling down the pier. "I'll run back and grab the baskets."

Before Shelby could protest, he was sprinting back toward the boat. "Come on, Rio," she said, taking the little boy's hand. "Let's keep going. Uncle Michael will catch up with us."

The sun dipped behind the horizon and dusk settled around them. The docks were quiet except for the constant gentle sloshing of water against the sides of the boats. Shelby was tired. It had been a long, emotionally exhausting day and she wanted to go home and crawl into bed. But Michael had promised to take them out for pizza, and that was one promise she knew Rio wouldn't let him forget. She inhaled deeply, filling her senses with the strong scent of saltwater and sea air, steeling herself for a few more hours in Michael's company.

A scrawny man in a black ski mask jumped in front of them, catapulting Shelby out of her lethargy. He lunged toward Rio, and Shelby's screams split the night air as she spun Rio behind her, praying he wouldn't be thrown off the pier and into the water. She kept herself between the child and the man, clumsily backing up as he slowly advanced.

"Run!" she screamed to Rio as the man moved toward her. "*¡Corre!* Run!"

He was much taller and undoubtedly stronger than the punk who had accosted her on the street, and Shelby knew there was no way she could defeat him. But if she could just hold him off long enough for Rio to get safely to Michael . . .

A click and a glint of light drew her attention to his hand. A long, cold blade of steel gleamed menacingly. He jabbed the air as he crept steadily forward, forcing her to back up.

More than anything, she wanted to look over her shoulder and see where Rio was. But she didn't dare. Even in her panicked state she knew that turning her back on a man wielding a knife would be nothing short of stupid. She offered up a silent prayer and continued her step-by-step retreat.

A blur of color flashed by, tackling the man in the mask. A sob tore from her throat, and only the adrenaline surging through her bloodstream kept her from hysteria. A mixture of relief and renewed fear seized her as she watched the two men rolling on the deck, grappling for control of the knife. Michael struggled to his feet, dragging the man with him. He smashed him hard into a wooden post and Shelby heard a satisfying crack. But the advantage was short-lived.

The silver blade slashed through the evening sky, and Shelby watched in helpless terror as Michael crumpled to the dock.

Chapter 12

"I heard screaming."

"It came from over there."

"Somebody call the cops!"

"Come on!"

A half-dozen voices echoed along the pier, sounding for all the world to Shelby like a chorus of angels.

"Here," she screamed. "Help us!"

The dazed assailant hovered over Michael's body, staring at her through narrowed eyes. If she lived to be a hundred, she would never forget the look of pure evil radiating from those eyes. He raised the knife over Michael's crumpled form.

"I see them!" shouted a voice. "Over there."

The man glanced over his shoulder and in that split second, Shelby made her move, hurling herself into him. Her lunge wasn't professional but it was effective. The man landed on his backside with a dull thud. As he fell, the blood-streaked knife slipped from his hands and slid across the wooden dock. An eternity passed as the knife teetered precariously on the edge of the dock before it finally tipped and plopped into the deep water. With a final look in her direction, the man stumbled off into the gathering darkness.

"There he goes!"

"Get him!"

Shelby dropped to her knees where Michael lay, a steady stream of blood pouring from his left shoulder. Dear God, no. "Call an ambulance," she screamed. "Hurry!" She looked around for something to stop the bleeding, but there was nothing. She grabbed the bottom of Michael's cotton shirt and tore off a long strip. Blood soaked her own top as she tried to wrap his shoulder, praying the makeshift bandage would stem the bleeding. She didn't want Rio to see his uncle like this.

Rio! Shelby jumped to her feet and dashed down the pier. "Rio!" she cried. "Rio, where are you?"

A small whimpering off to her right drew her attention to a large blue-and-white yacht. Rio sat in a chair under a canopy as still as a mouse.

"Thank God, you're all right," Shelby said, reaching for the child. "Come here, honey."

Rio shook his head.

"It's okay, now," Shelby crooned. "The bad man is gone." She glanced back down the dock to where Michael lay frightfully still. "Please come with me, Rio."

The little boy's eyes were filled with tears and fear. "Tío Michael said stay here and don't move," he sobbed.

Shelby jumped into the boat and scooped Rio into her arms, her own eyes filled with tears. "You were a good boy, honey." She hugged him fiercely. "Uncle Michael will be very proud of you."

A crowd was gathering around Michael as Shelby hurried up the pier. Where the hell was that ambulance? She spotted Pasig at the dock entrance and rushed toward him.

"What in the world is going on here? I had to leave the car—"

"Michael's been hurt," she said. She thrust Rio into the chauffeur's arms. "Take Rio home and ask Mrs. Hodges to look after him."

"No!" Rio shouted.

"Yes," Shelby said firmly. She took the little boy's face in both her hands. "Uncle Michael will be fine. I promise."

Please God, let that be true.

"I'll call you from the hospital," she said to Pasig. "And I'll see you later, honey." She kissed Rio on the top of his head.

"No!" he screamed again. He struggled to get out of Pasig's arms, but the chauffeur held tight.

"Rio, my man," Pasig said, easily restraining the thrashing child. "What say we move that little seat of yours up front with me? I've got more buttons and gizmos up there than you've ever seen. In fact, I've been meaning to show you how they work."

Shelby smiled her thanks to Pasig, then pushed through the crowd to where Michael lay. She knelt beside him and cradled his head in her lap. His face was as white as new canvas sails, and his dark hair fell like an angry slash across his forehead. She moved her fingers to the base of his throat. A shallow but steady pulse beat beneath her fingertips as the shrill noise of sirens resounded in the distance. *Hurry,* she begged. *Please hurry.*

"You don't have to be that quiet," Michael said three hours later, as Shelby tiptoed into the room. "I'm awake."

"How are you feeling?" she asked, sitting next to him on the hospital bed.

"Just dandy," he groused. "Hand me my shirt."

Shelby picked up the discarded shirt—the top soaked with blood, the bottom torn into shreds. "I don't think you'll be wearing this shirt again. I'll have Mrs. Hodges put together a set of clean clothes for you, and I'll bring them by tomorrow."

He struggled to sit up. "I'm going home now."

Shelby tossed the shirt on the end of the bed, just outside his reach. "What did your doctor say?"

"I didn't ask him. I don't have to. I know what I'm doing."

"Oh, really?" she asked, folding her arms across her chest. "And which medical school did you say you graduated from?"

"I'd like an answer to that question myself, Michael." A tall man with copper-colored hair and a matching beard stopped at the foot of Michael's bed and thumped his chart. "You're spending the night."

Gingerly, Michael swung his legs over the side of the bed, ignoring the pain in his shoulder that burned like hot coals. "I'm going home...even if I have to walk."

"Is he always this charming?" the doctor asked, introducing himself to Shelby.

"Oh, no," she replied blithely, shaking the man's hand, "usually he's petulant, pigheaded and downright cantankerous."

"You two can joke all you want," Michael said. "But I'm leaving." A wave of dizziness swept over him and it took every ounce of strength at his command to keep from falling flat on his face.

"Michael, be sensible," his doctor said. "You need to rest."

"I'll rest a lot easier in my own bed."

"You need someone to keep an eye on you, give you medication, check for fever or infection."

"I have a very competent staff, and, if I have to, I'll hire a private nurse."

"I know you, Michael. You wouldn't hire a private nurse if your life depended upon it...which it just might. That knife wound wasn't deep, but even so, you've lost a fair amount of blood, and it's going to take time for your body to replenish that blood supply. In your weakened condition, there's always the risk of infection. I won't sign your release until I'm convinced you'll be well cared for."

"You trust her, don't you, Doc?" Michael draped his good arm casually around Shelby's shoulders—it was either that or make a complete fool of himself by passing out. "Tell her what you want done, and she'll do it."

The doctor turned his stare on Shelby. "Are you willing to assume responsibility for him?"

Michael flashed her a grin that cost him a lot more than he'd let on. "Say yes, and I'll double your salary," he whispered loudly.

"Do you promise to do exactly what I tell you?"

"Yes, yes, anything. Just get me out of here."

"Okay." With the doctor's help, she eased Michael into a nearby chair. "If you could give me a moment, Doctor, I'd better call his driver. Then I'll be happy to take down all your instructions." They headed out the door and toward the nurses' station. "And you," she said, turning around and shaking her finger at Michael, "you stay put until I get back."

Michael saluted with his good hand and kept a smile plastered on his face until they were gone. Then he slumped back against the chair and swiped an arm across his forehead.

How quickly the day had turned around. What had started out as one of the best days of his life, had ended in a nightmare. The memory of Shelby's screams and the vision of the man with the knife still haunted him. He didn't give a damn about his shoulder, the doctor, or anything else. All he cared

about was Rio and Shelby. He already knew Rio was safely
back at the estate, and he wanted Shelby there, too. He knew
damn well what would happen if he stayed here. She'd never
call Pasig to come and get her. She'd take a taxi...standing
alone outside on the street or in the parking lot waiting for it to
come. Anything could happen to her out there...and that was
a risk he wasn't willing to take.

What he'd told the doctor was true. He wouldn't have a moment's rest in the hospital, knowing she was alone. Granted,
there wasn't much he could do for her in his present condition,
but at least he'd have a little peace of mind knowing there was
someone else to look after her. The hospital attendants would
see them safely in the car, and once they were back on the estate, he could rely on Callahan, Pasig, even George at the front
gate, to handle any problems.

Michael drew a sharp breath and steeled himself for the long
trip home. Once they reached the estate he would relax. But
until then...

A shudder racked his damaged body. Maybe tomorrow he'd
hire a security team...just to be sure.

"Hurry up, we don't want him to get chilled...careful now...
I'll hold the door...watch his shoulder...gently."

"Will you stop that," Michael muttered to Shelby from his
awkward position between Callahan and Pasig as they helped
him from the car to his bedroom. "You're making me feel like
an old man."

"Not an old man, an injured man—although at the moment, there probably isn't much difference." She dashed into
his bedroom, flipped on the lights and drew back the covers on
his bed. "Get him up here," she barked. "Easy now...that's
it."

Michael groaned loudly. "If I had known you were going to
act like a drill sergeant, I would have stayed in the hospital."

"You should have thought of that before you made such a
big stink about coming home. It's too late to change your mind
now." She threw open the door to one of his closets. "Where
do you keep your pajamas?"

"Who said I wear any?"

The images that danced through her mind made Shelby want
to turn tail and run, but she refused, on principle, to give him

that satisfaction. With her hands on her hips, she turned slowly to face him. "John," she said, addressing her comments to John Callahan, but never taking her eyes off Michael, "please help Mr. Chandler get ready for bed, in whatever mode he finds most comfortable. I'm going to check on Rio, but I'll be back shortly to give Mr. Chandler his medicine."

Michael's rich baritone laugh followed her all the way down the hall.

She rapped softly on the door to Rio's room, then stepped quietly inside. She needn't have worried about waking him, for the little boy threw himself into Shelby's arms the moment she entered the room.

"What's this?" she asked, extricating the small arms that clutched her neck. "What are you doing up at this hour of the night?"

Mrs. Hodges lifted her portly frame out of the rocking chair and put the storybook she had been reading back on Rio's shelf. "I'm sorry, miss, but that wee one's been worried sick about Mr. Michael. Even after we got your call from the hospital, I couldn't persuade the lad to eat a bite or lie down, either."

"Is that right?" Shelby asked, looking into Rio's wide eyes. They were filled with fear. He said nothing, but continued his death-grip hold on her hand.

"And he's been fit to be tied ever since he heard all the voices. He wanted to be with you, but I was afraid to let him go out, not knowing and all."

"Well, I can certainly understand that," Shelby said soothingly. She sat down on the edge of Rio's bed and lifted the little boy into her lap. "Do you know what happened to Uncle Michael?"

Rio shook his head.

"He hurt his shoulder very badly right here," she said touching the comparable part on Rio's small body. "We took him to the hospital and the doctor put a bandage on it. He also gave Uncle Michael some medicine that would stop the hurting. He's going to be fine, but he won't be able to go swimming or boating or play with us for a while, and we'll have to be very careful not to bump his shoulder. Do you think we can do that?"

Rio nodded solemnly.

Shelby smiled. "Do you know where Uncle Michael is right now?"

Rio shook his head.

"He's in bed...which is where you should be," she said, tweaking the little boy's nose. "If I take you in to say goodnight to Uncle Michael, do you promise to come right back here and hop into bed?"

Rio nodded his head vigorously, but still didn't speak.

"Okay, then," Shelby said, sliding him off her lap and taking his hand, "but we'll have to be very quiet just in case Uncle Michael is already asleep."

They tiptoed down the hall and were about to knock on Michael's door when it opened and John Callahan stepped out.

"Is he all set?" Shelby asked.

"If you mean, is he decent," John replied, "the answer's yes. You can go in."

Shelby poked her head around the door. "Are you up for some company?" she asked. Rio squeezed in front of her and peaked around, too.

Michael brightened at the two faces who peered at him. "Absolutely," he said. "You two look like a lopsided totem pole. Come on in."

Rio walked hesitantly over to where Michael lay, propped up by several large pillows. "Climb up here, sport," Michael said, patting the bed beside him. "How are you doing?"

Rio said nothing, but stared at Michael and at the bandaged part of his bare chest. Michael glanced at Shelby with unspoken questions, but she shrugged her shoulders and shook her head. This time she couldn't help him; he was on his own.

"Yes, well...did you have fun today on the boat?"

Rio nodded, his eyes regaining a little of their brightness.

"I did, too," Michael said. "And I'd like to go out again, just as soon as my shoulder feels a little better. Would you like that?"

The little boy nodded again.

Michael took a deep breath, ignoring the pain that ripped through his shoulder. "Were you frightened by what happened when we got back?" Rio looked down at the bed, his small hands drawing invisible pictures on the quilt. "I'll be honest with you, sport. I was scared." Rio looked up at Michael slowly, skepticism clouding his precious face. "There's no explanation for why some people act the way they do or why they try to hurt others. I'm sorry that man in the mask scared us, but I'm not going to let him ruin my fun or keep me from going boating again." Wordlessly, Rio looked back down at the bedspread, tracing the pattern with his fingers. "You know," Michael continued, "Shelby told me how brave you were, staying right there where I left you. I'm very proud of you."

Silently, Rio's gaze wandered around the room, looking everywhere except at his uncle.

"Sorry, guys," Shelby said, glancing at her watch, "but it's time for all men named Chandler to get some sleep." She stood from the armchair she'd pulled close to Michael's bed and picked up two prescription bottles that lay on the nightstand. "You," she said to Michael, "have to take two of these and one of these." She dropped the tablets into his palm and held out a glass of water. "And you," she said to Rio, with continued mock severity, "made me a deal. You've got exactly two minutes to get your body into bed." She watched as Michael made a face, then tossed the pills into his mouth and washed them down with half a glass of water. Shelby put the glass on the nightstand with a satisfied smile, moving to the door. "I'm going to turn on your night-light, find teddy and open your bed," she called to Rio over her shoulder. "Remember...two minutes."

"You better listen to her, sport," Michael said, ruffling the boy's curls. "She's stronger than both of us."

Rio climbed down from the bed and walked slowly to the door. At the entrance to the room, he hesitated, his hand on the doorknob. Without a word of warning, he spun around and flew across the floor, flinging himself against Michael's rib cage, hugging him with all his might. "I love you, Uncle Michael," he sobbed, but before Michael could answer, he was gone.

Michael rubbed the spot on his lower chest where Rio's body had been just moments before. *I love you, Uncle Michael.* It had been a long time since anyone had said those words to him...and longer still since he had returned them.

It was just one more in a series of events that had brought a host of long-buried emotions surging to the surface. First, there was Shelby. She had done the impossible. In less than two months, she had driven him out of his self-imposed isolation and tossed him right back into the mainstream of life. Now, he spent a lot of his time fantasizing about her...but the experience they'd shared on the boat was no fantasy. Who knew where it might have led under other, less crowded, circumstances?

And that brought him to Rio. Being with Shelby and Rio reminded him of the things he'd given up on a long time ago—things like marriage and a real family. Marriage with someone who was a friend as well as a lover, and raising a family where the kids were taught about trust and love and emotional security.

And that led his thinking straight to the villainous man who threatened to destroy his dreams for the future. Bile rose in his throat every time he thought about how close he'd come to losing Shelby or Rio.

A yawn crept up on him, but he stifled it.

The officer who had questioned him in the hospital said Michael had foiled a probable kidnapping. Maybe... but he doubted it. He wasn't about to mention it to the police, but more likely, the attack was the second attempt to recover the statue, perhaps by the original thief.

He yawned again and his lids lowered. His chin fell to his chest and with a jerk, he forced his head upright again.

As long as he had that statue, Shelby and Rio were in constant danger. He had to do something... but what? Maybe tomorrow... maybe tomorrow he'd call Ingersoll... he'd call Ingersoll and ask him to...

Shelby laid her hand against Michael's cheek, his forehead and his neck. His skin was cool to the touch. There was no sign of a fever. His covers had slipped to his waist, revealing a broad, bare chest and a furred line of dark curling hair that ran over the taut muscles of his abdomen and disappeared under the waistband of his pajama bottoms.

With shaky hands, she reached down and pulled the covers up over his chest, up to the heavy bandage that covered the wound. She ran her fingertips over his forehead, smoothing away the worry lines between his thick dark eyebrows. A low sound of contentment escaped his lips and she smiled.

His lips looked cracked and dry. She filled the glass on his nightstand with cool water, then dipped her fingers into the glass and dribbled the water across his lips. Reflexively, his tongue darted out, catching the drops on her fingers. Her breath caught in her throat, then broke in a rush of air.

Get a grip, she chided herself. But there was no denying it. Even sleeping, the man had a powerful effect on her.

Shelby put the glass back on the nightstand. There was nothing more she could do tonight. Her only reason for staying was to watch him . . . to touch him . . . to be near him. She turned down the light and tucked the blankets in around him.

"Shelby . . ."

His eyes were closed and in the dim light, his lashes cast smoky shadows across his cheeks. "I'm right here," she said, taking his hand in hers. "What can I do?"

"Will you stay . . . ?"

The reality of how close she had come to losing him hit her with the force of a sledgehammer and she swallowed around the large, painful lump in her throat. She would have done anything in her power to protect him from being hurt. A tear dropped from her cheek and was absorbed by the bedclothes. "Don't worry, Michael," she said, her voice soft and low. "I won't leave you."

She pulled the armchair that was next to the bed closer and sat there, holding his hand. The Michael Chandler who had hired her was arrogant and domineering—the type of man who pushed his way through life, intimidating everyone who came in contact with him. She had slowly come to know a different Michael Chandler, though, one who was lonely and vulnerable, one who could be loving and passionate, who struggled with the tender side of his nature. But nothing had prepared her for this. Seeing him injured and helpless, touched another side of her, as well. Her fingers entwined with his, she felt connected to Michael in a way that went beyond caring for a friend, beyond maternal instinct . . .

And that was a dangerous sign.

There had been other men in her life, and one or two with whom she had fleetingly thought she was falling in love. But nothing that compared to this. With Michael, all her senses seemed alive—colors were more vibrant, sounds were richer, smells were more fragrant. Everything around her was like living in a 3-D movie.

She was falling in love with this man.

And there wasn't a damn thing she could do about it.

Shelby pressed her lips against the back of his hand. None of this would have happened if Michael didn't have that stupid little statue downstairs. Or would it?

Maybe the attack had nothing to do with the statue.

Shelby turned the possibility over in her mind, examining it from every angle. Michael was a powerful businessman and he had undoubtedly made more than his fair share of enemies over the years. Maybe someone was trying to get even.

But why now? Michael had admitted to the police that in fifteen years, nothing like this had ever happened, and suddenly there were two attacks in as many weeks. Shelby shook her head. Angry people didn't generally wait fifteen years to get revenge.

Maybe the police were right. Maybe it *was* an attempted kidnapping. Everyone in the English- and Spanish-speaking worlds knew about Michael and Rio. And there were plenty of lunatics out there looking for an easy way to make a quick bundle.

She thought about the young kid who had attacked her outside the pediatrician's office. With slow-motion clarity, she replayed the scene over and over in her mind, looking for evidence to corroborate her theory. There simply wasn't any. That punk had never even looked at Rio. He had gone straight for Shelby, or more accurately, straight for the teddy bear she was holding. She was absolutely convinced of it.

Shelby took a deep breath and continued her step-by-step analysis. Okay. She was standing on the street and a teenage boy tried to steal a ripped-up, broken-down old teddy bear out of her arms in broad daylight. Short of the fact that the kid may have been insane, there had to be a logical explanation for why he wanted that particular toy.

And the only reason she could come up with was the statue.

Tonight's attack wasn't as easy to justify. The man had definitely lunged toward Rio...but he could just as easily have been trying to grab the bear.

Shelby shook her head. The man in the ski mask continued to haunt her. All evening she'd had an eerie feeling she couldn't shake. Something about the man was frighteningly familiar. She hadn't seen his face or heard his voice, but the memory sent chills racing down her spine.

The police may have settled on attempted kidnapping, but that creep wasn't after Rio. He was after the statue he thought was inside Rio's bear. It was the only theory that made any sense.

The medicine had kicked in and Michael was in a deep, drug-induced sleep, his breathing relaxed and even. Shelby released his hand and slid his arm under the covers, then curled up in the chair next to the bed.

Oh, Michael. How did you get your hands on that statue? Why can't you see how much trouble it's causing? Why don't you get rid of it?

Shelby looked at Michael sleeping peacefully near her. As soon as he was better, she was going to personally throttle him. There had to be a way out of this miserable mess...and she had to find it before the man in the ski mask tried again.

In the cold light of early dawn, it took Michael a full minute to remember what had happened. The dull ache in his left shoulder as he struggled to sit up brought it all back with astonishing clarity.

That was when he saw her. In all of his forty-one years, he'd never experienced a moment as wholly wonderful as waking up to Shelby McMasters asleep in the chair beside him. A soft yellow blanket was tucked around her, completely covering her body from neck to ankle. Only her bare feet peeked out at the bottom, and her golden hair fell in swirls across the blanket at the top.

He'd never met anyone like her. The girls he had known as a kid growing up on the streets were no different than he. They were all tough and lonely, fighting just to survive. After his meteoric rise to the top, the women in his life had all been like Gina, party girls who hung around until the money or the fun ran out. Never was there any sign of trust and affection or any of the other things Shelby had grown up on. He had heard it in her voice yesterday when she talked about her parents. He had seen it in the way her eyes sparkled when she mentioned her grandfather and his crazy love of cars.

How many nights had he lain here in this bed, wondering how it would feel to have someone talk about him that way, someone who cared, someone who would still be there through bad times and good?

Last night he'd had a small taste of what life with Shelby would be like. He had felt comforted and cared for as she'd held his hand. He had felt loved and cherished as she'd touched his cheek and forehead. He couldn't remember what she'd said, but he remembered the way she'd touched him—with tenderness and compassion. And he remembered her touching him in other ways, as well, and the thought was enough to send his blood rushing due south.

In the quiet of early morning she was still here, sleeping only an arm's length away, her breathing sounding velvety and sweet.

Where was it written that Michael Chandler was doomed to a life of loneliness? Whose decision was it to deny him the joys of marriage and family? Why shouldn't he take a chance on a future that was better than anything he had ever imagined?

All he had to do was make Shelby McMasters a permanent part of his life.

"Lord, you're bossy." Michael crossed the room and eased himself back onto the bed late one afternoon ten days after the stabbing.

"It's one of my more redeeming qualities," Shelby said, dropping the last pill from a medicine bottle into Michael's palm and handing him a large glass of juice.

"Not from where I stand."

Shelby's eyebrows shot toward her forehead and a smile flickered at the corners of her mouth.

"All right, from where I sit. It's still not high on my list." He swallowed the pill and set the glass on the nightstand. "The last time I took orders from an employee was..." He cocked his head to one side. "I don't think I've ever taken orders from an employee."

"Well, you are now." She held the empty bottle up to the light and frowned.

"Seems to me I'm doing a lot of things with a certain employee that I've never done with my employees before." Without a word of warning, he reached out and grabbed her around the waist, pulling her into his lap.

"Michael, no." She tried to pull away, but he held her fast.

"Why not?"

The question was simple. The answer wasn't. A half-dozen reasons why she shouldn't be here, why they shouldn't be doing this sprang to mind. She was a paid nanny, not a concubine. Her first responsibility was to take care of Rio's needs, not Michael's...or her own. Michael was still recovering from the stabbing, and...

"And don't give me any feeble excuses about your job or Rio or my shoulder," he said.

Shelby blinked and said nothing.

"I think we should talk about that day on the boat," Michael said softly. "What might have...what almost happened."

Shelby struggled to get out of his arms, but he refused to release her. "There's nothing to talk about," she said firmly.

"I think there is." He shifted position in the bed, turning her to face him. "Shelby, we didn't plan this, but you can't deny there's something happening between us. Something we can't go on ignoring." He cupped her chin in his hand and forced her to meet his unflinching stare.

Ever since that day on his boat, she had imagined how it would feel to have him hold her and touch her again—and now that he was, she wasn't at all sure she could handle it. "Rio might—"

"Rio is helping Pasig polish the limousine. He's probably having a grand time, and they won't be finished for hours. But this isn't about Rio. It's about us."

Us. He made it sound so simple. As though there were no problems, no obstacles, nothing to stand in their way. Resentment flared as she thought of Michael Chandler Businessman, snapping up companies and corporations without so much as a by-your-leave. When he saw something he wanted, he took it. It was that simple. And she was just one more thing he wanted.

She searched her mind, but found the answer in her heart. Michael wasn't like that, and she knew it. He was patient and caring and gentle. And he would never maneuver her into something she wasn't ready for.

"You need more time to recover," she said feebly.

"My shoulder's fine," he said, "thanks to my fantastic nurse. See?" With his injured arm, he stroked her back in slow, indolent circles. The caressing stopped as quickly as it started. "Maybe you're the one who needs more time."

His face was so close, she could smell the orange juice on his breath. "Actually," she stammered, "I should be..."

"You should be honest about what you're feeling. Shelby, if you don't want this to go any further, say so, and I'll never bother you again. But don't make up feeble excuses or run away. Don't lie to me. Don't lie to yourself."

Michael held his breath until he thought his lungs would explode. She looked so helpless and soft and vulnerable. He had no doubt that if he tried to seduce her, he would succeed. But when it was over, there would be hate and regret in her icy-blue eyes. And that would kill him more than having her get up and walk away. He drew an unsteady breath.

Shelby didn't answer. How could she? He had backed her into a corner, pinned her down as neatly as if he had used his own body. She looked down at his hands, no longer clamped on her arms, no longer restraining her, not touching her in any way. She was free to leave, and he wouldn't do anything to stop her.

"Shelby, will you stay?" His voice was a whisper, dark and full of promise.

The last time he said those words, she had spent the night holding his hand. But this time it would not be so simple. He was asking her for much more. He wanted to make love to her, and heaven knew she wanted it as much as he did.

But sex wasn't everything, and Michael hadn't promised anything more. She knew he liked her, admired her, and there was enough chemistry between them to blow up a science lab. But did he love her the way she loved him? And if he did, what would become of that once he found out the truth?

"Shelby, please talk to me." He had been watching her—watching her struggle to find an answer that would satisfy them both. He didn't know how much more of it he could take.

The lemony sun dipped a little lower in the sky, and the bed was bathed in sunlight. She was thirty-three years old, and had spent most of her life in the safety and seclusion of her job. Maybe it was time to be reckless, to risk an affair with a man who might not love her. Maybe he did love her, after all, even though he'd never said it. She hadn't told him she loved him, either, but she did.

And maybe that was reason enough to say yes.

With a nervous smile, she touched his dark hair with her fingers, brushing it off his forehead. "I'll stay."

He pulled her close and lowered his head. She pressed her lips to his, briefly, hesitantly, then with certainty and desire.

Clasping her hands between his, he pulled away, his eyes boring into her with an intensity that was both frightening and exhilarating. "Are you sure?" he asked, his voice husky and thick with desire.

Shelby looked at the man before her—the man who was tender and compassionate. The man whose touch set her skin on fire. The man who cared enough to let her make her own decision. The man she loved.

"I'm very sure."

He closed the distance between them, his mouth covering hers in a shattering kiss that was demanding and urgent. His tongue stroked her bottom lip, then plunged into her mouth, exploring every crevice, coaxing her into joining him in a sensual battle. She needed no further persuasion. Her lips softened and began to move with his, kindling the desire that flamed between them.

He dragged his mouth roughly across her cheek, kissing her neck, her ear, her temple. Shelby's hands slid around his neck, lightly forcing his mouth to hers again.

Michael groaned and pulled her closer, crushing her breasts against his chest, his good hand sinking into the thick mass of hair at her nape. He gentled the kiss, his warm lips tasting and shaping hers in a way that drove her blissfully out of her mind.

He watched as her lids fluttered open. Her blue eyes were filled with intense longing, making them as deep and lovely as lapis.

She pressed her lips against the tiny scar on his neck and let her mind go blank. She didn't want to think about the statue, or her petition or the elaborate ruse she was caught in. All she wanted was to be with Michael, wanted him with an intensity and urgency that banished everything else from her mind.

Her arms stole around his neck once more and she returned his kisses with a passion that matched his own. A low sound broke from Michael's throat as she slipped her hand inside his robe and ran her fingers lightly down his chest and across the taut muscles of his abdomen.

He spoke her name and pulled her close, fitting her body against the hard length of his, their curves and angles blending together like pieces of a jigsaw puzzle. Shelby's breath caught in her throat as Michael's hand covered her breast with hard warmth. His lips traced her jawline from temple to chin, and when he reached her mouth, he kissed her with a slow deliberation that sent the blood rocketing through her veins.

With her palms braced against his chest, Shelby kissed him soundly and firmly, then pushed herself away. The sound of heavy breathing suspended erotically between them. Slowly he removed her halter top, the look in his eyes turning to smoldering desire as he took in the sight of the soft swells of creamy flesh. His breath fanned her overheated skin as he bent his head to kiss the silken curve, and she shivered with delight.

Michael unzipped her shorts and eased them over her hips. "You're so beautiful," he murmured, when she lay naked before his admiring gaze.

Shelby felt beautiful. In his arms she felt cherished. She watched with unabashed pleasure as Michael slipped out of his robe and pajama bottoms. She loved to look at him, to touch him. She ran her fingers along his square jaw, across his broad shoulders, and down the flat plane of his belly.

She quivered as his hands roved her breasts, gently caressing and arousing, stroking the ridge along her spine, touching the curve of her buttocks. His warm breath stirred the tendrils of hair that framed her face, and she gasped as his hands moved over her with a knowledgeable firmness, filling her body with raw desire. She felt more alive than she ever had. Every sense was achingly acute as her body arched toward the warmth and strength of his.

His lips tasted and teased the secret places that made her gasp with pleasure. And when Shelby could no longer bear the exquisite tension that wound her stomach into coils, her fingers tightened on his back and she drew him to her. His breathing was rough and shallow as his mouth covered hers in a hard kiss that was both demanding and giving. Her hips arched to meet his thrust and when their bodies joined, he filled an emptiness she hadn't dreamed could ever be filled. As her body drew him deeper inside, her arms tightened around him, trying to hold him even closer, making them one.

They found their own unique rhythm that gradually shifted from slow and giving to demanding and urgent. And when the pace had accelerated to a frenzied, fevered pitch, their bodies shuddered, grew taut, then exploded in a final shattering union.

The roar of the ocean pounded in her ears and waves of pleasure shimmered through her. Michael's arms tightened around her and his head dropped to her shoulder. When the trembling passed and her breathing slowed, a drowsy contentment swept her away and nothing existed for her but Michael and a magical sense of oneness.

Michael cradled her in his arms and listened to the soft sound of her breathing as she dozed. He bent his head and pressed his lips to the tiny dimple in her shoulder. For as long as possible, he wanted to hold her and imagine what it would be like to never let her go.

He suddenly realized he had used nothing to protect her against pregnancy, but oddly the thought didn't bother him. After Gina had left, he had given up hope of ever having children in his life. Then Rio arrived and Michael had found a new joy in being an uncle and a surrogate father. Now the thought of creating a child with Shelby thrilled him beyond words. He kissed the top of her head, loving the way the golden curls framed her face.

She stirred against him and he dropped a second kiss on her nose, then leaned on an elbow to study her. "Do you know what I like most about you?"

She looked up at him with sleepy eyes. "Well," she said, sighing, "I can't cook, I hate balancing my checkbook and I'm a terrible dancer." She snuggled into the warmth of his arms and rested her cheek against his chest. "It must be my sense of humor."

His laughter rumbled deep in his chest. "Besides that," he said, smoothing back her tumbled hair and kissing her forehead. "You're not a user. You don't let me intimidate you and you don't want me for what I can give you."

Shelby raised her head to look at him, her eyebrows lifted in wry amusement. "Oh, no?"

He swatted her playfully and pulled her back down on top of him. "What I meant was you don't want my money..."

"I don't need it," Shelby mumbled.

"...or my name..."

"I like my own."

"...or my power or my prestige or..."

Shelby pushed away from him and frowned. "You think you're pretty hot stuff, don't you, Chandler?"

His grin was wicked as he rolled on top of her, covering her with his body. "You tell me."

Chapter 13

Shelby awoke by degrees, feeling safe and warm and surrounded by love. She hugged her pillow and squeezed her eyes tight, trying to hold on to the wonderful dream that would vanish with the dawn. It had been a long time since she'd felt this happy, and she was reluctant to let it go.

She opened her eyes to a room, not gray with the first rays of morning, but orange with patches of sunlight and shadow formed by the setting sun. It wasn't a dream. She truly *was* safe and warm—and lying next to Michael.

She lay very still, not wanting to disturb the man or the feelings he created. Being in his bed, in his arms, in his life, felt so natural that anything less would be incomplete.

Gently easing away, she tucked an elbow under her head and watched him sleep. His dark hair was rumpled, and she couldn't resist brushing a curl off his forehead with the tip of her finger. Sleep seemed to soften his features. His face was smoother, the angular bones less harsh, the firm mouth gentled, the tight muscles relaxed. He looked...younger...more vulnerable...almost innocent.

She chuckled softly at the thought. Michael Chandler was anything but innocent.

Without making a sound, Shelby slipped out of bed and quickly dressed. Her body ached pleasurably from his hands and mouth and body. Delicious sensations still coursed through her and for the first time in years she felt truly loved.

It seemed strange thinking about love. The years alone had left her with an aching emptiness that she'd tried to fill by relentlessly pursuing a career. It hadn't worked. It took being in Michael's arms to feel whole. It took being loved.

She crossed the room and pushed apart the French doors that opened onto a small balcony. As twilight settled around her, a cooling breeze drifted in from the ocean, offering a respite from the summer heat. Shelby inhaled the fresh air deep into her lungs. Heady fragrances of hibiscus, bougainvillea and hydrangeas filled her senses.

Distant shouting and a beeping horn drew her attention to the driveway. Rio was sitting on Pasig's lap behind the wheel of the silver limousine waving wildly to her through the driver's open window. Smiling, Shelby returned the gesture and watched the car creep slowly toward the garage.

For now, for this very moment, and for a few moments to come, she had it all. She had her nephew—the child she had sworn on her brother's grave to love and raise, the little boy she adored and who adored her in return. And she had Michael—the man she wanted to be with, to be a part of, to share her body, her life, her heart and her soul with.

Assuming that was what Michael wanted. He hadn't said he loved her, but sometimes words didn't come easily. It took a great deal of courage to admit your love, to open yourself to rejection and ridicule, to reveal your deepest secrets. How could she condemn Michael for something she herself wasn't brave enough to do? There were other ways to show love without saying the words. And Michael had shown her several of those this afternoon.

Shelby slipped back into the room and studied the man sleeping just a few feet away. He lay on his side, his head sharing the pillow she had occupied only moments before. The sheet and comforter had slid down to his waist, exposing his broad back and one strong arm. She pulled the covers up over the relaxed muscles, her palms tingling as she remembered the feel of their rippling strength under her hands. She tucked the sheet around his shoulder, her fingers lingering in the hair at the nape of his neck.

What wouldn't she give, what wouldn't she do to spend every day for the rest of her life with the two people she loved?

She heard Rio bounding up the stairs. Quickly she left Michael's room, quietly closing the door behind her. Halfway down the hall, she intercepted Rio clutching an armload of papers. With a finger to her lips, she led him back downstairs well out of earshot of Michael's room.

"Did you see me?" he bubbled, talking half in English and half in Spanish. "I shined *el carro grande* and drived it, too."

Shelby smiled and nodded her head. "I saw you driving," she said. "Where did you go?"

"I drived it to see George and get *el correo.*" He opened his arms, showing Shelby the pile of mail. "I want to give it to Tío Michael," he said, heading for the stairs.

Shelby caught him by the arm. "I'm sorry, honey, but Uncle Michael is sleeping. Why don't I take the mail and we can give it to him later. Okay?"

Rio shook his head stubbornly and grasped the pile a little harder. Several envelopes slid to the floor.

Shelby frowned and knelt to pick up the scattered pieces. "Well then, how about this. You carry the mail to Uncle Michael's study and we'll sort it into piles. Then you can deliver the mail to Mrs. Hodges and Mr. Callahan right now."

Rio beamed. "Like a real *cartero?*"

"Like a real *cartero,*" Shelby echoed.

Rio skipped into the library while Shelby followed, retrieving pieces of mail that trickled from his arms. They dropped the whole bundle in the middle of the floor and sat down to examine it.

"This one is for Mrs. Hodges," Shelby said, pointing to the letters on the front of the envelope. "And this one says Michael Chandler."

"Read this," he said, stuffing an advertisement into her hands.

Shelby laughed. "This one is for you." She watched as the delighted child started a stack of junk mail, which quickly became the largest stack of all.

"One more," he said, dropping a plain white envelope in her lap. Shelby turned it over and a chill crept up her spine. In crude, handwritten block letters were the words "The Nanny" followed by "Chandler Estate" and the rest of Michael's address. There was no return address, but it was postmarked San Francisco.

"Is it for me?" Rio asked, climbing into her lap and leaning his head against her shoulder.

"Not this time," Shelby said, swallowing reflexively. She struggled to her feet, then bent down and picked up two piles of mail off the floor. "I think you should deliver these to Mrs. Hodges and John Callahan. Then get washed up for dinner. I'll leave your mail and Uncle Michael's mail on the desk and after dinner you two men can go through your papers together."

"Good idea," he said, nodding solemnly. He took one stack in each hand and hurried off like a real mailman.

Shelby smiled after the child who had filled her life with joy. As promised, she put the two remaining stacks of mail on the desk, then sat down in Michael's leather chair to study the letter. In the two and a half months she'd been here, she'd received no mail. Even her attorney was under strict orders not to contact her at Michael's home.

A sudden fear hung over her, suspended like the blade of a guillotine. Grabbing Michael's letter opener, she sliced open the envelope and withdrew the thin single sheet. With icy fingers, Shelby placed the paper on the desk in front of her and smoothed out the creases.

The same primitive block letters appeared inside as on the envelope:

COME ALONE TONIGHT AND BRING THE BEAR OR THE CHILD WILL FOLLOW IN HIS PARENTS' FOOTSTEPS

A time and location was scratched at the bottom of the page.

Shelby's hands shook as the vile words and all they implied took shape in her mind. She felt physically ill, yet she couldn't stop reading the letter, over and over again.

Somebody knew.

Somebody knew she was more than a nanny. Someone had deliberately sent this malicious letter to her rather than Michael. Someone knew that mentioning Rio's parents—her brother—would tear her apart.

But who? And why?

Shelby glanced up at the jadeite statue. The why was easy.
Like nearing the end of a jigsaw puzzle, the pieces began falling into place. Faster and faster, she picked them up and
dropped them into position. Someone knew about her phe-
nomenal archaeological find. Someone from the dig or maybe
from the commune. That someone had stolen the statue and
hidden it inside Rio's bear. And now he wanted it back.

The note was clear. The thief would do whatever it took to
get his hands on that statue—even if it meant killing Rio. The
words jumped off the page and seared her brain. FOLLOW IN
HIS PARENTS' FOOTSTEPS. Another piece snapped into
place. The bus crash wasn't an accident . . . Linc and Rebecca
had been murdered. Horror and pain racked her body and a
numbness settled around her heart.

No. Not them. And not Rio. She had to do something. Ever
since the attack on Michael, she had felt helpless, as much a
victim as he was. Now she could change that. She'd meet this
bastard and . . . and . . . and what?

And find out the truth.

If, as the note implied, there was more to the accident than a
blown tire, then she had to know why . . . had to know if Linc
was involved in stealing the statue . . . had to know if he'd lied
to her one last time.

The initial paralysis was wearing off, and the numbness that
had frozen her emotions was melting as quickly as snow in a
spring thaw. Violently, Shelby pushed away from the desk. She
was suddenly angry—ragingly, explosively, screamingly mad.
Mad at the thieves and liars and users who ripped apart peo-
ples' lives like so many pieces of paper. And she put her own
name at the top of the list.

COME ALONE . . . COME ALONE . . . COME ALONE . . . .

The words echoed in her brain, beckoning, luring, calling her
out. Her anger was stoked to a white-hot fury, a madness bor-
dering on insanity that forced reason aside. Oh, yes, she'd meet
this vile creature and lay to rest, once and for all, the doubts
about her brother that gnawed at her soul.

Somehow she managed to get through dinner. As soon as it
was over and Rio and Michael were safely occupied in the library with their mail, Shelby sought out Mrs. Hodges and
asked her to keep an eye on Rio while she ran an errand.

"At this hour?" Mrs. Hodges asked skeptically.

"Yes, please," Shelby begged. "I won't be long. I'll take the Jaguar and be back before Rio knows I'm gone. I'm sure he won't give you any trouble."

Mrs. Hodges shook her head. "That child hasn't been a lick of trouble since the day he arrived." She wagged a finger at Shelby. "It's you I'm worried about. You're as pale as death and you didn't eat more than two bites at dinner. If you're sick, you should get yourself upstairs to bed."

"I'm not sick, Mrs. Hodges," Shelby insisted. "But there's something I do need to take care of tonight. It's very important."

Mrs. Hodges wiped her hands on her apron as she contemplated Shelby's request. "All right," she said finally. "But you don't have to hurry. I'll watch over the wee one for as long as you're gone. And I'll call Pasig for you, too. He'll take you wherever you need to go."

"Thank you," Shelby said, slipping into her jacket and picking up her purse, "but please don't call Pasig. I don't mind driving myself."

Mrs. Hodges folded her arms across her ample bosom. "Does Mr. Michael know about this? He doesn't want you left alone, you know. Not after what's happened."

"Michael and Rio are in the library and I don't want to disturb them. Besides," she stammered, "it's a . . . surprise." Shelby flinched and tried to keep the look of guilt off her face.

"A surprise, is it?" Mrs. Hodges studied Shelby with knowing eyes and then smiled. "All right, but you be careful."

Borrowing Michael's Jaguar, Shelby sped into the velvety darkness, leaving behind the safety and security of the place she now called home. Stars glistened overhead like chips of diamonds, but there was no beauty in their sparkle, only a coldness that belied the summer night.

Checking the address on the bottom of the letter, Shelby pulled into the parking lot of a small drugstore. The plan, or more accurately, the lack of one, hadn't bothered her until now. But the anger that had bolstered her earlier was slipping away and common sense was rearing its ugly head. Nervously, she glanced around.

There were a few cars scattered about the lot and she held her breath every time one drove past. But no one stopped, no one got out, no one came near. After a while, she flipped on the interior light and looked at her watch. Twenty minutes and nothing. She double-checked the address and then frowned. Maybe the person didn't know she was here. Maybe he was waiting for her to get out of the car.

Shelby turned in her seat and searched the dimly lit parking lot. Still nothing. But then, what had she expected? Surely the person wasn't going to be wearing a neon sign that flashed on and off like an advertisement on a shady motel. Shelby shivered. Maybe getting out of the car wasn't such a bad idea. She'd park as close as possible to the store, wander in, buy something and wander back out. Nothing could possibly happen in that short a period of time, and if anyone was watching, at least he would know she was here.

Shelby started the engine and eased the car into a parking space within bolting distance of the front door. She got out slowly and looked around, scanning the parking lot for any sign of movement. The quiet was too quiet, too eerie, too nerve-racking. Shelby took a deep breath to steady herself and locked the driver's door. An old Chevy careened into the lot and her heart slammed into overdrive as the car screeched to a halt a few spaces away. Before she had time to react, two high-school girls climbed out, giggling and whispering.

Shelby gulped. What a waste of good adrenaline.

She hurried into the drugstore and wandered aimlessly up and down the aisles. Finally, an attendant approached her. "Excuse me, miss, but we're about to close."

Shelby selected a bottle of vitamins to replace the ones Michael had finished earlier in the day and hurried to the checkstand. She nearly laughed out loud at the irony. Michael needed vitamins about as much as a bald man needed a haircut. If this afternoon's performance was any indication, he was quite well recovered.

Shelby paused at the door of the drugstore, all of her senses on full alert. The high-school girls pushed past her and climbed back into the Chevy, their laughter eclipsed by the roar of the noisy engine. A moment later the lights in the drugstore went out and she stood in darkness.

Shelby tried to shake the confusion from her head. Maybe this was all a mistake. Maybe she'd misunderstood the note.

Maybe she was meant to misunderstand. Her heart rose in her throat. Maybe this was an elaborate ruse to lure her away from the estate. Maybe at this very moment Rio and Michael . . .

Shelby sprinted across the parking lot, her mind racing out of control, her fingers fumbling with the keys. She forced the tiny piece of metal into the lock and flicked it to the left. A soft click sounded in the empty parking lot, and she yanked out the key and reached for the handle.

Bony fingers grabbed her elbow and a low harsh voice rasped close to her ear. "Hello, Shelby," he said, as a sudden icy chill scraped along her spine. "Long time no see."

Michael paced the library floor. He stopped in front of the desk and picked up the phone, then dropped it back down. He had called the front gate three times in the last hour. Calling again wouldn't get her home any faster.

Where the hell was she?

Mrs. Hodges had said Shelby had left to run an errand . . . alone. Damn. She knew how he felt about her being unaccompanied, unprotected, and yet she still went traipsing off in the middle of the night. If anything happened to her . . .

Michael raked a furious hand through his hair. Ever since he woke up from their glorious lovemaking, he'd wanted to talk to her, to hold her, to touch her again. But the best he could do was leer at her from across the dining-room table, and after dinner he had spent time with Rio, all the while counting the minutes until he could tuck Rio into bed . . . and then take Shelby back to his.

Michael sighed and collapsed into a chair. Desire had driven them into each other's arms and now there was no turning back. He wanted her—all of her. He wanted to see the sunshine in her eyes and hear the laughter in her voice. He wanted to bury his face in her fragrant, honey-colored hair and feel her smooth, warm skin against his own. He wanted to slip inside her mind and know her secret thoughts and wildest dreams, wanted her heart and soul. He wanted a family—a mother for Rio, a wife for himself.

A wife?

He couldn't believe he was even considering it. After his disastrous marriage to Gina, he had decided never to marry again, never to run the emotional risk. But he and Gina were different people who wanted different things from life. She'd wanted a husband who would provide her with prestige and money and standing in the community. He'd wanted a family and someone to share it with. Someone who loved him for himself and not for the things he could give her. Someone like Shelby.

He looked at the clock one last time, then grabbed a book and turned out the lights. He'd wait for her upstairs, but there'd be no sleep until he knew she was safe. And even then sleep might not come. His bed, his very life, were incomplete without her.

Shelby spun around, her heart thudding painfully against her rib cage. Her mind went blank as she stared at the wiry man. "Who are you?" she whispered. "What do you want with me?"

He leaned against the side of the Jaguar and pulled a pack of cigarettes from his pocket. A thin humorless smile crossed his face. He tapped the cigarette against the hood of the car, then stuck it between his lips.

Shelby glanced around uneasily. The parking lot seemed suddenly deserted and his colorless smile raised goose bumps on her skin. She reached for the door handle, but he slid in front of the door blocking her way.

"This is a real nice little car you've got here." He ran a dirty hand along the roof and down the side. "Can't imagine how you can afford this." His stare heightened the chill that had settled on her skin.

Shelby folded her arms across her chest. The least she could do was not give him the satisfaction of knowing he was terrifying her. "The car belongs to my employer."

"Is that so?" He squinted against the smoke that clouded around his head. "Your employer is at an archaeological site in Mexico, and he doesn't have a Jaguar in San Francisco."

Her mouth went dry. He knew. He knew she was an archaeologist. And maybe he knew a whole lot more. In which case he had the advantage because for the life of her she couldn't figure out who he was or where she may have met him. He wasn't Mexican and she was sure he had never worked at the dig. Shelby wet her lips nervously. She had acted hastily in coming here alone. Stupidity reigned. The smartest thing now would be to get back to the estate and tell Michael everything... before it was too late.

"I've taken another job," she said. "Temporarily—to tide me over until I can return to the dig." She waved the paper bag in the air. "In fact, I just ran out to get these for my boss. He's expecting me, so I'd better get going." She waited, but he didn't budge from the door.

"I'm sure Mr. Chandler won't mind if you're a little late." The menace in his tone was so chilling, it took her a full minute to realize what he had said.

"How do you know about Michael Chandler?"

"I know many things, Shelby. I know of zoos and museums, of pediatricians and schools. I know of boats and docks, of..."

Her heart slammed forward against her ribs. A small choking sound escaped from her throat. Average height. Thin, scrawny build. The stench of old cigarette smoke. Piercing eyes, ugly and malignant. Her stomach cramped and gagged. Her hand flew to her face, clamping over her mouth.

"It w-was you," she finally stammered. "You were the one in the ski mask. You tried to kill me." Anger and adrenaline surged through her bloodstream. "You almost killed Michael."

"Almost killed him?" The man shook his head. "I don't think so. In the first place, the newspapers claim it was hardly a scratch. 'Entrepreneur Michael Chandler foiled the attempted kidnapping of his nephew,'" he quoted. "And in the second place, he's lucky I *didn't* kill him after he tried to bash my head against the dock post."

Her mind recoiled at the words he was saying. As if of its own volition, her hand lashed out to strike him, but he caught her wrist and gripped it painfully.

"Let me go!" Shelby said, trying to wrench away.

"Not yet, sweetie. Not until I get me a new teddy bear."

Her pulse thundered in her ears as she violently jerked at her wrist. "Who are you?"

"You really don't know, do you?" He stared at her, his eyes unblinking. "Consider yourself lucky. After all," he said, his voice dropping to a silky threat, "what you don't know can't hurt you." He gave her arm one last twist, then released it suddenly. "Look, I don't give a damn about Chandler or his brat. There's only one thing I'm interested in."

Shelby swallowed hard, and stopped massaging her aching wrist. "The statue," she said, her voice barely a whisper.

He smiled, an ugly, malignant smile. "The statue," he echoed. He glanced toward the front seat of the car. "Give it to me."

She shook her head. "Surely you don't think I'd be stupid enough to bring it with me."

"Is that right? Well, now, that poses a little problem, doesn't it?" His voice was terrifyingly pleasant, but there was no mistaking the anger and resentment simmering beneath the surface. "I went to a lot of trouble to get that statue and I want it back."

"It belongs to the people of Mexico," Shelby said, clenching and unclenching her fists, her arms rigid at her side. "You have no right to it."

"Shelby, Shelby," he said with a long sigh. His voice was deathly soft, his tone patronizing. "You are so naive. You simply don't understand the greater rules of life."

She didn't want to hear any of this. She only wanted to get away—as far away as possible. But for the moment, she had no choice. "What rules?" she reluctantly asked.

"The law of economics, for one. Right this very minute, there is a gentleman interested in purchasing that little figure for a very handsome sum. And, as it so happens, I find myself in need of a very large amount of money. So there you have it. The law of supply and demand. And now I'm demanding you give me that statue."

"Never," Shelby snapped. "If I return it to anyone, it will be to the Museum of Anthropology in Mexico City, where it rightfully belongs."

Nansen laughed, a sound that was caustic and grotesque. "Tsk, tsk, my dear. You're letting your feelings cloud your thinking. Let me explain. You have something I want, and I have something you want. Think of it as a simple trade."

"There's nothing to trade. I want nothing from you."

A sly look narrowed his pale green eyes. "Are you sure? What about that little boy you're so fond of...your nephew, to be exact."

Panic stuck in her throat and she swallowed hard. He even knew about her relationship to Rio. But how? No one knew that except Amelia and Zenith and...and a few of the people at the commune. He wasn't a commune member, but there had to be a connection. Shelby searched his face, looking for something, anything, to jog her memory.

"Leave Rio out of this," she said flatly.

His smile twisted in hatred. "Ah, but he's the reason I'm in it."

"I . . . I don't understand."

He studied her a long moment, then gave her an affected shrug. "Best leverage I ever had. It's amazing what people will do to protect that kid. First your brother, and now you."

Shelby blanched. "You're Thomas Nansen," she blurted out, immediately regretting her stupidity. Thomas Nansen had been her brother's partner, the one who carried out all Linc's scams and schemes. Shelby had seen his name more than once on police reports . . . usually in conjunction with the words "armed and dangerous."

"My reputation precedes me. I'm flattered." Nansen tossed away the cigarette butt and pulled a new cigarette from the pack. The flame of the match licked the night, leaving an eerie reflection on his face. As he bent toward the flame, his mouth and chin were clearly visible, but his eyes were half-hidden in shadow.

"You were at the commune, weren't you? That's where I've seen you."

"I was just visiting," he snarled. "Just trying to talk some sense into that lunatic brother of yours . . . trying to talk him out of retirement." He smiled hideously. "But he wasn't interested. It seemed Mr. High-and-Mighty had found something else to occupy his time . . . until I threatened to take that something away . . . permanently." He grinned in response to Shelby's look of disbelief. "Anyway, we made a deal. I promised to leave him and his family alone, and in return he told me all about the pretty little jadeite statue you found, and what you'd done with it, and how you'd packed it and where it was going . . ."

White-hot pain sliced through her as her worst fears came true. Linc was involved. He'd sworn it was over, promised her never again. And like all the other times, she'd fallen for his lies. All the talk about changing, about finding what was important in life, about starting over . . . lies . . . all lies. Shelby blinked back the tears, refusing to let Nansen see her cry.

"How did you get it away from the dig?"

"I made the most wonderful switch," Nansen gloated. "I found a stone about the same shape and weight as the statue, wrapped it and crated it with so much care. Oh, I would have loved to have seen the curator's face when he unwrapped a new and worthless rock instead of an old and priceless figure." He threw back his head and laughed at his own cunning. "It was so perfect." He gave Shelby a look that chilled her blood. "Until I found out my old partner couldn't be trusted. He wanted to turn me in. Imagine that." His casual shrug belied the fury in his eyes. "What's that old saying? 'Let sleeping dogs lie.' Always remember that, Shelby."

Shelby's voice was barely audible. "You killed him?"

"Of course not," he crooned. "Well, not directly. That bus was so old, the tires so worn, the road so steep…anything could have happened . . . all it took was one . . . little . . ."

Shelby jumped reflexively as a pop sounded near her ear. Thick, dark clouds had gathered overhead and the air was getting colder. Two storms were brewing—and one of them stood directly in front of her.

"The accident was in all the papers, along with the fact that Chandler's nephew had survived and was being shipped stateside. Once again, the kid came through for me. When I found out which kid it was, I watched him and soon figured out he didn't go anywhere without that stupid bear. So I stole it, hid the statue inside and left it where I was sure they'd find it again. The rest you know."

Shelby shook her head. "Why, Nansen? Why would you do it?"

His laugh was short and derisive. "I'm only in it for the money…which brings us right back to you."

The air and the conversation were both frightfully cold, and Shelby rubbed the goose bumps on her arms. "Me? What have I got to do with any of this?"

His eyes were stony, his smile a thin line. "For one thing, you have twice foiled my attempts to get the bear." Shelby shrank back at the menace in his voice. "But I will forgive that slight indiscretion since I now know it wouldn't have made any difference." He took a long drag on the cigarette and blew the smoke deliberately in her direction. "But now, you're going to get that little statue and turn it over to me."

"I won't do it," Shelby said defiantly. "I'll…I'll…"

"You'll what?" he mocked. "Call the cops and have me arrested?" He shook his head and sneered at her. "You can't prove a damn thing." With an angry slash of his hand, he threw down the cigarette. "Look, Shelby, let's cut the crap. You've got two choices. You get that statue and bring it to me tomorrow morning, nine o'clock. There's a deserted warehouse a few miles from here." He scribbled the address on a book of matches and forced it into her hand. "I'll meet you at the north entrance."

"Or?" Shelby asked, not really wanting to hear the answer.

"Or that kid won't live to see his next birthday."

"You bastard!" Sanity fled as rage filled her soul and she lunged for Nansen. She hit him once, twice, her nails raking his cheek. Then he backhanded her across the face, knocking her to the ground.

A streak of lightning ripped through the night sky, giving the low-hanging clouds an iridescent glow. A clap of thunder shook her car, drowning her cry.

"Remember, Shelby. Tomorrow morning. I'll be waiting."

And then he was gone.

Shelby picked herself up off the asphalt, retrieved her purse and package, and climbed into the car. Holding a hand to her bruised face, she closed her eyes and leaned her head back against the seat.

Another clap of thunder cracked overhead. What should have been a gentle summer rain was now a frosty sting as it pelted down. Every drop that pinged against the windshield felt like an icy hypodermic needle piercing her skin.

Shelby wrapped her arms around herself in a futile attempt to keep out the cold. The enormity of all that had happened was slowly sinking in—Linc's role in the theft of the statue, his attempt to atone for it, the deaths that weren't accidental. It was more than she could handle, more than her mind and her heart could absorb. Deliberately, she blocked out the pain and anger and anguish, and focused on the one thing over which she had control.

There was another flash of light followed by booming thunder and a cloudburst directly overhead. The skies seemed to open up and a heavy rain poured down, drenching the area.

Shelby gripped the steering wheel, and drove as fast as she dared on the rain-slick highway. Rio's life was in danger and she would do anything . . . anything at all to protect him.

Chapter 14

The thunderstorm stopped as quickly as it started, leaving behind small puddles of water along the driveway. Shelby pulled the Jaguar into the garage and dashed across the back lawn of the estate.

She slipped in through the patio doors of the dark kitchen, and hurried through the dining room, the living room, the entryway, around to the other side of the house. All the lights were out and the house was deathly quiet. It was late, much later than she'd realized and apparently everyone had gone to bed. Hopefully, that everyone included Michael.

Quickening her steps, Shelby ran past the sun room. A feeling of dread exploded in her chest and she stopped outside the library door. *Please don't let him be in here,* she prayed. She couldn't face him right now, couldn't explain what she was about to do.

She pushed gently against the door, and indescribable relief caught her breath as darkness surrounded her. She stepped inside the room and quickly closed the door behind her. Rejecting the idea of switching on the bright overhead light, she walked in darkness, crossing the room with sure steps. She ran her fingers along Michael's broad desk until they bumped against the small desk lamp. The click resounded loudly in the night and the room was bathed in a soft, dim light.

Shelby hurried to the display case that held Michael's collection of Mesoamerican figures. The jadeite statue was still there, staring at her from behind the glass wall. She touched the case, hesitantly at first, then with conviction. Her first priority... her only priority... was Rio. And if giving the statue to Nansen was the price she had to pay to buy Rio's life, she would do it gladly.

She traced the outside edges with her hands, seeking entry to the case. She had never seen Michael open it, but there had to be a latch or knob or button that would release the door. Her fingers fumbled in the near dark, tripping over bumps and bulges in the casing that held the glass cabinet to the wall. Desperation drove her on. She had to get that statue... had to save Rio.

And then there was a click—a small noise really, yet thunderous in the silence of the empty room—and the glass door swung open. For a long moment Shelby just looked at the statue. Its crevices were still filled with dirt and bits of sediment, a testament to the hundreds of years it had remained buried deep underground. An archaeologist could look for a lifetime and never find an artifact this rare... this precious.

Slowly her hand reached out. Tears blurred her vision as she grappled with what she was about to do. A huge shudder racked her body and she slammed shut the door of the cabinet.

Fresh tears streaked down her face and she pounded her fists against the glass in silent defeat. She couldn't do it. She couldn't commit one atrocity to prevent another. And that was the end of it.

But she had to do something. She had to protect Rio and find a way to make Nansen pay for what he'd done. He had stolen a Mayan artifact and smuggled it out of the country. He had attacked her outside the pediatrician's office and he could have killed Michael on the dock at the yacht club. He was responsible for the deaths of Rio's parents.

And she couldn't prove a blessed thing.

Nansen was right. If she told the police, she would only succeed in getting herself in trouble. There was no proof against him, no proof at all. It was his word against hers, and given the lie she'd been living for the last two and a half months, her word wouldn't mean much to anyone.

Except maybe Michael.

She had to tell Michael.

She had to tell him about Nansen and the statue and the threats against Rio. She had to tell him about her career as an archaeologist and how the statue he'd found in Rio's bear had come from a dig in the Yucatán. She had to tell him that Linc was Rio's father and her brother.

Shelby took a deep breath. Telling Michael everything meant admitting her duplicity in becoming Rio's nanny. She would have to explain how she'd intended to oppose his petition for custody and how she had hoped to gather information she could use in court that would prove him unfit to be a guardian.

It was a risk. A big one.

But she would also tell Michael how wrong her first impressions were. During their time together, she had come to see a different side of him. He was strong and compassionate, deeply caring and sympathetic. He was the type of man who would make a wonderful father, and she would not oppose his petition on any grounds.

Oh, yes, there was a risk. There was the risk that Michael would not forgive her for betraying his trust. He had always applauded her honesty and straightforwardness, and her actions would be a slap in the face. And if he couldn't forgive her, if he made her leave the estate, she would find a job in the area and still see Rio as much as Michael would allow. Of that much she was certain. Michael knew how much Rio loved her, and he would never punish Rio for her mistakes.

Shelby pressed her bruised face against the cold glass as a wave of exhaustion swept over her. She needed him now—needed his strength and wisdom and mind-drugging kisses. Shelby smiled weakly. An archaeologist could look for a lifetime and never find a man this precious, this rare.

The door crashed open and bright light flooded the room while Michael's thundering voice shattered the stillness. "Where the hell have you been?"

Shelby spun around to face him, the bright light blinding her. She froze, like a deer paralyzed by the headlights of an oncoming car. His voice was furious, his stance menacing. And in that moment, she knew she didn't have it in her to face yet another angry man. All she had gone through tonight, all that still lay ahead, was suddenly too much.

The realization that Shelby's knees were buckling galvanized Michael into action. He sprinted across the room and caught her just before she hit the floor. He carried her to the couch, nestling her among the cushions. He settled a pillow behind her head, and bent to brush the hair away from her face.

"My God, what happened to you! Who did this?" Shock and fury registered on his drawn face. "I'm calling a doctor."

"No." Her voice was cold and strong, much more so than her body. She reached out and clutched his arm with steel fingers. "Sit down, Michael. Please. We have to talk."

Fear formed a choking lump in his throat and left a vile taste in his mouth. All night he had waited for her to come home, listened for her light step on the stairs, anticipated the moment he would take her in his arms, take her to his room, make her a permanent part of his future. The last thing he'd expected was the battered dispassionate specter sitting before him. Reluctantly he sat down beside her. "About what?" he asked tonelessly.

"About that statue." She nodded her head in the general direction of the glass case.

His body went rigid as he tried to control the dread exploding in his chest. She was involved. It was the only explanation. "What do you know about the statue?" he asked woodenly.

Shelby took a deep breath. She spoke slowly, choosing her words with great care. "I know it's a priceless Mayan artifact that was stolen about three months ago from an archaeological site near Xpujil. It was smuggled out of Mexico in Rio's teddy bear. The two attacks, outside the pediatrician's office and at the marina, were not purse-snatching or kidnapping incidents. They were attempts to get Rio's bear."

Panic squeezed Michael's heart. "How do you know all this?" he whispered hoarsely.

Wordlessly, she withdrew the crumpled envelope from her pocket and offered it to him. He eyed her suspiciously, and took the paper with an obvious reluctance, holding it between his thumb and forefinger.

"Read it," she commanded. Her throat was tight and her voice husky. If she couldn't make him understand this much, about Rio's life being in danger, then there was no hope of explaining the rest.

She watched his face as he unfolded the single sheet and scanned the page. His eyes were cloaked, guarded, revealing nothing.

Relief, joy, anger and outrage surged through his blood-stream—one after the other—as comprehension dawned. He jumped to his feet and waved the letter in front of her. "This was the errand?" he shouted. "You went to meet this…this… person. Tonight? Alone?"

Shelby nodded, nerves robbing her of her ability to speak.

"Good Lord, woman, what were you thinking!" She was curled up in the corner of the sofa, looking small and helpless, and he wanted to shake her for acting so foolishly. Instead, he pulled her into his arms and crushed her to his chest. "Why didn't you tell me? Don't you know how much I…" He started to say "love you," but he wasn't sure she was ready to hear that. He wasn't even sure he was ready to say it. "…care for you?"

He felt the flutter of lashes against his throat and then she pushed back, looking up at him, her eyes filled with hesitant hope, her smile oddly uncertain.

"You could have been killed," he rasped. His gaze focused on the large blue and purple bruise spreading across her cheek. He touched the spot with his fingertips and cursed when she flinched. He sat down on the couch, pulling her with him. "Who did this, Shelby? Tell me."

Shelby released a long breath. "His name is Thomas Nansen, and he's evil. He…he admitted following us and even listed all the places we went, so I know he wasn't making it up. He said he was after Rio's bear. He arranged for the attack outside the pediatrician's office and he confessed to stabbing you on the dock." Shelby looked away as the memory of that afternoon came back in vivid detail. "He fits the general description and I remember his eyes…" She shivered and Michael put his arm protectively around her. "It was him," she said simply, "and there's no doubt in my mind he would have killed us if he'd had the chance."

Michael took one of her hands and squeezed it gently. It was as cold as a tomb. He took the other hand and began to chafe some warmth into her freezing fingers. "Go on," he encouraged.

The caring she heard in his voice touched her more than the physical contact of their hands and Shelby drew another shaky breath. "He told me about stealing the statue and hiding it inside Rio's bear. You accidentally found it, didn't you?"

Michael nodded. "The night it was trampled at the airport."

"I guessed as much, especially since I was the one who put it back together, and there was nothing in the bear then." She pulled her hands away and turned to face him. "Michael, why didn't you do something right then? Why did you keep it?" Her hand flew to her mouth and her pale face grew whiter as realization dawned. "You thought *I* was the smuggler."

Michael's hand sought hers again, gently tightening before he answered. "Yes, I did."

At least he was honest about it. That was more than she had been. But maybe now he would understand how deadly suspicions could be. "What made you change your mind?" Her eyes came back to his as she searched his face. "Or have you?" Even now, she feared his investigators were probably digging into her past, uncovering her secrets. Secrets that she wanted to tell Michael herself.

"*You* changed my mind," he said softly, his smoky gray eyes even softer. "The way you relate to Rio...take care of him...love him." His voice was husky. "The way you are with me."

A wave of dizziness swept over her and in the distance she heard sirens, swelling louder, like orchestral violins. His arm slipped around her, pulling her unresisting body closer. His hand stroked slowly over her soft golden hair and he whispered a kiss teasingly over her mouth.

"Michael..." Her breath drew in sharply as he traced her lips with the tip of his tongue. "There's more," she gasped. "We have to talk." She could feel his restrained hunger as the kiss deepened, and she tasted him, dark, hot, insistent.

A tiny voice at the back of her brain was telling her to stop the madness, to tell him the truth now. But her heart silenced the noise, giving in to the sweet, confusing, dangerous urges he aroused.

"Shelby?"

His voice came to her in a dream as the sirens screamed louder and louder. "Hmm?"

He pulled back, his dark gaze eyeing her quizzically. "You didn't touch the statue, did you?"

Gauzy moonlight now turned red and flashing. "Of course not," Shelby protested, curling back into the warmth of his embrace. "I considered it, I even opened the case, but I couldn't bring myself to take—" He was off the couch and across the room before she could finish the sentence.

With an explosive curse, Michael ripped open a metal cabinet, nearly tearing the door off the hinges. The electronic display was ablaze with colored lights all winking and blinking. Michael's head went back, his shoulders shook, and laughter erupted in the sedate room.

Shelby struggled to her feet. "Michael?"

Her voice was soft and soothing, the kind one used on a hysterical child, and that thought alone was enough to make him double over with laughter.

"Michael, what's wrong?"

She stepped around the sofa and slowly reached for him as a half-dozen police officers burst into the room. Two of them dropped to their knees, the rest took a braced stance. "Freeze, lady," one of them barked, his gun trained directly on her.

He didn't have to say it twice. Shelby froze dead in her tracks, her face ashen white, as one of the officers came up behind her and grabbed her arm.

"It's all right," Michael said, quickly waving them off. "She works for me."

"¡Tía Shelby!" Rio bolted across the room and threw himself into Shelby's arms.

"Mr. Michael, what on earth is going on?" Mrs. Hodges appeared in the doorway wearing a chenille robe and huffing broadly, with John Callahan behind her.

"Please, everyone," Michael said. "It's all right. There was a small...malfunction...in the alarm system. The police thought someone was...breaking into my collection." He grinned at Shelby, who blanched and gripped the back of the chair for support. "Rio, come give me a hug, then let Callahan take you back to bed. Mrs. Hodges, some coffee for the patrolmen, and Sergeant, since you're here, there's a matter of great importance we need to discuss."

Having dispatched the crowd, Michael informed the officer of the stolen statue and the threats against Rio's life.

"Mr. Chandler, I'm a patrolman with the Marin County Sheriff's Department. I think this should be turned over to my lieutenant and maybe even the San Francisco Police Department. But I guarantee I can get them here."

True to his word, the lieutenant and two S.F.P.D. detectives arrived at the Chandler estate less than thirty minutes later and Michael quickly filled them in.

The lieutenant shook his head. "You took a big risk meeting this guy alone, ma'am. You should have called us the minute you received the note."

Michael cleared his throat and frowned at Shelby. "Yes, we've already been over that. What happens now?"

The detective slipped Nansen's letter into a plastic bag. "We'll have the lab check for fingerprints and any other information they can come up with. Are you two the only ones who have handled it?"

"We're the only ones who touched the letter," Shelby said. "But the envelope came through the mail, so there could be dozens of fingerprints, including those of the gate attendant and my nephew...I mean...Mr. Chandler's nephew." Shelby ventured a look at Michael, then took a deep breath and felt the color come back into her cheeks. If he had picked up on her error, he probably attributed it to her shattered nerves—which wasn't far from the truth.

The truth.

Shelby looked down at her hands clenched in her lap. She couldn't tell Michael now—not in front of all these people. Maybe after they left...

She jumped as Michael's touch branded her shoulder. "What?"

"Did Nansen set up another meeting?"

Shelby nodded. "He said to bring the statue to him tomorrow morning, nine a.m., at a deserted warehouse." She fished through her purse and pulled out the book of matches, then handed it to the officer. "This is the address."

The lieutenant looked at the address and scribbled something in his notebook. He gave the book to one of the detectives who nodded and asked permission to use the phone.

"How did you know which statue Nansen wanted?" the lieutenant asked.

"What?" Shelby looked at him blankly as though seeing him for the first time.

"Mr. Chandler has a lot of statues," he said, pointing to the collection. "How did you know which one Nansen wanted?"

Shelby bit her lower lip. "He…um…described it to me. It's fairly distinctive and quite different from the others."

The detective who had gone to the phone rejoined the group. "Ms. McMasters, we'd like you to keep your appointment tomorrow morning with Nansen."

Before she could answer, Michael's deep voice cut through the silence. "No." He stood behind Shelby with his hands on her shoulders. "Absolutely not."

"Mr. Chandler, I think you should hear us out and then let Ms. McMasters decide for herself." The detective sat down next to Shelby and spoke directly to her. "While you were talking, I ran a computer check on Nansen and your description fits. I'll be very honest with you, Thomas Nansen is about as bad as they come. He's wanted in four different states for everything from insurance fraud to armed robbery and assault with a deadly weapon. His story about Mexico checks out, too. Nansen's been working alone for the past five years, but prior to that he had a partner named Kelland. Interestingly enough, Kelland died about three months ago—in Mexico. It's just a bit too coincidental, don't you think?"

Shelby couldn't think at all. She felt as if the air had been knocked from her lungs. She gripped the edge of the sofa as the room began to spin.

"Shelby, are you all right?"

"Yes…I mean…no." She covered her eyes with a shaky hand. "It's so hot in here."

One of the officers offered her a glass of water, which she gratefully accepted. The cool water soothed her parched throat and helped clear her head.

Michael's cool fingers touched her fevered cheek. "You've been through enough tonight. You need to rest. I won't allow you to meet Nansen or anyone else tomorrow."

"No, Michael. Wait." Shelby put the glass on the coffee table. "I'd like to hear what else the detectives have to say."

The officers eyed each other in a way that made Shelby very uneasy. Finally, the lieutenant nodded and the detective continued. "Ma'am, quite frankly, you're the best chance we have of catching Nansen."

"Forget it," Michael said. "She's not going to do it."

"Ms. McMasters, we need solid proof. You would be wired for sound before your meeting with Nansen. When you get there, you would have to get him to tell you again how he stole the statue. Then, when you hand him the wrapped statue, which, by the way, would not be the real thing, the police will arrest him. What do you say?"

"Tell them no, Shelby," Michael urged, his voice close to her ear. "It's not worth the risk."

"I assure you, you will be in no danger. We will have plenty of men there to protect you."

Shelby swallowed around the lump in her throat. She didn't ever want to see Nansen again. Just thinking about him made her blood run cold. But neither could she sit around wringing her hands. In fact, the only thing she wanted to wring was Nansen's neck.

"He threatened Rio," Shelby said softly, talking more to herself than the men in the room. "He almost killed you, and he won't stop until he makes us pay. We can't live locked up on the estate. And I can't spend every minute Rio and I are off the estate, looking over my shoulder, wondering if Nansen is behind us, waiting for him to strike. I won't let him destroy us." She looked up at the officers and nodded. "I'll do it."

The detective stood up and shook her hand. "We appreciate your help. You're doing the right thing. We'll get everything set up and be back early tomorrow morning."

Michael showed them the way out, then stormed back to the library. Somehow he would change her mind, make her forget about this madness, even if he had to. . .

She was still on the sofa, right where he'd left her, with a vacant, faraway look in her eyes.

Michael crouched in front of her, taking her hands in his and forcing her to meet his gaze. "I don't like this, Shelby. I won't let them use you as bait."

Shelby saw the depth of caring in his eyes, and loved him all the more for it. "You're really worried about what Nansen might do, aren't you?"

Michael nodded, his throat too constricted to speak.

She ran her hand through his thick, soft hair and brushed the side of his cheek. He took her hand and pressed his lips to her palm in a way that made her insides turn to butter.

She pulled her hand away and stood quickly. "I'd better go," she said.

"Shelby. . ."

"You can't stop me, Michael. Don't waste your time trying."

"That's not your job, damn it. You're supposed to be here, playing with Rio or fixing his teddy bear, not hanging around a deserted warehouse trying to catch a smuggler who's handy with a knife."

"Not that handy," Shelby quipped, "or you wouldn't be standing here lecturing me."

"Shelby, this is no joke." He was angry, and worse than that, he wasn't getting through to her. "I don't like it. I don't like the idea of your being anywhere near that man again."

Shelby silenced him with a kiss, gentle and light, and meant to reassure. "When this whole thing is over, we'll celebrate." She backed away slowly and started to leave.

"Shelby, don't do it." His voice was raw and his gray eyes blazed with anger.

"Please, Michael, try to understand."

"Understand what . . . that you're willing to take a senseless risk with a man like Nansen?" He shook his head. "I'm a risk-taker, Shelby. I always have been. I know all about putting myself on the line. But not like this." He sucked in a quick breath. "Damn it, Shelby, I love you."

There. He'd said it. He'd taken the biggest risk of all, hoping, praying that she would say it back to him. An electrified silence crackled between them and pain ripped through him at her lack of response.

Shelby's stomach churned and clenched into a knot. "I'd better go," she said weakly. She turned around and headed toward the door.

He covered the distance between them in three quick strides and hauled her to him so fast, he knocked the oxygen from her lungs. His mouth slammed onto hers, making her blood race. With one arm he held her tightly around the waist, his lower body ground against hers. With his other hand he held the back of her head, so his mouth could plunder hers again and again. The pressure against her head made her neck ache, and his overpowering strength could have toppled mountains.

She should have knocked him clear into next Tuesday for such ruthless behavior, but she didn't . . . couldn't. She succumbed. She accepted his searing kiss, brutal and selfish though it was. She absorbed it, then tilted her head back even farther, inviting, welcoming, demanding more.

A kiss that started in fury, ended in passion. He was still angry, but Shelby knew it was not with her. His kiss was laced with the desperation and frustration and fear that came from caring. And when she gave herself up to him, he kissed her with consuming desire.

His mouth tore free, and they both gulped in air. Through half-open lids, Shelby gazed up at him, marveling at the depth of love she saw in his smoky gray eyes. The look he gave her was an unspoken plea, begging her to turn back from what he perceived to be madness.

She wished with all her heart he would understand. If she could get Nansen out of their lives and tell Michael the truth about her motives for becoming Rio's nanny, then there was a chance they could share a future. But until then . . .

His expression tore at her heart, and she couldn't bear to look anymore. In silence, she lowered her gaze, studying the checked pattern of his shirt.

His thumb stroked the side of her jaw. His touch was tender, his coarse voice sank to a raw whisper. "Good night, Shelby." And then he was gone.

Shelby stood in the middle of the library, staring out into the darkened hall. Like a huge wave rolling and rumbling and gathering strength out in the ocean, the emptiness crashed over her, flooding her with a soul-wrenching hurt.

Tomorrow.

She'd tell him tomorrow.

And then it would all be over.

Chapter 15

Shelby threw open the windows of Michael's study, then curled up in his leather chair and swallowed the last of the cold tea, which had been piping-hot sometime around dawn. Sleep had been impossible and she had spent the better part of the night tossing and turning and staring at the ceiling. When a lemony glow arched its way across the eastern sky, she had given up and come downstairs.

Last night's rain left a heavy, wet, clean smell in the air, and Shelby breathed in deeply. She closed her eyes and listened to the soothing liquid roar of the distant surf as it splashed against the cliffside. All she needed was for Michael to be here, to share it with her.

But he wasn't. She'd heard him leave the house early this morning, had seen him climb into the limo, had watched the car drive away. He was still angry. He had to be not to say good-bye, not to wish her luck, not to give her one of those kisses that left her breathless.

Shelby slid her hands through her hair, pulling it back from her face. He had given her one of those last night and where had it gotten him? *Nowhere,* she thought ruefully. He had even said he loved her, and her heart desperately wanted to return the words. But she couldn't. Not until all the secrets between them were out in the open. Still, she wished they could be together now. She longed to feel his strong arms around her, infusing her with his courage.

How very much her life had changed. After her parents had died, she had learned to make it on her own. She needed no one. She became strong and independent, and was proud of it—just like Michael. They were like two marble pillars standing side by side, each being pummeled by life's cold winds and fierce storms. But she was tired of standing alone, and once or twice she had leaned toward him, and felt him bending to meet her. Together they formed an arch that was much sturdier than either of them alone.

That was what this was all about—not being crushed under the weight of another, or being absorbed to the point of losing your identity, but learning to support and brace each other. She had needed that this morning, to feel close to Michael, and so she had come to his study. She ran her fingers along the arms of the chair where his muscular arms often rested. She fitted her body into the curves of his chair, snuggling against the imprint made by his own large form. The room, the desk, the chair— everything felt or smelled or was somehow part of Michael. It was a poor substitute for the real thing, but it was all she had. And somehow it would be enough to get her through the day.

The buzzer on the intercom interrupted her reverie. She leaned forward and punched the button. "Yes?"

"Ms. McMasters? This is George at the front gate. Two officers from the L.A.P.D. are here to see you."

"Send them right up," Shelby said. She clicked off the intercom and rose to meet them. From here on, there was no turning back.

The area around the warehouse was deserted as Shelby pulled the Jaguar to a stop near the entrance on the north side. The sight that greeted her chilled her to the bone. The old brick building was about three stories tall, with weeds growing up around the outside. The windows and doors had been boarded up long ago, and spray-painted graffiti covered much of it. The entire block was filled with seedy, run-down buildings, but that wasn't what scared Shelby. What frightened her the most was the feeling of utter isolation. She hadn't expected to find black-and-white police cars, but she had thought she'd see some sign of life. Instead, there was nothing—no cars, no people, not even a stray dog. She felt as though she had been dropped in the middle of a ghost town on the set of a western movie. But this was real and only her feelings for Michael prevented her from throwing the Jaguar into reverse and getting the hell out of there.

Cautiously she opened the car door and got out, clutching her shoulder bag. She started to lock the door of Michael's new car, then thought better of it. If anything went wrong, her chances of jumping into the Jaguar would be a heck of a lot better if she didn't have to fumble with finding her keys and unlocking the door.

A short burst of humorless laughter escaped from her lips, and pierced the silence of the morning. If anything *did* go wrong, her chances of getting away from Nansen, let alone making it to the car, were pretty remote.

Determined not to let Nansen see her fear, she marched boldly to the boarded-up warehouse door. She stopped short as the revolting stench of sweat and liquor assaulted her senses. Two bums slept in the doorway, an empty wine bottle between them. Slowly she began backing up, never taking her eyes off the sleeping forms. One was bareheaded and nearly bald, the other had a hat pulled down over most of his face. Both wore torn coats caked with dirt and filth.

What had possessed her to agree to do this? Gingerly she continued backing away, praying that they wouldn't wake up, that they wouldn't see her and...

The back of her leg banged against the bumper of the car and she sat down with a thump on the hood. If there were any cops listening in on the transmitter she'd been wired with this morning, they were probably grinning at her choice of words. That was assuming they could hear anything at all over the pounding of her heart.

She pushed back the cuff of her shirt and glanced at her watch. It was already after nine. Maybe he wasn't coming. She felt for the fake statue through the leather handbag and clutched it a little tighter. Maybe he knew about the police. She glanced quickly around the area. What police? There wasn't a soul around for miles... or was there?

She stared intently at a figure in the distance running toward the warehouse. Her heart rose in her throat. Maybe it was Nansen...maybe it was a cop. She held her breath as the figure swept by on the other side of the street without even a glance in her direction. It was only a jogger. Red shorts, white T-shirt, fancy running shoes and the obligatory headband marked the guy as one of those crazy people who ran for fun, not because they were scared half out of their minds. No nightstick, no gun and holster, not even a pocket in which to hide a knife.

Shelby's heart slowed and her shoulders dropped as she slumped against the car. *Wonderful,* she thought dejectedly. If she got into trouble, she could always hope the jogger would hear her screams and come running back to hit Nansen over the head with his Walkman. She glanced at her watch again. "Where are you?" she said out loud.

"Right here."

Shelby spun around at the sound of Nansen's icy voice. "I didn't see you drive up. I mean, I—I thought you'd be in a car," she stuttered.

"You thought wrong." His smile was feral. "Let's cut the pleasantries. Do you have it?"

Shelby patted her handbag. "Yes, it's right here." She glanced furtively around the area. Were they here? Could they hear this? She didn't want to get close enough to Nansen for him to spot the microphone, but she didn't want to be so far away that the police couldn't hear what he was saying.

"What are you looking for?" he asked roughly.

"Nothing. I'm just nervous, that's all."

"So hand it over and I'll be on my way." He reached for her handbag and she shrunk back.

"What guarantee do I have that you'll leave me alone?"

"What guarantee do I have that you even have the statue?"

Without taking her eyes off him, Shelby unzipped her shoulder bag and retrieved the figure wrapped in cloth. Nansen's eyes gleamed with avaricious delight, then hardened again as she slipped the covered statue back into her purse. "I risked everything bringing this statue here." The words tasted sour in her mouth. Another half-truth. She was becoming disgustingly good at telling lies. "I'm sick of jeopardizing my future for scum like you." That much was pure truth, and so help her God, if she ever got out of this mess, she would go straight home to Michael and tell him everything, *everything*. And she'd never lie to anyone again.

"Well, isn't that the pot calling the kettle black?" Nansen scoffed. "Seems to me we're two of a kind. I stole the statue from the dig and you stole it from Chandler. That makes you no better than I. Now hand it over."

"No," Shelby said. Where were they? Didn't they hear that? He admitted stealing it from the dig. What were they waiting for? And then she spotted something. "We've got company," she said quickly, half under her breath.

Nansen jerked his gaze to the sidewalk, where an old woman was walking an even older terrier. Images of people looking like their dogs sprang into Shelby's mind as she watched the gray-haired lady, her shoulders hunched forward, wobble down the sidewalk with her equally gray-haired and wobbly dog.

Shelby wanted to laugh—not because the scene was so comical, but because her own situation was so pathetic, and at the moment, laughing seemed eminently preferable to crying. She hugged her purse and watched as the twosome disappeared around a corner.

"All right, Shelby, they're gone. Now quit stalling. I want that statue. I already told you, I have an acquaintance who has set aside a very large sum of money with my name on it. After I give him that Mayan statue, I'm going to take a nice long vacation."

Out of the corner of her eye, Shelby noticed the two bums were no longer asleep. They were watching the scene with open curiosity and now one of them had struggled to his feet.

It was time to get out of here. Something must have gone wrong with the wiring system. If there had been any police listening to the conversation, they surely would have grabbed Nansen by now.

"And what about Michael and Rio?" Shelby asked, edging toward the car door. "I want your word that you won't try to hurt them ever again."

"My word?" Nansen's laugh was short and derisive. "As long as you do what I say, he and the kid will be just fine."

"Hey, mister." One of the bums staggered toward them. This was her chance. Nansen was distracted. If she could get to the car . . .

"Can you spare a few do-dollars? My buddy here n-needs a drink." He stumbled into Nansen, who shoved him easily aside.

"Get lost," Nansen snarled. He spun around as Shelby bolted for the car. He was faster. "Where the hell do you think you're going?'' He ripped the bag from her shoulder and seized the figure. The cloth fell away, revealing a phony statue. "What the... Why, you double-crossing bitch!"

A small cry emerged from her throat as he grabbed her arm and threw her to the ground. In a split second, thick hands encircled her throat... tightening... choking. Desperately, she clawed at the hands, trying to gulp air into her oxygen-starved lungs.

Michael. Her heart cried out to him and, in her mind, she saw him running toward her. The fingers constricted another notch and she felt herself slipping into blackness.

And then she was free.

The stench of liquor and sweat enveloped her as the bum with the thinning hair helped her to her feet. The shrill whine of sirens hurt her ears and, in a daze, she watched as the jogger tried to stop Michael from battering Nansen.

Jogger?

Michael?

Nansen lay on the ground, curled into a tight ball, clutching his stomach and coughing. Blood trickled from his nose and he whimpered like a whipped dog.

Shelby swayed unsteadily and would have toppled if the bum beside her had not held her upright.

Michael shook off the restraining arms of the jogger. "Get up, Nansen," he barked to the figure on the ground. "I'm not finished with you yet."

Nansen struggled to his feet and took a wild swing, which Michael neatly deflected. Then he drew back his arm, and with one swift blow knocked Nansen senseless to the ground.

"Michael?" Shelby touched his arm and he turned to find the tears streaming down her cheeks. As if she couldn't trust her eyes, she moved her fingers over his chest, across his shoulders, one now aching from the fight, and stroked the quill-like bristles on his cheek and jaw. "Oh, Michael," she said through her sobs. She threw herself into his arms and buried her face in the torn and smelly coat.

He held her. Her body fit snugly against his own and he wanted to hold her like this forever. He wanted to kiss her and caress her and love her. His lips brushed her hair, her temple, her face.

She opened her eyes and tipped her head back to look at him, to make sure, and her words tumbled out in a rush. "It's really you, isn't it? How did you get here? Why didn't you tell me?'' Her nose wrinkled as the offensive odors invaded her senses, removing the last vestiges of doubt that this was a dream. ''Michael, you smell!''

He threw back his head and laughed, hard and long, an explosion of all the tension that had been building inside him since last night. ''Don't you like it?'' He held open the coat and pirouetted to give her the full effect. ''It's the very latest in police undercover wear.''

Shelby waved her hand in front of her face. ''Don't spread it around,'' she said, laughing so hard the tears ran down her face. ''It makes my eyes water.''

''Nice work, Ms. McMasters.'' A police officer handed her the purse, which had been dropped in the scuffle, and Shelby sobered at the sight of Nansen being put in the back seat of a black-and-white police car.

''Were you able to hear him?'' she asked the officer.

''Every word. We have enough evidence to convict Nansen on charges of grand theft, smuggling, extortion, assault with a deadly weapon and maybe even attempted murder.'' He pointed to the ugly red swollen marks on Shelby's neck. ''You might want to have that looked at by a doctor.'' He turned and offered Michael his hand. ''Thanks for your help, Mr. Chandler.''

Michael took the hand and shook it warmly. ''My pleasure. Oh, and here...'' He shrugged out of the heavy overcoat and returned it to the officer. ''I won't be needing this anymore.''

The officer grinned. ''You sure? If you want, you can keep it as a souvenir.''

Michael shook his head. ''Thanks, but no thanks. We've got plenty of memories. In fact,'' he said, dropping his arm around Shelby's shoulders and pulling her close, ''I think it's time we put a few of those memories behind us, and start some new ones.''

They watched in silence as the officers climbed into the police cars and disappeared down the street. ''Come on,'' Michael said, leading her toward the Jaguar. ''Let's go home.''

''I couldn't believe you were there,'' Shelby said.

''I couldn't believe you took my Jaguar again,'' Michael groused good-naturedly. ''Every time I turn around, you're running off in *my* car." He rubbed his hair vigorously with a towel, then tossed it carelessly on top of his desk in the library. He settled his large form on one end of the sofa, and patted the cushion beside him.

"So then what happened?" Shelby asked, snuggling into the arms of her clean-smelling, freshly shaven hero.

"Well, there was no way I was going to stay here while you risked your life with that creep. So I told the police I was going to be at the warehouse either with or without their permission." He dropped a light kiss on her forehead. "After a few minutes, they were persuaded it would be smarter to make me part of their plan instead of running the risk of having me ruin it. By eight-fifteen, Officer O'Connor and I were lying in the doorway waiting for you."

"And the jogger?"

"He was another cop who was sent around to watch for Nansen. He was also wired and his Walkman was really a transmitter. We knew Nansen had arrived before you did."

Shelby shook her head, clearly impressed. "And the old lady with the arthritic dog?"

Michael chuckled. "She was a fluke, but her timing was perfect. Wherever she and her dog are, they have my blessing. I hope they both live to be a hundred."

"Amen."

Silence settled around them and for a long moment neither of them spoke. "You're awfully quiet," Michael said stroking her hair. "Is something wrong?"

Shelby hesitated before answering. "I was remembering what happened. If you hadn't gotten to Nansen when you did, he might have killed me," she said softly, fingering the red welts on her neck. "You saved my life."

Her words died in her throat as he gently stroked her cheek. "That works both ways. If you hadn't knocked the knife out of Nansen's hand, he would have killed me on the dock. You saved my life, too." He sat up suddenly and propped his elbow on the back of the sofa, resting his head against his hand. "Do you realize what that means?"

"We cancel each other out?" Shelby teased.

Michael shook his head. "An old Chinese prophet once said if you save someone's life, you're responsible for that person forever."

"Is that so?" she asked with feigned innocence.

"Scout's honor," he quipped. He made an X across his chest and held up two fingers.

"You were never a Scout."

"That's beside the point." He drew her back into the warmth of his arms and ringed a necklace of kisses along her jawline.

"You also don't know any old Chinese prophets."

"You're changing the subject." His mouth covered hers in a kiss that affirmed what they'd almost lost. He pulled her tight against him as if trying to absorb her body into his. He kissed her with a raw hunger that left her weak. The taste of his lips and tongue was fiery and sweet, and she sagged against him in surrender.

"Forever?" she murmured.

"Uh-huh."

Her arms wrapped around his chest and her cheek found a natural pillow in his shoulder. "I could get used to that."

He drew back suddenly and gripped her forearms with his hands. "Could you, Shelby?" His tone was needy and desperate, almost sharp, as he forced her to look at him.

"Wh-what?"

"Could you get used to spending forever here, with me?"

It was the moment she had been longing for and dreading at the same time. She put a trembling hand against his chest, keeping a small distance between them. "Michael, there are a lot of things you don't know about me—"

"I know everything that matters. I love you, and I think you love me." Michael Chandler, the last of the loners, formed the words that he had carefully avoided and flatly refused to say to anyone else for the last decade. "Will you marry me?"

What had started out as an opportunity to spy on Michael Chandler had turned into something so much more. Shelby couldn't ever imagine leaving this place, the place she now called home. Living with Michael had given her a sense of permanence and oneness. His was the first face she wanted to see in the morning and the last face she wanted to see at night.

Being with him was like celebrating the Fourth of July every day of the year, full of skyrockets and fireworks, and she had never realized her heart was capable of such overpowering feelings. Even though she had never said it out loud, the simple truth was she loved him.

"Shelby?" She raised her head to look at him. His face betrayed no emotion, but there was an anxiousness in his dark gray eyes and his powerful shoulders were tense.

She took a deep breath. "We need to talk."

"We'll have the rest of our lives to talk if you'll just say yes. I can't take this suspense. Please, give me an answer."

"Yes, but—"

"Yes? Really?"

"Yes, really, but—"

He let out a whoop that could be heard halfway to the Bay. Pulling her up from the sofa, he swung her around in his arms, and when he set her down she was breathless. "We need to celebrate," he said, pulling two champagne glasses from the bar. "We'll do it right. I'll make reservations tonight at Stars and we'll get all dressed up." He removed a bottle of champagne and unwound the wire from the plastic cork.

"Michael, please wait a minute."

A loud pop was accompanied by a bubbly fizz. "And a ring. First thing tomorrow morning we'll go looking for a ring." He poured the effervescent liquid into two glasses.

"Michael . . ."

He handed her a glass, then clinked his own against it. "And Rio," he said, after swallowing a large sip. "We've got to tell Rio. Just think, before long, his 'aunt' and uncle will be his mom and dad."

Shelby put her glass on the table. "That's what I want to talk about. I want to tell you about Rio and me."

"Mr. Michael?" Mrs. Hodges poked her head around the library door. "Mr. Sid's here to see you."

"Sid! Come on in." Michael sprinted across the room and grabbed his old friend by the elbow. "You're just in time to help us celebrate. This charming and beautiful young woman has just agreed to marry yours truly. What do you think of that?"

"I think you'd better sit down, Michael," Sid said, his eyes narrowing as he studied Shelby.

"Look, Sid, if this is about that Tokyo company . . ."

"It's not about Tokyo . . . it's about your nephew." He threw an envelope on Michael's desk. "A petition has been filed opposing your request for permanent guardianship of Rio."

Michael's drink stalled halfway to his mouth. "Who filed it?"

"His aunt," Sid said, "Shelby Kelland."

Chapter 16

Dread exploded in Michael's chest and he braced his hands on the bar for support. His mind knew the answer before his mouth could ask the question. His voice was a strangled whisper. "What did you say?"

A tomblike silence settled over the group.

"Answer me, damn it!" The thundering order was directed to Sid, but Michael never took his eyes off Shelby. A moment ago her eyes were bright and animated, her color high. Now she stood there trembling, eyes wide and helpless. Guilt and shame were written all over her face.

Sid picked up the document he had thrown on the desk. "According to the petition filed by her attorney, Shelby Kelland claims her brother, Lincoln Mark Kelland, was Rio's father..."

Panic gripped Shelby's heart. "Please, Michael, I can explain..."

"It further states that she is seeking guardianship of the child based on the fact that she is Rio's natural aunt, she is bilingual and she is able to provide the nurturing love and caring that a young child needs..."

"You don't understand..."

"... and she further questions your fitness to be appointed guardian because of your recent involvement in the smuggling of Mexican artifacts."

Michael's voice was strangled with pain, his face contorted with betrayal. "You lied to me."

"No, Michael—"

"No?"

"I mean, yes." The rage and hatred blazing from his eyes terrified her. "Please," she implored, "let me explain."

"Explain what?" His right hand curled and uncurled into a fist at his side. "Kelland was your brother. You knew he and Nansen were partners, didn't you?" He slammed his fist onto the bar. "Didn't you!"

Shelby nodded, too weak to answer.

"Lies, all lies. You could have told me the truth that day on the boat when we were talking about your real name. Instead, you joked about it. You thought it was funny." The champagne glass was still clenched in his hand, and he squeezed harder, sending the anger and bitterness shooting down his arm until the glass shattered in his hand. Shards of glass and drops of blood spilled onto the carpet, but Michael didn't notice.

"I was going to tell you, Michael," she cried, genuinely alarmed at the callousness she saw in his eyes. "Honestly."

"Honestly?" Michael repeated with jeering sarcasm. "When, Shelby?" he asked scathingly. "When? After we were married?"

"No, that's not how it was." Feverishly she tried to explain. "I hired the attorney because I really believed you weren't the right person to raise Rio. But when I got to know you, I realized I was wrong. You would make a great father. You *are* a great father." She reached for his arm, but he jerked back, recoiling at her touch.

"That's it, isn't it?" he asked as another, more devastating thought racked him. The rage drained from his face and was replaced by bitter contempt. "Why risk losing a court battle when there was another, easier way to get what you wanted?"

"I don't understand," Shelby said hesitantly.

"Don't you?" His scathing look quelled her. "Admit it, lady, the easiest way to insure your getting Rio was to marry me."

"No, Michael! That's not it at all." Her chest and shoulders heaved with silent, choking sobs. "I love you."

There it was. The words he had waited to hear. But they were too late. His eyes were like chips of gray ice and his voice cracked like a whip. "You're a liar." He sat down at his desk and opened the center drawer.

"No, Michael," she begged wildly, "don't say that. Think about us. Think about Rio."

"There is no 'us,'" he said coldly, slamming the drawer closed. "And I *am* thinking about Rio. You lied to me from the first day you walked into my office, and *you* are the one who is unfit to raise a child. If you persist in trying to get guardianship of Rio, we will fight it out in court. But I will tell you right now, you don't stand a snowball's chance in hell. And I'll never let you near Rio again." He finished scribbling out a check and tore it from the register. "You're fired," he said silkily, his face a controlled mask, void of emotion. "I'll call you a taxi. You've got thirty minutes to pack your things. Consider this your severance pay." He stuffed the check into her hand and strode quickly toward the door. His voice was like an icicle as he wrenched it open. "Now get out."

Shelby tried to swallow the lump of desolation that stuck in her throat. She looked down at the check in her hand, and a single tear dropped from her cheek and plopped onto the paper. Through pain-dazed eyes she watched as the salty liquid swirled the blue ink on one of the digits in the ridiculously large number. Mesmerized, she watched the ink bleed and run until all that remained of the once crisp digit was a lifeless blob. Slowly she raised her head. Mustering every ounce of dignity at her command, she crossed the room and stopped directly in front of Michael.

"I made only one mistake, Michael, and it wasn't lying. Under the same circumstances, I would do the same thing all over again. My only mistake was in not telling you sooner. I think it would have made a big difference to both of us—but...but..." For a moment her composure slipped a notch and a cache of tears threatened to spill onto her cheeks. "...but now we'll never know." She blinked back the tears and surrounded her heart with a blessed numbness.

"As for this," she said, holding out the check with a trembling hand, "I don't need or want your money, and, for that matter, neither does Rio. He just needs your love."

So do I, screamed her heart. But no one heard it.

With frozen hands, she tore the check into a dozen little pieces that, mingled with the torn remnants of her heart, fluttered to the floor at Michael's feet.

"Don't let your hatred of me get in the way of your love for Rio. It's too big a price to pay, and it may be the only thing in the world you can't afford."

She turned and walked out of the library, never looking back.

Michael slammed the door closed behind her and headed for the bar. He pushed aside the bottle of champagne that was supposed to be a celebration of his engagement and reached instead for a bottle of scotch.

"That's not going to help."

Michael looked up, surprised to see Sid still there. "Go home, Sid," he said woodenly. "You've done your duty."

"I'm not so sure." Sid crossed the room and leaned against the bar, watching Michael pour the scotch into a glass.

"No? You stopped me from once again making a fool of myself with a woman." He threw the scalding liquid down his throat. "I should have listened to you years ago when you warned me about Gina. But don't worry, I never make the same mistake twice. I'm indebted to you for pointing out the truth." Michael laughed bitterly at his own use of the word. "I was so damned sure that I'd finally found someone who didn't want me for my money, and what happens? Turns out she wants me for my nephew. Isn't that rich?" Another humorless laugh broke from his lips. "Rich, get it?" He reached for the bottle, but Sid beat him to it.

"You're a real comedian," Sid said, shoving the bottle out of Michael's grasp. "But you don't need this. And furthermore, I'm not sure I did you any favor. I watched her the whole time. She was as hurt by this as you were. I think she really loves you."

Michael's oath was pithy and eloquent. "You don't betray the trust of people you love. You don't lie to them and play them for a fool. There's only one thing she wants—Rio—and damn it, she's not going to get him." He stuck his hand under the faucet and winced as the water stung the cuts. He draped the damp towel around his hand and headed for the door.

"Where are you going?" Sid asked his friend.

"I'm going to have Pasig take me to the doctor and get this hand cleaned up. Then I'm going to hire an army of private detectives to investigate every aspect of the life of Ms. Shelby

McMasters Kelland...or whatever the hell her name is. I want to know everything that ever happened to that bitch. By the time I'm through with her, there won't be a skeleton left to rattle in her closet. We'll see who's fit to be Rio's guardian."

"What about your staff? What are you going to tell them?"

"You talk to them. Tell them the truth. Tell them we've all been taken in by a lying, deceitful fraud."

"And Rio?"

Michael's face and voice softened at the mention of his nephew. The child had already endured more tragedy than most people suffered in a lifetime. It would be devastating for him to lose Shelby, too, but eventually he would get over it, and in the long run, he'd be better off without her. "I'll talk to him myself when I get back," Michael said quietly. The fierceness in his voice quickly reappeared as he remembered who was responsible for Rio's latest pain. "In the meantime, I want you to call a cab and see that she gets in it." He felt the anger surging through his limbs again and he wrapped the towel more tightly around his hand, making it look like a large red mitten—and making it less likely that he would do anything else stupid. He issued Sid a final warning before storming out of the house. "Just make sure every trace of her is off this property by the time I get back."

Shelby closed the lid of her suitcase and snapped the locks. The resounding click echoed in the empty room, forcing home the finality of what was happening. She dragged the suitcase off the bed and put it with the other one next to the door. In a few more minutes she would be gone and this part of her life would be reduced to memories. She looked slowly around the room, memorizing every detail—the lemon-yellow wallpaper and pristine white curtains, the dark walnut furniture, the sunlight streaming through the windows that looked out over the back lawn.

She had made such a mess of things. Any chance of explaining to Michael her reasons for lying to him had disappeared the moment Sid revealed she was Shelby Kelland. If only she had told him the truth the day they went boating. If only she hadn't been so afraid of losing the best thing that had ever happened to her.

But all the "if onlys" in the world wouldn't chase away the pain that was steadily gnawing at her heart. God help her, she loved him—loved him with a passion she never knew she had—loved a man who despised her for her treachery and deceit. Tears formed in her eyes and blinded her. She had to get out of here now, before her body collapsed along with her world.

"¿Tía Shelby?"

She dashed the tears away with the back of her hand and turned to face the child who had given her the happiest moments of her life. Never would she forget their time together. Always would she regret her part in bringing that to an end. Michael had sworn she would never see Rio again, and she had no doubt he would make good on that promise.

"What are you doing?"

Every feature of Rio's face, every golden curl, every gesture, every look, was permanently etched in her mind. Right now, the wide-eyed expression of fear preyed upon his young face. It was painfully clear that he already understood she was leaving. She opened her arms and he ran to her, hugging her fiercely.

He pulled back suddenly and looked up at her with eyes the color of thick, heavy fog, filled with pain and fear and looking just like Michael's. "Don't go," he begged. "Please don't go."

"I have to, honey."

"Why? Don't you love me anymore?"

Shelby swallowed back the tears. How could she explain to a child what she barely understood herself? She wrapped her arms around Rio and pulled him close, burying her face in his soft blond hair. "I'll always love you," she said simply, as the throbbing ache in her heart began again.

"Then why are you going away?"

She sat down on the bed and held Rio on her lap. "Because I did something that I shouldn't have done. I lied to your Uncle Michael and now he is very angry with me."

"That's all?"

The innocence of his words crushed her. "I lied a lot, about many different things, and I'm afraid I hurt your Uncle Michael very much."

"You could tell him you're sorry and not do it anymore."

Shelby smiled at Rio's wonderfully innocent vision of life. If only adults could see their problems through the eyes of a child.

"I wish it were that easy, honey. But once you start lying to people, they don't trust you anymore. I could promise never to do it again, but how would Uncle Michael know that I'm not telling another lie?"

Rio's small forehead wrinkled as he considered the dilemma. It was apparent from the look on his face that he couldn't come up with an acceptable solution. "So he's making you go away?"

Shelby chose her words carefully. Rio was going to have to stay with Michael and they had already formed a wonderful relationship. She didn't want to say anything to jeopardize that, or to instill a fear in Rio that if he did something wrong, Michael would send him away, too.

"Rio, I want you to listen carefully to what I'm going to say, and try to understand. Lying was only the first mistake I made. Everyone makes mistakes from time to time—you, me, even Uncle Michael. But when you do something wrong, you have to go to the person and explain what happened, tell the person why you did it and say you're sorry."

Rio's eyes were wide, his face solemn. "Didn't you do that?"

Shelby shook her head. "I made an even bigger mistake by trying to cover it up. Someone else found out what I had done and then told Uncle Michael. It would have been so much better if I had told him myself." The words stuck in her throat.

"I'm going, too."

The fierceness in his young voice alarmed her. No matter what she said, Michael was going to have his hands full. "You can't, honey."

"Why not?" He eyed her slightly bulging suitcases with skepticism. "I won't bring much. Just my teddy."

Shelby felt what was left of her heart shatter into a million pieces. "It's not that I don't want you with me. I do, more than anything. But I don't have a place to live yet, and I'll have to get a job. You already have a lovely place to live, with toys and books and a jungle gym and a Big Wheel. If you go, your Uncle Michael will miss you very much, and think about John and Pasig and Mrs. Hodges—they'd be very lonely without you here."

Rio looked down at the carpet for a long time. The topic Shelby had been dreading finally surfaced. "Will you ever come back?" he asked softly.

She took a deep breath. "I'd like to come back and visit sometime, but I don't know when that will be."

John Callahan appeared in the doorway. "Shelby, Sid Bryce is downstairs. He said to tell you the taxi's here." He looked from her face to the two suitcases and back again. "What's going on?"

"I have to go," she said simply. "Could you help me carry my bags downstairs?"

Denial replaced the shock on the younger man's face. "But—"

"Not now, John," Shelby interrupted. She inclined her head toward Rio, who had backed away into a corner of the room, and was standing there trying hard not to cry. "Please tell Mr. Bryce I'll be right down."

After a moment's hesitation, John nodded mutely, then picked up Shelby's bags and disappeared down the hall.

"I have to go now, Rio." She held out her hand to him. "Will you walk downstairs with me?"

Wordlessly, he took her hand and together they left the bedroom. Before they even reached the landing, Mrs. Hodges's stern and heavily accented voice drifted up to them.

"I don't care what you say, I won't believe a word of it. Not one word. It's all a mistake, I tell you." She planted one hand on her portly hip and shook the other one under the attorney's nose. "Mr. Michael's taken leave of his senses, that's what, and I'm going to tell him so as soon as he gets back." She stopped abruptly as Shelby and Rio reached the bottom of the stairs. Her face was flushed with anger and there was a determined set to her chin.

Shelby let go of Rio's hand and hugged the housekeeper. "You've been very good to me, Mrs. Hodges, and I appreciate your wanting to help, but in Michael's current frame of mind, he's angry enough to fire you and Jules and everyone else. I wouldn't want that. I'd feel better knowing you were still here to keep an eye on Rio. Promise me you'll do that."

The woman's frown shifted to a faint smile and she dabbed her eyes with the edge of her apron. "Aye, I'll take care of him, and Mr. Michael, too. But I don't mind telling you it's going to be mighty lonesome around here without you."

Shelby nodded and glanced at the attorney.

"Ms. Kelland . . ."

"Please don't apologize, Mr. Bryce. You were doing your job and I don't fault you for that. But you don't know me very well, because if you did, you would realize I never intended to hurt Michael. I had hoped to tell him before the day was over, and whether or not you believe me, that's the truth."

Finally, she turned to Rio who was again backing away from the little group. She stooped down in front of him and held both his small hands in hers. "Goodbye, honey," she said as tears stung the inside of her eyelids. "Be a good boy for Mrs. Hodges, and keep an eye on your Uncle Michael for me, okay?"

Rio nodded and looked down at his feet.

"I love you, Rio." Shelby gave him one last hug and kiss, then fled through the door and down the steps to the waiting taxi. As the cab pulled away from the house and started down the long driveway, Shelby heard a noise and turned to see Rio chasing after the taxi. With tears in her eyes, she watched as John swept him into his arms and held him tight with one hand while waving with the other. Rio stopped his struggling and also began frantically waving. Shelby waved and blew him a kiss...then the car rounded a curve and they disappeared from view.

Slowly, she turned around in the seat and faced front again. George had the gates open, and the cab rolled through. Shelby felt rather than heard the gates click shut behind them.

"Where to, miss?"

She had never grieved when her parents died—she'd had to be strong for her little brother. And when Linc had been killed in the bus accident, she had been too busy trying to get Rio to take the time to mourn. Now she had all the time in the world. Her life stretched out before her like a deserted road. She had no place to go...nothing to do...no one who cared.

The driver cleared his throat. "Miss?"

"I don't know...anywhere. It doesn't matter," she said dejectedly. "Just keep driving."

The shock was wearing off and an intense and overwhelming sense of loss was setting in. There were only two people in the world she loved—two people for whom she would have gladly given up her career, her dreams, her very life.

One of them now despised her. And, because of that, the other one would be kept from her forever. The dream of a fu-

ture with Michael and Rio, filled with joy and laughter and
magic and romance had suddenly vanished.

And that's when the tears began.

In the last month, Michael had ripped everything to do with
Shelby out of his life. He tore down her swimming pool fence
and installed his own. He replaced the carpeting and the wallpaper in her yellow-and-white bedroom and made the decora-
tor redo the room in brown. He even sold the Jaguar because
every time he drove it, he swore the scent of her perfume still
lingered—even though everyone else said the only odor *they*
smelled was the disinfectant he had made Pasig use on the car,
every day for a week. He threw out everything she had ever
touched or admired. He erased every shred of her from the estate . . . but he couldn't tear her out of his mind.

The other day, he had been at a directors' meeting at the
Wells Fargo Bank in downtown San Francisco, and suddenly
he'd heard a woman laugh. It was Shelby's laugh—light and
musical—and he had leaped out of his chair and flung open the
door of the boardroom. Two secretaries had turned their
stunned faces to stare at him, and when he realized it wasn't
Shelby, his heart had sunk.

Today he stood in his own office looking out over the blue-
green water of San Francisco Bay. This was where he'd stood
four months ago when Sid had first told him he'd been granted
temporary custody of Rio.

Rio. Poor Rio. So many losses in such a short time. Michael
had suspected Rio would react strongly to Shelby's departure.
He had expected him to cry and scream and lash out the way he
had the night he lost his teddy bear. But there had been none of
that. Rio was quiet and somber—almost morose. He spoke
very little, and what little he did say was usually in Spanish.
Michael had tried to engage him in games and outings, but Rio
was wholly disinterested. According to Mrs. Hodges, he spent
most of the day in his room looking at books or playing quietly with his dinosaurs.

He couldn't forget Shelby, either.

From his office window, Michael watched the tiny white tri-
angles bobbing up and down on the water. It was perfect boating weather, and the Bay was dotted with an incredible
assortment of vessels. He hadn't put out to sea since the inci-

dent at the yacht club, and he didn't relish the flood of memories that being there would bring back. But he had put it off far too long. He and Rio both needed a vacation, and as soon as this hearing was over, he was going to take Rio boating.

A gentle knock on the door was followed by Sid's gravelly voice. "Are you ready for this, Michael?"

Michael turned from the window, straightened his tie and buttoned the two buttons of his dark blue suit jacket. "As ready as I need to be," he answered smoothly. "After all, you're the one who's doing all the work."

Sid made himself comfortable in one of the chairs facing the desk, ignoring Michael's impatient look.

"Shouldn't we be going?"

"We have plenty of time before the hearing, and there are a few final points I want to cover with you."

Michael scowled. He knew damn well what Sid wanted to talk about. Sid wanted to talk about her. The last time Sid had started in on him, Michael had threatened to ram his fist down Sid's throat. "If you're going to give me another lecture on misunderstandings and forgiveness and second chances—"

"I wouldn't waste my breath," Sid retorted. "I just want to go over a few topics that may come up at the hearing."

"Fine," Michael said tersely.

Sid pulled a pad from his briefcase and scribbled down a few notes. "First, have you hired a new nanny?"

Michael turned toward the window. "No."

"No? Michael, you've had a whole month. You found Shelby in less than a week."

"Right," Michael said bitterly. "And look what a great job I did on that one. I'm being more careful this time."

"Careful is fine, but one of the things the judge will want to know is if you can provide the proper care for Rio. Have you interviewed anyone?"

Michael picked up a stack of twenty files off the credenza and threw them onto his desk. "I've seen them all," he said sullenly. "They're not right for the job."

"Not right for the job?" Sid picked up a handful of files and flipped through them. "What's wrong with this one?" he asked, shoving a résumé across the desk in Michael's direction.

Michael gave it a cursory glance. "She was too old."

"And this one?"

"Lousy sense of humor."

"And this one?"

"Her Spanish was weak."

Sid's jaw dropped open. "Michael, her previous experience includes working as a translator at the U.N. Her Spanish can't be *that* weak." Exasperated, Sid closed all the files and shoved them aside. "You wouldn't hire Mary Poppins if she walked through that door." The normally soft-spoken man fairly shouted at his friend. "Admit it, Michael. You're not looking for a nanny. You're looking for another Shelby McMasters. But she's gone, and you're too pigheaded to do anything about it."

"We've been over this before," Michael said in a low, deadly voice. "And I've told you *exactly* what I want done. I want that woman publicly flogged. I want every tidbit of her life laid out for public display, and I want to make damn sure the judge awards me sole and permanent guardianship of Rio." He ripped open the buttons on his suit jacket and sat down behind the desk.

Sid sighed and his voice dropped to its normal level. "No one can guarantee how a judge will rule. But I've already told you that, in my professional opinion, you *will* be appointed as Rio's permanent guardian. I also appreciate the fact that you have been deeply hurt by her betrayal." He held up his hand as Michael started to protest. "However, if you persist in name-calling, mud-slinging or slanderous behavior, you will only harm yourself." Sid stood and slapped a file on Michael's desk.

"I've been over this investigator's report a dozen times, and there's nothing here...*nothing*...that will strengthen your case. She was a model teenager, which is an aberration in itself. She put herself through college after her parents died. She is a dedicated archaeologist and a staunch supporter of preserving the histories of lost civilizations. In short, she has led an exemplary, albeit solitary, life until the day she walked into your office with falsified credentials certifying her as a professional nanny. If you try to attack her in court, you will end up looking stupid and petty."

A muscle clenched in Michael's jaw. "And what if she attacks me? What if she brings up that mess about smuggling artifacts?"

"I seriously doubt that's going to happen. The police have Nansen's taped confession, and if I have to, I'll subpoena him from his jail cell. He's so mad at Shelby, I guarantee he'll testify you had nothing to do with the smuggling."

Unconvinced, Michael pushed himself to his feet and began pacing the room.

"Please, Michael. As your attorney and your friend, please listen to me. When you get into the courtroom, sit there with your mouth shut. Don't say a word unless you are asked a question, and then answer it as succinctly as possible."

"I'm convinced she's up to something. She wants Rio and she'll stop at nothing to get him. I don't trust her, Sid."

"I know that, and I think you're dead wrong. I think she really loves you and you're too damn stubborn or too afraid to admit that you care for her, too." He paused, but a stony silence greeted him. "Talk to her, Michael," Sid begged. "Talk to her before we go into court. Tell her how you feel. Give her a chance to make it up to you, now, before it's too late. Damn it man, don't throw it all away."

But it was already too late. There was too much between them—too many angry words and bitter feelings. It was over, and it was best left that way.

Sid rose from his seat and shook his head. "Okay, my friend. Let's get this over with."

Michael sat in the courtroom at a table next to Sid, his heart hammering uncontrollably in his chest. He glanced over his shoulder at the crowd filing in. There were a bunch of reporters and a couple of artists with sketch pads and a whole roomful of nosy onlookers.

But no sign of Shelby.

The table across the way was empty. No doubt she and her attorney were waiting to make a grand entrance, he thought grimly. His eyes riveted on the back door as he watched for her. What would she be wearing? Maybe the plain red knit dress with the wide belt—no, too flashy for court. No doubt she would wear the suit she had worn the day she interviewed at his office. He remembered clearly the slim, navy blue skirt that emphasized her long, shapely legs, and the prim, ascot-style blouse that accentuated the curves of her breasts. He remembered the long, golden honey-colored curls that were pulled back in an intricate braid. He remembered her eyes so blue that a man could lose himself in them, and a smile that seemed to glow from the inside out.

"Are you all right?" Sid asked.

"I'm fine," Michael lied, refusing to admit to any of the anguish he felt.

Sid inclined his head toward a small man with glasses who had pushed his way through the crowd and was now sitting down at the table across from them. "Looks like we're ready to start."

Where was she? Why wasn't she with her attorney? Michael jerked around in his seat and searched the crowd for that achingly familiar form who haunted his dreams nightly. A feeling of apprehension coursed through his body.

"All rise."

The judge took the bench and the clerk announced the case and the names of the parties involved.

"Mr. Bryce," said the judge, "are you and your client ready?"

Sid stood. "We are, Your Honor."

"And you, Mr. Whittaker? Are you and your client ready?"

The small man stood and straightened his glasses on the bridge of his nose. "Your Honor, after working for the petitioner for over two months, my client, Shelby Kelland, believes Mr. Chandler is a fit and proper person to raise a child, and that he has only the child's best interests and welfare at heart. My client has therefore directed me to withdraw her petition, and she respectfully requests that the court place the child known as Rio in the permanent guardianship of his uncle, Michael Chandler."

Chapter 17

A loud murmur hummed through the courtroom and the judge banged his gavel on the desk. "This court will come to order or all spectators will be removed." When the courtroom was again quiet, the judge addressed the attorney. "Mr. Whittaker, do I understand that your client is no longer seeking guardianship of the child?"

"That is correct, Your Honor. Ms. Kelland believes Mr. Chandler will be better able to provide the necessary care for her nephew."

The buzz of voices filled Michael's head again and left him hypnotized. For the next thirty minutes, he sat transfixed, answering questions with robotlike automation.

And then it was over. Rio was his. No one could ever separate them. The spectators filed out of the courtroom and Michael watched in stunned silence as Sid gathered all his documents and returned them to the briefcase.

"Congratulations," Sid said without much enthusiasm. He stood and closed the lid of his briefcase. "You got what you wanted." He clicked the locks with a deadly finality and stalked out of the room.

Michael stared blankly at the retreating figure. Sid was right. He had gotten what he wanted. He'd won. So why didn't he feel triumphant? Why couldn't he gloat and celebrate? He'd beaten her—so why did he feel so defeated?

Because, in fact, he'd lost. He'd lost his heart, lost the part of him that had come alive when he was with Shelby. He'd lost the one thing that mattered more to him than life itself. He'd lost her.

Until now, he hadn't realized how much he wanted to see her again. Why hadn't she shown up today? Why hadn't she fought for Rio? Why had she turned tail and run? Run out on him like everyone else had. He dismissed the thoughts as quickly as they entered his head. Shelby wasn't anything like the others. With astounding clarity he understood the fallacy of his thinking. His father was a good-for-nothing drunk who didn't deserve the time of day, and Gina wasn't much better. They had stripped him apart as if they'd been pulling bark off a tree, and when there'd been nothing left, they'd taken off.

And then Shelby had come along. And she loved him. She hadn't said so, but her body had told him long before she spoke the words. She had done more than just withdraw her petition. She had supported *his,* publicly endorsing him, stating he was better able to provide for Rio than she was. It was the ultimate declaration of love.

She'd made a mistake, a big one, but he had never given her the chance to atone. It was almost as though he was *looking* for an excuse and if it hadn't been this one, he would have found another. It was much easier to throw her out than to take the chance of *her* leaving *him.* Like everyone else, he was a product of his experiences, and his experiences had taught him some pretty ugly lessons—such as what it felt like to be abandoned, and how no one would ever really love him for himself.

And then there was Rio. Their childhood experiences may have been different, but what Rio was feeling and the way he dealt with those feelings made him a carbon copy of Michael. Rio was filled with pain and fear and loneliness, but he hadn't shed a tear—not one. He was suffering in silence and dying inside just the way Michael had. And why? Because Michael was too damn stubborn or too afraid to admit Shelby could really care for him. Shelby hadn't run out. He had driven her away...and he was the only one who could bring her back.

A muscle jerked convulsively in Michael's neck. Memories overtook him and he was powerless to keep them at bay. He remembered the day she stood up to the cement truck driver and the countless times she stood up to him. He remembered all the breakfasts they'd shared in the cozy light of Mrs. Hodges's kitchen. He remembered the time they spent together—the three of them, as a family—at the zoo and the park and the museum.

He could see the sparkle in her bright blue eyes and smell the clean fragrance of her golden hair. His fingers remembered the softness of her skin, and he could taste her lips moving hungrily against his own.

He remembered how much he wanted her—wanted, not just to love her, but to spend his days and nights in her company, sharing their dreams and planning their future.

He loved her.

And he had to believe it wasn't too late to get her back.

Shelby leaned against the side of the trench she had been working in for the last week. After spending so many exciting, hectic, fun-filled days with Rio and Michael, she had forgotten how slow and tedious her archaeological work could be.

Not that it really mattered. There was nowhere else she needed to be...no one waiting for her to finish her work and come home...no home to go to. Whether this job took another week or another year, it really didn't make much difference. She had all the time in the world.

The tough part about having all the time in the world was having all the time in the world to think. And, as much as she tried to avoid it, that was what she had been doing a lot of lately—thinking and crying.

The tears came easily now. She grieved for the deaths of Linc and Rebecca. She mourned giving up her dream of raising Rio and losing the man she loved. More than anything, she cried for how badly she had hurt him.

It had taken losing Michael to force her to face all the other losses in her life. In the past, she had ignored the open wounds, refusing to attend to them, letting them eat away at her insides. Now, finally, all the old wounds had been treated and were healing, with only a few thin scars to remind her of what she had survived. Eventually, she felt strong enough to leave the commune where she had been staying and return to her archaeology. Like a phoenix rising from the ashes, she felt restored...at peace with her past.

But if losing Michael had helped lay to rest the ancient demons, it had left her with a more present and powerful one. The anguish and loneliness were not easily dealt with. The dreams of what might have been were not easily forgotten. She tried to tell herself that healing takes time. But given the way she felt, an eternity wouldn't be long enough to absorb all the pain.

The midday sun bore down upon her and she swiped her forehead with the back of her arm. She remembered vividly the last time she had basked in the sun—that glorious day spent on Michael's boat when he had laughed and teased her about wearing a bikini. She glanced down at her belt cinched a full two notches tighter. The only good thing about heartbreak was the weight loss that went with it.

Oh, how she wished she could transport herself back to that time. To share one more day with the two people she loved most in the world.

Shelby glanced at her watch. It was probably all over. Today was the day of Rio's hearing, and by now, no doubt, Michael was celebrating his victory. For one brief, irrational moment she had considered going back for the hearing . . . just to see him again. But she had tasted more than enough of his anger and disgust. It was better to remember the happy times than to create more ugly ones.

Maybe next month she'd take some time off . . . go to Mexico City and visit the Museum of Anthropology . . . see a certain little jadeite statue . . . and remember . . .

He had been here nearly two weeks, and he still couldn't get used to the heat. Sweat ran down his neck and soaked his shirt. Although, if the truth be told, this afternoon he was sweating as much from nervousness as from heat. The van had arrived in Xpujil, and even though it would be late afternoon when they got there, he and the driver were going to the dig. There was no way he could wait until morning. Getting a loaded moving van halfway across Mexico, through a tropical rain forest, and up to a half-dug-out archaeological site was the easy part; facing Shelby was going to be much more difficult.

He made the driver stop near a stand of trees, just before the last bend in the dirt road, about two hundred yards from the clearing. Slowly, Michael climbed down from the cab and walked the rest of the way alone. He had come this far a dozen times in the last two weeks, always stopping at the edge of the clearing, watching them work without his being seen. A couple of times he had seen her, and it was all he could do to keep from dashing across the vine-covered terrain and pulling her into his arms. He wanted to hold her and kiss her and love her. He wanted to beg her forgiveness and heal their pain with his mouth and hands and body. But he had forced himself to wait until the time was right. And that time was now.

He crossed the distance with sure, swift steps that belied the way he felt. The setting sun blazed around him in red and gold as he searched the area for Shelby. A number of workers were calling it quits, climbing out of shallow pits or coming down from half-uncovered mounds of stone. And then he spotted her. She was standing in a waist-deep trench, chipping away at a small section of sand and stone. Her honey-colored hair was pulled back in a simple ponytail and she wore cutoffs and a light cotton blouse. She looked heartbreakingly young and beautiful and Michael cursed himself again for ever letting her go.

Shelby paused to wipe a trickle of sweat from her face. Out of the corner of her eye, she glimpsed a pair of men's boots. "What do think, Felipe?" she asked. She moved her face closer to the embedded stone and blew away some of the dirt and dust. "Do you think we've been through enough today?"

"I think we've been through enough to last a lifetime," said an achingly familiar, deep voice.

Shelby twisted around and squinted into the setting sun. The tall, solemn man stepped closer, putting himself between Shelby and the sun. The shadow of his tall, broad body fell across her, and the color drained from her face as she stared up at him. His features were engraved upon her mind—the thick, sablelike hair now curling a little in the hot, humid air; the blunt dark eyebrows above gray eyes darkened with emotion; the square cut of his chin and jaw; and the firm, generous mouth set in determination. This was the vision that stalked her empty, desolate days, and haunted her dreams every night.

But this was no vision. Michael was here in Mexico and there could only be one reason for that.

"Rio's fine," he said, easily reading the thought that clouded her face.

Intense relief flooded her body and a tiny flame of hope flickered uncertainly. "Then why are you here?" She tried to keep her voice calm and casual, turning back to her work, hiding her face from his scrutinizing gaze. A small gasp of shock tore from her throat as his strong arms pulled her effortlessly from the pit and turned her to face him.

"We have to talk, Shelby."

Her heart wrenched at the sound of her name on his lips, and she swallowed hard against the violent swelling of emotion. She dragged her gaze to his face, and met the stare of his fathomless gray eyes. "There's nothing left to say, Michael." *We've already hurt each other terribly by what we did—and didn't—say.*

His whole body tensed at the deadly calm of her voice, but he wouldn't let her walk away. "Oh, yes, there is," he said firmly. "We have some unfinished business to clear up."

Shelby's chest ached from the wild thumping of her heart. "I don't understand."

"I told you I always adhere to the strict letter of the law. According to paragraph 16a of the employment contract, which we both signed, an automobile would be made available for your personal use. I was supposed to provide you with your own car, and since I failed to do so, I stand in breach of contract."

Shelby blinked and looked at the man standing before her as though he were an apparition. "Michael, you're not making any sense. Surely you didn't come all the way to Mexico to apologize for not providing me with a car."

"No, I came here to fulfill my part of the contract."

"What?"

Michael whistled loudly and Shelby watched as a large moving van lumbered around the corner and up the hill. As it chugged to a stop, Michael pulled a set of keys from the pocket of his jeans and dropped them into Shelby's hands.

Shelby made a face. "You're giving me a moving van?"

"Not exactly," he said. He waved to the driver, who hopped out of the cab and opened the rear doors. Shelby watched in stunned silence as the driver laid out a ramp, then disappeared back into the van. A moment later she sucked in her breath as out rolled a beautifully restored, shiny red, 1968 Shelby Mustang GT500.

"It has a V-8 engine, 335hp and is guaranteed to go zero to sixty in 5.2 seconds flat," Michael said, grabbing her hand and pulling her toward the car. "You can't imagine how hard it was to find one of these."

Shelby looked from Michael to the car and back again in total confusion.

"Don't you like it?" He looked nervous and terribly vulnerable.

It's a beautiful car, Michael. But that's all it is . . . just an assemblage of metal and plastic and rubber. I don't want your car. I want you.

"I can't accept this," she answered, neatly avoiding his question.

"Why not?"

"Well, to begin with, you don't owe me a car, or anything else. And second, this car is a classic. You can't leave it sitting here in the middle of the Mexican jungle."

"I don't have any choice. It's not mine to dispose of. Here's the title and owner's registration." He handed her two pieces of paper that indicated the car was definitely hers. "You can do whatever you want with it."

Why are you doing this? Why have you come here to torment me with yet another reminder of what we might have had?

"Michael, you're a very generous man—"

"As I recall, you told me that the first day you arrived at the estate."

Was that a sparkle in his eyes?

"This time your generosity is misplaced." She raised her hands and gestured helplessly. "This is where I live and work. It's very hot here and when the wind kicks up, it blows dirt and dust and bits of stone everywhere. The paint would blister and the stones would pepper it in less than a week."

Michael nodded his head solemnly. "Looks like you've got a problem."

"I've got a problem?" she sputtered. "Michael, you're being unreasonable."

"You think so?" He paused to consider it. "Well, maybe I could offer you some suggestions. If you don't want to keep the car, you could always sell it. Of course, I'm sure you realize you're forbidden by Mexican law to sell it here, so you'd have to drive it back to the States to sell it."

Shelby folded her arms across her chest as exasperation overwhelmed her. "Wonderful. That shouldn't take long. One whole week to drive there, another two or three to find a buyer and a fourth week to get back."

Was that a smile tugging at the corner of his mouth?

"Not a good idea, huh? Well, another option would be to quit your job and move to a place where the climate is a little more temperate. In fact, you might want to find a place that has a garage, so the car would be protected from the elements."

Shelby's heart soared and a full-blown grin danced across her face. "Really? And can you recommend someplace that has just such a temperate climate?"

"Now that you mention it, the San Francisco area is well known for its mild winters and delightful springs. The summers aren't too hot and the autumns are glorious."

"Is that so? I've never seen San Francisco in the fall."

Michael leaned back against the car and pulled her between his legs and into his arms. "Then come back with me. Please." He cupped her chin in his hand and looked her straight in the eye. "I've been a fool and I've hurt you, hurt us both, and I'm so sorry."

Shelby closed her eyes for a moment as the wall around her heart crumbled. "I'm sorry, too, Michael," she said softly. "Sorry for all the lies and deception, for betraying your trust and causing such pain..." Her words were silenced as Michael took her face between his hands and kissed her.

She felt the warmth of his breath and then the sudden thrust of his tongue between her lips. His lips moved hungrily against hers and the world around her shattered. Her arms circled his neck and she leaned against him. A shudder ran through his body as she kissed him back with all the love and passion in her heart.

"I love you," he whispered against her mouth.

"I love you, too, Michael, and I don't need a new car or a fancy house or anything else your money can buy. I just need you." She wrenched away from him and stepped back, putting distance between them. "But there's still so much you don't know about me. So much I haven't told you."

"Really?" Michael grabbed her hand and put it to his lips. "I know you were ten years old when you started wearing glasses, and sixteen when you switched to contact lenses. I know you played volleyball and basketball in high school and sang in the choir. I've spent two weeks living in the commune learning all about you and Linc and my sister, Rebecca. I probably know more about you than you know about yourself. And do you know what? I realized I loved you before I knew any of those things. In fact, I think I've loved you from the first time I met you. I want to spend the rest of my life learning about you . . . and teaching you all about me.''

He knelt down in front of her in the midst of all the dirt and trampled foliage and took her hands in both his own. "I asked you this once before, and I'm going to keep on asking until we get it right. Shelby McMasters Kelland, will you marry me?''

"Yes!'' she cried. And her laughter rang through the jungle as he rose to his feet and enveloped her in his arms.

"You've got too many names,'' he grumbled. "The second thing we're going to do is change your name to something simple . . . like Chandler.''

"Is that right?'' Shelby gave him a wide-eyed look. "And what's the first thing we're going to do?'' she asked with feigned innocence.

"We're going to get some help celebrating.'' With a mischievous look, he opened the door of the Mustang and gave the horn three quick blasts.

Shelby waited, but nothing happened. "So, now what?'' she asked.

Michael pointed to the stand of trees that the moving van had hidden behind earlier. "Look.''

Shelby watched curiously as the outline of a familiar figure in a long cotton skirt emerged from the growing darkness and picked her way across the tangled underbrush. Shelby's voice was barely a whisper. "Zenith?''

Michael's voice was soft and close to her ear. "Keep looking,'' he coaxed.

Shelby strained her eyes in the gathering darkness until she spotted the small figure stumbling toward her as fast as possible in the thick vegetation. "Rio!'' Her cry pierced the night and she bolted forward at a dead run, with Michael only a step behind. In a mass of laughter and tears and kisses, she hugged the little boy . . . and her old friend . . . and the man who was to become her husband.

But the joy didn't diminish as she surfaced to reality an endless time later. "How did you know to bring Rio here?'' she asked Michael. "How did you know I would say yes?''

Michael grinned. "I didn't,'' he admitted sheepishly. "But I figured maybe Rio wasn't the only one with a guardian angel.''

With a heart full of happiness, she watched Michael swing Rio high up on his broad shoulders. Then, hand in hand, they headed back to the car to begin the long ride home.

* * * * *

Rugged and lean...and the best-looking, sweetest-talking men to be found in the entire Lone Star state!

Diana Palmer

LONG, TALL TEXANS

In July 1994, Silhouette is very proud to bring you Diana Palmer's first three LONG, TALL TEXANS. CALHOUN, JUSTIN and TYLER—the three cowboys who started the legend. Now they're back by popular demand in one classic volume—and they're ready to lasso your heart! Beautifully repackaged for this special event, this collection is sure to be a longtime keepsake!

"Diana Palmer makes a reader want to find a Texan of her own to love!" —*Affaire de Coeur*

LONG, TALL TEXANS—the first three— reunited in this special roundup!

Available in July, wherever Silhouette books are sold.

Take 4 bestselling love stories FREE

Plus get a FREE surprise gift!

Special Limited-time Offer

Mail to Silhouette Reader Service™

3010 Walden Avenue
P.O. Box 1867
Buffalo, N.Y. 14269-1867

YES! Please send me 4 free Silhouette Intimate Moments® novels and my free surprise gift. Then send me 6 brand-new novels every month, which I will receive months before they appear in bookstores. Bill me at the low price of $2.89 each plus 25¢ delivery and applicable sales tax, if any.* That's the complete price and—compared to the cover prices of $3.50 each—quite a bargain! I understand that accepting the books and gift places me under no obligation ever to buy any books. I can always return a shipment and cancel at any time. Even if I never buy another book from Silhouette, the 4 free books and the surprise gift are mine to keep forever.

245 BPA ANRR

Name	(PLEASE PRINT)
Address	Apt. No.
City	State Zip

This offer is limited to one order per household and not valid to present Silhouette Intimate Moments® subscribers. *Terms and prices are subject to change without notice.
Sales tax applicable in N.Y.

UMOM-94R

©1990 Harlequin Enterprises Limited

MONTANA Mavericks™

Stories that capture living and loving beneath the Big Sky, where legends live on...and the mystery is just beginning.

Watch for the sizzling debut of
MONTANA MAVERICKS in August with

ROGUE STALLION

by Diana Palmer

A powerful tale of simmering desire and mystery!

And don't miss a minute of the loving as the mystery continues with:

THE WIDOW AND THE RODEO MAN
by Jackie Merritt (September)
SLEEPING WITH THE ENEMY
by Myrna Temte (October)
THE ONCE AND FUTURE WIFE
by Laurie Paige (November)
THE RANCHER TAKES A WIFE
by Jackie Merritt (December)
and many more of your favorite authors!

Only from ▼ *Silhouette*®
™   where passion lives.

SILHOUETTE® Shadows™

Join award-winning author Rachel Lee as

CONARD COUNTY explores the dark side of love....

Rachel Lee will tingle your senses in August when she visits the dark side of love in her latest Conard County title, **THUNDER MOUNTAIN, SS #37.**

For years, Gray Cloud had guarded his beloved Thunder Mountain, protecting its secrets and mystical powers from human exploitation. Then came Mercy Kendrick.... But someone—or something—wanted her dead. Alone with the tempestuous forces of nature, Mercy turned to Gray Cloud, only to find a storm of a very different kind raging in his eyes. Look for their terrifying tale, only from Silhouette Shadows.

ROMANTIC TRADITIONS

Barbara Faith heats up ROMANTIC TRADITIONS in July with DESERT MAN, IM #578, featuring the forever-sultry sheikh plot line.

Josie McCall knew better than to get involved with Sheikh Kumar Ben Ari. Worlds apart in thought and custom, both suspected their love was destined for failure. Then a tribal war began, and Josie faced the grim possibility of losing her desert lover—for good.

October 1994 will feature Justine Davis's LEFT AT THE ALTAR, her timely take on the classic story line of the same name. And remember, ROMANTIC TRADITIONS will continue to bring you the best-loved plot lines from your most-cherished authors, so don't miss any of them—only in V■INTIMATE MOMENTS®

Silhouette®